Bel...

"Ms. Potter has given us another thrilling drama. Every page proves the reason for her award-winning success . . . *Beloved Impostor* travels at a fast pace with outstanding characters and an expertly developed plot."   —*Rendezvous*

"A wonderful Scottish tale wrought with emotion, tender in its telling and heart-wrenching in its beauty. Ms. Potter captures our hearts and gifts us with another beautiful story."   —*The Best Reviews*

"[A] superb romance . . . It's Potter's unique gift for creating unforgettable characters and delving into the deepest parts of their hearts that endears her to readers. This is another masterpiece from a writer who always delivers what romance readers want: a love story to always remember."   —*Romantic Times*

"The story was riveting, the execution and the telling of it and the characters involved showed spirit, courage, chemistry, and mostly they had a heart and held on to hope. It held my interest and kept it."   —*Pink Heart Reviews*

"Ms. Potter is a very talented storyteller, taking a much-used theme, lovers from warring families, and manipulating it, adding plenty of new ideas and twists, until the end result is the original, highly satisfying *Beloved Impostor* . . . Ms. Potter very adeptly whetted this reader's appetite for more about these two Maclean brothers, but for now, there is *Beloved Impostor*, which I highly recommend."

   —*Romance Reviews Today*

continued . . .

The Heart Queen

Beloved Stranger

PATRICIA POTTER

BERKLEY SENSATION, NEW YORK

THE BERKLEY PUBLISHING GROUP
Published by the Penguin Group
Penguin Group (USA) Inc.
375 Hudson Street, New York, New York 10014, USA
Penguin Group (Canada), 90 Eglinton Avenue East, Suite 700, Toronto, Ontario M4P 2Y3, Canada
(a division of Pearson Penguin Canada Inc.)
Penguin Books Ltd., 80 Strand, London WC2R 0RL, England
Penguin Group Ireland, 25 St. Stephen's Green, Dublin 2, Ireland (a division of Penguin Books Ltd.)
Penguin Group (Australia), 250 Camberwell Road, Camberwell, Victoria 3124, Australia
(a division of Pearson Australia Group Pty. Ltd.)
Penguin Books India Pvt. Ltd., 11 Community Centre, Panchsheel Park, New Delhi—110 017, India
Penguin Group (NZ), Cnr. Airborne and Rosedale Roads, Albany, Auckland 1310, New Zealand
(a division of Pearson New Zealand Ltd.)
Penguin Books (South Africa) (Pty.) Ltd., 24 Sturdee Avenue, Rosebank, Johannesburg 2196, South
Africa

Penguin Books Ltd., Registered Offices: 80 Strand, London WC2R 0RL, England

BELOVED STRANGER

A Berkley Sensation Book / published by arrangement with the author

PRINTING HISTORY
Berkley Sensation edition / February 2006

ISBN: 0-425-20742-0

BERKLEY SENSATION®
Berkley Sensation Books are published by The Berkley Publishing Group,
a division of Penguin Group (USA) Inc.,
375 Hudson Street, New York, New York 10014.
BERKLEY SENSATION is a registered trademark of Penguin Group (USA) Inc.
The "B" design is a trademark belonging to Penguin Group (USA) Inc.

PRINTED IN THE UNITED STATES OF AMERICA

10 9 8 7 6 5 4 3 2 1

With gratitude to Carolyn McSparren, Phyllis Appleby, Kenlyn Spence, and Barbara Christopher for all their support, advice—sometimes painful but always on target—and, most of all, their friendship. I love you all.

Prologue

Flodden Field, England
September 9, 1513

The promise of redemption had turned into a descent into hell.

Lachlan Maclean moved his mount closer to his liege, King James IV of Scotland, and watched disaster unfold beneath him.

Redemption.

This battle, this invasion by King James into England, was to have been Lachlan's final redemption, the act that might somehow undo the fact he had caused his father's death years earlier. In taking the Macleans into battle, he'd hoped to spare his older brother their father's fate.

He'd never forgotten the look on his father's face as he died. He'd died because Lachlan, who'd wanted to be a priest, could not raise his sword to fight off the Campbells. Despite his training since early childhood, he had frozen, and his father died protecting him.

His clan had considered him a coward.

He wondered even now whether he could take a life, whether he would freeze again . . .

The cannon roared again, and the scene below was worse than any vision of the underworld. Horses screamed as they fell, their cries mixing with the more guttural shouts of wounded and dying men. Acrid, lung-blistering smoke turned the afternoon mist dark, and its bitter smell commingled with the sickening sweet odor of blood.

The view below was chaos. And a disaster that never should have happened. Superior English cannon destroyed Scottish cannon, then turned to fire on the rows of Scottish pikemen waiting to attack. Hector, Lachlan's second-in-command and a man as close to him as a father, was on foot with the pikemen.

Lachlan exchanged somber glances with Jamie Campbell who also accompanied the king. In the past two years Jamie had become his best friend, and the two of them had often visited King James's Court. Now, Jamie led his contingent of loyal Campbells, while Lachlan led the Macleans.

Jamie's cocky grin was gone. Until an hour ago, his eyes had shone with anticipation. He'd left his bonny wife behind, but he was a man called to adventure. Now adventure turned to horror.

They'd all thought the battle won. The Scots held the high ground. They had the larger numbers. They would force the English to approach from below. At one point, aides told James he should attack the English as they gathered in disarray beneath them.

"There is no honor in that," James said. And waited.

Waited too long.

In the name of honor, James had been surrounded, giving up the advantage he once had.

Honor always bore a price, and this time Lachlan wondered whether it was worth it.

Still, he waited at his liege's side, his spirits sinking as the English fired their cannon with an accuracy the Scots couldn't meet.

A messenger galloped to James's side and delivered a message. The king frowned as he read it, then told the men around him. "Lord Home has disobeyed orders and started down the ridge toward the English."

Lachlan knew what that meant. King James and Lord Home were close friends. To keep his friend from dying, James, too, would surrender the superior position to attack the enemy.

"For Scotland!" James roared and started down the hill.

Lachlan's heart sank. He knew the main army was still above. James was leaving them without a leader.

He and Jamie followed James as he charged down the hill. Spurred by the sight of their liege fighting like a man possessed, Lachlan thrust and hacked his way toward Surrey, who led the English in the battle. A cannon ball exploded just in front of him, and his horse shied away as the smell of death and blood grew denser, and the level of noise crescendoed.

What am I doing here?

Better me than my brother with his wife and new babe.

With that one thought in mind, he rode beside Jamie and his king. Honor. Honor and duty were what mattered. He had failed once. He would not fail again.

The horsemen met the enemy. Lachlan leveled his pike at an Englishman. The jolt jarred his body as it hit the man's shield, tearing it away. He thrust again, and this time the pike entered the enemy's body. He'd learned well as a lad how to kill. And kill well. He'd hated every moment of the training.

Now he welcomed those hard-earned skills. *Thrust, pull out, thrust again.*

"English," cried one of his companions. "At our rear."

He turned around. English horsemen were approaching from the south.

"To me," cried James.

Lachlan fought his way to the king's side. Then he was surrounded, his pike forced from his hand. He reached for his sword. He was fighting now for his king, his honor, for Scotland, and, aye, his life. Masses of men on horseback and on foot enveloped them.

He looked for Jamie Campbell and saw him on the ground, overwhelmed by men on foot. He started toward him, when he heard an anguished cry, "The king is down!"

Before Lachlan could turn, pain sheared through his leg, and a lance hit his chain armor. His horse screamed and went to its knees.

He tried to jump free, but he had no strength left. His horse, which he'd raised from a colt, fell on his leg, and Lachlan lay there helpless next to his king, as the English swarmed around them, plunging their swords into James, then turning on him.

Honor was not all it was said to be, he thought, before pain turned into nothingness.

Chapter 1

Flodden Field, England
September 9, 1513

Kimbra Charlton steeled her resolve as she accompanied the women who combed the fields of dead. Dressed in her mourning gown, she huddled against the side of the pony cart with other reiver women.

Cedric Charlton, her late husband's cousin, had ridden to her cottage hours earlier to say that tens of thousands—both Scots and English—lay dead on Flodden Field. They had to rush to beat other reiver families if they wanted the best that could be gleaned from the battlefield.

The Charltons had been called to fight with the English, but Cedric had no wounds, no blood on his jack. She suspected that he, and most of the reivers, had left the field before the battle, only to return later to rob the dead and dying after the battle was spent.

She concentrated on the squeaking wheels and tried not to cough in the acrid smoke that grew denser with every turn of the wheels. She inched away from the other women who talked excitedly about what they might find. She didn't share their anticipation.

How much lower could she sink?

She tried to think instead of better days, of riding with her husband, Wild Will Charlton, on raids across the border. It had been rare, a woman riding with reivers, yet Will had been an unusual man. Reiver through and through, he'd been bemused by what he considered her adventurous nature, had given in to her pleading and taught her to ride and aim an arrow.

He'd never known the fear inside her, the knowledge that someday she might have to run for her life, just as her mother had fled many years ago. She'd never shown the fear her mother had taught her.

He might never have married her if she had.

Though she had learned to enjoy the raids, the freedom of them, to her they were not the game they were to others. She'd picked up a bauble here and there for herself and had hidden them away. That was something else her mother had taught her.

In the two years since Will had died, she had sold them all to support her daughter and herself.

She thought back to her first raid. She had asked Will to take her, but he'd just laughed at her "fancy," just as he'd laughed at her dream of reading. But then one night, she'd disguised herself as a man and had stolen Magnus, one of the finest hobblers on either side of the border. Will had said she was the best of the lot and with a great bellow of laughter defied his friends to say nay on future rides.

But motherhood had ended those adventures.

A pang of loss struck her as she thought of her husband. Tall and handsome and strong, Will had had a devil-may-care smile and a broad humor that sent a room roaring into laughter. He'd loved their daughter, even as he yearned for a son. He had regarded her in men's clothes with a broad grin on his face. "No one else has ever had a lass like you," he said.

And she had indulged *him,* admiring her husband who was among the boldest of the Border Reivers, and who had chosen her—a woman without dowry and with an unknown past—to be his bride. He'd always fought for her, and now she would fight for his daughter.

Reiving was a family business for the Charltons. They raided both their English neighbors as well as the Scots across the border. The Charltons had been reivers for a century or more and considered it a respectable profession. It had been a fine game as well. Stealing cattle. Taking hostages for ransom. Each side took its share, and rarely was anyone killed. In truth, even when the Scots and English met in battle near the border, 'twas said the borderers often protected the same neighbors they'd raided the week before.

But one raid went wrong. Will was hit with an arrow. The wound, despite all her ministrations, had turned to inflammation. She would never forgive herself for that. If only she'd done more . . . or known more. Those terrible days were burned in her mind like a brand . . .

There had been fifty raiders that night. Having heard of a great black horse said to have an Arabic sire, they'd attacked an Armstrong holding. She hadn't ridden, staying home instead with her ailing daughter. She'd helped Will dress in his customary clothing: a jack covered with leather, a doublet of fustian, and dark hose. She'd placed his steel bonnet over his dark hair.

She'd been there with him in spirit, knowing exactly

when they would cross the Bewcastle Waste, a wild area of fell and moor. Their hobblers—small, swift, hardy horses—were black and gray, chosen to blend into the darkness.

She'd waited as the night slowly passed and dawn came, and fear started to tug at her. It had been midday when the riders came and Will stumbled as he'd dismounted. Blood covered his hose.

"'Tis nothing," he said and submitted mildly enough to her cauterizing the wound. But it had been too late. The poison had spread, and despite all her herbs, all her poultices, he'd died three days later in agony he obviously tried not to let her see.

A jolt of the cart brought her back to reality. She smelled death now as they neared the place of battle. An eery silence had settled over the countryside. She heard only the creak of wheels, the occasional whisper of the men riding to the front of them. There was no sound of night birds, no rustle of animals running from humans.

God forgive her for what she was about to do, but she had no choice.

No longer was she allowed to join the reivers. No longer did she share in the plunder. She raised herbs—a skill her mother had known and used as a servant—and vegetables in her garden. She'd planted a field of oats, but half of the yield went to the Charltons, and she did not have enough to buy seed next year. If there was an early frost she would lose her herbs.

Since Will's death, she'd fought to keep their small cottage and Magnus, the horse she had stolen. Will's horse had died the year before his death, and he had taken Magnus as his mount. Now Audra and Magnus were all she had left of Will, and she would fight to protect both of them.

Yet she dreaded tonight. Reiving was one thing. It was a way of life on the border. Stealing from the dead was something else. A shudder ran through her body.

I can do it for Audra.

I can rob the dead and go to hell for it. For Audra.

Flodden Field. She'd heard the cannon throughout the evening. She had smelled the smoke that melded into the light mist, turning it dirty and sticky and heavy. She wore her mourning gown, both because it would blend into the night and because she was mourning the loss of part of herself.

The cart continued to bounce along the trail, then over a field. It took hours traveling this way, where a horse would reach it in a quarter of the time. She longed to be riding Magnus, but the animal—as well as her cottage—was the subject of great conflict between her and Will's family, and she could not, would not, wave it in the faces of the Charltons.

She was but a woman, she was reminded readily enough, and not worthy of owning such a mount, even though it was she who had stolen him. In English law it belonged to Will. Nor, according to Will's family, did she deserve to remain alone with her daughter in a much coveted cottage. She was not a Charlton by birth. It should go to a true Charlton who could farm the land.

Her one option was marriage. The Charltons had urged her to choose among the bachelors, but they all repulsed her, particularly Cedric, Will's cousin, who had always consumed her with greedy eyes. Yet she feared Cedric was Thomas Charlton's choice. And Thomas Charlton's wishes ruled among the Charltons.

She would take Audra and flee first.

But where would she go?

She had no family of her own. Her mother, now dead ten years, had been the daughter of a physician when she was raped by a noble. When she found herself with child, she threatened to tell the magistrate, the noble laughed at her and said no one would believe her. The next day her home burned with her father inside. She'd been in the woods picking mushrooms with her maid, or she would have been inside as well. They had seen the flames and hurried back, only to see the noble on his horse, watching the cottage burn.

They'd fled to the border, to her maid's family, and her mother had taken up service under a different name. She had a knowledge of herbs, but she'd feared using it. She always feared the earl's son would find her and kill both her and her child.

Yes, Kimbra knew the power and ruthlessness of nobles.

She still remembered the pinched look of fear on her mother's face when a stranger came to the Murray peel tower. Kimbra was thirteen when her mother died, and after her mother's death, the Murrays employed Kimbra as a maid for their daughter.

Without a dowry and with a parentage of questionable character, she had little hope of marriage until Will had seen her at a gathering of border families for traditional games. She had been serving tankards of ale when she saw someone beating a horse. She threw the contents of a tankard at the offender, and Will rushed to assist her when the man turned on her. Minutes later, he had smiled at her and declared she would be his wife.

She smiled at the thought. He'd defied his family to make it happen. He'd even fought her own reservations. While not a noble, he was cousin to the head of the Charlton family, far too fine for a maid.

The sound of moans and cries erased her smile, as the cart came to a halt. The stench grew stronger. She knew the smell of blood, but that of so many men and horses numbed the senses. Figures, made wraithlike by the mist, moved from one fallen body to the next. The land was smothered with them.

Cedric rode over to them, handing each woman a large sack and a torch. "Take jewelry and weapons," he ordered. "Ye might take boots as well or any fine clothing. The English commander has ordered all Scots be killed. If someone is still alive, call for one of the men." He looked toward her. "Unless ye want to finish him yourself."

She ignored the jibe. He had always resented her presence on the raids.

Her hand dug into the rough cloak she wore and felt the dagger she carried, along with the water flagon.

She took one of the bags. Cedric started after her.

She turned. "I wish to do this myself."

"I should protect ye. There might be some alive."

"You can protect the others. I need no help. I can use a dagger as well as any man."

"Ye should not need to. Ye need a man."

"I had a man. I wish no other."

She turned her back on him and veered away from the others. 'Twas a miserable deed she was doing, and 'twas easier to do it alone. In truth, Cedric made her flinch inside. She had managed to evade his intentions thus far, but he was becoming more and more insistent.

Neither did she join the other women. There was no glory in what they were doing, and she didn't want to hear nervous chatter—or worse, excitement over unexpected finds. She knew she would be allowed to keep one or two items for herself, and she intended to make the most of them. She could sell them if she had to leave.

Torches spread a glow among the field of dead. Bodies sprawled out in any number of positions, and the ground was muddy with blood. She moved quickly between the fallen, looking for rings, a jeweled belt, a coat of mail. Anything of value.

She'd heard that the Scottish king had been killed. She was sure his body had already been stripped of anything of value, but perhaps those around him would have items of value as well.

She heard a moan and turned. *An Englishman.* She leaned over him, and from his wounds knew she could do nothing except offer some water from the flagon she had brought with her. He thanked her with his eyes, and then he died.

She sat next to him for a moment, feeling hot tears in the back of her eyes. She fought them back. She could not indulge herself.

Kimbra stood again and renewed her search. There seemed to be little left. Others had already been here and stripped most of the bodies. She had to look under piles of bodies for an item overlooked. She found two rings, several daggers. Each time she took something from a body, she uttered a prayer on their behalf. Perhaps that would mitigate her guilt, find her some forgiveness for what she had to do.

Kimbra moved on, trying to ignore the stench of the dead, the sensation of spirits moving around her. She stopped, leaned against a tree, trying to breathe normally again.

A dark figure darted toward her, grabbed her bag. She ran after the fleeing thief who had her night's work. Kimbra was faster and jerked the thief's jacket, spinning him around, and grabbing her sack back.

She'd expected a man. Instead, she looked into the thin face of a woman. She didn't know her, yet there was something she recognized. Desperation. And stark fear.

The woman turned to flee.

"Wait!" Kimbra commanded.

The woman stopped, turned.

Kimbra reached in her sack, took out a ring. "Take this," she said. "Bargain wisely."

The woman stared at her. "Why?" she said.

"You look as if you need it more than me," Kimbra said simply.

The woman stared at her, then gave her a brief curtsy. "My name is Mary Armstrong," she said. "I meant you no harm, but my mon died here, and my bairns ha' nothing."

An Armstrong. A member of the family that killed her husband. Yet this woman was like her. Doing what she must for her child.

"Go, Mary," Kimbra said. "Leave before someone takes that from you."

"Thank ye, lady." The woman turned and ran.

Kimbra watched her go, then turned back to her work. The stench, the bodies, the sadness overwhelmed her. She bent over and retched. She kneeled there in the mist, amongst the dead. She thought of Will and all the women waiting for the lords to return.

A keening wail broke over the field. A wife had found a husband.

God help them.

She forced herself to stand and renew her search. If she didn't take what was there, someone else would. She hurried her steps. The first rays of dawn lightened the sky. This was something best done in the shadows of night.

She started to turn when her gaze detected the slightest movement behind a clump of trees not far away. She wasn't certain what she'd seen and was about to move on when a barely audible groan came from that direction. Taking the dagger from her belt, she moved toward the sound.

A man lay still, his body mostly covered by a thicket of dense brush. He had clearly escaped the notice of earlier reivers, since he was still dressed in a finely woven plaid, his upper body covered by chain mail. His legs were bare except for leather boots, and she saw the jagged, open wound on his leg. She set down her bag and stooped next to him. His breath was ragged, but he was alive.

And a lord. She knew that by his clothing.

He had multiple wounds. The side of his head bore a wide purple bruise. His arm was sliced, and his leg had been ripped open by some weapon.

Yet he apparently had dragged himself over here, away from the soldiers and scavengers going from man to man to deliver final blows.

His eyes opened, and she noticed they were blue. Bloodshot. Clouded with pain and suffering. "Water," he whispered. "Please."

She gave him the flagon. He greedily swallowed several gulps.

She heard her name called from a distance. She looked at the eyes staring up at her with gratitude. *A Scot.*

A Scot was an enemy of her country.

She knew her duty. She knew she should call Cedric or one of the others. Her duty was to end this man's life.

She could not do it. Nor could she call for someone else to kill him.

He would probably die in any event, she told herself.

"Thank . . . you," he mumbled. Then closed his eyes.

What to do?

She looked at the man's leg, which had been torn by a sword. It had stopped bleeding but would probably start again if he was moved.

Suddenly making up her mind, she struggled to remove his helmet from his head, then the mail. Both would have attracted attention. Under the mail she found a jeweled crest, and she slipped it into the bodice of her dress. Then she set her flagon next to him. He should find it when he regained his senses.

She covered him with leaves and underbrush. Perhaps he would survive the next day. Then she could return on Magnus and take him back to her cottage. Perhaps he was a great lord and would be grateful. Perhaps he would be her way out of the Charlton hold.

If he lived.

"Kimbra!"

She started at the sound of her name.

Cedric. And not far away.

Her heart pounded. He couldn't find the Scot.

She finished covering him, knowing that only God could save him over the next day. She couldn't return until night, and then not until late.

She leaned down. "Stay still. I will return," she whispered. "Tonight. Sometime tonight."

Then she covered the last of his face with leaves and stood.

"Kimbra!"

The voice was nearer. She grabbed her sack and the mail and helmet, then moved swiftly to her right, past several trees, before answering him. Cedric would be pleased with the mail. Even she could see that it was of the finest metal.

"I'm here."

"Where have ye been?"

She held up her chain mail. "See what I found."

He looked at her through narrowed eyes, then reached out for the chain mail.

She drew it close to her body. "It is mine."

"Nay, me lady," he said mockingly. "'Tis Charlton property."

"You should remember that as well. It will not be yourn."

His lips turned into a smirk and turned. "Be careful, Kimbra. I have asked to the Charlton for yer hand, and he looks kindly on my suit."

"I do not believe you."

"He wants ye wed." His eyes bore into her. "The cart is leaving. Unless ye wish to ride wi' me."

Kimbra didn't. She clung to the chain mail even as she twisted the top of the sack around her hand and lifted it to her shoulder, then made her way between the bodies. She knew she would never forget the stench.

She also knew she would be back this eve.

She wondered if the Scot would still be alive then.

She also wondered why she cared enough to risk her life.

She only knew she must. This man had tried desperately to live. And if she could save one life in this sea of death, mayhap God would forgive her the other sins.

Chapter 2

WHEN the cart arrived back at the Charlton tower, Kimbra added her sack—and the chain mail—to the jewelry and armor and clothing in the center of the courtyard. Well aware that every day she had to prove worthy, she made sure the Charlton noted that she brought more than many of the others. But she kept the jeweled crest hidden in the bosom of her gown, even though it seemed to burn a hole in her chest.

She was given leave to take one item for her own, and she chose a gold ring. If she was going to participate in thievery, she was going to make sure that at least some small part of it protected her daughter.

Once all had been collected, she walked to her cottage. Bear ran gleefully toward her. The huge dog, named because he'd looked like nothing so much as a bear cub when he was a pup, stopped at her gown, sniffed the dried blood, and looked up anxiously.

Engulfed with the enormity of what she'd just done this night, she hesitated for a moment, then leaned down to pet him. "It is all right, Bear." But he took several steps back and looked around.

"She will be home soon," Kimbra assured him. Audra was Bear's charge as well as playmate.

She fed the dog some leftover stew, then changed her gown, quickly washing the bloody mourning gown she had worn to the battlefield. She wanted to throw it away—to never look at it again—but every possession was valuable now. She did not have the luxury of destroying a garment. Instead she hung it outside over the branch of a tree.

Then she fed the chickens and milked the cow. Bess bellowed with disapproval at the lateness of what was usually a morning ritual. Kimbra pacified her with soft words and fresh hay. She then saddled Magnus, leading him from the small stable that housed the two animals.

It was far into the day now. There was no way she could reach the wounded man until dark. She would need Magnus to bring him back, and a hobbler as fine as Magnus would attract notice.

Would the Scot even live that long?

She didn't know. She did know that the longer he went without attention, the more risk there was of infection. His face haunted her as she walked swiftly down the path. It had been wracked with pain, but his eyes had been as pure a blue as she'd ever seen.

The image did not leave her as she rode over to Jane Carey's small hut.

Jane, a widow who often looked after children, was adored by them all. She was a Charlton by blood and had been permitted to keep her small abode.

Audra came out the door, and Kimbra slid off the horse and leaned over to hug her. Her daughter had but seven years, and she wriggled with delight.

"Mater," she said, holding up her arms for a hug.

Kimbra gave her one. "My pretty love," she said. "Did you have a good day? Did Jane make you a sweet?"

Audra made a face. "Porridge."

"Oh dear," Kimbra said. "I will tell her to make you one tomorrow."

"Are you going away again?"

"Just for a while tonight."

Audra looked at her with disappointment in huge blue eyes.

"When we get back, you can help feed Magnus and Bess."

Audra's face brightened. She loved animals and always wanted to feel useful. Magnus had always been gentle with both Kimbra and Audra. Kimbra had seen Cedric with horses and knew he had a cruel hand—another reason to despise such a match.

Kimbra would never let him have control of the horse, nor of their elderly cow, which was giving less and less milk. Bess was more like a pet now. Cedric would not hold such sentimentality.

After telling Jane she would be bringing Audra back this night, she lifted her daughter onto the horse, then mounted herself. Her daughter's warm body cuddling against hers comforted her.

She would give her life for Audra. This past night's work was little enough if it would help keep her daughter safe and fed.

They reached the stone and wood cottage Will had built for them. Unlike most, it had two rooms as well as a loft. She loved the cottage—the large room with a huge fireplace and the furniture he had built with his hands. It had a second room, which she and Will once shared. Now she shared it with Audra. The loft was for visitors.

It was not a large dwelling, but it was well built. She'd sewn curtains for the window, and during the spring and summer, she always kept flowers from her garden in several bowls.

It was *hers*.

Audra helped her unsaddle Magnus, or at least Kimbra let her daughter think she helped, handing her the bridle and bit to put away. Together they fed and watered both Magnus and Bess. Then, holding hands, they went into the cottage.

The day went quickly, though her thoughts continued to wander back to the battlefield, to the Scot so badly wounded. She didn't know why he preyed so heavily on her mind, except he had been a breath of life on a field of death. Perhaps help would be a modest redemption for what she had done.

When it grew dark, she and Audra rode Magnus back to Jane Carey's. Audra went to sleep in her arms, and Kimbra was consumed by overwhelming love for her daughter. Audra should come first in all things.

So why was she risking so much for a man who was an enemy?

She had promised him. It was as simple as that.

After she returned to her cottage, she changed into the men's clothes she'd once worn on raids. She pulled on leather breeches, then a doublet followed by a jack, a quilted coat of stout leather sewn with plates of horn for protection. Finally she tied her hair in a knot and placed a steel bonnet over it. Except for those few who had once ridden with her husband, no one would realize she was a woman.

A woman on a horse would be questioned. A borderer, a raider, would not, especially one with a sword at his side and a wicked-looking dagger on his belt. She started to leave, then returned to bundle several of Will's garments together.

It was well past midnight when she mounted Magnus and rode toward the battlefield. She felt the horse's unease as the odor of death enveloped them. As yesterday, figures moved among the dead, looking for anything of use or value. By now, the pickings would be slim. The weapons, the jewelry, the clothes and boots would be gone. It did not take the border reivers long to find whatever was valuable.

To the poor, anything was of value.

The moon was visible this night, though sometimes shaded by clouds drifting across the sky. The smoke had disappeared, but the acrid scent remained.

Magnus picked his way through the dead, prancing nervously at the smell. He was well trained, but horses didn't like the smell of blood, nor did they want to step on the dead.

Kimbra had memorized landmarks. The place where the cart had stopped. Her own journey through the dead. Several of the bodies near the spot where she'd found the Scot were gone. They must have been of importance or they, too, would have remained here like so many others.

Had her Scotsman been found? Or if he hadn't, was he still alive?

She dismounted and led the horse to the silent clump of trees. Below it was a stream she had not noticed the night before.

She saw the outline of bodies down there as well.

In the light of the moon, she found the place where she'd left the Scotsman. Kimbra knelt and brushed off the leaves and dirt.

He moved and opened his eyes. He looked startled, then apprehensive as his gaze focused on her, on her clothes. He tried to sit up but fell back with a moan.

A streak of emotion ran through Kimbra. *He was alive!*

" 'Tis only me," she said. "The one who found you last eve. I left the water."

His face relaxed slightly. "You . . . came back."

"Aye. I said I would."

"Thirsty."

She glanced around him and found the flagon. It was empty. He would have to wait.

"Later," she said and put an arm under his shoulder. "Can you sit?"

He didn't answer, merely tried with her help to raise himself. A groan escaped his lips, yet she felt the determination in him. He fell back, then tried again.

"I have a horse and a litter. But you have to help me," she said to him. "I cannot get you on it myself."

With a grunt, he managed to heave himself to a sitting position, though she knew by his harsh breathing that every slight movement was agonizing. She handed him Will's clothes. They would be too large for him, but they were certainly safer than the plaid and shirt he wore.

She used her dagger to cut the plaid from his body.

He held out his hand, stopping her.

"I am English," she said, careful of her speech. "My husband's family is English. You must also be English. The plaid says otherwise."

He stared at her for a moment, then nodded.

"Why?" he asked suddenly. "Why . . . are you doing this?"

She couldn't answer, because she wasn't altogether sure herself. "Does it matter?"

"Nay," he said. "I am . . . grateful."

She continued to cut the cloth, even as she saw him struggle to stay in a sitting position. Each time he moved to try to assist her, pain flicked across his face. A low involuntary moan came from deep in his throat.

"Who are you?" she asked as she continued to work.

There was no answer.

"Your name?" she said again, this time more sharply.

She saw a bewildered look settle in his face. "I do not know, mistress. I canna remember. You said I was a Scot. I donna remember that, either."

Her heart sank. He was addled. How could she get a ransom or reward if she knew not who he was?

He spoke well. His clothes, speech, and manner all bespoke of rank and nobility. But she would need his name.

She remembered the jeweled crest that had fastened the plaid. Should she mention it? No, he would want it back. She surely deserved something for her trouble, and he was a noble. He probably had many such baubles in Scotland.

She decided not to mention it for now.

As for not remembering, he could be lying. But the confusion in his eyes belied that.

She should leave him here and keep the crest. She knew she would not, though. In this field of death, one survived. Surely God had had a hand in that. There was also something vulnerable about him.

She ignored his nakedness once the plaid and shirt was cut from him and helped him into Will's jack and breeches. She had to pull them over the large gaping wound in his leg, and she heard the swift intake of his breath. No outcry, though, and she was grateful.

The next problem was getting him on the litter.

"You will have to help me," she told him again. "Once I get you to my cottage, I can tend you."

He nodded.

She stood and offered her hand. For a moment he looked at it helplessly.

"I am strong," she said.

He took it and tried to stand. He fell back. She heard voices and stooped beside him, quickly pushing the plaid and shirt underneath the dirt and leaves that had covered him.

"If anyone challenges you, say nothing. If someone

questions me, I will say you are addled but obviously from your dress you are an Englishman. Your life rests on that."

He may have forgotten his name, but she saw intelligence in his eyes. He did not question her, but merely nodded. He was very still, and the voices faded again.

She stood again. "We must go. Every moment is dangerous."

She offered her hand, and he tried to stand again. He got to his knees. Pain and determination stiffened his face as he rose on his good leg, then managed, with her help, to get to the other. He put his arm around her and hobbled to the litter, collapsing on it. She tied him there so he would not slip off, then—on foot—guided Magnus toward her cottage.

She tried to think. She needed to get the Scot to the cottage and tend his wounds. The wound on his leg was the greatest concern. But he had other injuries as well. His breath was short, and it was obviously painful for him to breathe. She had noticed the deep purple and red bruises on his chest, where he'd been struck by a pike or spear. She prayed those injuries would not lead to the lung sickness.

Then there was the huge knot and bruise on his head that had evidently cost him his memory.

She urged Magnus forward. She kept looking behind, afraid the Scot would fall off the litter. She didn't know whether she could get him back on it again, and if she could not . . .

After safely avoiding the bodies on the battlefield and staying afoot to keep the horse calm, she spotted a fallen log that she could stand on to help her get up on the horse. Once mounted, she kept Magnus at a slow pace to prevent any unnecessary joggling of her charge.

She prayed she would arrive without meeting anyone on the way. It could well mean his death and her banishment. Or worse.

* * *

$\mathcal{E}$VERY step the horse took sent waves of pain through him.

He stifled groans. Instinct warned him of danger. It also told him to trust her.

She said he was a Scot. He knew the word, *Scot,* but he could not relate it to himself. All he knew was a black void, and the woman's voice was the only thing he had to hold on to.

He started to drift away, and then a hard bump sent a new jolt of agony through him, bringing him back to a present he wasn't sure he wanted. Darkness was easier. Darkness didn't require answers to questions pounding in his brain.

Still, he tried to remain conscious. Tried not to allow the darkness to overtake him. He yearned to be drifting into a gray netherland where there was no agony, where the fierce need to understand what and who he was would fade away.

Think. Remember.

After what seemed forever, the movement ceased and he was aware of the woman leaning over him, trying to help him to his feet as a dog barked. He tried to stand but couldn't quite do it, and then he was falling.

She broke his fall, and he was aware they were both on the ground. New pain rolled through him in continuous waves, almost blinding him in its intensity.

"Can you move?" she after a pause.

"Aye, I . . . think so."

"A few steps," she said. "Just a few steps, and we will be inside. There is a bed. I can tend those wounds."

With her help he struggled to his feet and managed to stand there. His legs barely held him.

A step.

Another.

He forced himself to keep moving, to ignore the agony streaking down his leg, the sharp pain in his chest that made every breath an effort.

Then he was inside a dwelling. Where?

And who was he? It was like a long wail in his head. She lowered him onto something soft. And the need to move, to stay awake, was gone. His eyes closed, and he drifted again into a dark void.

Chapter 3

K IMBRA looked down at the Scot lying in the feather bed she and Will had shared.

The second he sank into it, his eyes had closed, and she knew he had used every bit of his fading strength to get inside. She was relieved that he had lapsed into unconsciousness again.

Fire. She needed fire. There were no embers left, and starting one was always difficult, even after all these years. She finally got a fire going, and hung a pot of water over the flames. Then she went into the other room to check on the Scot. Will's breeches were soaked with fresh blood from the wound, and like her own clothes yesterday, she couldn't afford to destroy them. The stranger—if he lived—would need the garments. She would have to clean them, then make adjustments to the size. She hoped that, if anyone came, they would not recognize them as belonging to Will. The borderers—both English and Scots— wore much the same clothing and spoke with similar accents.

His speech, though, was not that of the border. She would have to warn him to be cautious in what he said and how he acted.

She realized she was expecting him to live now. She was thinking about his future.

Kimbra undid the laces on the breeches, pulled them off him and examined the leg. It had been a day without treatment, more than long enough for poison to spread. She covered him with a blanket, then went back to the other room, where she took out the herbs she'd gathered earlier and stirred them into the steaming water. In minutes she'd made a poultice. She would try that before burning the wound.

She pulled back the blanket, averting her eyes from parts of his body other than the wound. She applied the poultice of comfrey and aloe. That was one of the few benefits of centuries-ago Roman occupation. They'd left their herbs when they moved on.

The Scot's body flinched, then relaxed as she secured the poultice to the wound.

She carefully removed Will's jack from his body. His harsh breathing told her there had been damage to his ribs. When he woke again, she would bind his chest and pray the ribs were only bruised.

In addition to those to his leg and ribs, there were other wounds. Slices in his left shoulder and right arm. A huge lump on the back of his head.

His body was dark with dried blood and dirt. She found a towel and poured more hot water in a bowl, then returned to his side and started to clean the filth of battle from his skin. She had to repeatedly throw out the dirty, bloody water and refill the bowl. She stitched the worst of the wounds and tried not to think about what she had done in trying to save this man. He was the enemy.

It was dawn when she finished spreading a thick salve on the last of the wounds. She could do nothing about the lump on the back of his head.

She straightened and fought off weariness. She had to shed her man's clothes and change into a gown. Audra was expecting her.

She hurriedly washed the blood from the clothes the Scot had worn and spread them out in front of the fireplace. She added several logs to the fire, praying they would be sufficient to keep it going until she returned.

She would have to bring her daughter back, and she had to warn the Scot to be cautious in anything he said.

She leaned over him. His breathing was still raspy.

Kimbra studied him as he slept. His body was lean. There was a scar on his shoulder, so he'd obviously battled before. Yet his face was more saint than warrior. His eyes drew her to him. They had been so blue. So tortured. Her heart had reacted, and she—and more importantly Audra—could not afford that.

She tried to wake him several times, before his eyes finally opened and focused on her. She put the palm of her hand against his cheek. Miraculously it was not warm. He had escaped fever thus far.

God must be looking after him.

"I will fetch water," she said. His thirst would be a mighty thing after a day lying on the battlefield.

"My . . . thanks."

She mixed water with rosemary and poured the mixture into a cup. She returned and handed it to him. He took a sip, made a face at the bitter taste.

"It will help you sleep," she said.

He took another sip, then another, until the cup was empty.

"Do you remember who you are now?" she asked.

Frustration filled his face, bewilderment his eyes. He shook his head.

"I have to leave you here and fetch my daughter. She is seven. She must think you English," she said. "You must have a name."

"I . . . do . . . not know."

She had been thinking during the time she had bathed him. "You are Robert Howard. 'Tis a large and scattered family, and no one would want to question a Howard overly much. It is said they have powerful friends at court."

She stared at him for a long moment, then repeated, "Robert Howard. Can you remember that?"

He nodded, then said, "But I have to know—"

"Later. I have much to do."

"Your . . . husband?"

"He is dead. By the hand of a Scot." She stood.

"Your name?"

"'Tis Kimbra Charlton."

"Kimbra Charlton . . . I am sorry about your husband."

She stood, aware that his eyes followed her every movement.

"My thanks," he said again. "I do not know why you are doing what you are doing but—"

"'Tis not for you," she said abruptly.

"Then why?"

"You have the look of a noble or man of wealth. There may be a ransom. A reward."

A light in his eyes dimmed, and an unexpected stab of self-disgust went through her. She had purposely rebuked him, wanting to distance herself. She had tended wounded men before, men not her husband, and she had never felt anything but pity and a fierce desire to defeat death.

She felt something more now. She told herself it was pity, but pity was no longer a part of her. She admired his fierce determination to live. Anyone else with his wounds would have succumbed. There was something indomitable about him, and it reminded her of Will.

She hadn't saved Will. Mayhap she could save this man.

He closed his eyes. The rosemary slowly took effect, and finally the Scot slept, though fretfully.

Would he remember what she had told him? It was ever so important. Audra had no guile, nor did Kimbra want her to have it.

Anxious to return quickly, she left and rode Magnus to Jane's hut and found Audra sitting on a stone in front of the door. Her daughter's worried face creased into a toothy smile.

"How's my love?" Kimbra said as she dismounted and swept her daughter into her arms for a hug.

"I have to talk to Jane," she said, setting her daughter down. "Can you wait here and watch Magnus?"

Audra beamed.

"Remember what I told you. Do not get too close and do not make a quick movement. It could startle him."

"I will sing a song to him."

"I think he would like that very much." And he would. Audra had a sweet and true voice.

The door opened as she started to knock. Jane welcomed her with a smile.

"Thank you for keeping Audra."

"She is a joy."

"I will be home this night, and hopefully the next nights." Jane's face fell. "I will miss her."

"I suspect you will see her soon. I will bring her over to visit, along with some bay leaves for your legs."

Jane nodded. She had pain in her legs, and Kimbra's bay leaves could be made into an oil that relieved it.

Kimbra said her farewell and hurried out to Audra. It had been only seconds, but she worried about her daughter, nonetheless.

The sweet sound of her daughter's voice stopped her. She was singing an old lullaby to the horse. The picture, and melody, sent pangs through Kimbra's heart. What if she was endangering her daughter by shielding the Scot? She should forget this fancy and ride immediately to the Charlton, the acknowledged leader of the family, and tell him she'd found a Scot. Let *him* decide whether he would be kept as a hostage.

But she truly didn't know what he would do. And the hours she had spent nursing her patient had created a responsibility. She would wait until he had more strength. Then she would decide her next step.

She waited until Audra had finished her song, then swooped down on her, lifting her high and into the saddle. She walked the horse to a block and mounted. Cuddling her daughter on the way home, she asked what she had done the night before.

"Baked bread," Audra said with no little pride.

"You can bake mine," she replied.

Audra turned her head to face her.

Was she doing the right thing?

She had to tell Audra now about the stranger. She couldn't let Audra walk in on a strange, naked, and badly wounded man without warning.

"There is a man staying with us," she said. "He was hurt in the battle two days ago. You must be very quiet so he will get better."

"May I help?"

"Not now," she said. "Mayhap later."

"Who is he?"

"He is a Howard," she said, hating herself for lying to her daughter. She doubted Audra would know the name, but she would remember it. She remembered a great deal.

"Was he a friend of father's?"

"Aye," she lied again. It would be as good a tale as any. Will had had many friends.

"Then I am glad we are helping him."

"You will have to be very good. And very quiet."

"I will," Audra promised. "I will fetch some flowers for him."

"I think he would like that very much."

Then she had to say one other thing, for she wouldn't be surprised if she had a visit by Cedric. "You cannot say anything about him," she said.

"Why?"

Kimbra had known that question was coming. Every statement prompted a "why."

"Because the Charlton may not approve of a man staying with me, and I fear no one else can care for him as I can." That, at least, was true.

"Is he sick like Papa was sick?"

"Aye."

"Could he die?"

She would not lie about that. "Aye, he could, but I will do everything I can to see that he does not."

"I want to help."

"You can sing to him later," Kimbra said.

"I can help with the fire."

That was the last thing Kimbra wanted.

"No," she said more sharply than she intended. Yet she had a fear of fire. She always had. She had conquered it because she had to. But the fear of it never went away, and she didn't want her child near it.

Audra's eyes started to tear at the unaccustomed rebuke.

Kimbra's heart cracked. She leaned over Audra. "I want nothing to happen to you, love. But there are other ways you can help."

Audra's small back had slumped, but now it straightened. "I will be very careful."

They arrived back at the cottage. Bear happily barked a welcome and gave Audra a wet kiss when she was back on the ground. Audra hugged the big dog, as he frantically waved his tail.

"You can help me tend Magnus," Kimbra offered, and Audra happily followed her into the small stable.

Kimbra took off the bridle and asked Audra to hang it up. Then she lifted the saddle and lowered it to the ground. "Can you get Magnus some water?"

"Aye," Audra agreed happily.

Kimbra handed her the empty bucket hanging in the stall. Hopefully, fetching water from the barrel would distract her from asking any more questions about the stranger.

Kimbra rubbed the horse down, then put a blanket on him, just as her daughter appeared, carrying a bucket that looked as heavy as she was. Water sloshed as Audra tried to balance it, walk a step or two, then set it down again. Kimbra leaned over and took the bucket and hung it up for Magnus.

Then she took Audra's hand and they walked to the cottage. She tried to hide her anxiety. Though she had not been gone long, she found herself hurrying so fast that Audra practically had to run to keep up.

They went inside, and she gave Audra the wooden horse Will had carved for her. It reminded Kimbra again of Will. Two years gone now. The pain was fading, but then there were moments . . .

Kimbra hugged Audra and went into the room where she'd left the Scot. He was awake. Not only awake but sitting up with naught but a corner of the blanket covering his man parts.

His forehead was wet with effort, and his eyes were clouded with pain as he looked up at her.

"I cannot stay," he said.

"And where will you be going?"

"I thought about . . . what you said. I must be . . . putting you in danger. I should leave."

"You would not be getting far," she said, softening the sharp edge by touching his shoulder. The contact sent a jolt of heat through her, and it was not from a fever.

She stood there stunned. There was awareness in his eyes as well.

"I do not want anyone finding me here," he protested.

He was the first man other than Will who had ever cared about her safety and well-being. She resented the fact that she was drawn to him because of it. She did not want to like him. She did not want to admire him. She wanted nothing to do with him but make him well to spite all the death she'd seen, and mayhap collect a reward.

"My clothes?" he asked.

She wondered if he remembered that she had cut the plaid from him and left it behind. "They are still on the battlefield. The ones I used to replace them—they belonged to my husband—are drying in front of the fireplace. They were bloody."

He looked down at himself, the bandage around his arm, the poultice tied to his leg, the blanket partially covering him. He looked up, his eyes searching, looking for something that she couldn't give him.

"I cannot take them."

"You prefer wandering about without clothes?" Her voice was sharper than she intended. But she wondered what would have happened if she had not arrived when she had.

"I cannot repay you. I do not even know my name, nor where . . ." He stopped, bewilderment and frustration again filling his eyes. "I do not even know if I have a wife, bairns."

She did not know what to tell him. She had never encountered anyone who had lost their memory.

She wondered whether she should show him the jeweled crest she had taken from him. Mayhap it would spark a memory. But that and the ring the Charlton had allowed her were all she had of value for that night's work, the only protection that might save her from a marriage she feared, the only assurance she could care for her daughter.

He will get his memory back.

He must. Without it, he would be of little use to her. Or to himself. What would happen to a wounded man wandering about the dangerous border without horse or arms or memory?

The thought chilled her. Especially now when he seemed more concerned about her welfare than his own. While he healed, she could listen. If he was a noble, surely someone would be looking for him.

Did he have a father, a brother who would pay for information as to his whereabouts?

Did he have a wife and children waiting for him?

"You must lie down again. My daughter is outside and might decide to enter at any time."

He glanced down at his nakedness and nodded. "I suppose I *would* need those clothes," he said wryly.

"You will have them later. When they dry. For now, you must promise you will stay quiet. 'Tis the only way you will heal."

His gaze caught hers. Troubled. Filled with pain. Confusion. Stubbornness. He did not want to give in.

She touched his face lightly. The skin was only slightly warm under the bristle on his cheeks and chin. He wore no beard, which was most unusual, but it appealed to her. His hair was shorter than fashion, too, but she could not tell its true color at the moment. It needed a good washing.

He surrendered and lay back down with a sigh that was more groan, though she suspected the surrender would be short in duration.

"Tomorrow," he said. "I will be on my way."

He would not get far. Not today. Not tomorrow. Even with that will that was so evident. There was only so much a body could tolerate. He had lost a great deal of blood. The pain from his ribs and his leg must be almost beyond bearing.

Once he was lying down, she checked the poultice. It had soaked up fluids. She would fix a new one as well as a potion for the fever. She would pray, as well.

She went into the other room and slumped down on a chair. Audra had left the wooden horse and was playing with her straw doll. "Is he going to die, too?"

"Nay, love. Not if I can help it." She suddenly thought of something Audra could do. "Would you pound these herbs for me?"

"Aye," Audra said eagerly.

"You will have to be careful not to hammer your own fingers."

"I promise," Audra assured her.

Kimbra put the herbs on the table and gave Audra a small wooden mallet with which to pulverize them, then added a log to the fire and heated more water. She was beginning to move slower and slower, the loss of sleep weighing on her.

But the Scot's injuries couldn't wait. As the water started to boil, she looked at Audra who leaned over the table with concentration, trying very hard to reduce the greens into powder. And doing very well.

"That is very good," Kimbra praised, taking the powder and mixing it with hot water and oatmeal. She took the mixture into the other chamber. The Scot was still awake, his eyes on her.

"I've made a new poultice," she said. She pulled down the blanket covering him and placed a towel underneath his leg as she took the old poultice off and wiped the foul-smelling substance from his leg. She spooned the fresh mixture onto his leg, seeing his body tense as the poultice touched the raw wound. She then tied a cloth around it to hold it in place.

"Are you a soldier?" The small voice came from behind her. Audra had followed her inside. She'd been too weary to remember to close the door.

She looked at her patient. Would he remember what she had told him?

"Aye, I expect so," he said. He hastily pulled the cover over the lower part of his body.

"My papa was one, too."

"And a very brave one," the Scot said.

Audra gave him a lopsided grin. "Aye. He was handsome, too. My mater told me so."

Audra went to the side of the bed and gazed down at him. "You do not have a beard."

He felt his face as if unaware of that fact.

"Nay," he simply agreed.

"Why?"

That look of bewilderment flooded his eyes again, as he sought to find a reason and could not.

"'Tis a rude thing to do, asking a man about his appearance," Kimbra scolded.

Audra's smile disappeared, and she ducked her head, her bottom lip trembling.

"That is all right," the Scot said. "It is a perfectly reasonable question."

Audra gave him a grateful smile.

"In truth, it feels good," he said.

An explanation that could or could not be the real reason, but it satisfied Audra. At least for a moment.

He moved slightly, winced again, before smiling slightly. "And whom do I have the honor of addressing?"

Audra giggled. "I am Audra."

"A bonny name for a bonny lass," he said.

Every word was a struggle. Kimbra heard it in his voice,

yet he wanted to make a child feel better. She saw Audra smile in a way she hadn't for a long time.

Her heart thumped harder. For her daughter who missed her father. For the man still very ill.

Then she heard Bear barking, the bark that foretold visitors.

Fear ran through her.

Cedric? As much as she wanted to, he was not a man to ignore.

The barking increased. *Thank God for Bear.*

She stooped down to Audra's level. "I want you to go up to the loft and stay there until I tell you to come down. I want you to be very quiet."

Audra's eyes were solemn as she looked up at her. She knew about quiet. The Charltons had been raided, just as they had raided, and her cottage was away from the peel tower. They had practiced quiet before.

She nodded.

"No matter what you hear," she added. "Promise?"

"I promise." But it was a tiny uncertain voice.

"Go, then," she said.

She watched as Audra left the room. She turned to the Scot, "Be very quiet."

He nodded.

Kimbra hurried out of the room, closing the door behind her. She was grateful that Will had insisted on a door. He'd planned on many more bairns and had said a bit of privacy might prove fruitful. For a moment, she smiled inwardly at the memory. She looked up at the loft. Audra had disappeared, probably into the pallet there.

Then Kimbra turned her attention to the pounding on the door.

It wouldn't be a raid, not in the middle of the day. But her visitor could be far worse. She glanced out the window.

Cedric Charlton stood there.

She went to the fireplace, took up the nearly dry clothes the Scot had worn, and quickly ducked back into the sleeping chamber. His eyes were open. She put her finger to her lips, asking for silence and placed the clothes on the bed then left.

Her stomach clenched, but she readied herself for battle as she went to open the door.

Chapter 4

$\mathcal{B}$EAR continued barking a warning, then she heard a sudden yelp.

She opened the door. Cedric stood above Bear, a whip in his hand. Teeth bared in a snarl, Bear crouched as if to leap. Blood showed in his fur.

"Bear, no," she said.

The dog whined in protest, but sank to his belly.

Kimbra turned on Cedric. "What did you do to my dog?" she demanded, fighting to control her temper.

"The bloody animal would not stop barking."

"He is not supposed to."

Bear growled.

She leaned down and petted his head. "No, Bear," she said again.

The dog continued to growl.

"You should keep that dog tied up."

"He protects us." She stood in front of the door.

"I came to see you," he said, obviously deciding to ignore her hostility. "I have something for you."

"I have no need of anything."

"I would like to come inside."

"My daughter is asleep."

His eyes flamed, and she almost took a step back from the anger in them. But she was not going to show fear. Not to the likes of him.

He took an object out of his pocket and held it out.

She had no choice but to look at the brooch lying in his palm. It was a pretty trinket with a dark gray stone.

"It matches your eyes," he said.

The words surprised her. She knew he'd lusted after her, even while Will was alive, but he'd never offered sweet words before.

"It came from the dead?"

He looked startled, then defensive. "Ye were taking goods yourself," he said.

"For the family." A lie.

"Take it," he said.

"Nay."

His face mottled with anger, and he took a step forward. Bear snarled again.

Cedric stopped. He was not much taller than she, and more stout than the Scot, though some would say handsomely formed. His hair was dark, almost black, and his beard was black as well.

"The Charlton gave me permission to pay court," he said.

"'Tis too soon. I still mourn Will."

"Your daughter needs a father. A woman needs a husband."

"I am not ready."

"The Charlton has given you long enough to mourn. He grows impatient. The cottage should house a man, a soldier."

"It was my husband's."

"And a widow has no right to it. The land reverts back to the Charlton."

"Will meant for me to have it." She knew her protests would make little difference, but she had to try.

"A refreshment," he said, suddenly coaxing. "A glass of ale. We can talk."

He was a different man—or was trying to be—than the one who had prodded her two nights ago to steal from the dead. Will had always disliked him, had always said he wore many faces.

"I told you my daughter sleeps."

"Ye cannot avoid me forever."

"I have no feelings for you," she said desperately.

"They come in time, Kimbra. I am lonely. I want a son."

He wants the cottage. And Magnus.

He might want her as well, but she doubted whether love—or even affection—had anything to do with it.

"Please leave," she said. "I have promised some herbs today, and I must get them ready."

"You would not have to work so hard, were ye my wife."

Harder, more likely. She glanced down at Bear who was eyeing her visitor balefully. If she gave the word, the animal would charge Cedric and probably die in the doing.

"But I am not your wife, and I do have chores and a daughter that will be waking shortly. Mayhap later." She hated pleading with him but was afraid to antagonize him too far. He might well barge into the cottage.

He frowned. He did not want to accept rejection, and she knew he was weighing possibilities. Should he force her? Then a marriage would be a necessity.

But she knew she had the Charlton's affection as had Will. Cedric would be taking a risk, and he seemed to her a cowardly man.

"I will leave, but I will be back," he finally conceded. "Think about all I can give ye. Ye would have my protection against raiders. I can provide for ye. Most women would be grateful for my attentions."

He ran his finger beneath her chin and tipped her head upward. His finger moved along her cheekbone, but there was little gentleness and much possessiveness in the gesture. Before she could move away, he turned and mounted his horse. She opened the door for Bear, then she stepped inside before Cedric changed his mind and returned.

Cedric would not be deterred. He'd made that plain. Mayhap she would visit Thomas Charlton on the morrow and make her own plea. But how could she leave the Scot alone in the cottage? What if Cedric paid another visit? Walked in? She would not put it past him.

She had to wait until the Scot could leave the cottage, or at least move up to the loft.

She went to the window and watched as Cedric rode away.

"Audra," she called.

Audra peeked out from the loft, then climbed down the ladder. "Who was it?" her daughter asked.

"Cedric." Kimbra leaned down and checked Bear. There was a gash at the side of his neck, but it was not bad, and she didn't believe it needed stitching. Still, it must have hurt. She would make a paste and spread it on the wound.

"Ah, brave Bear," she crooned.

Bear preened as if he understood every word. Audra was looking at the blood on Bear with horror, then she gave the dog a huge hug, careful not to touch the wound. Tears filmed her eyes. "Why would he hurt Bear?"

"Mayhap he was afraid of him."

"Bear would not hurt anyone."

"He would if he thought you in danger, love."

"But I wasn't."

"Nay, but Bear did not know that."

Audra put her head against Bear's fur. "I do not like Cedric."

She wanted to tell Audra that she shouldn't say such a thing, nor even think it. But she couldn't. Not when she felt the same way.

"Go outside," she said, "and I will see to the . . . Howard."

She'd almost slipped and said "the Scot." That's the way she thought of him.

She watched as Audra and Bear went through the door. In seconds they were chasing each other around the yard. Though Bear was gentle with Audra, Kimbra knew the dog would protect Audra to the death if anyone tried to touch her.

Pain twisted inside as she watched Audra. Cedric was a cruel man. He used sharpened spurs on his horse, and the wound on Bear was only a small indication of what he might do if he had mastery here.

*R*OBERT *Howard.*
    He said it over and over again. It had been urgent to the woman, and he tried to make it real on his tongue.

But it had no familiarity. Neither did any other name. The more he tried to remember, the denser the cloud in his mind became. The more he struggled for memories, the more elusive they became.

Desolation filled him. The desperate loneliness of not knowing who he was, of feeling so thoroughly alone, rolled over him in waves. Pain pounded in his head, ached unbearably in his chest, and raged in his leg. But the greater torment was the recurring emptiness of anything before pain. Before the long night and day in the smoke-seared woods. Before the haunting cries.

He'd been fighting in battle. For whom? For what reason? He did not understand any of it. He didn't understand why the woman tended him. He did sense the fear under all that bravery in bringing him here.

He struggled to sit. Blood rushed to his head, and the agony from his chest was nearly more than he could bear. Only too aware of his nakedness, he reached for the clothes the woman had left on the foot of the bed. His world instantly went dark as waves of new pain assaulted him. After a moment the intensity lessened, and he managed to pull the clothes toward him.

He did not want to take what had belonged to the woman's husband. She had kept them. They must have meant something to her.

But he had no choice. Vaguely he remembered her cutting cloth from him. His own clothes must still be on the battlefield.

He'd heard the knocking that took her from his room. Her urgency had told him to remain silent, and there had been apprehension, even fear, in her movements. He worried it had something to do with him. He could not allow someone to suffer on his behalf. If someone entered the room, she would be compromised. He knew that, even though he didn't know how he knew it.

If he were dressed, he could always say he forced her.

Using every bit of strength he still had, he pulled on the rough, woolen shirt. Every movement was agony, but he did not like the sense of helplessness he felt. His nakedness made him feel even more vulnerable.

He couldn't hear voices. He did not know what was happening as he shook loose the poultice, letting it drop to the floor, and painfully drew on a damp pair of breeches. He stood, swayed slightly and used the wall to move to the door. It was solid, though, and he could hear nothing. He dared not open it. Instead, he looked around for a weapon and found a dagger. He lifted it, balanced it in his hand.

He obviously knew how to use it.

He sat in a chair. He was so bloody weak.

Useless to her if there was danger.

He tried again to remember. He *had* to remember!

The door opened, and the woman returned.

He questioned her with his eyes.

"It was my husband's cousin," she said. From the tone of her voice, the visitor had not been a welcomed interruption.

"You should be in the bed," she said.

"You . . . seemed concerned. I thought . . ." Then he realized he must truly be addled. What would he have done? He would be precious little protection.

"He is gone. You should not have left the bed," she scolded.

He rose painfully from the chair. In truth, he didn't know whether he could make it back to the bed or not. His leg wanted to buckle under him, and his ribs . . . he felt as if an anvil had landed on them.

Almost instantly she was at his side, adding her strength to his. She was surprisingly strong for a woman.

He sank back into the bed.

"You do not obey well."

"I feared for . . . you."

"I can take care of myself," she said sharply. "And you cause me more work when you do something foolish. Now I must make another poultice."

He wanted to say nay. That he would leave immediately. Yet it had taken all the strength he had to dress and take the few steps to the door. The best thing he could do now was heal enough *to* leave.

"Mistress Charlton—"

"Kimbra. Call me Kimbra."

He smiled slowly. "'Tis easy to do. Like Audra, it is a bonny name."

He saw a glimmer of tears in her eyes then, making them almost luminous. She turned away from him.

He cursed himself. She was crying. This strong woman who seemed undaunted by anything. He didn't know what he'd said to provoke tears, but it appeared he had done exactly that.

"My pardon. I did not mean to—"

She turned back to face him, and he saw a sheen of tears in her eyes. Her jaw moved slightly as if she were trying to control her emotions. " 'Tis none of your doing," she said.

She obviously wasn't going to explain further. And there was little he could do to console her.

"Where am I?"

"On the border in Northumberland."

Northumberland. It meant nothing to him. A chill invaded him. It should. *It must.*

"What happened?"

"A battle between your Scottish king and our King Henry. A great battle."

"Who won?"

"The English. They say the Scottish king is dead, along with most of his army."

"The Scottish king? His name?"

"James."

James.

He had apparently fought for a king. King James. For a fleeting second, he thought it was coming to him. But then, it vanished like smoke. Mayhap he only *wanted* to recognize it. To recognize something. Anything.

"You said a Scot killed your husband."

"Two years ago. On a raid across the border."

He looked at her. She was a handsome woman. Not beautiful, but pleasing.

Her eyes were gray, and her hair raven black. It fell in unruly curls to frame a face more interesting than pretty. Her chin was determined, her mouth wide, her eyes taking on different hues of gray according to her emotions. Under a black, almost shapeless gown, her body was slim

but strong, her back straight. She'd not smiled once, and
her manner seemed deliberately distant. But he'd seen a
kindness when she talked to her daughter, and her hands
had gentleness in her care for him. It belied the curt
speech and short answers.

"Why then—"

"I told you. You might bring a ransom. Or reward."

Someone might ransom him? Would he not remember
someone close enough to do that?

"Why do you think someone would pay a ransom?"

"You were near the king. You wore a fine plaid and fine
mail."

Think!

A plaid. He remembered it, soaking in his own blood.
Or was the blood someone else's? Had he lost a brother? A
friend?

The questions pounded at him. From what she said, he
was alive when many Scots died. The hunger to know more
gnawed at his heart.

"I must look after my daughter," Kimbra said, her voice
unsteady. "Please do not move again. I cannot spend the
day making poultices."

"I am grateful for what you have done."

"Then stay still," she said.

And then she left the room, leaving a scent of roses behind her.

Tis a bonny name.
        Will used to say that but a little differently. Pretty
instead of bonny. She'd liked the way "bonny" rolled off
the Scot's tongue. A flicker of warmth flared inside her.

And regret. The words had sparked too many memories.
The Scot lying in their bed did not help.

God help her, she had almost shed tears. It was the tension. Nothing else. Will had been dead two years now, and

she'd grown used to the loneliness. Then why did something as simple as an innocent observation bring on this rush of emotion?

Tired. It was because she was so tired.

She had heard of people losing their memories, but she had never before encountered it. She had no idea what to do, how to bring back bits and pieces of a life.

Still, despite his loss of who he was, there was a quality that attracted her, a gentleness she rarely saw in the borderers. There was also an attraction that stunned her, since there had been none before Will and none after. Why a stranger? A Scot. And particularly someone who apparently was of noble blood?

Nonsense. She should not think of such things. He represented a way for her to be independent, to be free of an unwanted marriage. She had to find out who he was, without anyone else knowing. She could not reveal the crest without someone wondering why she had not surrendered it with the rest of the plunder they'd collected the night after the battle.

He *had* to regain his memory. He had to tell her who he was. Then perhaps whoever cared about him would give her enough money to find a cottage someplace safe, someplace where no one would demand she marry.

She did not have much time. Cedric had made that plain.

She looked out the window. Audra was sitting next to Bear, singing one of her songs to him.

Kimbra went outside and knelt beside her. "Would you pick some comfrey for Mr. Howard?"

Audra nodded.

"Do you want me to show you which it is?"

"I know where it is."

"Show me."

Audra went to the herb garden and immediately went to the plant with the long narrow leaves, then looked up triumphantly.

Pride surged through Kimbra. Audra had been helping her tend the gardens since she was three years of age. Still, she'd not realized how much Audra had learned. She'd always thought Audra extraordinary, but she'd also considered the fact that Audra was blood of her blood, and therefore she was wont to think Audra the most exceptional child. "That is very good," she said.

Audra bent down and started picking the herb. Kimbra would mash the leaves together with aloe for poultices. Both were said to have healing powers, especially in stopping infections.

They had not stopped Will's.

She prayed it would stop the Scot's.

*K*IMBRA napped on and off during the afternoon. She sat in a chair next to the Scot's bed. His face and body had warmed, and she feared infection.

He slept on and off as well, though she recognized it was a dark sleep. He mumbled words, not clear enough to understand. He thrashed about, and at times she laid her body across his to keep him from falling from the bed. She thought she heard a woman's name—or was it a child's?—but she wasn't sure.

At one time when he moved restlessly, she brushed her fingers across the stubble of his beard and let them linger there, a gesture of comfort. He seemed to still, and she held her hand there for a moment, willing her strength into him. In that moment, he became more than a Scot who represented her only chance for an easier life for herself and her daughter. He became a person whose life was intertwined with hers. Warmth radiated between them, a warmth that had nothing to do with the fire in the other room.

She jerked her fingers away. He meant nothing to her but the funds he could bring. He could not mean more. 'Twas quite obvious he was noble. He spoke well. His manners, even without knowing who he was, were finer than she'd ever seen.

Do not even think about it!

The Scot's station was obviously so far above hers that she knew she could not have even the slightest feelings for him. If he ever regained his memory, she would be less than nothing to him. She knew how nobles treated their servants, those they regarded as less than themselves. It was unlikely that he would be any less treacherous.

He moved violently again. Then began shivering, even though his skin was still hot. She lay next to him, warming him with her own body.

Will had suffered the same way. Fever. Tremors. Violent shaking. Thank Mary in Heaven she didn't see the same red streaks running from the wound.

When the shivers subsided, she left him and went into the other room. She mixed more willow bark with water, and put water over the fire for a new poultice. The room had darkened, and she lit an oil lamp. Audra was sound asleep on a sheepskin before the fire, one arm around Bear. Kimbra put a warm hide over her. Since Will's death, Audra had slept in Kimbra's bed, each of them a comfort to the other.

She went outside and stretched. The air was cool this late summer evening and finally clear of the smoke that had hovered over the land for days. But she knew she would never again think of the wet, boggy valley bottom without smelling death.

She went back in. The water was hot enough, and she made the new poultice. She changed them often, wanting to draw out the infection in his body. Holding both the poultice and cup of the foul smelling willow bark mixture, she reentered the room. The coverings were gone, and he lay there half naked, his eyes open.

She leaned over. "Lift your head," she commanded. She put a hand behind his head and supported his back slightly. He tried to help her. His body was hot with fever, and she heard—and felt—the intake of breath. With his help, she finally got his head high enough to enable him to drink.

He was weaker than he was yesterday, the fever sapping what strength he had. When he finished drinking, she inspected his leg. The wound was ugly, and much of his leg was red.

The leg should come off. She knew that. But she had no skill in cutting. She only knew herbs. She felt his gaze on her. He knew the danger as well as she, even though he may not know how he knew.

"No," he said.

"You could die," she said.

"But I will go to God—or the devil—with two legs." His words were raspy.

"Are you wed? Do you have a wife?" She knew she had to keep trying to kindle a memory.

He simply stared at her, the familiar frustration filling his eyes.

"I know I would want Will alive, with one leg or two. Someone must be waiting for you."

She could see the strain in his face as he struggled to find answers that he could not.

She closed her eyes. What would God want her to do?

She would wait another day. If he did not improve . . . if his leg grew redder, she would have to go to the Charlton. She would have no choice.

She had tonight.

"Can you eat anything?"

He shook his head.

But he must. He must have enough strength to fight the demons in his body.

He thrashed suddenly, then his breath caught from what must be terrible pain in his bruised ribs.

She leaned down and put her hands on his shoulders. "Try not to move," she said. "The poultice must stay in place, and the ribs will heal only if you are still."

He nodded, his eyes thanking her.

She sat down until the willow drink and his own exhaustion lulled him back into sleep. She closed her eyes, wanting to join him. Then she opened them again.

She needed to tell the Charlton that she had found an Englishman and had nursed him back to health, but how could she explain that she'd waited so long to tell anyone?

First of all she would have to coach the Scot in the ways and speech of the English.

If he got well.

He *would* get well. She would not allow anything else.

Chapter 5

FOR three days, the Scot hovered between life and death.

His eyes were sometimes open, but unseeing. He moved restlessly, and his breath came in small labored gasps.

He said things in a language she did not understand. It might have been Gaelic, but then it might well have been French. She had no knowledge of language other than her own.

"You will be well," she insisted over and over again, as if the words would work their own cure.

Audra brought water to her, even mixed the willow bark into a cup, and then the child sat quietly in the corner. Watching. Clutching her straw doll. Once, she went to sleep in Kimbra's lap, and they both jerked awake when the Scot stirred and uttered a cry.

Kimbra continued to bathe him with cool water, trying to bring down the fever. Sometimes she had to rest her body against his to quiet the violent shivering and thrashing. He muttered words she didn't understand.

She often touched his face to judge the course of the fever. Once she ran her fingers through his hair, the thick, damp wayward strands wrapped around her finger. He was so warm.

Though his leg appeared to be getting better, the fever remained, and she feared an infection in his lungs. She continued to urge him to drink her mixture of herbs, even as she washed his body repeatedly. She came to know it intimately, the new wounds and an earlier one—a jagged scar across his left arm. His chest remained different shades of purple from the blow struck there.

On the fourth day, she knew she had won. She had defeated a fever for the Scot that she'd been unable to defeat for her husband.

It was a bittersweet thought.

JAMIE Campbell paced his cell in the dungeon of an English castle.

He had been allowed to pen a message to his father in Edinburgh, telling him that he was being held for ransom. He also related that he had seen Lachlan Maclean go down near his king.

He knew that King James was dead. He'd heard the celebrations, even as his heart ached for the monarch he so admired. The king had attended his marriage to Janet Cameron and had played a part in bringing Jamie's cousin Felicia and Rory Maclean together after a century-long feud between the two families.

James had known how to draw the nobles together, how to charm even the most reckless of them. He'd loved music and poetry and literature. And he'd admired law, insisting

that the clans end their ancient feuds and work together for
the good of Scotland.

Now there was only a bairn to rule a Scotland that had
just lost the best of its nobles. Jamie knew Scotland's
weaknesses. There would be chaos as clans tried to manip-
ulate the queen and her young son.

God's love, but he'd sworn to protect his king, his
Campbell soldiers, and his friend Lachlan. He had failed at
all three.

He'd seen Lachlan's horse go down, then he'd been
swarmed by the English as well. A pike had tumbled Jamie
from his horse, and when he tried to get to his feet, a sword
was at his throat.

He had been taken as hostage for ransom, while archers
and pikemen were systematically killed. He wished now
that the sword had gone through his throat. The flower of
Scotland died at Flodden, and he should have been among
them. He should have died protecting his king and his
friend.

His self-loathing competed with his need to get free and
discover exactly what had happened to Lachlan. Was his
friend, too, being held for ransom? Or was he still lying on
the Flodden killing ground?

Jamie thought of Janet, of her smile and blond hair and
eyes so blue they put the summer sky to shame. She hadn't
wanted him to go, but he'd looked forward to war with anticipation. What a fool he'd been.

How many Campbells died at Flodden? He had brought
200 of them: archers and pikemen. How many would return to Dunstaffnage?

He shivered in the dampness. In Scotland, hostages
were held as guests, but he had been brought to a cold,
damp cell and told to write to his family.

How long would it take for a rider to reach the island
and return? Then he could begin his search for Lachlan. He
had sworn to Rory that he would look after Rory's younger

brother. He could not return home until he knew what had happened to the man once his enemy, then one of his closest allies.

If he spent his entire life doing so, he would bring Lachlan, or his body, home.

Inverleith on the Sound of Mull

The news of the disastrous battle reached Inverleith by a messenger on horseback.

The king was dead. The messenger knew nothing about Lachlan Maclean. Neither did he know about Jamie Campbell, the heir to the Campbell clan. It was believed, though, that all the men at the king's side died with him.

Rory Maclean bowed his head. His wife, Felicia, who had been with him when he heard the news, put her arms around him and lay her head close to his heart. She was very close to Lachlan as well as to Jamie Campbell, her cousin, who was as dear to her as a brother.

Then she moved back.

"I do not believe it," she said. "Not Lachlan and Jamie."

"If the king is dead, so is Lachlan," Rory said heavily. "And probably Jamie as well. They would have been with James."

Her eyes filled with tears. "Lachlan surprises everyone," she protested, "and Jamie . . ." She paused, then said brokenly, "I must go to Janet."

Rory touched her cheek. "Aye. Both she and Angus will need you." He paused, then added vehemently, "I should have gone." Guilt sapped his heart. He should never have allowed Lachlan to take his place, but his younger brother had begged to go. And Rory believed in King James, knew he would have a far superior force and thought that for once and all this quest might drive the final demons from Lachlan.

And Rory had a new bairn and a wife he loved dearly.

He closed his eyes. How much did they have to do with his decision? It had been his place as the Maclean to lead his soldiers into battle. And how many of them had lost their lives? How many widows and orphans?

He would provide for them all.

Lachlan. His troubled brother who'd hidden his torments behind a smile and a song. Rory had not known how deeply scarred his brother had been until Rory had returned to Scotland after ten years at sea.

He could not lose another brother!

Patrick, his older brother, had disappeared somewhere in Europe years ago. Then Rory's father died. Now Lachlan. He had thought the Campbell curse on his family conquered, but now he wondered whether it hadn't been waiting out there, seizing one after another of the Macleans.

He swallowed hard. He had to find his brother. Mayhap he was wounded somewhere, or had been taken for ransom. *He couldn't be dead.*

He knew one thing. He would not leave his brother on the border. He would find out what had happened, and he would bring him back to Inverleith.

The Border

He kept retreating into the dark cave. Pain didn't follow him there. Nor did the terrible void that had become his world.

A voice called him back. Over and over. She would not let him go.

He grew angry. Anger gave him strength.

He knew when his eyes opened, she would be there. The woman who refused to let him die. His body was cold, and he had a terrible thirst. Every movement was a supreme effort. Even opening his eyes seemed too difficult to do.

He felt as weak as a kitten.

A kitten. He knew kitten. He knew water. Light. Darkness. He recognized voices. The woman's voice. A child's voice. A sweetness in the latter. Determination in the former.

Why didn't he know anything else? Why did everything else retreat behind a curtain he could not raise?

"Can you take water?"

He knew the words. He'd heard them over and over again.

He opened his eyes. The woman had haunted his fevered dreams until he'd believed her to be naught but a figment of them. But she was real, her long dark braid falling over her left breast, her gray eyes intense.

"Aye," he whispered.

He took the water she offered him, a drip at a time, then a swallow.

"The fever is fading," she said. She put fingers to his cheek. He felt calluses on her fingers, yet her touch felt good. So good he was disappointed when she withdrew her hand.

He asked the question that had been plaguing him. "How did you happen to find me?"

She hesitated. Her eyes would not quite meet his. "I was gathering items from the battlefield, along with the rest of the Charlton family. It is what we do."

She must have seen something in his eyes, because she continued defiantly. "Aye, it is what we do. Steal. Smuggle. Ransom."

He saw her shoulders tense. She did not like what she was doing. That was clear. He wasn't too fond of the idea, either. He remembered the cries for water. Had anyone slaked the thirst of the dying as she had his?

And why him and none other?

Ransom, she'd said, but there must have been others who offered similar opportunities.

Why him?

She did not offer a defense, but she looked ready to take a blow.

"You must have your reasons," he finally said.

"I do. Audra."

"There is no one to take care of you?" he asked. "Your family, your husband's family?"

"I have none of my own. Will's family wish me to remarry. I will not do that."

"You loved your husband." It wasn't a question but a statement of fact, as if he already knew.

"Aye. I cared for him."

Not exactly the same thing as love. He changed the subject. "I heard singing," he said.

"My daughter. She decided to sing you back to life. She would have been very sad if she had failed and you died."

He absorbed that, but it required too much effort to answer. It was a sweet thought, and it was rather comforting to know someone would be sad if he died. But it also brought back the loneliness of a mind empty of memories.

"You need food. Do you think you can eat?"

He was ravenous. "Aye."

Almost immediately she was back with a bowl of soup. He took as many sips of soup as he could, then he shook his head.

"I will keep it on the fire. Mayhap in an hour or two you can eat more."

"You have not slept."

"Aye, a little." She looked at him. "Do you remember anything now? Your name?"

"Howard?" It was the only name he recalled.

"You do not remember anything before that? Where you lived?"

She looked so hopeful he hated to say the truth. But he had nothing to offer her. "Nay."

She hesitated, then asked, "Do you read?"

Read? Did he? Then suddenly he knew he did. "I think so."

"Do you think you can show me?"

"I do not know," he said.

"I will find a book." She knew it would not be easy. Books were rare, and were kept as precious objects. But the priest might well help. He had tracts. Perhaps if the Scot read something familiar . . .

Words were on the crest, and that might bring back a memory. But what if he claimed the jeweled crest when he regained his senses?

No. She needed to protect the crest. She would try to help him remember in other ways.

Or would he ever remember?

*S*HE brought him a rough crutch she'd fashioned for him. Because of the wounded right hand, he tried to use his left arm but discovered a weakness there, probably from an older wound. He wondered how he had received that one, then put away the thought. It was only one of many questions he had, and probably among the least important. He tried his right hand. Pain shot through it, but he managed to get to his feet.

Each movement was agonizing. If he was upright, his chest did not hurt so badly, but his leg was pure agony. If he favored the leg, his chest felt as if it was crashing inward on him. But he managed a few halting steps with the aid of the crutch.

Those few steps required every bit of strength he had. But movement was one thing he had control over. He had none over any other part of his life.

He kept thinking his memory would return. It didn't, though he strained every moment to find something familiar. A name. A place. Even a language.

He knew English and probably several more languages, according to Kimbra Charlton. She said he spoke words during the fever, but she had not understood them. She thought several of them were Gaelic, which she'd heard on the border. But others were strange to her.

After his faltering steps, he collapsed back on the bed while she coached him on the speech of the borderers. She'd already told him much about the clans on the border, the English and the Scot, and their tradition of raiding across the border. He must understand them, she said, if he was to survive. He must be able to pass for an Englishman until she discovered his identity.

The speech came easily to him. He seemed to have an ability to ape words and the way they were spoken. Lessons stretched from one hour to several.

Later, Audra would enter the room and shyly ask him questions.

"Can you sing?" she asked after gifting him with a song.

He did not know. He started to hum the song she'd just sung, then the words came. But his were different from hers. A word here and a word there. A song he'd known? One he might have sung to his own child?

He looked up, and Kimbra was in the doorway, surprise on her face. "Do you know any other songs?" she asked.

"I did not know I knew that one," he said.

"Can you play anything?" she asked.

He shrugged.

"We have a lute. Will . . . found it on a raid and kept it, but he never learned to play. Still, he could never bring himself to give it up. He always thought Audra would play it someday."

"He sounds like a good man."

"He was. Some would say he was a thief, but to border-ers raiding is a way of life."

"How was he killed?"

"An arrow. He died of infection. I could not stop it."

"Is that why you tried so hard to stop mine?"

"Aye, part of it, I think."

"I owe you much, madam."

She seemed flustered by the address. "I will fetch the lute."

For the first time since he woke in this strange world, he was aware of amusement. Kimbra Charlton did not seem to be the kind of person to be flustered. Her competence and stubbornness awed him. The fact that she had plundered the fallen did not bother him as much as it first did. He supposed he would do the same, if necessary, to feed his own.

Did he have his own? He evidently knew a lullaby. A powerful loneliness swept over him. Did someone believe him dead? Did he leave a wife without the means to survive? Each question was like another sword in his gut.

Audra had not left his side. "I will take you to our waterfall," she said.

"A waterfall?"

"Aye, it is ours, Mater's and mine. No one else knows about it."

"A magic place then," he said.

Her eyes danced with conspiratory glee. "You must never tell anyone."

"I will not," he pledged.

"Mayhap you can milk Bess, as well."

"Bess?"

"Our cow."

"I am not sure I know how to milk a cow."

"Everyone knows how to milk a cow," she said. "I do."

"All by yourself?"

"Aye. I like Bess, and she likes me."

He could not imagine anyone—man or beast—not liking the lass. "I am impressed," he said.

She giggled. "I like you," she confided.

"Is there anyone you do not like?"

"Cedric," she said readily.

"Who is Cedric?"

"He was here three days ago. He wants us to marry him."

"Why do you not like him?"

"He hurt Bear."

"I would not like him then, either," he said and found that indeed he did not. Something inside him was repelled by cruelty.

The woman returned then. No, not the woman. Kimbra. Kimbra Charlton. He did not know quite what to call her, either to her face or in his mind. Kimbra was too intimate for their positions. Healer and patient. Jailor and prisoner.

Except despite all her protestations that he was here because she wanted a ransom, he did not feel like a prisoner.

She held a lute in her hands and handed it to him as he sat up in the bed. His hands ran over the instrument, then he fingered the strings with familiar ease. He found himself playing a melody and after a moment started to sing. The words came naturally, but they were not in English.

He finished and looked up at her. "It seems I do play the lute."

"Aye," she said, but there was no accompanying smile. Her gray eyes were intent on the lute. "Could you teach Audra?"

"I am not sure I could teach anyone. I do not even know how I learned, but I will try."

Her eyes sparkled then for the first time. He had not thought her lovely before, but he did now, even in the black mourning gown she wore and the proper cap covering her dark hair. He remembered her in the warrior's clothes she wore the night she had brought him here. He had been nearly unconscious, but he remembered seeing her kneeling beside him.

Even then, she'd radiated with a passion for life.

He realized he was beginning to feel more than gratitude toward her. He also knew he had to stifle those feelings. He might well be wed and have bairns of his own. But no matter how hard he tried, he couldn't conjure up a face in his memory. Not of a woman. Not of wee bairns. Surely if someone was important to him, an image would surface.

"We should let Mr. Howard sleep now," Kimbra Charlton said.

He placed the lute at his side.

"I do not want to leave," Audra pleaded.

"He will be here in the morning."

She left with Audra, closing the door behind her.

He picked up the lute again. Even that movement hurt. He had not wanted to show pain to the child, but it remained in every movement. Yet the lute felt so familiar in his hands. He strummed again, his hands fingering the strings with surety.

What else did he know?

KIMBRA put Audra down on the thick skins near the fire, then made bread for the next day. She heard the sounds of the lute through the door, and her heart ached at the beauty of the notes. He was accomplished with the instrument, as much so as many minstrels who came by the peel tower to tell their tales and sing their songs.

She did not know if such a talent was unusual in a man of rank. She only knew there was something about the melody that made her heart ache with longing.

Bear barked outside, and she looked out the window, praying it was not Cedric. She had thanked God every day he did not appear.

Jane was walking stiffly up to the cottage, leaning heavily on a cane.

Guilt ran through Kimbra. She should have checked on her friend and renewed her supply of bay leaves. She'd promised. She quickly went to the door to the room where the Scot was abed. He was still holding the lute, his fingers touching the strings.

"I have a visitor," she said. "You must be quiet."

He nodded.

She left the room, closing the door behind her, then went to the front door and opened it. Again she stepped outside and closed the door behind her.

"Jane, what brings you here?"

"I feared something must have happened. I have not seen ye."

"Nay, I just needed some rest."

"They should not have made ye go to the battlefield."

"Many went," Kimbra replied. "And I was able to keep a ring."

"You should be able to keep much more. Will would be turning over in the ground if he knew how they were treating ye."

"I have to do my share. Just as Will did."

"Yer Will worked hard for this place. For ye. Thomas Charlton should respect that instead of selling—" She stopped suddenly.

"What have you heard?" Kimbra asked.

"Cedric and several others are fighting to wed ye."

"He was here three days ago. I feared he would return, but he has not."

"He is gone. He and others have gone after the few Scots who survived."

"How many lived?"

"I do not know, but there is a bounty for Scots. They are picking up occasional stragglers and turning them over to the crown, which is executing them."

Horrified, Kimbra could only stare at her. "But there could be ransoms."

"I hear a few have taken highborn Scots for ransom, but the Charlton wants to appease the warden. There have been accusations that the Charltons did not do their fair share in the battle. He would not risk disobeying now."

Kimbra did not doubt that at all. The Charltons were

brave enough when enriching themselves, but they saw little reason to risk life and horse for the English king.

Kimbra knew the Charlton family was ruthless, that they had little regard for life. She suspected they killed some of the wounded in the aftermath of the great battle. She would have suspected it of Cedric readily enough, but not of Thomas Charlton, who talked much about the honor of the borderers.

Her stomach sinking, Kimbra invited Jane inside, knowing not to do so would raise suspicions, all the time wondering how much longer she could keep the Scot's presence a secret. She might well need help. Could Jane provide it?

Jane glanced down at Audra sleeping on the hearth. "Ye must tell her I came to see her."

"I will," Kimbra said, then offered some ale and fresh bread she'd just baked, along with butter she'd churned.

"Do you know when the men will return?"

Jane shook her head.

"Is the Charlton at the peel tower?"

"Aye, 'tis getting more and more difficult for him to ride."

"I may need to see him."

"Take him some of your bay leaves."

"He has his own physician."

"He is not helping, by all I hear."

Kimbra considered the words. Perhaps that would be a way to approach Thomas Charlton, the head of the family. He held no official rank. He was no baron or earl or duke. But he ruled the family and had the respect of the border families.

"I will take over the bay leaves," she said. She fetched some that Audra had picked earlier in the day and tied them in a piece of cloth. "These are for you. And take a loaf of bread."

She realized she was almost shoving her friend out the door.

After Jane left, she leaned against the door. She'd almost

told Jane about her Scot until her friend explained the Charlton order to turn any over to the crown.

She would not be able to go through Thomas Charlton for ransom.

And if anyone discovered who he was, her Scot would die.

She couldn't bear that. Not after all the hours she'd spent trying to save him.

But what now?

She did not see too many choices.

She could get him well, then help him escape from here and hope that he might be grateful enough to send her some money.

But if anyone discovered that she harbored an enemy, she could be killed and Audra orphaned.

How long could she keep his presence a secret?

And how important was his life compared with her daughter's? She had to think of Audra first. Even a heavy ransom or reward would not justify the chances she was taking.

She fully realized now what a dilemma she had created for herself. She had no idea how to solve it.

Chapter 6

Inverleith, Scotland

Rory prepared a troop to head south to search for his brother. Archibald, his captain of the guard, would accompany him. Douglas, his steward, would stay and protect the castle. And Rory's wife.

It had taken him several days to call in what few men were available. So many had gone with Lachlan.

In those few days, he'd also delivered food and seed to those crofters who'd lost their men. He'd mourned with widows and their children and reassured them that they would always have a place at Inverleith. The most difficult visit was to Hector's wife, Fiona, who was now probably a widow. Hector, with Archibald Maclean, had led Maclean forces for thirty years. Hector had left with Lachlan, and

Archibald—who was nearing sixty years—had stayed at Inverleith to train more Macleans for battle.

Hector had been as much a father to Rory as his own had been.

"I will look for Hector on the border," he told Fiona, "as well as for Lachlan and Jamie."

"God bless you," Fiona said. "I knew you would no' leave him there."

"I canna promise anything. Only that I will try to find your husband, but failing that, you will be cared for all your days."

Then he and Felicia visited Dunstaffnage, the stronghold of the Campbells and home to Jamie and Janet Campbell. He half expected the old chief, Angus, to have returned, but he had not. He surely, though, had heard about the defeat.

Someone had evidently seen them coming, because the gate was up, Janet standing just inside. Felicia slid from her horse and embraced Janet. Not only was Janet her cousin by marriage, but they were very good friends. One of their joint adventures, in truth, had led him to Felicia. For that reason alone, he'd always had a soft spot for Janet.

The sorrow on her face told Rory that she had heard news of the defeat.

"Have you heard anything of Jamie?" Felicia asked.

"Nay. His father said that King James had been killed and most of the army destroyed." Her lips quivered slightly. "I know so many who went, and Jamie . . . and Lachlan . . ." She stopped. "Have you heard anything? Is there any news of Lachlan?"

Felicia shook her head.

"I am so sorry," Janet said. "Come in and eat with me. I can barely stand being alone."

Rory and Felicia followed her into the great hall, then into a small, intimate room.

"I have news," Janet said after asking a servant to bring them refreshments. "I am with child."

Felicia hugged her again. "How long have you known?"

"I knew before Jamie left, but I did not wish to worry him. Now . . ."

"He'll be back. So will Lachlan," Felicia said.

Rory wished he had the same confidence. He had taken the messenger aside and had heard that at least thirteen Scottish earls were dead, as were more than fifteen lords and many clan chiefs, along with thousands of Scottish soldiers. Lachlan would be back by now, if he had survived, or at least sent word. Jamie as well.

"Does Angus know about the child?"

"Aye, and I hope it gives him some peace. He never showed it much, but he loves Jamie dearly."

"Will he return here?"

"I think not. He says the vultures are swarming around little James V. He fears to leave the queen and lad."

"Not much more than one year old, and Margaret, God keep her safe, is no match for the power hungry," Rory said.

"She loved the king so. She must be devastated." Janet's hand went to her stomach, to the child inside.

"Perhaps you should travel to Edinburgh and have your bairn there," Felicia suggested.

"I will wait here," Janet replied. "I want to be here if . . . when . . . Jamie returns."

They ate and exchanged what little they knew about the battle. None of it boded well for Scotland or their families. "'Twas said that Lord Home turned and ran," Felicia said.

"If true, he will live his days paying for it," Rory said grimly.

"Will the English come north?" Janet asked.

Rory noted how hard she was trying to maintain her composure. She had a quiet dignity, but her eyes glittered with unshed tears.

"Nay, I doubt it. They had many killed as well, and much of their army is in France."

Rory and Felicia lingered another hour longer, then had to leave. It would be a long journey back to Inverleith.

They were quiet most of the way back. As they approached the walls, Rory turned to his wife, and her eyes met his. They knew each other so well now that words were often unnecessary between him.

"Find them," she said.

"I will." And he would if it took his own life. Lachlan had gone in his stead. The least Rory could do was to bring him home.

$\mathcal{K}$IMBRA continued to instruct her Scot in speech. She was astounded at how quickly he lost his dialect and remembered the English turns of phrase when he could not remember anything about his past.

She was equally as startled at how she responded to him as she wrapped his chest tightly to ease the pain and changed the bandages on the leg that still barely held him. Her heart jolted when he looked at her, and heat sparked in her every time she touched him.

At the same time, she knew how much danger they were all in. Even if there had not been orders to kill all Scots, her hopes of ransom had faded. He remembered no more today than he had the day she'd found him. And he could not yet leave. His leg would not hold him more than several steps, and that with the crutch she'd made. He had no money, no horse, no memory.

She had outwitted herself. In thinking to reap a financial benefit, she found herself responsible for someone who had no value and could bring disaster upon herself and Audra.

She could ask him to leave. He would. But where would he go? How would he survive in hostile England? She would have to find a way to get him across the border.

But if she could transform him from noble into an English borderer, mayhap she could save all three of them. With time, he could walk again and start back to Scotland where someone would recognize him.

But he would not be strong enough for several weeks.

She finally reached a decision. Every moment he spent at her home without the knowledge of the Charlton was dangerous. She would tell the Charlton that she found him just two days ago, that he was an English borderer of the Howard family.

She told the Scot what she planned, asked if he could carry the ruse.

"I will try."

"You will have to be a bastard, banished by your family, and thus you became a soldier. That way no one will wonder why you are not sending word to someone."

"You have a devious mind, mistress."

"Ah . . . be careful when you talk. No borderer would say that." She should have been offended but she was not. She wanted to be mistress of her fate, and if it took deviousness, then so be it.

"Aye," he agreed. "I would not want harm to come to you—"

"Then you must always think before you talk." She softened her tone. "In several weeks you can leave."

"I thought you wanted to claim a ransom," he countered, now not entirely sure he *wanted* to leave.

"It is too dangerous for you now. The king has ordered all Scots killed."

He stared at her. "And still you care for me?"

"Only until you are well enough to go."

"Where?" he said in a voice that made her heart cry.

"To Scotland. Your clothes were very fine. You must come from a wealthy family, probably a noble one. In

Edinburgh someone will know you." She paused. "You probably have a wife and children."

She watched his eyes and saw something flicker there. Because he had remembered something, or had he merely considered the possibility?

She hesitated. What if the wrong word slipped accidentally from his mouth? She was going to tell the Charlton that he'd had a bad head wound and his thoughts were addled at times. She told the Scot that he should say he was from the southern border, a place far enough away that he would not have met any Charltons but close enough to Scotland to share a common speech.

"I do not think I have children. Or a wife," he said.

"Why?"

"Surely I would have some memory. Some token."

She said nothing. She suddenly realized she didn't want him to have a wife—and that frightened her. She shouldn't care. She should care about naught but a reward. And her own child's safety.

Especially since he would have naught to do with a border reiver's widow once he regained his former life. He was obviously educated, and she could not even read. Yet she felt the same spark in him she felt in herself, saw the way his eyes followed her, and how they softened when his gaze met hers.

"I must go," she said. "I may well have company on the return."

"Audra?"

"She goes with me. I could not leave her alone."

"She would not be alone with Bear and me."

"You could not protect yourself, much less her."

She saw the light leave his eyes. "You are right, of course."

She wanted to lean over and touch him, reassure him. He was a warrior. His wounds proved that. He went down with his king, fighting to the end. But to touch him would be to cross that barrier she'd tried to build.

"I will be back shortly," she said, then stepped outside.

She prayed she was right.

HOMAS Charlton—the Charlton—was sitting in a chair, one leg up on a padded stool. The leg looked twice its normal size.

"Mistress Kimbra, how kind of ye to stop in and see an old man."

"Posh. You will never be old."

"Flatterer."

"I brought some bay leaves. A good hot drink should help your legs."

"Now that is very kind of ye."

"And to tell you something."

He simply nodded his head and waited.

"I found an Englishman near my cottage three days ago. He was very badly wounded. I got him inside, but he had a terrible fever, and I did not feel I could leave him."

"English, ye say?"

"Aye, he wears border clothes and says he is a Howard."

"He is one of ours, then, and ye did the right thing. He should be moved here. There will be talk if he stays with ye."

"There is always talk."

"Aye, but it is time for ye to marry again. I have been approached by several men."

"Cedric said you favored him."

"Did he now?" he said. "I do not believe I expressed that thought, only that I felt it time you wed again."

"It is my choice then?"

"Unless ye wait too long. There is grumbling that ye are favored over others, that the cottage should go to a fighting man and his family."

"Will was loyal to you," she protested.

"Aye, he was, and that is why I have not pressed ye, but I cannot and will not wait much longer. It is a distraction to my soldiers, and distractions are never good. And they may not approve of a man living in your cottage out of wedlock."

"He is very ill."

"I will drink your bay leaves tonight," he said, "and ride over to see your Englishman in the morn, if possible. I will decide for myself where he should go."

She nodded, knowing she had done all she could, and any more protestations might well anger him. Thomas Charlton was not known as a patient man.

She curtsied to him and fled.

She had received more than she had hoped. Now if only the Scot could do his part.

Kimbra collected Audra, who had been waiting outside, her hands primly crossed in her lap. She sensed the importance of the occasion.

She looked up with worried eyes, and Kimbra realized her own apprehension had transferred to her daughter. "Everything is perfectly fine," she said.

"Then Mr. Howard can stay?"

"A few days. No more."

"I like him. So does Bear."

"He has to go to his own family."

Audra's lips trembled. "I do not want him to go."

"He probably has children just like you," she said as she led her daughter outside. It was a long walk, but she'd feared that someone might have tried to claim Magnus if she had ridden him.

She found herself hurrying. She'd hated to leave the Scot by himself. Audra was lagging behind, and Kimbra picked her up and started to carry her. For some reason, apprehension crawled up her spine.

She walked even faster.

* * *

*H*E used her crutch to walk. Every step required every ounce of strength he had. His chest both burned and ached. His leg would barely hold him.

He had struggled to his feet after the woman and child left.

He would not put them in danger. He would go into the woods and rest, then try to make it to the border. She must be right. Someone beyond the border would know him, recognize him.

And she would not regret helping him. He would make sure she was amply rewarded.

He knew he had to leave, even though a voice deep inside him told him he belonged here, or at least with Mistress Charlton and her young lass.

Kimbra felt it, too. He knew that. Which was why he had to leave until he could discover who and what he was. He was drawn to her, but what if he had a family of his own? He would not dishonor someone who had helped him, and he knew every day he stayed could lead to exactly that.

Yet where would he go?

North. The day was cloudy. He had no idea which direction was north.

Bear followed him, as though it was his job to protect him. He tried several times to send him back, but the infernal dog refused to heed him.

His clothes felt unfamiliar, and he regretted the necessity of taking them. They did not belong to him; he felt that to his bone. He wondered whether he would have felt that before his head injury. Had he been a just man as well as a warrior?

He stumbled, the pain in his leg crippling him. His chest was a fiery inferno. How long had he been gone, and how far had he come? Not far, yet he could not see the cottage, and trees were closing in around him. He prayed he was going in the right direction.

He took several more steps, then found a fallen log to sit on. He knew if he went all the way to the ground, he could not rise again. But he had to rest.

Bear sat with him. "Go back," he said.

The dog sat and stared at him.

Frustrated, Lachlan stared back in a battle of wills. He did not know why Bear was following him and refused to go home. He was Audra's dog, meant to protect a child, not a warrior.

Warrior. Somehow the word did not ring true to him. He wanted to read and sing songs and play the lute. He had no urge to kill another human being, yet he probably had. Many times.

As for being fierce, not even a dog obeyed him.

The thought did not relieve him. Why did nothing seem familiar?

"Go home!" he ordered again.

Bear lay down and rested his head on his paws, all the while looking at him.

"God's tooth," he muttered. He could not take the child's dog.

He would have to go back. Put the dog inside or tie him up.

He tried to stand. Weakness flooded him. He grabbed for the crutch, but it fell. He noticed his breeches were wet with blood.

Kimbra Charlton had been right. He was not . . . ready.

He tried again to rise, but his legs would not hold him, and he fell beside the log. He looked up through the trees. The sun was fast disappearing, and he shivered from the damp air that seemed to be growing colder.

He would rest a few moments. Just a few.

He reached out for the dog, but the animal moved out of reach, watching him with dark eyes. Then Bear bounded away.

Lachlan's eyes closed.

* * *

*I*T was dusk before Kimbra and Audra reached the cottage.

No welcoming bark greeted them. She went inside. She'd left two large pieces of log in the fireplace, but they were down to embers now, and the cottage was cold and dark.

Kimbra placed her sleeping daughter down on the pallet. She didn't want to alarm her, and when Audra slept, she slept deeply. She probably would not move for hours.

She hurried into the solar chamber. In the darkening gloom, she saw the bed was empty.

What had happened to him? He was too weak to go anywhere.

She returned into the main room and added some smaller pieces of wood to the embers. In moments they flamed, and she lit a candle.

Audra stirred and mumbled something.

She knelt by her daughter and comforted her, even as her thoughts were in turmoil.

Where was the Scot? And Bear.

The dog would never have left without a good reason.

Had someone come by and taken the Scot, and Bear thought he should follow?

Yet nothing was out of place. The stick the Scot had used to hobble around with was gone.

Had he gone on his own?

But how could he? His wounds had been too severe. She had seen and tended too many wounded men not to know that determination would carry them only so far.

She remembered his insistence that his presence not harm her or Audra.

She placed the candle in a lantern, then went outside to look around. Dusk was quickly turning into night, every moment further darkening the sky. A wind blew, and clouds raced across the sky. The air had turned cold.

She would have to look for him.

But that meant leaving Audra alone.

She closed her eyes for a moment. She didn't want to make decisions like this. She couldn't. Her heart ached. Her conscience hurt. She couldn't leave her daughter. She couldn't leave the Scot somewhere to die.

She heard a bark, then saw Bear running toward her, stopping at her feet and looking up at her.

"Bear? Do you know where he went?"

Bear barked again.

"I can't leave Audra."

Bear ran a few feet toward the woods, then looked back again, obviously begging her to follow.

The Scot couldn't have gone far. Audra should be safe for a short period of time.

She followed Bear through the woods, though she could barely see. A mist was falling, and it eclipsed all but the few feet illuminated by the lantern.

Bear would run ahead, then bark and wait until she reached him. Then he would bound ahead again, barking again, encouraging her.

He could not have gone this far.

She started to call Bear and turn back, when the dog's barking changed. It was high-pitched and frantic.

Still holding the lantern with one hand, she slowly moved forward, the branches of trees brushing against her skin. She stopped suddenly.

A body lay next to a log.

She hurried over to the still form.

Her Scot's breathing came in short rasping sounds, and blood had spread over the ground. She muttered one of Will's favorite curses and stooped down.

She tried to wake him. He moaned slightly, and his eyes flew open, but they appeared unseeing.

Fury at him rose up in her. He had been improving, and

now he'd been lying on the cold ground in a mist, and his efforts had opened the wound just newly closed.

She said fool in every way she knew, then decided that didn't help much.

He was losing blood and could catch an infection in his lungs if he had not already. She told herself she should leave him here. She knew she couldn't.

She shook him as gently as possible, and he started up, a roar in his throat rather than a moan, his arms thrashing about.

Go, and leave him here. He is not worth it.
Audra is waiting for you. She's all alone.

"Scot," she demanded loudly.

Nothing.

She shook him harder. This time his eyes seemed to concentrate.

"You cannot stay here," she said. "You will die. You must help me."

"Tired. So tired."

"You should be," she said. "You were addled enough to walk far from the cottage when you could barely move this morning. Where did you think you were going?"

"Did not want . . . you . . . to risk . . . more."

"Well, now you and your bloody conscience or whatever it is are going to cause more problems." Her voice was harsher than intended, mainly because of worry.

The mist turned into rain. She should have brought Magnus with her, and the litter, but she hadn't fancied dragging it through the woods. She had hoped he had not gone far, and that he could return on his own.

Obviously, he could not.

He shivered, his entire body moving.

She made her decision.

"Bear, stay with him. Lie down and keep him warm. I'll be back."

Using the lantern for what little illumination it provided

in the rain, she ran as quickly as she could back to the cottage.

It wasn't long before she reached the stable and quickly saddled Magnus. She hitched the litter she'd made days earlier to the horse, then started back.

She was reminded only too well of her other journey a few nights earlier. This was a short distance, and not so dangerous, but her heart pounded, and she knew it pounded with fear for him.

Chapter 7

H E didn't stop shivering, even when she got him back to the cottage. He was unconscious. She knew she couldn't get him up on the bed. It had been all she could do to roll him onto and off of the litter.

She dragged him into the main room next to the fire and covered him with everything she could find.

The weather hadn't been icy cold, but the damp cool ground and rain could be deadly for someone so weak.

She put more wood in the fireplace, then tried to pull off his breeches. When she couldn't, she used her dagger to cut the cloth around his wound. His leg was gapping open, the stitches she'd so carefully made pulled away.

Kimbra left his side and went to Audra. Her daughter was still sleeping. Bear was inside and had settled down next to her.

She reached down and picked up Audra and took her into the other room, settling her in the big feather bed. She closed the door behind her as she returned to the Scot.

She probably should have cauterized the Scot's wound when she first brought him here. But now she had no choice. It was bleeding badly and had torn too far apart to be sewn back again. She thanked God he was unconscious. If only he remained that way.

She went over to the fireplace and placed the dagger in the flames and watched until she thought the metal hot enough.

Her stomach turned over. She had done the same thing for Will, had seen his body react though not a sound escaped his lips. And he had still died.

She wrapped her hand with a piece of cloth, picked up the dagger and approached him. "Stay unconscious," she pleaded softly.

Kimbra kneeled beside him, steeling herself to do what needed to be done to staunch the bleeding and close the wound.

She pressed the dagger against the wound, heard the sizzle of heat against skin and smelled the odor of burning flesh. His body jerked, then relaxed. But she knew the agony he would feel when he woke.

He shivered, and she lay down next to him, putting one arm around him, letting his body absorb her body's heat.

She rose several times during the night to fuel the fire. She wiped his damp face with a towel, pushed back strands of his hair, felt the stubble of new beard.

She willed him to fight, willed him to live with all the strength of her body. It was as if his death would be hers as well. As if they had become one.

By now she knew every scar on his tall, lanky body. She didn't know the scars in his mind.

And so she prayed as she had not prayed since her husband died.

Inverleith

Rory planned to leave the next morning when two messengers arrived. One came from Janet at Dunstaffnage. She had received a ransom demand for Jamie and had sent it on to Jamie's father in Edinburgh. Jamie Campbell was alive!

If Jamie was alive, then Lachlan could be as well. Perhaps a messenger was on his way with the same demand for his brother.

The second message came from Queen Margaret. It was a summons to Edinburgh, a plea. She needed counsel about her infant son, now king, and there were few people she truly trusted. Most of those had died at Flodden.

Rory had not been a confidante to either the king or his bonny queen, but King James had granted him the greatest boon of all, his wife. The king had mended a century-long feud between the Campbells and Macleans, and for that Rory had vowed fealty. There was no question of refusal, even now. He would have to journey to Edinburgh.

Archibald would accompany several Campbells to the border with the ransom. Rory would join them as soon as possible.

Felicia wanted to go with him, but she could not leave Maggie and little Patrick that long. Her children were yet too young.

Rory saw the longing in her eyes as he bade her farewell. "I wish you were going with me," he said.

"My days of adventuring are over."

"I think not, love. They will come again."

She looked mollified by the observation. Until the babes came, she'd created chaos wherever she went, a quality that had amused and befuddled him. But since the bairns came, she had been the model of motherhood. Still, he sometimes glimpsed a longing for adventure in her eyes. Someday, he'd promised, he would take her back to sea.

Now she shared his concern for Lachlan. She loved his brother as much as he did.

Rory blessed every day he'd had with Felicia and would miss her greatly.

"Why do you not ask Janet to come stay here with you until Jamie returns?"

Her eyes brightened. "I will."

He'd already saddled his horse, and the animal was waiting in front of the entrance. He could tarry no longer. He leaned down and gave her a long lingering kiss.

As he reluctantly drew away, he touched her face, memorizing its feel. He did not know how long he would be gone.

"Hurry back. I do not want to come after you."

And she *would*.

He left then. If he hadn't, the look in her eyes would have delayed him even longer.

*B*EAR'S barking warned Kimbra as she loosened the damp cloth binding the Scot's chest.

She looked outside. Thomas Charlton was dismounting slowly and obviously painfully.

She had hoped he would not be able to come. She never would have gone to him had she known the Scot would worsen, that fever made him unaware of words coming from his mouth. He had quieted through the night, and the shivering was gone, though his breath was still raspy and frightening.

Audra had wakened early, and Kimbra had given her porridge and milk. She tried to get some milk down the Scot's throat as well, but he had gagged it up. He hadn't entirely gained consciousness, though he had muttered several times during the night.

Audra curtseyed prettily to the Charlton, and his severe face broke into the smallest of smiles.

The Charlton entered the cottage and immediately went to the man on the floor and regarded him for several seconds. "A Howard, you say."

"It is what he said," she lied, hoping God would forgive her the untruth. It was, after all, to save a man's life.

"He said nothing more? Not which Howard family?"

"Nay."

"He appears next to death."

"He became worse last night."

"I will send for my physician."

"He will merely bleed him," Kimbra replied. "He has lost enough blood."

"Ye are willing to look after him?"

"Aye."

"Why?" he asked bluntly, even suspiciously.

"I think Will would want me to take care of someone wounded. I would hope that someone would have cared for him had he required it."

The Charlton frowned at that, then returned his gaze to the wounded man.

The Scot mumbled something that she believed might be French.

The Charlton's frown deepened. " 'Tis not English."

"He said he has fought against the French in Europe. Mayhap . . ."

Charlton used a foot to stir the Scot. The Scot groaned but did not open his eyes.

"He probably will not live through another day," the Charlton said. "If he does, we will move him to the tower. I would not like your reputation darkened for helping an English soldier. It could destroy your chances of a good marriage. Even with the cottage as a dowry."

Which might be a way out.

But she only agreed. "Aye."

He started for the door, then turned back. "The bay leaves? Do ye have more?"

"They helped, then?"

"Aye."

"Send someone over, and I will have some ready."

"Ye are doing well here, on your own?"

"We have a cow for milk, and I have my garden. I trade my herbs for what I need."

"Ye still need a husband. Ye and Audra are alone here. The Armstrongs have been raiding isolated farms and cottages."

"I have Bear. And you know I can use a dagger."

" 'Tis not enough. Ye need protection. I will send someone here to help you."

She hesitated. The last thing she wanted was someone to spy on her, and yet she thought he meant it as a kind offer. But until the Scot was lucid enough—if he became lucid enough—to realize what he was saying, she had to take care of him alone.

"Audra is helping me. I will call if I need help."

He looked from her to the Scot and back again. "If he lives, I will send a messenger to the Howard family. Mayhap there will be a reward. It will be yours."

She said nothing. She couldn't say anything. Pray God, the Scot would be gone before an answer came.

She watched as he disappeared down the path, then returned inside.

She made a new poultice of aloe for the burn, hoping it would relieve the pain when he woke. And he *would* wake. She was determined about that.

Audra helped as much as she could, handing her cloths and taking used ones to a big pot where they would be boiled and used again to draw heat from the wounds.

He woke again as evening came. Once she knew he would survive the night, her anger grew. He'd nearly killed himself.

She tried to contain it when he opened his eyes. They

fastened on her, and he grimaced. "You do not give up, do you, Mistress?"

"And you do not stop being foolish," she retorted.

His eyes fluttered for a moment as he reacted to her anger.

"I am . . . sorry. I thought I was stronger—"

"So you decided to take a walk, fell, and lay in the bog and rain for God knows how long. If not for Bear you would be dead now."

"I tried to send him back."

"He has more sense than you. He knew you could not go far. You have no sense in your head, and not just from the blow on it."

He tried to move, lifted himself slightly, then fell back down, a grimace crossing his face.

"You lost even more blood and tore open the wound that was about to heal. I had to burn it to stop the bleeding."

"You should . . . have left me."

"Bear did not think so. He would have stayed out there with you and broke Audra's heart."

"I . . . did not want to put you in danger."

"And now there is even more," she said, unwilling to forgive him after the night and day of such intense worry. "You were getting better. Now you will have to stay in England longer."

His eyes met hers. They were bloodshot. Full of pain. She knew that despite the salve she'd mixed, his leg must feel like white hot coals packed inside. She put her palm to his head. He was still feverish but not as much as earlier. Her herbs were working their magic. But why had they not done the same for Will?

"My apologies," he said, a contrite expression on his face. " 'Twas not what I intended."

Her fury faded away. She had no doubt he had left to save her trouble and danger. His intentions had been good, even as the result had almost been disastrous.

"You will not try it again?"

"Not without telling you first," he promised.

She frowned. It was not the promise she wanted, but she suspected it was the only one she would get. He may not know who he was, but 'twas clear he was more used to giving orders than taking them. He was gentry, or royalty, or noble. That was clear.

"I will get a potion for the pain."

"You have done enough."

"There is no sense in suffering more than you must."

"Do you . . . ever take any rest?"

"Not when men do foolish things."

He looked contrite. "I will try to keep any further foolishness to a minimum," he said solemnly.

She sighed heavily. "You do not want to use such words," she reminded him. "You are a borderer now. You would not use fancy words."

"Are they fancy?"

"Aye," she said, then realized he was teasing her.

He was obviously better.

Still, she persisted. "You must remember. And you cannot stay here long. The Charlton wants to take you to the peel tower, and then they may well learn you be a Scot if you do not watch your speech. Without a name for ransom, they will kill you. They showed no mercy to those wounded on Flodden Field."

He tried to move again, and the effort showed on his face.

"Stay where you are."

Audra entered then, and she could say no more. "Audra, take an oatcake to Bear as a reward for finding Mr. Howard last night."

Audra smiled shyly at the Scot. "I am glad he found you."

"He did not let me out his sight," the Scot said wryly.

"He knows I like you," Audra said.

The Scot gave her a crooked smile. "That must be . . . why."

It was obvious even those words required as much strength as he had.

"Go," Kimbra told her daughter.

Audra glanced at the Scot and appeared reluctant, though ordinarily she would have been delighted at the prospect of playing with Bear.

The Scot nodded, and Audra headed toward the table, found an oatcake, and went out the door, Bear at her heels.

Kimbra felt a momentary resentment that her daughter obeyed the stranger more readily than she did her own mother, but then she was angry already. She had spent too much effort for the Scot to throw it all away.

She said nothing more as she found the chamber pot and started to help the Scot as she had her husband. A man's body was a man's body and nothing to be shy about. But the Scot refused to help.

"I will do it myself."

"And do more harm?"

"I swear not."

She gave him a look that she hoped told him what she thought of that promise.

But his gaze—so blue—held hers, and she knew he would not relent.

"I will be outside the door," she surrendered.

She went out, but stayed at the door, ready to reenter at the first groan and cry, or bump, or crash. There was none.

She allowed her attention to wander over to Audra and Bear who were chasing each other, or Bear was pretending to chase. She couldn't imagine Bear leaving the cottage and following the stranger. The beast must have thought the Scot was important to them.

He was not important at all. There would be no ransom or reward. How could you collect one for someone who didn't know who he was? And she was certainly in no position to discover his identity on her own.

Yet there was something about the Scot that had made her care far more than she should. She knew that when she searched for him last night. She'd been frantic, far more than she should have been for someone she'd known only a short time.

She did not wish to explore her other reactions to him. The way her heart fluttered around him. The warmth that crept through her when she touched him. The odd sensation in her heart when he smiled.

Enough daydreaming. She knocked, then went inside. He was lying back down, his breath coming more rapidly and his face white with strain, but the pot was in a new spot.

She moved it away and sat next to him, taking up the cloth and wiping the moisture from his face. Then she made a potion that should ease him into sleep. She lifted his head as he drank it willingly enough.

As she put the cup down, he raised his hand. It brushed her arm, and she felt as if she'd been touched herself by that white-hot dagger. Heat coursed through her body. She jerked away and stood.

"I am sorry. I did not mean to offend—"

She knew her face must be red with shame. "You did nothing. It is just no man has touched me since Will died."

"How long . . . ?"

"He died two years ago."

"You've lived alone these years?" His voice was surprised.

"Is that unusual where you come from?"

A look of puzzlement passed over his face. She had hoped that an unexpected question might stir a memory.

"Yes . . . no . . . I . . . God's tooth but I cannot—"

"Are you from Edinburgh?" she asked.

He shook his head in obvious frustration.

She wished she knew more about Scotland, but all she

knew was what came from the minstrels who played songs for a roof overhead and a meal. The tales were of wild Highlanders and rape and pillage.

Yet this man appeared in no way wild. Still he was a warrior, or he would not have been at the side of a king.

"You need rest," she said. "And I have work to do. The Charlton wishes some herbs."

"You are a healer then?"

"I just know herbs," she said, "as my mother did."

His eyes studied her face. "You are a most unusual woman," he said.

"Nay, I am just trying to take care of my daughter."

"Then you would not have brought me here."

"I wanted a ransom," she defended herself.

"You knew that was unlikely when you came for me last night."

"It was not good manners to leave that way," she said primly.

"Now that is a fearsomely strange reason to haul someone back. But I apologize, Mistress Kimbra."

"I do not want your apology. I want you to get well."

"Why?"

"So you can leave, and my daughter and I can have our cottage back."

"After all your efforts, I will try to do my best."

His slow smile made her heart pound faster. She forced herself to rise. "I have chores to do."

She went out and called for Audra. She knew she should have milked the cow earlier but she'd been too tired. Bess would be heavy and sore, and rightfully short-tempered over the neglect. There were several chickens to feed as well. She eyed one as the possible source of soup for the Scot, but they had become pets, and she and Audra depended on the eggs for barter.

While Kimbra saw to Bess, Audra fed and watered

Magnus. Together they scattered seed for the hens and one rooster, then gathered several eggs.

The Scot was sleeping when they returned to the cottage, and she breathed deeply in relief. She still felt heat where he had touched her so briefly. It was only, she told herself, because she had been without a man since Will died. And while his lovemaking had often been fast, leaving her wanting something more, she had grown used to his arms, to his warm presence beside her.

But he had not stirred the wild feelings that the Scot did. She felt traitorous to Will's memory, especially since this man was a Scot, an enemy to Will's family and to England.

He did not look like an enemy. She couldn't rid herself of the fact he had almost died to prevent harm coming to her and Audra.

Her heart was becoming far more involved than she'd thought possible.

And that, she knew, was far more dangerous than his physical presence in her home.

Chapter 8

*K*IMBRA woke to a shout.

Audra, who was sleeping next to her, did not move.

It took her a moment for everything to come flooding back. She and Audra were back on the pallet. They had moved the Scot back into the other room. He'd protested, but she'd argued it was safer. People came to her for herbs. Until he knew more about the borderers, he should keep out of sight.

The shout still rang in her ears, but there was not another one. She rose and went to the door. The fire was still burning from the several logs she'd added just a few hours earlier.

She listened at the door, not wanting to wake the Scot if he slept. He needed as much sleep as he could get. But then she heard another cry, more a moan. She lit a candle from the fire and went into the room.

He was thrashing across the bed, his face screwed into grief. He had kicked or torn the blankets from his body, and he wore only a long wool shirt that had belonged to her husband. His eyes were closed, and she realized it was probably a nightmare.

"Maggie!" he cried out.

A woman's name. Someone from his past?

She hesitated. She was far too involved already. But mayhap his memory was returning. If so, she could send word to someone.

She wasn't sure how, but she would find a way. Then he would be gone, and hopefully return a reward for her and Audra. Oddly, the idea was not as appealing as it had been days ago.

He uttered a guttural cry. She could no longer stand and watch. She placed the candle on the table and went over to him, put a hand on his shoulder.

His arm swung out and hit her across her mouth. It was so unexpected she cried out.

He came awake then with a sudden, violent movement that frightened her, dulling the pain of the blow against her lips. She was aware of something wet and salty in her mouth.

She was also aware he suddenly went quiet.

"Dear Mother," he muttered as his gaze found her lip. He half sat, his face indicating the effort it took. "What happened?"

"You had a nightmare. You flailed out. Do you remember any of it?"

He ignored the question as he stared at her lip. "Did . . . I do that?"

"You did not mean it."

A stark bleakness darkened his blue eyes.

"The nightmare," she pressed, ignoring the blood dribbling down her chin. "Do you remember anything from it?"

He closed his eyes. "Fighting," he said.

"At Flodden Field?"

"I . . . I . . . do not . . . think so. I . . . God's tooth, there is something. I . . ."

"You mentioned a woman's name. Maggie."

She watched him strain to remember. It was painful to watch. Finally, he just shook his head.

No matter how much she wanted to know his name, she could not ask him more questions, not with the torment she saw in his face.

She sat down on the bed and placed the back of her hand to his cheek. It was cool. She allowed it to linger there, trying to comfort him.

He jerked away. "Your lip," he said. "Your lip needs tending."

" 'Tis nothing."

" 'Tis a great deal when you have done so much for me. I cut you."

"It will heal quickly. I startled you. I should not have tried to wake you, but you were . . ."

"Were what?"

"Shouting. I thought you were in pain."

He struggled to sit, swaying as he did so. He brushed her lip with such gentleness that his touch soothed rather than hurt. "I wish I could care for that as well as you cared for me."

She felt her face grow warm. Not only her face but the core of her. Something shifted inside as an almost palpable attraction leapt between them, filling the air with its intensity. "You are not well yet," she said in a shaky voice.

"But soon to be," he said. "Because of you."

"You started to say that you remembered something."

"Jumbled images. Feelings. Fear." He hesitated, then

added in a soft voice, "Something worse. I feel it. But everything is shrouded by a mist. Not solid enough for me to catch it."

He dropped his hand. It came away with blood on it. She rose and found a piece of cloth and wiped her face with it. The cut was of little matter. She would, though, have a bruise she might have to explain.

"I will get you something to help you sleep," she said.

"Nay, I will sleep on my own. You must get some rest." He looked at her quizzically. "Have you slept since you found me?"

"Aye, I have. I have never needed much sleep. I used to ride with my husband on raids. We would ride two days straight." She heard the longing in her voice. She had loved the feeling of freedom on those rides, galloping across the march and splashing across creeks.

"You liked it?"

"Aye, I did."

She found herself sitting back on the bed, reluctant to leave. "I always thought it unfair that women had to cook and sew and work the crops, while men slept all day and rode all night. Will taught me to ride, and I loved it. Because we are isolated here, he taught me some warrior skills. To shoot a bow and arrow. To use a dagger. Even a sword.

"But then he would ride out alone, and I imagined all kinds of things. I cut down some clothes he'd outgrown and joined the group of riders as they left one night. By the time someone discovered who I was, they'd ridden too far to return. I took Magnus from the Armstrongs that night, and I was otherwise useful."

"And your husband?"

"Angry at first, then he thought it amusing."

The Scot's eyes lost some of their bleakness. "And himself fortunate," he said, his meaning quite clear.

"Nay. He died too young. He loved Audra, but he prayed

for a son. I wish I could have given him one. 'Twas the least I could do when he took me without a dowry and against the wishes of his family."

The conversation was becoming far too intimate. His hand rested on her lap, and she liked it there. It felt natural. She hadn't realized how much she missed that kind of contact with a man.

But this could not be with an enemy. With a noble who was as far above her station as anyone could be.

She rose abruptly. "I must go," she said, taking the candle and almost running from the room.

*H*E lay back in the darkness. His hand still tingled where she'd touched him, and he'd touched her.

Since she had first brought him here, she had puzzled him. Though his past was a blank, he was quite sure that there were few women like her. Then that brought back the worry that he might have a wife.

If so, was she anything like this woman who wore men's clothes, dragged strangers off battlefields, and took them in? Who rode with bandits and stole from the dead, yet had such a gentle way with her child?

She intrigued him, attracted him, challenged him.

If he had a wife, he hoped she was like Kimbra Charlton.

Was he now betraying her with lustful thoughts of another woman?

Despite his lack of memory, he knew that Kimbra Charlton must be unusual. And even as weak as he was, she aroused a yearning inside him so deep that it dwarfed any physical pain.

He turned over. He did not want to sleep again. The images, the emotions he'd felt during the nightmare haunted him. He tried to remember more of the nightmare, the faces within it, but they evaded him. A heavy sense of failure, of despair lingered instead.

* * *

*K*IMBRA lay next to her sleeping daughter and pulled her into her arms.

Remember what's important.

Life was important. Audra's and—because of Audra—her own.

She had to look out for herself and her daughter. That meant getting the Scot well and extracting what information she could. She had to prompt those memories.

She wasn't sure how long she lay there before first light seeped through the windows and Audra stirred next to her.

Kimbra rose, piled more wood on the fire, then looked in on the Scot.

He was sleeping, but the bedclothes were strewn all over. She worried there had been more nightmares.

She watched him for several moments. She didn't understand why he so intrigued her. Even beguiled her. He was nothing like Will. Yet something inside melted as she watched him. She'd tried so hard to resist her reaction to him. She'd tried to be curt with him. Even unlikable. But he always seemed to see beyond that.

She tore her glance away and put another piece of wood on the fire. Audra sleepily got to her feet and plodded over to her.

Kimbra hugged her close. "I love you," she said. "Forever and forever."

Audra rested her head against her mother's heart, and tenderness flowed through Kimbra. Each moment with her daughter was so precious, she was shamed that sometimes she didn't have more time to play with her, to tell her stories, as her own mother had not. She had so longed for her mother's attention as a child, but her mother had never had time—nor the heart—for it. She had never quite understood, not until Will died. Now she, like her mother, had to spend nearly every moment of the day trying to keep them both fed and housed. The few picnics at the pond were the exceptions.

She'd thought the Scot her only way to provide better for her child.

Now he was more of a curse than the blessing she'd hoped. She dared not leave the cottage, and the Scot, alone.

She squeezed Audra, then set her down. "If you dress quickly, you can help me milk Bess and feed Magnus."

"Can I ride Magnus?" Audra asked, trying to enlarge her share of the bargain.

"Aye, but just within sight of the cottage."

It was a promise she'd made weeks ago but had continued to put off. She remembered herself as a child, wanting so much to ride, but as a maid's daughter, she was unable to do so. When she'd married, Will taught her, and riding had given her so much joy that Kimbra wanted her daughter to share that pleasure. She knew Audra should have a pony to learn, but that was a luxury she doubted would ever be within her grasp.

She would be careful, but Magnus seemed to recognize that Audra was a child, and Kimbra would be at Audra's side. It was the best she could do.

She prepared boiled barley and added honey to sweeten it, poured some in a bowl for Audra, and more in a bowl for the Scot. Then with a cup of ale, she took it into the Scot's room. She had to learn to call him—even think of him as—Robert Howard, but he remained *the Scot* in her thoughts.

He was sitting up, looking better than he had the day before, though as he turned toward her, she saw a muscle throb in his throat as if stifling a groan.

"I have some barley with honey," she said, handing him the bowl and placing the ale on a table next to him.

The side of his mouth twitched up in a forced smile as he took it and tasted it.

" 'Tis probably not what you are used to."

His gaze met hers. "It is good, and I do not know what I am used to."

"I hear the nobles have fine feasts to break morning."

He took another bite. "This is a feast to me."

"That is because you have not had much to eat."

"And I am taking what you have."

"We have enough. I have gardens and a field of barley."

"Who tends them?"

"I do."

"Is there naught you cannot do?"

"Read," she said wistfully. "I want that very much, though there is little to read."

"Did your husband read?"

"Nay, though he could write his name."

"I will teach you to read," he said. "I swear it. 'Tis little enough in repayment."

Hope leaped inside her and caused her to start. Then it faded. She had nothing here to read. He would not be here long enough . . .

"I will teach you letters," he said, obviously reading her thoughts. "Once you know those, you can learn on your own."

"Audra, too?"

He grinned. "Aye."

His grin was that of a young boy given a present. A warm glow flowed through her. She believed then he could do it.

Then mayhap she could decipher the words on the crest. That thought sent her back down to earth. She had no right to it.

She sought to extinguish the glow still warming her heart. "We probably will not have time," she said. "You want to leave. You tried to leave. You said you would try to leave again."

His grin disappeared. "Aye, because it is safer for you. But I will find a way to make good the promise."

But not, most likely, if he regained his memory and returned to a fine castle and an old life. "A fine promise," she said, hearing the doubt in her voice.

Why did she care if he didn't keep his promise? She had his jeweled crest. She could sell that.

Once again she thought about showing it to him. It might bring back memories. But then she would have nothing. That crest, and the gold ring from the night's plunder, were Audra's only hope for a safe future.

Guilt ate into her, though, and it was an ugly feeling. She rose and went to the door. "I have work to do, but I will stay around the cottage. If anyone comes—"

"I am a Howard," he finished for her, the smile gone from his face.

She merely nodded and left.

K IMBRA stepped back but kept Magnus on a long rope as the horse trotted around in a circle, a happy Audra proudly sitting upright in the saddle. She was a natural rider.

Will had said Kimbra had been, as well. She'd learned quickly under his instructions. Within a year she'd felt confident enough to fool his companions on that first raid.

Kimbra looked up at the sky. They had been out an hour, and it was past Bess's milking time. Yet the joy in her daughter's eyes was difficult to resist.

She stopped the horse, lifted Audra down and let her lead the horse back into the stable.

Kimbra unsaddled the horse while Audra fetched oats and water. Then she addressed the needs of Bess. The cow, still obviously disgruntled at the recent neglect, swished her tail. Kimbra ducked, spilling some of the milk. She muttered an oath she'd heard Charltons utter only too often, then heard Bear bark.

Bess was still heavy with milk, but Kimbra had no

choice but to leave her. She moved the pail, just missing an aimed kick from a hoof, and hurried outside.

To her dismay, she saw two horsemen and recognized one as Cedric, the other his brother, Garrick, who was nearly as odious. Bear ran by their side, obviously trying to keep pace.

She called to Audra.

Audra ran over to her.

"Tell Mr. Howard that we have visitors."

Audra ran into the cottage.

Kimbra prayed the Scot would remember everything she had told him. She stood where she was as the two riders approached. Cedric reached her first and leaned down.

"I hear ye have a Howard here."

"Aye."

"Ye said nothing about it when I visited you."

"I found him after your visit."

He stared at her, his dark eyes soulless. "I want to see him."

"He is very ill. He should not be disturbed. Even the Charlton thought so."

"I will see for myself."

"You have no right."

"Nay? I have every right. Ye are my cousin's wife, my responsibility." He dismounted.

Bear growled.

"No!" she said sharply to the dog, not wanting him hurt again. Bear slunk back, his teeth bared.

"I will see this man," Cedric repeated, starting toward the door, his brother behind him.

She had no choice but to follow.

Chapter 9

$\mathcal{A}$UDRA burst into his room.

Robert Howard—he kept trying to remind himself that he *was* Robert Howard—had just returned to the bed when the door opened.

"Mater said to tell you that Cedric is here."

"Cedric?"

Audra's lips pursed in disapproval. "We do not like him," she pronounced with the gravity of a magistrate handing down a death sentence.

He recalled the name, remembered the tone with which the Charlton lass had said it a few days earlier. Contempt had been mixed with anger.

He also remembered the words of the Charlton chief. Unless very ill, he could not stay here. He was no longer that ill, only weak.

Memories were flashing through his head. They did not

yet make sense, and yet he felt that, given time, they would. But the Charlton lass had said he mumbled words, even names, in his sleep. Although Kimbra had drilled the border accent and words and customs into his head, he could not risk making an unconscious lapse in an enemy camp.

He did not want to think that there was any other reason he wanted to stay, that the woman, despite her often sharp tongue, gave him a sense of belonging, even of peace.

He had to make himself appear more ill than he actually was. Suddenly he knew exactly what to do. *Something remembered.*

"Can you go out and distract him?" he asked Audra.

"D'stract?"

"Make him think of something else?"

She gave him a grand smile. "Aye."

"I will need a wee bit of time."

She nodded, then sped out of the room, her dog running and barking behind her.

He managed to get to his feet and with the crutch stumbled into the next room. He dared not look out the window for fear of being seen. He could only trust to luck. Howard, he reminded himself. He was Robert Howard.

He thanked God there remained a fire in the hearth. He looked around, saw a cup, and quickly put it among the coals. He waited only several seconds, then picked it up with a piece of cloth. Holding it with one hand and the crutch with another he made it back to the bed, and pressed the wrapped cup against first one side of his face, then the other. The heat burned through the cloth, and he felt it color his face.

He heard voices in the other room, pushed the heated cup under the bedclothes, and feigned unconsciousness.

The door opened.

Kimbra Charlton's protests were indignant. "He is still ill."

"'Tis not fitting that he stay with ye." The voice was angry.

"Thomas Charlton knows he is here."

"The Charlton is not Will's cousin. The responsibility is mine," her visitor countered.

"Nay, but he *is* your chief."

Robert Howard groaned and opened his eyes. "Hot. Water."

He was aware of her soft scent as she leaned down over him. She touched his face, and he felt her sudden concern.

"The fever is back." She turned to the man hovering beside her. "You can see he is still very ill."

Her visitor was stocky but had the appearance of strength. Muscles bulged under the shirt he wore. His face was heavily bearded, and his eyes were a dark, malevolent brown. "Yer name?" he demanded.

"Robert . . . Howard." He prayed that her coaching on accents had been sufficient.

"Ye do not have the look of a Howard about ye. And I do not remember ye."

"I have been . . . on the continent, and at sea." He desperately tried to remember every word Kimbra had suggested to him. She had said fighting the French. Yet the word *sea* had just popped out.

"I know of no Howard who went to sea." Suspicion was deep in his visitor's voice.

"Do you know everything?" Kimbra Charlton interrupted.

The man named Cedric glared at her. "I know enough, Kimbra, and ye have not learned respect. Will was much too lenient with ye."

"You will say nothing about Will."

"I will say what I wish to say."

"You have seen what you came to see," she said. "I must tend to him."

"There is a physician at the peel tower."

"The Charlton came to me for herbs," Kimbra said

doggedly. "The physician did not help *him*. He agreed the stranger should stay until he improves."

"He is a stranger. He could be dangerous."

"I think not. A finger would knock him over."

Cedric studied her face for a moment. "Your lip is bruised."

"Aye. In his fever, his hand hit me. But it was not his fault," she hurriedly added. "He did not know what he was doing."

The words swirled around the man called Howard, as did sudden flashes. They roiled around his head so quickly he couldn't grab any one of them. *Howard*. He had to think of himself that way. Howard. He felt the heat fading from his face. He groaned again.

"Please go," she told Cedric. "He needs rest. I assure you that as soon as he is well enough to walk, he will leave."

"What if he were to strike you again?" Cedric said. "Yer safety is important to me, though he don't look like much of a soldier to me."

"It was nothing," she replied, "and I have managed well enough these two years," she said sharply. She turned to the door, obviously hoping Cedric would follow.

He did not. Instead, he looked around the room. "He had no weapon with him?"

"Nay."

Doubt was in his eyes. "Ye had chain mail with you the night of the battle."

"Aye. It came from a dead Scot."

Cedric Charlton's gaze flitted down to the man who called himself Robert Howard.

Howard did not meet his eyes for fear he might see the lie, and anger, in them. Instead he closed them, waited for Kimbra to answer.

"Are ye sure the owner of the chain mail is dead?" Suspicion was in his voice.

"He did not breathe. Neither did many more who fought. Did *you* fight, Cedric?"

The challenge echoed in the room. It was an insult deliberately thrown to take attention away from the man on the bed. He didn't like her taking the brunt of anger from him. But he feared he would only worsen things if he spoke up.

"Thomas Charlton has already sent a messenger to the Howards," Cedric said in a tone icy with fury. "We will know soon enough if they are grateful for your saving him, or if he is a Howard at all."

He left then, but the threat hovered in the air.

Kimbra Charlton did not follow him out but went to the window. After a moment, she turned back. "He is gone."

"He will be back."

"Aye, and I will not be able to stop him."

"You must tell me more of the Howards."

"They are spread out over the border. I once worked as a maid for a Howard. That is why I chose them. You are from a branch far away, a . . . a bastard who has not been seen in years." Her eyes locked with his. "You said nothing to me about the sea."

"It just . . . came out."

"Are you a sailor then?"

"I . . . see the sea in my mind. I do not know if I sailed, or lived near the sea. I know it, though. That is all . . ."

She went over to him and felt his cheek. "It is not so hot." Her eyes narrowed. "How did you . . . ?"

He brought out the cup from underneath the bed covering. "I heated it in the flames."

She regarded him with something like admiration. "How . . . ?"

"I do not know. I just remembered—" He stopped suddenly.

"You remembered . . . ?" she prompted.

"A hot brick. A laugh. That is all."

"A woman's laughter?"

"Aye."

"You do not remember a face? A name?"

"Nay."

"Could she be your wife?"

"I do not know," he said, his voice harsh with frustration.

"You have had other memories?"

"A few. But they are phantoms. They do not stay long enough to grab on to."

Her gray eyes had darkened, and he was reminded again of a frothy sea. He could see that sea now. Why couldn't he see anything else? Her face looked intent on solving the puzzle of his memory. Strands of black hair escaped the long braid she wore and framed her face. Her cheeks were still pink from the cool air outside.

He longed to hold out his hand to her, but he had no right. Not as long as his past remained a mystery.

"What do you remember of the sea?" she asked.

"The colors. Gray at dawn, like your eyes. The feel of the wind . . ."

"You liked it then?"

"Aye, I think so. I . . ."

He did like it. He knew that. But there had been something else, something that had beckoned to him. He knew longing. He knew grief.

For what? For whom?

Something of his torment must have shone on his face, for she looked as if she was seeing something she shouldn't see.

"I will keep the cup near the fireplace," she said.

"Did I d'stract him good enough?" came a small voice from the door. "I asked him a question."

"What did you ask?"

"Why he was so mean?"

He smiled. "No wonder he was scowling. Did he tell you?"

"He said children should not be heard. He said other things as well but I did not listen."

"You d'stracted him very well," he told Audra.

"Bear barked at him."

"Then I should give my thanks to Bear as well."

"I stayed with him till Cedric left. Bear does not like him."

"I did not like him, either," he confided.

Her lips widened into a grin. "I knew you wouldn't."

"Come with me while I prepare some food," Kimbra said. "And you, little love, were very brave, but you should not ask people such questions. I want you and Bear to stay away from Cedric."

"Mr. Howard told me to d'stract him."

"*I* will d'stract him in the future."

They left him then. The door did not close, and yet he felt as if another door had closed. He had used a child. He had used a woman. What had he done in the past?

He struggled to sit again. He was wearing the long shirt that covered the private part of him but no more. He found the breeches and pulled those on.

Then he stood, grabbed the crutch Kimbra had made for him, and took several steps. His ribs were still sore, and the pain in his leg intensified, but he made his way into the main room. He had not noticed it before. He had been too ill when he came to the cottage, and too determined to leave when he'd left it several nights ago. And when he was here seeking embers, he'd been too intent on his task to notice anything.

The cottage was obviously well crafted of wood and stone. Solid. He could not miss that. It was full of flowers and greenery and bright window coverings, and that, he knew, was the doing of Kimbra Charlton. There was nothing of defeat in the cottage, only of hope.

I was a maid. But she spoke well, and she had such a

longing for learning. He knew that from her questions, from her wistful comment about reading.

She turned and saw him. "You should not be out here. Someone might come."

"Your Bear will warn us."

"If you fall, I cannot lift you."

"I will not fall."

"Just as you thought you could walk miles the other night?"

"A bit of overconfidence," he said ruefully.

She continued to glare at him.

He feared he might have sounded as if he were humoring her, when, in truth, he admired her tremendously. He sat down before he fell.

"You do not follow instructions well," she accused.

"I do not know whether I do or do not," he said. "You work hard enough without having to bring food and drink to me, as well."

"Rather that than try to lift you if you fall."

"I will not do that again."

She glared at him.

God's tooth, but she was pretty when she glared. Those gray eyes smoldered. He wanted to reach over and . . .

Their gazes met. Held. Heat radiated in the core of him. An exquisitely pleasurable type of heat.

Audra broke the spell. "Do you like stories?"

Did he like stories? He did not know.

"I think so," he said, unwilling to disappoint her.

"Can you tell me one?"

"Mr. Howard does not remember things," Kimbra broke in.

Kimbra. He had tried to think of her as a Charlton, the Charlton lass, anything but Kimbra. But he knew now it was hopeless. She was Kimbra. A pretty name for a pretty lass. An English name.

A chill ran through him. She said he was a Scot. Her husband had been slain by a Scot. Most likely, his king and friends had been slain by her people.

They were enemies.

And yet no one ever seemed less like an enemy than this woman who had saved him at the risk of herself and her child.

She placed a plate of bread and cheese in front of him, then served her daughter before sitting down herself. "We will have a pie tonight. There are berries nearby," she said with a bit of defensiveness.

He bit into a hunk of bread. It was cold but filling, and the cheese was good. "I have never tasted anything so good."

Surprisingly her mouth broke into a smile. "That is because you do not remember anything."

He was enchanted. There had been many things he liked about Kimbra Charlton, but he'd not seen her humor before, nor the smile that lit her face, mayhap because she'd been so determined to save him. But he should have guessed it. Any woman who rode with reivers was a most unusual lass.

His gaze met hers, and she stilled. The air filled with expectancy, with a need that boiled between them. It was so powerful that he had to force himself to move, to push back the chair.

He breathed again, unaware until that second that his breath had caught in his throat. She stood, turned away, but her step was unsteady, almost as unsteady as his had been walking into the room. He did not take his gaze from her as she returned with a pitcher of ale and refilled his cup.

He sensed that, like his movement, it was an attempt to break the intense awareness between them, but instead her hand brushed his. He felt as if a streak of lightning struck and ran through his body.

Her hand was unsteady as she poured, as was his as he lifted his cup to his lips and sipped the bitter ale. The air was still dense, like that before a storm. God's tooth, it was a storm he ached for.

"Mater?"

The word shattered the cocoon they had unconsciously built around them. He looked toward Audra. She glanced between her mother and him, a puzzled look on her face.

He suddenly realized that she must have felt an outsider. He knew that feeling. He just did not remember when. Or why.

He forced himself to turn all his attention to her. "I hear you rode today."

Audra's face lit, the momentary uncertainty obviously chased away by a happy thought. "Aye. Mater said I am very good."

"I would expect so."

"Why?"

"Because you are very much like your mother, and I understand she is a very good rider."

"She rode with my father."

"I heard about that. It was very brave."

"I am going to ride with the reivers when I am old enough."

He looked up at Kimbra. A flicker of fear was there. She did not want her daughter to be what she was, what she had been.

He'd heard apprehension, even fear, in her voice when she talked of Cedric Charlton, but now he understood it was fear for her daughter, not for herself. She seemed to have none for herself.

He took another sip of the ale. He was endangering both of them. Every moment he stayed. And it was more than physical danger. He and Kimbra were like tinder and sparks together.

He took another bite of bread, then pushed back from the table. "I would like to go outside." Then he looked at her. "Mayhap it is time for our first reading lesson."

Unwise. He needed to put distance between them before he did something ungentlemanly. But he had promised.

"How?"

"We can use the ground to make letters."

She still hesitated.

"Someone might see you."

"Bear will warn us."

She hesitated, then that eagerness came into her eyes. "Aye."

He stood, ignored all the ripples of discomfort. He took the crutch and moved toward the door and opened it.

The sun was bright, the breeze cool, and he relished both. How long since he'd seen an autumn day bathed in sunlight? He could not remember. He only remembered darkness and pain and the rain.

He took several more steps despite the worry on Kimbra's face. She stayed at his side, and Bear bounded out in front.

"Keep watch," she told the dog. Bear barked, then sped out of sight.

The land was rolling and dotted with trees. A field to his left had been cleared. His gaze had been instantly drawn to it, and as he looked at it he immediately mentally compiled a list of what should be done.

Was he a farmer? A landowner?

Neither sounded right.

He found a stump and sat on it.

"Can you find me three twigs?" he asked Audra, who immediately ran off in search of them.

His eyes were drawn to a garden plot. Rows and rows of green plants of varying size and description overfilled the space. Did Kimbra Charlton ever stop working? His gaze moved on to a stone fence, which held a milk cow that eyed them malevolently.

"That is Bess," Kimbra said. "She feels neglected."

Audra returned with a number of twigs and piled them at his feet. Upon hearing her mother's words, she said, "Mater lets me milk her."

In another day, mayhap he could milk the cow.

But now he wanted to give Kimbra the one thing she'd asked of him.

"There are twenty-six letters," he said, "and when you learn them all, reading becomes easy." He sketched an *a* in the dirt, then a *b* and *c*. He asked each of them to do the same while reciting the letters. Then he used the twig to erase the letters, and asked them to draw them. When they finished, he moved to three more letters, and three after that.

He did not know how long they stayed in the sun as he finished the twenty-six letters. Then he asked them to repeat as many as they could, first Kimbra, then Audra.

He was stunned when Kimbra went through every one correctly. Audra hesitated on several. It was Kimbra who corrected her daughter, and he felt immense satisfaction. Tomorrow he would use the letters to form simple words.

He wished he had a book with him, or paper. Both of his students were astonishingly quick.

"I was good," Audra said.

"Aye, you were very quick. As was your mother."

He saw the pleasure in their eyes, the awakening joy of learning. He gloried in that moment, wanting to prolong it. He'd discovered he loved teaching.

"We should go back inside," Kimbra said regretfully. "I fear we have overtired you."

He tried to stand but was unsteady from sitting in one position for so long. Her hand went to his arm and steadied him while he got the crutch under his arm.

But God's tooth, he was tired. He was at the end of his strength. His chest hurt abominably. He made it back to the cottage without help, but once inside he nearly fell on the bed. Still, there had been progress. He had walked a small distance. He knew he could reach the stable, even the woods behind the cottage if necessary.

He had accomplished something else far more important, though, and that filled him with the first satisfaction he'd felt since being found.

Now if only he could remember his home. His family. His life.

England

Jamie Campbell lost track of days. In his dungeon cell, he could not tell day from night. He could only count days by the number of meals and those were few and certainly lacking in every way.

He was racked by images of the battle, the last sight of Lachlan Maclean going down, just before he himself was taken. He should have died with the other Campbells and Macleans. He should not have survived his king to whom he had pledged his life.

He thought about his wife. The golden hair that invited him to touch, to caress. The dusky blue eyes that invited him to her bed. He loved her, and yet he'd been eager to join his king, to participate in a great victory over the English.

How foolish he'd been. How lightly he'd valued her love.

He would change when he returned. He vowed it. But that vow would have to wait until he learned Lachlan's fate.

He heard a noise outside his cell, the scraping of a heavy door being opened. Another meal of beetle-infested bread.

"Campbell."

He recognized the voice of the baron in whose castle he was a guest. He stood, blinked as a torch filled the cell with light.

"The Campbells have paid your ransom."

He stumbled out, the light blinding him.

"How long have I been here?"

"Near three weeks."

"Milord!" The voice came from behind the baron, but Jamie readily recognized it. It belonged to a Maclean. Archibald. The Maclean's captain of the guard.

Jamie's eyes slowly adjusted to the light. Then he saw Archibald and went to him. "Any news of Lachlan?" he asked urgently.

"No, milord. We prayed ye might know something."

"I saw the king go down, then Lachlan. I was unseated by a pike and taken." The words sounded weak. He should have fought to the death, even if he had lost his weapons.

"Ye did not see him killed?"

"Nay. His horse went down. That was all I saw."

Archibald turned to the baron. "Do ye know of any other prisoners held for ransom?"

"I know of no others," the man said. "The king said no prisoners. Campbell is lucky to be alive."

"And you are far richer."

The baron shrugged. "I have some advice for you, young Campbell. Leave England as quickly as you can. There is a reward for Scots, particularly those of rank."

"Do not even think of trying to gain more," Jamie said. "My family knows where I have been."

The baron looked outraged. "I do have honor."

Jamie raised an eyebrow, then turned to Archibald. "Let us leave this place." He turned to the baron. "I thank you for your hospitality," Jamie said wryly. "I will remember it."

In minutes, he mounted a horse Archibald had brought with him. He had come with three men—two Campbells and a Maclean.

"I have clothes for you, milord."

"I want to see the last of this pigsty first," Jamie said. He used the heels of his boots to speed his mount on. The five of them cantered out of the gates, then galloped across a meadow, scattering sheep. When the keep was no longer in sight, Jamie pulled up.

"Tell me all you know."

"'Tis little. Rory wanted to come, but he was called to Edinburgh. The clans are quarreling over the young king, and Queen Margaret called for his help. He will meet us at the Armstrong tower."

"The Armstrongs?" He had heard of Armstrongs on the border but knew little of them other than the fact they were—had been—considered a thorn in the side of King James.

"Scottish reivers. Thieves," Archibald said with disdain. "But Rory said they owe him a debt. And they pay their debts. If anyone can find out anything about Lachlan, they can."

Jamie nodded, his heart pounding. God's tooth, but he was going to find Lachlan if it took a decade to do it.

They turned toward the border.

Chapter 10

KIMBRA tried to keep away from the Scot once he'd returned to his room. She washed her mourning gown and changed into her blue one, the only other gown she possessed.

She would change again as soon as the other one dried. She felt uncomfortable wearing the blue gown in front of the Scot. She still thought of herself as a recent widow, and she'd heard him call a woman's name. She'd prayed to God that the attraction that flashed so strongly between them would fade. 'Twas only because she was lonely.

Yet she couldn't remember responding to Will like that. She'd cared deeply for him, both for rescuing her and for his humor and good nature. But she had never felt the kind of electricity she felt with this man who had such deep blue eyes and a slow smile and inherent kindness. The latter did not match anything she knew about nobles.

To distract herself from such uncomfortable thoughts, she took Audra berry hunting for the promised pie.

"Is Cedric coming back?" Audra asked as they collected berries.

"I hope not," she replied.

"He did not like Mr. Howard."

"He does not like anyone."

"He likes you."

"He wants me, so he can have the cottage and Magnus. There is a difference."

"I do not want another father."

"I do not want another husband."

"But I like Mr. Howard. Do you like Mr. Howard?"

"Aye, but he will leave us soon."

"He will come back," Audra said with certainty.

"I do not think so."

"He said he would. I do not think he lies."

"He may not mean to, but when he remembers . . ." Her words faded away. She hadn't meant to say that.

"I believe him," Audra said, her lips pouting.

"Then he will be back," Kimbra said, not wanting to prolong this particular conversation. Apparently the Scot had bewitched her daughter as well as herself. Well, she planned to unbewitch herself.

"When can I ride Magnus again?"

"Tomorrow," Kimbra agreed. *Anything to get her mind off the Scot.*

They finished filling the bowl with berries and started back, Kimbra holding the bowl in one hand and Audra's hand in the other. It was near dusk.

They reached the cottage and went inside. She put the bowl down on the table and went to check on the Scot.

He was gone. Again.

His clothes were gone as well.

A sense of panic seized her.

She returned to the main room, trying not to let Audra see her concern. "He's not there," she told Audra.

"Mayhap he went to see Magnus."

The horse. What if he took Magnus?

She sped out the door toward the small stable with Audra behind her. As she approached, she heard singing. It came from the stable.

She slowed, her heart thumping normally again as she entered the stable. The Scot sat on the milking stool, his clothes soaked with milk.

He looked up and gave her a grin. "She does not like me," he said. "She has already beat me with her tail and kicked over the bucket. I thought a song would help. It did not."

"I could have told you she will not allow just anyone to milk her. *If* you had asked," she added pointedly.

"I wanted to help. I have learned something about myself. I know little about milking cows."

If not, he was learning fast. She watched as he finished and gracefully ducked another switch of Bess's tail.

"You should be in bed."

"Nay. I will get stronger if I am active."

"Someone might see you."

"I would have a sudden spell."

That momentary panic turned into anger. "This may be a game to you, but it is my daughter's life."

The light left his eyes, as did a little half smile from his lips. "I am well aware it is no game and what you have risked for me. My only payment can be to leave as quickly as possible. I cannot get stronger if I stay abed." His voice softened. "And I cannot lie in bed and watch you work so hard. The least I could do is milk a cow."

The anger seeped slowly away.

"Can you help me up?" he said. "I got down but . . ."

She held out her hand, and he balanced on it as he reached for the crutch and lifted himself to his feet. He *was* better than he had been in the morning, and even at noon when he'd taught Audra and her the letters. Steadier. Not well enough to leave on his own, but . . . soon he would be.

The sooner the better.

Kimbra stayed by the Scot's side as he limped toward the cottage. She had to stop thinking of him as *the Scot.* She had to convince herself, Audra, and him that he was a Howard. And yet . . .

They were almost to the door when he stumbled. She reached out to steady him and put her arm around him. He immediately righted again but his arm went around her shoulder.

The touch sent frissons of heat rushing through her. And something else.

It belonged there. The thought was so strong, and the emotion so clear that her breath locked in her throat.

She looked up at him. A muscle throbbed in his throat.

"I . . . thought I was steady enough," he finally said, slowly withdrawing his arm, though his fingers lingered at the back of her neck as if reluctant to end the connection. "I am sorry," he said. "I wanted—"

"To help. Aye, I know." Then his touch was gone, but not the heat that had flooded her.

She stood aside as he went inside. He started for the chair.

" 'Tis best if you stay in bed," she said. "If someone comes . . ."

But she was not as worried about someone approaching, as she was about being in the same enclosed space with him. Her heart pounded unsteadily, and her hand trembled.

What was wrong with her?

Audra didn't seem to notice anything, though. She frowned. "I want Mr. Howard to stay with us."

The Scot—Mr. Howard—glanced from Audra to her, then started for the other room. "Your mother is right. I need to rest this leg."

"Can I come with you?"

"I think your mother would like your company."

Audra's eyes opened wide with hurt. "You would not?"

"Indeed, I would, Miss Audra," he said, casting an apologetic look at Kimbra.

"Then you can teach me the song you sang to Bess?"

"I fear it did little for her mood," he said, his eyes suddenly alive with amusement. "I do not think your mother wants a cranky Audra."

"It was not you," Audra replied with great earnestness. "She is cross to everyone. She even tried to whack me with her tail."

"I hope you fared better than I."

"I ducked."

"I will have to learn to do that."

Kimbra listened with both a smile and ache in her heart. She'd never seen Audra respond so readily to another person. She held her tongue as Audra followed him into the other room. 'Twas obvious the Scot and Audra enjoyed each other. Audra had no children with whom to play, and few adults in her life.

It would only be a day or two more.

Only.

She wished the realization didn't hurt so. She would miss the masculine presence, the wry smile, the music in his voice. And he would go, not knowing where to go.

Mayhap the crest would help him find wherever he belonged.

You must wed.

The Charlton's words were like a sword over her head. She could not bear the thought of wedding any of those who had shown an interest in her. Without means, she would have no choice but to wed or surrender her cottage.

She told herself the crest would probably make little difference to him. If he could not remember his own name, how could he remember a crest? *But once he was in Scotland, others might recognize it.*

She wished the thoughts away as she prepared the pie and oat cakes and placed them in the hearth. Despite the wall separating them, she heard the song the Scot had been singing to the cow, this time with a young sweet voice accompanying it.

She felt something wet on her face. She wiped the tear away. She had not cried in a very long time.

Holy Mother, why was she doing it now?

THE oat cake was terrible, but the berry pie could have been the elixir of the Gods.

He ate the oat cake, though he had to work at it. He thought if he dropped it, it would bounce across the floor.

He had the pleasure, though, of watching the berry juice deepen the color of Kimbra's lips and seeing the berry-smeared grin on Audra's face. At that moment, he did not want to be anywhere else. He did not care about the past. Or the future. He only wanted today. This moment.

His eyes locked with Kimbra's. There was a smudge on her cheek. He longed to touch it, to run his fingers through her hair and feel her body against his. Blazes, he should feel nothing but a fierce need to return home. To his own country.

Tearing his gaze away from her, he looked at Audra who was trying unsuccessfully to swallow a big yawn. Her eyelids were fluttering back and forth. A wave of tenderness swept through him.

Almost as if Kimbra read his mind, she rose from her chair and went to Audra, picked her up, and hugged her close, before taking her over to the pallet on the floor.

She returned to the table, poured him more ale. He

drank it slowly, not wanting his mind to become addled. The fire in the hearth was roaring, the room was warm, the air dense with the attraction roaring between them.

"I am taking your bed," he said. "I can sleep in here."

"Nay. Audra's asleep now, and it is safer for you to be out of sight."

He asked the question that had been plaguing him. "What if the Howards say they have no one named Robert?"

"There are many Robert Howards, too many to count. They are scattered all over the border. It will take weeks to reach every branch of the family."

"But when they do not find one missing, will they ask questions of you?"

"I can only tell them what you told me."

That did not assuage his worry for her. She had risked much. At first she'd said it was for ransom, but even after she learned there probably would never be a ransom, she'd tended him.

He swore he would repay her. No matter what awaited him. She would never suffer for helping him.

He got to his feet with the help of the crutch. It was dark now, and Kimbra followed him with a candle lamp. He reached the bed and watched as she set the candle down.

"I should change the cloth around your wound," she said.

"It is doing well."

She was close to him, too close. The crutch slipped from his fingers, and his arm rested on her shoulder.

Her face, the bonny face that was usually so contained, was wistful. The smudge was still on her face, and he touched it, suddenly realizing it had been a tear. Her guarded eyes touched the core of his heart.

He unbraided her hair and watched as curls fell down her back. He touched it almost reverently.

He folded his arms around her as he balanced his bad leg with the good and held her tight. Relishing her scent of flowers mixed with berries, he lowered his head, his lips touching the soft skin of her face, caressing until he found her mouth and brushed a tentative kiss across her lips.

Her lips responded. She raised up on tiptoes, and the kiss turned feverish as her arms went around him and tightened around his neck. Need burned straight through him, and he knew by her response that she felt the same. The kiss deepened with a fierceness that nothing could break, a natural joining meant and destined.

He knew he should stop. But there was something so right about holding her, acknowledging the passion that was so strong it swept away every barrier. Need took over, need so great it threatened to consume him. He crushed her to him, his mouth insatiable as it tasted and wanted more, as heat sizzled between them.

His body arched as hers instinctively stretched against his, and her hands caressed the back of his neck.

Her tongue licked at his lips. Tension coiled in his body as he responded in kind, his mouth seducing hers. He savored the taste and feel of her.

A groan reverberated deep in his throat. He was aware of a craving he could not quite control. Lust mixed with something so much more tender.

He wanted her. He also wanted to protect her. The two were incompatible. Until he knew more about his life and future.

He drew away and looked at her. Her gray eyes smoldered. Her cheeks were flushed, her lips swollen by his kiss.

"Kimbra," he said raggedly.

He stroked the side of her face, then her neck in gentle movements, and then unable to resist, his mouth touched hers again. Everything in him wanted her.

With another groan, he drew his lips away. In the flickering light of the candle, he saw her face, saw the desire she couldn't hide, the same wonder in her eyes that he felt.

He lowered himself to the bed, his hand catching hers until she, too, sat. He bent his leg, feeling streaks of pain as wounded muscles pulled. He welcomed the pain. It was a reminder of forbidden fruit.

"I should not have done that," he said.

She fixed with that level gaze of hers. No blame. No regret. Instead, her fingers wrapped in his.

"I was as much at fault."

She reached up and touched his face as if memorizing it.

"If I knew I was free . . ."

"You are obviously of a noble family," she said, her face wistful but determined. "And you are a Scot. It would not matter if you were free."

He wanted to persist, but the determination on her face stopped him. He wanted to say he didn't care. But his mind was too full of holes. He knew nothing about his life. His family. The honorable thing was to wait until his memory returned.

He had no interest in being honorable. Not at this moment.

But she stood and took several steps backward.

He owed her enough to respect it.

"I *will* come back," he said.

But he saw that she did not believe him.

Instead, she headed for the door.

"I will milk Bess in the morning," he said.

"Nay," she said, then smiled wanly. "She will probably never give milk again if you do."

"That wounds me."

"The best thing you can do is rest. Or you will never get back to Scotland."

They were both ignoring what had happened minutes earlier, talking in strained tones to avoid the explosiveness still in the air.

"I am walking steadier. And breathing better," he said. "You are a fine healer."

"I just grow herbs," she insisted. "That is all. If I could have brought you a physician I would have."

Then she left, or fled, out the door.

Chapter 11

H E knew he had made a grave mistake.
He'd had no right to kiss her.

He went to the window. The night was soft. No clouds. Only a deep blue sky and millions of stars. 'Twas hard to imagine that so much violence and tragedy occurred weeks ago.

Then he saw her stride to the stable, her head high, her back straight, that glorious dark hair falling free.

I want her. I want her more than life itself. Thoughts of desire for Kimbra pounded through his head, heated his body. Had he ever wanted anyone else like this?

As if summoned, the image of a brown-haired lass flickered through his mind. She was running, her brown hair streaming behind her. She turned and tossed him a wide smile. Then as suddenly as she appeared, she was gone, vanished into a thick mist.

His wife?

He buried his head in his hands. Was that a true memory? A dream? Whatever it was, he had to find where he belonged.

He turned away from the window before the temptation of going to Kimbra became more than he could control. He'd done abysmally at controlling his actions earlier. If he stayed here, he surely would be damned. He could not use the woman who saved his life. Nor could he betray a woman to whom he might have given vows.

Bloody hell, what kind of man had he been?

Had he always been . . . so weak?

The questions didn't stop coming at him, and the few flashes of what might have been answers were only enough to tantalize him.

He used the crutch to walk around the room. He was steadier. The pain was still agonizing, but nothing he could not tolerate. The aching in his ribs intensified with any movement.

Could he sit on a horse?

Aye, if he had to.

He tried to concentrate on that. On the questions plaguing him. But his thoughts kept turning to Kimbra. The way she looked when he kissed her, then the stricken expression as she left the room.

In his mind's eye, he saw her returning to the cottage, a pail in her hand. He went to the bed. She would look in on him. She always did, as if she were afraid he might have wandered off again.

This time he would be asleep. He had to be asleep.

Honor demanded it.

And he was an honorable man.

Or—he wondered—*was he?*

* * *

*A*UDRA was asleep when Kimbra reached the cottage. The fire cast flickering shadows over the room. The door to the other room was closed.

She hesitated, then looked in. He looked asleep on the bed.

She closed the door quickly, remembering how his lips had felt against hers, how wildly she had responded. Then the way she had literally run from him.

She lit a candle from the fire and put it into a lantern, then climbed the ladder up to the loft. She looked under the pallet that had been available to Will's friends and found the crest and ring she'd hidden there. She left the ring and fingered the jeweled crest. She had but two clues to his identity. The crest. And the woman he mentioned in his dreams.

Who was Maggie? What was she to him?

And the crest? A shield, a helmet, a tower all encased in jewels. And words she could not read. Yet. Were they clues to his family? She wished once again that she could read. Never had it seemed so important.

Give it to him.

Then she would have nothing. He would leave, find his family and probably wealth, and forget all about his promises. She clutched it in her hand. Honor fought with survival.

His past against her daughter's future.

She hid it back under the pallet. He could not have it on him now, in any event. If it were to be found, it would be a sure death warrant.

But she knew she was only justifying the unjustifiable.

Kimbra climbed down, her hand still warm from the crest, and laid down next to Audra. Audra deserved a life free from fear, from hunger.

The Scot deserved his heritage.

It was the devil's own choice.

And she had no idea how she was going to make it.

* * *

*K*IMBRA rose after yet another restless night. All her doubts and fears nagged at her. She kept seeing the jeweled crest that had fastened the Scot's plaid and wondered whether she had the right to withhold it from him.

Maggie. No doubt a highborn lady with manners and wealth. Yet *Maggie* had an earthy, warm sound to it.

The Scot puzzled her. She had served nobles, and none had the quiet courtesy he did. Her mother had been destroyed by the son of an earl and had taught her to be wary of anyone of noble blood.

And yet the Scot was uncommonly gentle and patient with Audra and respectful always of her. Had her father been that way until he wanted to rid himself of someone not his equal?

Bear barked, and she went outside.

Jane, leaning on a walking stick, approached.

Audra ran toward her.

Jane leaned down and gave her a big hug. "I missed my lovey," she said.

Kimbra followed her daughter to Jane and greeted her. "'Tis good to see you. You've come for more bay leaves?"

"Aye, and to have a few words with ye." She glanced down at Audra, then back to Kimbra.

Kimbra understood. "Can you go and feed Bess and Magnus? Then you can help me get Jane some fresh bread and honey?"

Audra regarded them both somberly, as if she knew something of importance was to be said when she was gone. Then she turned and walked toward the stable.

"She's a good child," Jane said.

"Aye, she is."

Jane shifted on her feet, then blurted out some words. "There is talk of you and a soldier."

"And what is being said?"

"That he is a stranger, and you are disgracing your husband's name."

"Could Cedric Charlton be one of the talkers?"

"Aye, but he has others talking as well."

"The Charlton gave me permission to care for him."

"The talk is he is well enough to leave."

"Nay," she said, probably louder than necessary. "He is not."

"I just thought ye should know. Mayhap if I stayed with ye and help cared for him . . ."

"That is a generous offer," Kimbra said, "but he will be leaving soon."

Jane's gaze did not leave hers. "The talk is he is a Howard."

"Aye, but he's been away for years. I think he has little connection with the family."

Jane continued to stand there, and Kimbra realized she wanted to see the soldier in question.

Kimbra knew Jane would never betray her, and better now than ever to discover whether her Scot could pass as an Englishman.

"Come inside and see for yourself," she said.

Jane hesitated as if she realized her thoughts were entirely too clear. Jane had always been blunt. Honest. And protective of those she loved.

Kimbra went to the door dividing the two rooms. Once the older woman was settled into a chair, Kimbra knocked twice at the door, then went into the other room.

The Scot sat on the side of the bed.

"My friend Jane Carey is here," she said. "Jane looks after Audra when I cannot. She wants to meet you."

He raised an eyebrow in question.

"You *are* Robert Howard," she said softly.

He nodded as he ran his hand through his thick auburn hair, as if trying to tame the untamable. "I *am* Robert Howard," he agreed.

"She may ask many questions."

"I will try to answer them."

She prayed to Mary in Heaven that he was good at it.

She went back to the door. "Jane, come in."

In the seconds it took Jane to reach the door, the Scot was in bed, though he had his bandaged arm out from under the covers. There had not been time to prepare, and yet in those few seconds he managed to look truly ill.

He *was* ill, she reminded herself. But there was something about his will and determination that made him seem far stronger in her mind.

Now she tried to see him through Jane's eyes.

"Jane," she said to him, "has offered to help care for you. Jane, this is Robert Howard."

He focused on Jane and gave her the slow smile that always made Kimbra's heart shift.

"That is very kind of you," he said.

Kimbra looked at Jane who was staring down at the Scot with astonishment. Her cheeks went pink, then her stern lips stretched into a smile.

"'Tis not kind at all. Kimbra works far too hard and gives too much to everyone."

The effort he'd made earlier to walk was thankfully showing. His cheeks were flushed, shadows around his eyes were deep, and his face looked drawn.

Embarrassed by the praise, Kimbra took a step back. "His leg was sorely injured, and his ribs bruised, along with other wounds. He also had a terrible blow to his head."

"Kimbra knows more about herbs than anyone about here," Jane said.

"I owe her my life," he said.

"Then you owe her to leave," Jane said in her direct way. "She is being hurt by gossip."

"I will leave immediately."

"No," Kimbra said. "I worked too hard to save him. He cannot leave until he is well enough." She directed her reply to Jane.

"The Charlton would welcome another soldier," Jane said. "He could stay there."

"He knows naught of me," the Scot said. "Why would he take me in?"

"He is always in need of a fighting man. Ye have enough wounds to prove ye are that." Jane's eyes roamed over his bandaged arm.

The Scot's eyes turned toward Kimbra, then shifted back to Jane. "I will leave here tomorrow."

Kimbra felt a squeezing hurt. He seemed far too willing to leave and take up arms again.

She told herself it was for the best. Once he left, no blame could come to her and Audra if anyone discovered he was a Scot. He would be under another's roof, and she would still have the crest.

The cottage would seem empty again. A surge of loneliness, of loss, swept over her with unexpected strength and poignancy.

But it was Audra who voiced her dismay. "I do not want you to go," she said.

Kimbra turned around to see her daughter standing in the door, her mouth puckered in unusual defiance.

"I have to go soon, anyway, Miss Audra," the Scot answered. "I have imposed on you and your mother far too long. I am eating your food and taking your father's clothing, and using your room."

"Bear wants you to stay," Audra persisted.

Jane looked from Audra to the Scot with disbelief, and Kimbra suspected what she was thinking.

Audra had always been an obedient child and had been

more at ease with animals than people. Part of it had been Kimbra's doing. She had protected her daughter, never wanting her to know the fear she and her mother had once known. Now her daughter was protecting a stranger with the same passion she had for Magnus and Bess and Bear.

"I thank you and Bear," the Scot said in a voice soft with longing. "But it is time for me to go." He looked at Jane. "You can tell those who have interest in my whereabouts that I will move to the peel tower if the Charlton will permit it."

Jane looked both relieved and puzzled. Kimbra feared that though the Scot had caught some of the border inflection, he was far more well spoken than most.

"Come in the other room and have some bread and honey," Kimbra invited Jane. "I have your bay leaves ready as well."

As Jane went out the door, Kimbra turned and glanced back at the Scot. She'd never seen such stark loneliness before. But as he saw her glance, his expression changed to blankness, and she wondered whether she had seen it at all or whether it had merely been a figment of her imagination.

Once in the kitchen, Jane turned to her. "Ye did not tell me how handsome he was."

"I have not really noticed," Kimbra lied.

"Or how well spoken."

"I think he was the bastard son of one of the nobles," she said. Which would, she hoped, explain why the Howards wouldn't know about him. "He does not talk much."

"Audra is much taken with him."

"Probably because Bear is," she said.

"I see why Cedric is not happy with his presence."

"I worry he will appear any minute," Kimbra confessed.

"Mayhap ye should think about his suit."

A shudder ran through her body. "Never. Audra does not like him, and he is cruel to his animals. You get along well enough without a husband."

"I had one fer many years."

"Do you still miss him?"

"Aye. He was a rough sort, but he cared for me in his way. He stayed though I had no children."

Kimbra knew how Jane's childlessness had always hurt her. Jane had transferred her love to all the children in the village and beyond.

"Is Cedric still at the peel tower?"

"The Charlton has been pressed to send out men to search for Scots. The king wants no more uprisings and has posted a high bounty. Since Will died, Cedric is trying to take his place as Thomas Charlton's favorite. It would be a fine achievement if he could produce a Scot noble for the crown."

Kimbra wondered whether Jane suspected something and was giving her a subtle warning. Yet there was usually nothing subtle about Jane.

"I am just grateful he's busy elsewhere."

Jane ate the bread and honey contentedly. Kimbra added a hunk of cheese and a cup of ale to accompany it, and Jane took her time eating, obviously happy with the rare companionship.

Kimbra did not begrudge it, though her heart had pounded ever since Jane's latest revelation about a bounty. The Scot was right in leaving, but now he could not go to the peel tower.

Though it would break her heart, she would loan him Magnus and urge him to hurry over the border. If he wore Will's clothing, it was unlikely he would be stopped.

Loan?

Most likely it would not be a loan at all, but a gift. He would find his way, and someone would recognize him, and he would forget about a cottage on the border and a widow.

That eased her guilt in keeping the brooch. It would be little repayment for loss of the hobbler.

Jane finally left, and Kimbra went into the Scot's room. He was sitting up.

"You cannot go to the peel tower," she said. "They are hunting for Scots. There is a bounty for any who are found."

"You taught me to blend in."

"A small mistake, and they will discover you. I think Jane is a little suspicious, but she will not say anything."

"The more important then that I leave."

"You cannot walk far."

"I will rest often."

"They are combing the border area."

"I will not put you in any more danger."

"You can take Magnus."

He stared at her. "You cannot mean that. You—and Audra—love that horse."

"She will agree with me."

"I will not," he said.

"You will put us in far more danger by staying here or going to the peel tower," she said. "Having Magnus would not save our lives. You taking him will."

It was the one argument she thought would work with this man.

She saw the torture in his eyes, then surrender. "I will get him back to you. I swear it."

She remembered when a man had sworn love to her mother, only to betray her. Men with power made their own rules. She'd seen Thomas Charlton do it. Even her husband.

But she only nodded.

"Tonight," she said. "After dark. I can tell you how best to reach the border."

She left him then. She had made her decision. She would

not rethink it, or question it or regret it. But a huge lump was in her throat, and she didn't think it would go away.

*T*HE day crawled along. He did not want to leave this place of comfort, of peace, of belonging.

Yet he had no choice. He could no longer risk their lives by staying here, and he wasn't well enough to walk long distances. His last attempt proved that.

He wondered whether he should save his strength by staying still, or try to build it by moving around.

He finally rose and used the crutch. He again felt the weakness in his left arm. A scar ran along the upper length of it, and he wondered how it had been inflicted. Did it have anything to do with the flashes of violence, of panic, of an emotion so heavy he could hardly bear it? *Family. Something to do with family.*

Then Audra burst in with the lute. "Will you teach me to play?"

"Aye," he said, though not sure he was much of a music teacher. Still, with the large gray eyes on him, he could refuse her nothing.

He took the lute from her and ran his finger over the strings.

"Stroke it . . . lightly," he said. He had almost said something else. *Stroke it like a lover.*

The word *lover* conjured other images. The kiss he'd exchanged with Audra's mother, the internal heat he felt when she entered the room.

A lute was a thing, and yet he'd obviously once thought about it as a friend, even a lover.

"Can I try it?" Audra asked.

He showed her how each string had its own sound and how to hold her fingers as she strummed them. She was amazingly quick in finding chords.

He would remember her this way, her small hands

running over the strings, a bright smile in her eyes as well as on her lips.

Kimbra called. Audra regretfully placed the lute back into his hands. "Please do not go," she pleaded.

Going was the last thing he wanted to do and the one thing he must do. Would he find his way back? Could he find his way back?

"You best go to your mother."

She went to the door, then looked back. "I want to show you our waterfall before you go. It's our special place."

Her mother had mentioned a pool as well. "Where is it?"

"Not far. You can ride Magnus, and Mater and I can walk."

His common sense told him no. His feelings were already raw. Yet as he looked at her he could not deny her anything. "If your mother agrees."

She beamed at him, then ran out of the room.

He went to the window. Still clad in her widow's dress, Kimbra Charlton knelt in her herb garden, carefully cutting leaves and placing them in a basket next to her. She wore no cap this morning, and her long dark hair was braided as usual. As she worked, she occasionally brushed a strand from her face. There was a grace about her that beguiled him.

Kimbra looked up as her daughter skipped toward her. Her face lit with joy as she reached out her arms for her. Bear had bounded out behind Audra and now sat with a huge canine grin alongside his two favorite people.

How he longed to be a part of that small circle.

She had offered him one of her most precious possessions. He had watched her with the horse. *Hobbler.* He had to remember that. It had been an expression unfamiliar to him.

He continued to watch as the mother and daughter held hands and started back, Kimbra swinging her basket of herbs. He captured the image in his mind, knowing it was one he would not forget.

Where were the other images that should be there?

The door opened, and the two came into his room.

"Audra wants to show you the pool," Kimbra said. "Are you strong enough?"

"Aye." He paused. "I am grateful for all you have done. I will not forget it."

He saw the flicker of doubt in her eyes. He realized she thought it only a convenient promise. He wished he could let her know it was far more than that. He would die before betraying her trust.

H E was a horseman.
Kimbra knew that instantly. Because of his injury, he used her mounting block. Still, once he got himself into the saddle, he sat the horse well.

He leaned down and awkwardly brought Audra into the saddle with him. Then he looked at her.

"I prefer to walk. It's easier carrying this," she said, holding up the lute Audra had begged her to bring along. The better to avoid touching him, feeling his body against hers, hearing his heart beat. Better not to have those eruptions of flame in every part of her.

He had gentle hands on the reins. He guided by body weight, not by force, and Magnus, often contrary, responded to him.

She had been reluctant at first to bring him to the pool, fed by a tumbling waterfall. What if Cedric came? Or Thomas Charlton? She was already forming reasons in her mind.

But, according to Jane, Cedric was chasing phantom Scots, even as one was in reach. As for Thomas Charlton, she could explain she was trying to see whether the wounded Howard could ride well enough to reach the peel tower.

'Twasn't a great excuse, but she could think of none better.

And she wanted this afternoon for Audra. And for herself.

The pool was not much more than a brisk walk for her. The sun was bright, the sky clear, and the breeze warm rather than cool. Bear walked next to her until he caught a scent and chased after a rabbit. He would return, empty mouthed and panting heavily.

She gave her Scot directions, and the walk went entirely too fast. She enjoyed watching him bend his head to talk to her daughter. She felt part of a family again, even for these few hours.

The pool was sun-kissed, the blue sprinkled with gold.

The Scot lowered her daughter to the ground, then swung his leg around and slid carefully to his feet. He stood unsteadily for a moment. She realized then he hadn't brought the crutch with him. She went to his side.

"Lean on me," she said.

He put his arm around her, and they walked together to a rock where he sat.

Her hand found its way into his, while Audra played with Bear. His hand tightened around hers.

"Have you remembered more?" she asked.

She saw the answer in his eyes.

"A woman?" she persisted.

He turned to her. "Aye. Brown hair and brown eyes. I also remember screams. I do not think she still lives."

"A place?" she said, changing a subject that was painful.

"Nay. The sea, sometimes. I have been to sea."

"A tower?" she probed, recalling the crest.

He shook his head.

"Nothing of the battle?"

"Not from what you have told me of Flodden. Another, I think. I . . ."

She waited for him to continue.

"Someone died. Someone close to me. I think it was my fault. I see myself kneeling before him." When he looked at her, his eyes were full of turmoil, even agony.

Her fingers tightened around his. She would not ask any more questions. If only she could read. If only she knew what the words on the crest meant.

Tell him about it. The words might mean something to him.

"What are you thinking?" he asked suddenly. "You look so somber."

"'Tis nothing. Just that Audra will miss you."

"And you?"

Terribly. But she was not going to admit it.

Audra ran over just then. "I want to do the letters," she said.

"Have you been practicing?" he asked.

"Aye," Audra said. "I know them all."

"Kimbra?"

She nodded.

Kimbra hesitated on only one letter. Audra missed three.

He took up the lute and started singing the letters to a simple tune, then gave the lute to Audra. "You try it."

She had a few false notes, then found them, and sang the "letter song." This time she had them all right.

When she finished, he used a branch to make some words. He started with *dog,* then went to *Kimbra* and *Audra.*

"You can leave them in the earth," he said. "Mayhap they will be here the next time you come."

She thought he was right. The English had taken most of the game who watered here. She looked at the letters. She and Audra would come often.

* * *

ALL too soon it was time to go. There was Bess and the chickens to attend to, and it was especially important not overtiring him. "We should return."

Disappointment flickered in his eyes. "Aye, I have enjoyed it too much. But I will not forget you, lass."

"You probably have a wife and seven children at home," she said. "You will find them. Go to Edinburgh. Someone will recognize you."

His gaze met hers, held it. "I will find a way to reward you."

That had been so important to her several weeks ago. Now she did not want a reward. She felt low and unworthy for keeping the crest from him. She wanted nothing else.

Liar!

She wanted a great deal, but none of it was within reach. None of it was possible.

"Audra," she called. "It is time to return."

She avoided the Scot's gaze.

"It is a bonny place," he said.

"Do not use that word," she said sharply, far more sharply than she intended. "It is not common here."

This time she could not avoid his gaze. It caught hers and held. She had not the power to tear away. 'Twas as if he reached into her soul and saw what she'd tried to conceal. He reached up and touched a strand of her hair.

"But *bonny* fits so well," he said. "You, as well as the waterfall."

Transfixed, she was unable to move. She felt caught in time, in the magic of his eyes, in the connection that was like bonds linking them together. Heat pulsed between them, and her heart sped.

She stood, stepped back, almost stumbled on legs that didn't want to hold her. Then she straightened.

He stood awkwardly. "You are right to run," he said softly. "I have nothing to offer."

He had everything to offer. It was she who had nothing.

She tried to clear her mind, and her heart, though neither cooperated. She walked over to fetch Magnus who had been feeding on grass. She led the horse over to the Scot.

She watched as he mounted and helped Audra up. She walked by his side. The sun had lost its glow, and clouds had appeared. She tried not to think that tomorrow both the Scot and Magnus would be gone.

They had almost reached the cottage, when Bear barked and raced ahead.

A heaviness clogged her throat as she saw six riders and a riderless horse in front of the cottage. She searched for Cedric, but thank God he was not among them.

Another man she recognized as one of Will's friends rode toward her. He touched his forehead in respect to her, then gazed at the Scot.

"Thomas Charlton has sent us to bring ye to the tower," he said. "We brought a horse. It appears ye are able to ride," he added wryly. "I was told ye was near death."

She broke in. "He was going to the tower tomorrow, Richie. We wanted to see whether he could ride yet."

He cocked an eyebrow at her. "It seems, Kimbra, that he can."

Then he turned to the Scot. "Ye can ride that horse over there."

Her heart pounding, she watched the Scot painfully dismount and limp over to the other horse. She ran inside and fetched the crutch. By the time she'd returned he was astride the other horse.

She handed it to him.

"My thanks, again, Mistress Charlton," he said.

"And you, Miss Audra, keep practicing the lute."

Then he turned his hobbler and rode off with the others.

Kimbra stood there stunned. She'd known this moment was coming. Had thought it would be tomorrow.

But then she had hoped he would be free. Now he was in deadly peril.

Audra came over and clasped her hand.

Kimbra looked down and saw tears in her daughter's eyes.

She had to fight to hold back those of her own.

Chapter 12

❧

THE peel tower loomed over the marsh.

Robert Howard—he had to think of himself as that now—studied everything carefully as they approached a gray, bleak tower. A large stone wall wrapped around it. A barnekin, he remembered from Kimbra's lessons.

They went through an iron gate manned by men in the same uniform as he wore: breeches and a rough shirt under a leather doublet. He had not worn Will's jack on the picnic and had not been given time to take it.

They rode in silence. He was still weak, his chest burned, and his leg ached. The short ride to the pool had wearied him, but this last exertion sapped what remaining strength he had.

He had to keep his wits about him. One error and not only his life would most likely be forfeit but the consequences to Kimbra and her daughter could be as bad or worse.

He had memorized the story. He was a bastard Howard who had been away nearly his entire life before returning just before the battle. That would explain his speech and why Howards knew little of him.

The tower was four floors high, and the formidable entrance a double door. One was an outer iron grating and behind it one of heavy oak reinforced with iron. It would not be easy to breach, especially with windows overhead from which rocks and boiling water could be hefted.

As the riders neared the tower entrance, two young lads ran out and waited as they dismounted. He did it slowly, painfully. His leg buckled under him, and he used the crutch to steady himself. The well-armed Richie watched him carefully, but did not offer to help.

He limped to the door.

The outer grating was open, and, as he approached, the oak door opened as well. A huge man appeared at the door to regard him with suspicious interest. The giant stepped aside to allow him entry. "I am Jock."

He led Robert Howard and his escort up narrow, winding steps in silence.

Each step might well have been a mountain, but no one offered help. Leaning on the crutch and the inside wall, he took one agonizing step after another, stretching raw muscles. Sweat trickled down his cheek.

They stopped at the second level, and Jock led the way to an open door and again stood aside.

Robert Howard limped inside and faced the chief of the Charltons. He'd feigned unconsciousness when the man had stood over him before, and now he got his first look at the man who would decide his fate, and had Kimbra's and Audra's lives in his hands as well.

The Charlton sat heavily in a large chair. "I thought you were a dead man," the Charlton said. "God must have had a hand in your life."

"God and Mistress Charlton," Robert Howard replied. "I thank you for permitting it."

"She has a way with herbs," the Charlton said.

Robert Howard started to sway. He feared that he would fall soon.

The Charlton waved to a chair. "Sit."

Robert Howard sat.

"Kimbra told us ye were a Howard."

He hesitated, bowed his head slightly. "Aye but not one they recognize," he said bitterly.

"Your father?"

" 'Tis said he was Sim Howard. I am a bastard and not sure."

"He is dead."

"I learned that when I returned. I was fostered far away enough not to be an embarrassment to his wife."

"Your mother?"

"Died in childbirth."

"Ye speak with an accent."

"I have been a mercenary in Europe. I had no place here. It took me ten years to return."

"How did ye join the battle?"

That was the crux of the explanation. "I rode right into the English Army. I joined them."

'Twas a flimsy explanation at best, and both Kimbra and he had known it, but it was all they had.

The Charlton's gaze bore into him, weighing every word. "Where were you during the battle?"

"On the left flank. I saw several of the enemy fleeing and rode after them. I thought to claim some armor and weapons. Suddenly I was surrounded. I took two down, then I went down. When I woke, there were two dead Scots, and my horse was gone. I tried to move, but . . . I do not remember anything after that until I woke in Mistress Charlton's cottage."

He was thankful for his gift of mimic. Still, the Charlton's eyes remained suspicious.

"I've sent riders to the Howards. I thought there might be a reward."

"For me? I doubt many know of me, and if they do, I mean nothing to them."

"Yet ye were going to them."

"Is it so strange to want to see a father? Even if he did abandon you?"

"But to fight for them?"

"Not for them. For me. I sought to find favor. Mayhap some plunder."

"Ye dress like a borderer."

"As I said, I fostered on the border. I like the clothing."

" 'Tis dangerous to be a stranger here now."

Robert Howard said nothing. He did not want to protest or defend himself.

"Ye will stay here until ye are better. I told Kimbra that. And until we hear from the Howards. Jock will be looking after ye. I will also have my physician tend ye, though from the look of ye, I think Kimbra served ye better."

The Charlton turned away, and Robert knew he was dismissed. He wondered where Cedric was at the moment. *He* would be the greatest danger.

Cedric, and his own nightmares. What if he uttered words in his sleep?

It was obvious that the Charlton was not convinced he was who he said he was.

He rose and followed Jock out the door and down a dark hallway lit by sconces in the walls. He leaned on the crutch and made his way past five doors, praying he would not have to mount more steps. The prayers were answered when Jock stopped at a door and opened it.

The room was small and contained only a rough bed and a chair. A tall narrow window was the only source of light. He gratefully lowered himself onto the bed.

"Someone will bring ye water and food," Jock said.

Robert Howard nodded. He wanted to say as little as possible.

"I will be outside if ye need anything more." The large man left the room.

Outside.

For all the hospitality—required, he knew, by custom—'twas clear he was naught but a prisoner. One to be tended until the truth of his story was confirmed.

Or not.

*T*HE cottage was intolerably empty since the Scot left the day before.

Just as it had been two years earlier. She'd spent months trying to fill it back with life. Now even Audra and Bear appeared dispirited as they went through their daily routines.

When she milked Bess, she remembered the Scot's wry expression and his milk-drenched clothing. Other memories followed. The way he held the lute as he sang to her daughter. Drawing letters in the dirt. The story he'd told Audra. She prayed as she had not prayed in a long time that he would get back to Scotland and find his people. His family.

Later she found herself humming his lullaby to Audra as she went to sleep again in the big featherbed the Scot had occupied. Though she had washed the bedclothes, she thought the scent of him lingered. His jack hung from a hook on the wall. She had an excuse now to visit the Charlton tower and return his property.

But not today, and not tomorrow. Too much concern could well injure him as well as herself.

Once she was sure Audra was asleep, she went back up into the loft and pulled out the broach with the crest again. The stones included rubies along with some others she could not identify. But she knew the rubies. The Charlton

had a ruby ring he prized. It glowed like a living thing.
Other small stones outlined a tower within a double circle.
Three words were carved in gold within the double circle.

She traced them, wishing she'd had more time studying
with the Scot. Would they tell him what he longed to know?

She *had* to discover the meaning of the crest. She had
thought about the problem every moment since he left, and
now she settled on a course of action. She would take herbs
into the small village near the castle, bargain for some
meat and listen to gossip. She would stop by Jane's to see if
her friend had learned anything, as well.

There was a priest in the village who could read the
words on the crest, but he had flatly refused to teach her to
read when she had asked years ago. A reiver's woman had
no need to read, he'd said.

She certainly did not believe he would keep her secret
safe.

Nor could she trust the few other people she knew who
could read. They, too, had laughed at her when the priest
had announced to the entire village she wanted to learn to
read.

But mayhap she could learn more of the battle, more of
the clans that had participated, or the nobles who had ridden and died at King James's side.

Thus, decided on her first action, she replaced the crest
in its hiding place, then decided to get some sleep herself.
She'd had none the night before. She wanted that contact
with her daughter.

She wanted to assuage the guilt she had in not returning
the crest to him, or at least, showing it to him to see
whether it stirred memories.

But if she could learn what he needed to know to return
home, to where he belonged . . .

She would still miss him desperately, miss his touch, his
slow smile, the sound of his voice. But at least she would
not carry the guilt that ate like poison into her . . .

She told Audra the next morning that they would go into the village. "Can you gather some herbs while I milk Bess and collect eggs? Perhaps we can exchange my herbs for a piece of mutton."

Usually the prospect of a rare trip to the village brought some enthusiasm from her daughter. Today it did not.

"I want to stay with Bear," Audra said stubbornly.

"You cannot stay alone, and Bear can come with us. We will ride Magnus."

"Can we see Mr. Howard?"

"I think we should wait several days first."

Audra frowned. "Why?"

She decided to tell Audra the truth. "Because it could be dangerous if someone believes we are too close to him."

"Why?"

"Because Cedric wants to marry me and will do anything to accomplish it. Even try to destroy Mr. Howard."

Audra did not ask why again.

Kimbra did not want to frighten Audra, but her daughter had to be aware of what could happen if she said something that indicated a relationship that might be viewed as improper. Another load of guilt added to too many already. She should never have to burden her child like that.

"But we will see him again?"

"Aye, I imagine so."

Her daughter's blue eyes were so much like Will's. The familiar pang was not as great as it had been. Audra was quiet and curious, while Will had been confident that he knew all that he needed to know in his world. He'd never understood Kimbra's yearning to know more of people and lands beyond the border.

"We must go," she told Audra.

The ride would take them at least an hour and a half, probably longer, both coming and going. She did not want to ride at night with Audra.

In less time than she thought possible, they were

mounted on Magnus, a basket of herbs and eggs clutched in Audra's arms. Her small body snuggled against Kimbra's for warmth, as a wickedly cold wind swept the hills. Kimbra shivered. She knew the path well, had ridden it often with Will, then too many times alone.

The village was far busier than usual, and she saw men in English uniforms huddled in a small group outside the blacksmith's shop. The village was small, with only a little chapel, a butcher, the blacksmith, and the merchant Davie Carroll, who sold seed as well as cloth and household items. She went there first, knowing he heard everything.

Inside, Davie was talking to a soldier, saw her, then hurried over.

"Mistress Kimbra, it is good to see ye. And your pretty young miss."

"I have some herbs and eggs I thought you might buy."

He brightened. "I can always sell your herbs, and I am almost out of eggs." He named a small sum that would barely cover the mutton she coveted. But she had little choice. She nodded and handed him her basket in exchange for two coins.

"Have you heard anything since the battle?"

"They say ten thousand Scots died," he said in almost a wondering whisper. "They say Scotland's most powerful nobles and knights were killed."

"And the Scottish king?"

"Taken to the Branxton Church. They say it took time to know who it was. Stripped naked, he was. They say his head was bashed in."

"And the English? How many English died?"

"About half that, they say. Some are being cared for by local families."

"I found one," she said.

"I heard such," Davie replied.

So the gossip had spread rapidly.

"He's at the Charlton tower now."

Davie nodded.

"And prisoners. Were there any taken?"

She knew what Jane had said, and Jane was as direct as the sun. But she still could not believe her countrymen would order the slaughter of wounded and helpless men.

"Nay, the order was to kill all the wounded, though I heard several powerful borderers are defying the order and demanding ransom."

She absorbed the information, reluctant to ask more. But she had gleaned enough that a plan had started to form in her head. "Thank you."

"Come more often." He hesitated, then added, "We all miss Will."

She simply nodded.

"I heard rumors of a wedding. Cedric, mayhap?"

"You have heard wrong," she said.

She turned and left then. She wished she could ask him the meaning of the words on the crest. But she could only show it to someone who did not know her.

She purchased a piece of mutton for supper, then she and Audra headed toward Jane's.

*T*HE surgeon that the Charlton sent to his room wanted to bleed him.

He'd clucked over the wounds, obviously unwilling to give Mistress Kimbra Charlton any credit for the healing. "'Tis God's mercy," he mumbled as he took leeches from a box.

"Nay," Robert Howard said. "I think God had little to do with it and Mistress Charlton a great deal. And I have lost enough blood to cure a dozen men."

The physician looked at him as if he'd committed heresy.

"It merely needs a fresh cloth," he said more mildly, reminding himself to curb his tongue and be more injured than he truly was.

"Thomas Charlton said you were near death just a few days ago."

"The fever broke."

The physician regarded him much as Robert Howard thought he would regard a devil.

"My leg burns like the fires in hell," he grumbled, "and until yesterday I could not even stand alone. But I will not be bled. There are no more poisons in my body. Just lack of blood."

"I will tell the Charlton you do not desire my services," the physician said, his cheeks puffing out with indignation as he stalked to the door and walked out.

Once the door closed, Robert Howard sat up and used the crutch to stand, then walked across the room and back. Again and again. He had to find a way to leave before anyone discovered he was no Englishman, much less a Howard.

CLOTHED in her mourning gown with her hair hidden under a cap and the hood of her cloak, Kimbra started toward Branxton. She thought it was more than a half day's ride, but she had never been there before.

Jane, as agreed the day before, came to stay at her cottage to look after Audra and milk Bess for the next two days. Kimbra did not explain her reasons for going, only that she had to leave for several days. If anyone looked for her, particularly Cedric, Jane was to say she went to help a sick friend.

She would have to go past the battlefield, and she supposed that scavengers were still at work there. It would be dangerous, but she had a dagger with her.

She should be safe enough on Charlton land, but once

she left it, she would have to be wary. She would stop in some secluded place and change to her reiver's clothes, which she'd packed in a bundle. She did not wish a priest to learn who she was, and Branxton was far too close for comfort.

Lying to a priest was a sin.
But then so was robbing the dead.

She rode toward the woods where she'd found the Scot when he'd left the cottage. Finding a secluded place, she dismounted and changed clothes. She wrapped a piece of cloth tightly around her breasts, then pulled on the breeches and laced them. Finally she took off her woman's cap, replacing it with Will's skull cap, then pulled the steel helmet over it.

Once she was finished, she wrapped the gown and cloak together in a piece of cloth and tied it to the saddle. She mounted, grateful that she no longer had to fight her skirt.

As she approached the battlefield, she could smell the odor again. Now it seemed even worse. Ten thousand Scots, another four thousand English, and why? It had been three weeks and obviously many still lay in shallow graves. She veered away from the battlefield, but the memories had lodged in her head. She feared they would never go away, not any of it. Not the English soldier calling for water, nor her pulling a ring from a dead man's finger.

She finally passed the battlefield, and the odor faded. She joined a stream of people carrying bodies on horses or in carts.

She stopped one elderly man pulling a cart. A pair of bare feet stuck out from the end. "I am looking for Branxton Church."

"If ye want to see the Scot King, he's gone," the man replied and made the sign of the cross. "His body was taken to London."

"Is that your son?" she asked, trying to deepen her voice.

"Aye. He joined the English just before the battle. Foolish lad. He was my last." Then he apparently remembered the question. "Straight ahead."

Then he turned back to the road, his back bowed with grief. Her heart cried for him, and all the others looking for sons and fathers and brothers. Was someone looking for her Scot?

She turned back to the road. The man had not looked at her curiously.

She continued on as the sun started to dip. People on foot looked at Magnus enviously, or drew their eyes away. Then she reached the church. Grand compared to the small chapel in her village.

She dismounted, tied the reins to the post, and went inside. A handful of people were praying silently. A priest approached her.

"Can I assist you, my son, or are you here to pray?"

"I am hoping ye can help me," she said. She took the crest from a purse she'd attached to her belt and told the tale she'd rehearsed. "I killed a man on the battlefield. In his dying breath he asked me to return this to his family, but he died before he could tell me what family. I hoped ye might be able to help me."

She handed the crest to the priest who studied it for a moment. " 'Virtue Mine Honour,' " he read. "But I do not recognize it. You will probably have to go into Scotland to find the family name. I can take it and try to find whoever should have it."

"Nay, 'tis something I must do myself. I made a vow."

The priest did not voice the observation that rarely— if ever—did a borderer try to return an item, particularly one of value, but she knew it must be going through his thoughts.

However, he did not say so.

"Thank you, Father," she said, holding out her hand for

the broach, then fleeing as he reluctantly handed it back to her. She wanted no more questions.

She did not have what she needed—a name, a family, a title—but she had her first clue, something to give the Scot for his search. She did not know how she would explain how she discovered it, but she would.

By the time she left the church, it was dark. Magnus was where she had left him, and she gave a prayer of thanks, then mounted. She wanted to ask more people about the crest, but nearly all would be English in search of those killed by the Scots, and those who were not would probably not admit it. She did not like defeat. But more questions might endanger the Scot as much as herself. And she had something.

She had drawn the tower for him, but she had not drawn the letters. Mayhap those words would have stirred something.

Virtue Mine Honour.

Fine words for a noble. Her experience was otherwise, and yet her Scot seemed to reflect them. But then she warned herself that it may have been simply because he was made senseless by a blow to the head. Did character change with a loss of memory?

She was unsure whether to try to ride back this night or not. The sky was cloudy, and the night would be black, too dangerous to ride, even on established roads. But she did not have enough money to rent a room, and even if she did, to do so would be dangerous. Inns put their travelers in common rooms. She did not fancy sleeping in the steel helmet with ten or twelve soldiers.

Mayhap once out of the town, she could find a secluded place to rest until morning. She had the cloak for warmth.

Her decision made, she started back toward the battlefield and all its violence and tragedy. And mysteries. How many families would never know what happened to their

sons and fathers and brothers? At least, she had buried
Will, had told him she loved him.

Would the Scot's wife, if there was one, ever know the
truth?

She swallowed hard. She had tried her best to discover
his identity. Now she feared the only way to do it was to
surrender the crest. His escape might well mean the loss of
her own.

Chapter 13

※※

ROBERT Howard limped across the small room.
The more he used his leg, the stronger it became, though the pain was excruciating. He knew he would probably always have a limp.

His host had made it clear that while a guest he was also a prisoner. He spent most of the time walking back and forth in his room and on the third day was able to walk without the crutch.

He searched for memories, but they continued to elude him. When he looked out the long, narrow window at the wall below, another wall would dart into his mind. A thicker wall, and higher. But as he sought to hang on to the memory, it faded away. It was like grabbing a handful of fog.

And the nightmare. The same one over and over again. The man on the ground. The terrible guilt.

While the nightmares plagued his night, Kimbra haunted nearly every waking moment. She and her daughter. Was she all right? If he were to make a mistake, it would be Kimbra and Audra who paid the price.

Then on the third evening, the Charlton visited him.

The Charlton regarded him with something akin to wonder. " 'Tis miraculous," he said.

"Aye," Robert Howard agreed.

"The physician was convinced ye would be dead by now."

"So he told me, if I did not let him bleed me."

"Why did ye not?"

"I had been bled enough by the Scots," Robert Howard said. "I needed no more by my countrymen."

The Charlton grinned. "I have often made the same charge. Kimbra is a better healer, but she is reluctant to do anything but provide herbs. Except for Will. And," he added thoughtfully, "you."

"I am grateful."

"One of my riders returned from the Howards. No one knows of an auburn-haired Howard."

Robert Howard shrugged. "I would not be surprised. I have never met them. Neither do I know whether my mother was blond or redheaded."

"Sim was known to have bastards," the Charlton said thoughtfully. "What family did ye foster with?"

Robert Howard had a ready answer from Kimbra's coaching, a family that had feuded with the Charltons for years, despite the fact that they were both English. "The Forsters. John Forster."

The Charlton grumped his displeasure.

"I was happy to leave them," Robert Howard added.

"Cedric is suspicious of you," the Charlton probed.

"I did not like him, either," Robert Howard said. "I heard he did little fighting during the battle."

Charlton shrugged. "He fights for gold. He sees no honor in anything else." He paused. "Ye must feel the same, having fought in France."

"And Spain," Robert Howard said. "I like adventure." He thought he probably had. He found he did now. If it were not for Kimbra's safety, he may well have enjoyed this challenge of matching wits.

The Charlton left then, but Robert Howard—the man he was now—knew he had not entirely satisfied his host.

The next day, the Charlton appeared again with a servant carrying a tray with a pitcher of ale and two cups. In the Charlton's hands were a chessboard and a wooden box containing intricately carved chessmen.

"Do ye play chess?"

God's tooth, but he wasn't sure. Yet the board looked familiar enough. Why could he remember things and not remember his name, or his family's name, or from where he came?

He nodded, wanting the company and the challenge, even as he realized every moment he spent with the man meant risk.

"God bless ye, lad. No one around here is a challenge." The Charlton put the board down on the table and opened the box. His gout-swollen fingers moved the chessmen rapidly into place, but no more rapidly than Robert Howard did. He knew where every piece went. King. Queen. Rooks. Bishops. Knights. Pawns.

Robert had the white and moved the first pawn. The next move came automatically, and his mind sped several moves ahead, as his opponent took time to consider his.

How did he know how to play? Who had taught him?

In fifteen more moves, he knew he could checkmate the Charlton. He was not sure he should do that.

"Do not humor me," the Charlton said as if he knew

exactly what his opponent was thinking. "I do not like losing, but I like being patronized even less."

Robert Howard took him at his word. "Checkmate."

The Charlton looked at the board with amazement, obviously trying to figure out exactly what had happened.

"There is a lot of time between battles," Robert explained, not sure at all whether his explanation was true or not.

The Charlton's gaze pierced him. "Ye had little to wager, but ye won, and ye may choose a boon."

"A book." A book in English for Kimbra.

By God, he *would* see her again.

"Ye can read then?"

"Aye."

"How?"

He wished to the devil he knew.

"A priest taught me."

"Ye are a man of many talents, it appears."

Robert Howard said nothing.

"So be it. And ye will join us in the hall this night for supper." The Charlton rose, considered him for a moment, then said softly, "I hope ye do not disappoint me, Howard."

*K*IMBRA stayed away from the tower as long as she could.

She visited Jane and heard that the Howard was still at the tower. Cedric had returned from searching the border for fleeing Scots. The English soldiers were leaving the area. A brief truce had been declared locally, allowing Scots to come and carry off their dead.

Scots. There would be Scots in the area.

Was *her* Scot aware of that?

Mayhap one would know the crest.

As always, the thought brought mixed emotions. For his sake, she wanted him to find his family. But then he would no longer be her Scot.

"Is naught being said about Mr. Howard?" she asked.

"Oh, Cedric has a great deal to say, especially since the Charlton has invited Howard to sup with him, but he is careful. It appears, according to Jock, that the Charlton has taken a liking to yer guest."

She probably should be surprised, but she wasn't. Hadn't both she and Audra been taken with him? Cedric hadn't, because he'd sensed a threat to himself and his ambitions. But there was a very real danger to the Scot as long as he stayed at the peel tower, particularly if the Charlton was taking an interest in him.

She had to see him.

She left Jane's with Audra, and the two of them rode home on Magnus. It was noon, two days after returning from Branxton. She hurriedly gathered some herbs for the Charlton and folded Will's jack into a bundle.

Would the Charlton recognize it as once belonging to Will?

But so many on the border looked alike.

She would have to take a chance. If the Charlton did recognize it, she would merely say that Robert Howard's armor had been destroyed beyond repair.

She had just enough time to reach the Charlton tower and return before dark.

Audra was joyful at the possibility of seeing her friend again. She paced restlessly, Bear beside her, until Kimbra lifted her into the saddle.

Kimbra's heart raced ridiculously as they neared the tower. She feared doing something that might expose him, yet she had to judge for herself how well he was doing.

The first person she saw on entering into the barnekin

was Cedric, who was mounting his horse. His eyes undressed her as he rode over to her. "I was on my way to visit ye."

Bear growled.

"Ye still have that hound?"

"He is my daughter's dog. No one will touch him."

He arched an eyebrow, and she knew she would have to watch the dog.

"I wanted to warn ye. The Armstrongs are raiding again now that most of the king's army has left. Ye should not be alone. Ye should think of yer daughter."

"I am," she said sharply.

"Ye best not have interest in the Howard," he said.

"I have no interest in anyone."

"There is something wrong with him, and I will prove it to the Charlton."

"I do not know what you mean."

"Ye will," he said, then added, "I will wait for ye and accompany ye back to the cottage."

"We need no such assistance."

"I think the Charlton would want to know ye are safe, Kimbra."

"I will be a while."

"All the more reason for a guard. It will be nigh onto dark."

Better alone in the dark than with him.

A groom came out then and took Magnus's reins. Kimbra lifted Audra down, then dismounted. She untied the jack from the back of the saddle.

Be indifferent, she told herself. *'Tis only the return of an item. Nothing more.*

She was escorted up to Thomas Charlton's room, while a maid took Audra to the kitchen for a sweet. "Hope ye brought something to soothe him," said his man. "He be in a foul mood."

The Charlton was indeed scowling when she reached him. His ankle was stretched out in front of him, swollen and red and obviously painful. "I brought you some more bay leaves. I will brew some if you like."

"I would," he said. "Bloody leg. I cannot even ride."

"I also brought Robert Howard's jack. He was not given the chance to take it when your men came for him."

"I will see that he gets it."

"I would like to check his wounds."

"He is well. Ye are a good healer."

"I am not a healer."

"I never thought the Howard would live. We need yer skills, Kimbra."

She shook her head. "I could not save Will. I should have given him to the care of your physician."

"Nay. Nothing could save him once his blood was poisoned."

She did not say anything. Guilt was still a living pain in her. Why had she not been able to save her husband but could save an enemy?

"This Howard," the Charlton said, "he does not say much."

"He had a head wound. I think he forgot some things."

"He remembers enough to defeat me at chess."

She must have shown some surprise because he gave her a sly smile. "Not many around here can do that. I wanted to take measure of him. He apparently has little loyalty to the Howards. I can use a man like that. Since Will died . . ."

She was stunned. Of every possible outcome she'd imagined, this was not one of them.

"What about Cedric? His brothers?"

"They do not have the loyalty or trust of my men."

"You know nothing about Robert Howard."

"I am a good judge of men. He fought near to his death for King Henry. He meets my eyes when he talks to me." He grinned. "He can also play chess."

She did not reply, but her heart dropped. The last thing either she or the Scot needed was the trust and friendship of a man who did not like being fooled. On the other hand, it might make it easier for him to escape.

And worsen the sense of disloyalty roiling about inside her. She did not want the Charlton to trust him.

"Audra would like to see him," she said.

"I will take ye there."

"But your leg?"

He shrugged, lifted his bulk to his feet and reached for the cane. "I will send Jock for your daughter," he said. He led the way down the corridor to a door.

Jock, a particular friend of Will's, was standing outside.

"Jock," she said with real affection.

"Mistress Kimbra," he replied with a smile. "Where is your young miss?"

"She's in the kitchen," Kimbra replied.

"Is the Howard awake?" the Charlton asked Jock.

"Aye. Last time he was carving a trail on the floor. Back and forth."

"Go fetch Mistress Audra," the Charlton said.

As Jock disappeared down the hall, the Charlton opened the door and limped into the room.

Her Scot was in the midst of turning around, as if startled. He bent his head in acknowledgment of the Charlton, but his face was carefully neutral when he turned to her. Still, she thought she saw the faintest throb of a muscle in his throat. "Mistress Kimbra," he said.

"I wanted to see how your wounds were," she said, "and you left your jack in my cottage." She handed it to him.

"My thanks once again," he said, his eyes meeting hers

but revealing little, while her heart was beating far too rapidly.

She stood there awkwardly, not knowing what to say and, in truth, afraid to say anything with the Charlton present.

The Scot took several steps. He limped, but the steps were solidly made and without a cane. "You did well," he said, this time with a smile playing around his lips.

"Nay, I but gave you what God provided."

She felt the warmth of his gaze for a fleeting second before he turned to the door as Audra stood there, a broad grin on her face. She ran over to him. He dropped the jack he was holding and lifted her up.

"Have you been practicing the lute?" he asked, ignoring the sudden pain in his chest.

"Aye. Bear crawls under the table."

"All the better to hear," he said, a twinkle in his eyes.

Kimbra feared he was too familiar for a man at death's door just a few days earlier. But there was no preventing Audra from staring at him with rapt adoration.

"Lute?" the Charlton asked.

"Mr. Howard is teaching me," Audra said proudly.

The Charlton glanced at the Scot.

"Ye did not tell me that."

The Scot shrugged. "I do not play that well."

"Like chess?" the Charlton said wryly. "Is there anything else I should know?"

"Nay."

"I shall leave ye then for a while. Kimbra, you will sup with us tonight. Edith can take care of Audra, and Jock will accompany you home."

No Cedric. It was sufficient incentive to say aye.

"I have no gown with me," she protested.

"Claire will show you my wife's gowns, and you may choose one," he said.

Startled, she could only nod. The Charlton had lost his

second wife three years earlier, and he had mourned her, much as she had mourned Will. The first wife, she had heard, died in childbirth. The second wife, Mary, had produced a son, who had died of a fever, and a daughter, who had committed the unforgivable sin of marrying a Scot. He had not taken a third wife.

"Thank you," she said.

He left them abruptly then. She and her daughter and the Scot.

He put Audra down and reached out and touched her cheek. "I worried about you."

Heat coursed through her, and she feared her voice was shaky when she answered, "I can take care of myself."

"I fear that you may be in danger because of me."

She glanced down at Audra, and he clamped his lips closed. He knelt in front of Audra. "Have you been practicing the lute and your letters?"

"Aye," Audra said, and sang his letter song.

"Very nicely done," he said. "I have never had such a good pupil."

Audra's grin could not have been wider. Nor his.

Holy Mother, but she was beguiled by that smile.

She wanted to reach out and do what he had done: run her fingers down his face. And she wanted much more than that.

But she had to remember why she had come. "Audra," she said, "can you run down and see whether the cook has some sweets?"

Audra looked rebellious.

"I would like a sweet," he said, and Audra needed no more encouragement.

When she left, Kimbra said urgently, "The English army is leaving. Some Scots are coming over the border to claim their dead."

"I am watched every moment," he said.

She hesitated, then asked, "Have you remembered anything?"

"A man's face, that is all. I do not know if it is a memory or a nightmare."

"The Charlton said you played chess."

"Aye, though I do not remember who taught me." He pounded a fist in his hand. "It is so bloody frustrating. I can remember skills. I cannot remember people."

"But no one suspects you?"

"I think the Charlton has some doubts."

"Not too many, I think. He is thinking about bringing you into the family."

He stared at her.

"He believes he is a good judge of character."

The Scot's eyebrows furrowed together. "He insisted I join the clan for supper last night."

"Clan?"

He looked startled. "I should no' say that?"

"No."

"Was Cedric there?"

"Nay, but there were hostile looks from others."

"I still feel you should leave as soon as you find a chance."

"And where would I go?"

"Anywhere in Scotland." She hesitated, then asked, "Does 'Virtue Mine Honour,' mean anything to you?"

He repeated the words, then shook his head in denial. "Should it?"

Disappointed, she shook her head. "I just heard someone says it was a motto in Scotland. I thought it might make you think of something."

He repeated the words, tasted them, then shook his head. *The crest. Tell him about the crest.*

The door opened, and they both turned. Audra held a platter of sweets. Beside her was the Charlton's housekeeper.

Kimbra knew Claire well. She was Will's spinster cousin and had been housekeeper for Thomas Charlton since before Kimbra had married and come to the Charlton stronghold. She was a handsome woman of middle years, and often Kimbra had heard people wonder why Claire had not wed. 'Twas said there had been many suitors. She'd never been a friend, though Kimbra had never thought of her as an enemy, either.

Claire's sharp gaze had turned from her to the Scot, then back again. "The Charlton asked me to find ye a gown."

Kimbra desperately wanted a few more moments with the Scot, but she knew how dangerous that could be. His position here was full of risk, even more so now that the Charlton was taking an interest in him. She knew the infighting among the Charltons, especially since the head of the family had no living heir.

If the Scot was viewed as a danger to ambitions, there would be no limit to attempts to discredit him.

It made even more urgent his escape.

If only the motto—the words—had brought back a memory.

She left Audra and the Scot to eat from the plate of sweets and followed Claire down the hall to another room. Inside, Claire opened a chest and took out an armful of gowns, all of which were far finer than anything Kimbra had ever owned.

Kimbra eyed one of dark blue silk. It was of a modest cut and simple lines.

Claire helped her with the lacings. It was tight in some places, loose in others. Claire called for another woman, a seamstress, and within an hour, the gown fit far better.

Except for instructions, Claire was silent during the process. When the gown was altered, she looked at Kimbra's hair and shook her head in dismay. Minutes later, a young girl was twisting Kimbra's dark hair into an intricate knot.

When finished, the girl disappeared silently.

Kimbra turned to Claire. "Why is he doing this?"

"The Charlton?"

"Aye."

"He is lonely, I think."

The reply surprised Kimbra, not as much for the content as for the sadness in Claire's voice.

"The Charlton?"

"He was considering making Will his heir when he was killed."

Kimbra remembered the Charlton's visit when Will was ill, then the last one as Will lay dead. She'd always thought it was his natural concern for one of his soldiers.

"He always liked you," Claire added.

There was something in her voice that startled Kimbra, almost jealousy. She reached back in her memory. Claire was a cousin to Will, separated several times, but she was the Charlton's first cousin. Could she love . . . ?

The thought was impossible. It was forbidden by the church. But Claire was obviously privy to the Charlton's private thoughts.

"I thought he opposed our marriage."

"He did, at first. You brought nothing to the family, nothing to Will, but when you were found to have been riding with the family, he roared with laughter. He said you were worth two of most of his soldiers."

She was stunned. So that was why he'd allowed her to keep the cottage. Cedric had obviously been lying about Thomas Charlton favoring his suit, believing that if he convinced her to marry he'd find himself in favor.

She wondered now whether that was why the Charlton wished her to stay this evening, that he was making it clear she was under his protection.

She also remembered the fate of one of his favorites four years ago when he found himself betrayed.

A chill ran through her.

The Charlton was not a man to forgive betrayal. Nor one who tolerated lies.

Now that both the Scot, and she, had drawn his attention, both of them were in more danger than ever.

Chapter 14

❧

ROBERT Howard felt he was walking a dagger's edge as he sat among his country's enemies and tried not to look at Kimbra Charlton. She sat on the other side of the Charlton, a place of honor.

He was several seats down, among the reivers. Jock was on one side of him. A man called Davey's Son on the other. Cedric was on the other side of the table, his face set with resentment. A man looking very much like him was at his side. Garrick, he remembered.

Robert Howard, like nearly every other man in attendance, could barely take his eyes from Kimbra Charlton. The color of her gown turned her gray eyes blue, and her dark hair was pulled back, with several curls arranged around her face. She looked enchanting, and when she'd entered the room at the Charlton's side, he'd felt an odd jerk in his heart.

She was as bonny as the sun touching a Scottish loch and as challenging as a storm at sea.

Where had those images come from? Suddenly he was sitting on a cliff overlooking the sea, waves crashing beneath him. A rock jutted out of the sea. A feeling of malevolence jolted through him, settled in the pit of his stomach.

Then it was gone.

"Howard?"

He suddenly realized Jock had addressed him.

"Aye?"

"Ye do not look well."

"'Tis nothing. A momentary weakness."

"Eat well."

He tried to eat well. Platters and platters of food came. Mutton. Beef. Pheasant. As he ate, he tried to concentrate, to focus again on that rock. He saw it in his mind's eye, but the feelings were gone, the sense of evil he'd felt. The rock had once been important in his life. Of that he was certain.

He glanced up at Kimbra. She was smiling at something the Charlton was saying, and jealousy coursed through him. The man was nearly three times Kimbra's age, and he should have no such feelings. But the intensity of them were painful.

"No one has claimed ye yet," Cedric said on the other side of the table. "Appears strange that none know of ye."

He shrugged and did not reply.

"Mayhap ye are not a Howard at all," Cedric continued.

Robert Howard shrugged again, ignoring him and turning to Jock. "I hear most of Henry's army is leaving."

"Aye. They keep losing horses," Jock grinned.

"The Scots, no doubt," Robert Howard replied.

"No doubt," Jock agreed with a chuckle.

Cedric broke in. "It is said ye fought on the continent. For or against the French?"

"For whoever paid the most," Robert Howard said.

"The French are our enemies."

"Not always."

Cedric's face reddened. "I do not believe yer wild tale."

"That is your choice," Robert Howard said mildly and turned back to Jock, with whom he had developed somewhat of a truce in the past few days. They had even shared a pitcher of ale after the Charlton's first visit.

"It is as good as yer wild tales," Jock suddenly confronted Cedric. "Ye disappeared during the battle." He turned his glance away in obvious disgust.

Robert Howard glanced up the table. Kimbra looked down at the same time, and their gazes met. Held. God's tooth but she was lovely. Then her gaze returned to the Charlton.

He glanced at Cedric and knew from the fury in the man's eyes that he had seen the exchange.

Sweets came then. Pies and puddings and fruit.

Then he heard Kimbra's voice insisting she must go. She had a daughter to put in bed and a cow to milk.

"I will send someone to milk the cow," the Charlton said.

"You do not know my cow. She will allow none but myself to milk her."

Almost true, Robert Howard thought.

"I will accompany her," Cedric said, standing.

"Nay, Jock will do so," the Charlton said.

"I thought he was guarding this . . . man who calls himself a Howard," Cedric replied.

The Charlton frowned. "Are you questioning my decisions?"

"Nay, but . . ."

"We will talk later," the Charlton said curtly.

Kimbra rose, and Jock went to her. Kimbra glanced at Robert Howard. "I have not had a chance to check his wounds."

Jock ignored Cedric who was glowering at all of them. "Ye can do that while I get the horses ready."

He accompanied them up the stone steps and to Robert Howard's chamber. As they reached it, he turned to them. "I will see to the horses," he said, and left them.

The moment the door closed behind them, she moved closer to him. "You have to leave as soon as possible. If you can get to my cottage, take Magnus."

"I have thought about that, Kimbra. I cannot take your horse. If I am taken, you may well lose him."

"I will take that risk."

"I will not take it for you. I owe you far too much already. And despite the Charlton's hospitality, I am watched all the time."

He moved closer to her. She felt his breath against her cheek like a light breeze.

She leaned into him, and his arms went around her, his lips touching—barely—her cheek.

God's truth, but he felt as if he belonged there. How could he possibly be wed to another and have these feelings?

His lips moved along her cheekbone, then down to her throat. She made a soft purring noise. He wanted to make one as well. His lips found hers, caressed them with all the tenderness that had been building inside. She responded with a searching wistfulness, and suddenly the kiss turned demanding, the gentleness churning into a want so deep he could barely contain it. He crushed her to him.

Her lips sought his as greedily as his plundered hers.

He closed his eyes, soaking in memories. The way she felt. The light scent of flowers. The silkiness of her hair. He was consumed by a glow of light, of a warmth that pulsed through him, and he suddenly knew he had never felt this way before.

Loneliness was not a new companion.

She moved slightly, and he opened his eyes. Her gray eyes were tinged with blue as they looked up at him, sooty eyelashes unable to hide the smoldering passion stirring there.

Then he released her lips as his fingers touched the nape of her neck. "There is enchantment here," he said.

"Aye, but it cannot last."

"Why?" he whispered.

"It should be plain."

"Nay."

"You are a noble or at least of an important family. When you find where you belong, I would have no place."

"You have a place wherever I go."

She leaned her head against his heart for a moment or more, then stepped back, those striking eyes determined. "Nay. Dreams are for fools," she said.

Dreams are for fools.

He stilled. A tall man with dark brown hair, but the face eluded him.

We can never marry. Dreams are for fools.

The words had been bitter, laced with heavy grief.

Then the image disappeared.

He shook his head, trying to bring it back. But it was gone, lost with the other images that tortured him.

"Robert?"

It was the first time she had called him Robert. It was beginning to feel familiar.

"I remembered . . . I think I remembered—"

"What?" Her voice was suddenly sharp.

"A figure. A man."

"What did he look like?"

"I did not see his face."

"Did he say anything?"

He could not relate the words. They were like a brand on his soul. *We can never marry.*

"Nay," he lied.

"Your brother? Father? Friend?"

He shook his head. "Blast it, I do not know."

"Your nightmares? Have you seen him in any of those?"

"Nay."

"Anyone?" she persisted. "Have you seen anyone else?"

The laughing girl with brown hair. But he could not say the words.

Her gaze seemed to be reaching inside him, knowing there was something he was not saying.

Then she turned away. "I had best look at that wound," she said. " 'Twas my excuse for being here."

"Excuse?"

"Cedric and others will take any opportunity to hurt you if they think I, or you, are a threat to their ambitions." There was a coolness in her voice, and he knew it was because she sensed he was not being honest.

He was not sure why he could not tell her about the girl, or the words spoken by the man in that all-too-fleeting image. But he could not, not until he knew what they meant.

He sat on the bed as she checked his wound. There was no longer a need to wrap it. The scar was ugly because of the burn. Still a bit raw but well on the way to healing.

"I do not think you will be lame," she said.

"A good thing since my left arm is stiff."

"How did that happen?"

He paused. She did that, over and over again. She threw out questions which she obviously hoped would stir memories. He could only shake his head in bafflement.

He stood again. He wanted to reach out and touch her again, but he feared he could not stop himself from taking it a step further. God knew he wanted to. He wanted to undress her, caress her, carry her to the bed, and bury himself in her. He wanted to hear her laughter and see that all-too-rare smile.

"I wish I knew," he said, finally answering her question.

"It will come back."

He did not answer. He wasn't sure he wanted it to come back. For the first time, he wanted to quiet those disturbing voices inside.

He touched her cheek again, his hand cupping the determined chin. "I find I do not want to leave."

"You must," she whispered brokenly. " 'Tis so very dangerous."

"You are worth it." The words sprung from his mouth before he could catch them. He had no right to make declarations. She was right. He had to find his past before he could claim what he now knew he wanted above all.

He leaned down and kissed her lightly. "I will try to leave," he promised.

They heard Jock's heavy footfalls then, and separated.

"I will see you again," he said in a low voice.

But doubt was in her expression.

He wanted to kiss it away, but he could not. Instead he moved to the window as the door opened and Jock entered, a sleepy Audra in his arms.

"The horses are ready."

She nodded. "Good eve," she said, and went out the door, taking the light with her.

RORY rode into the Armstrong stronghold. It was near dark.

He saw Archibald, who was engaged in what looked like a battle to the death with a bearded, one-eyed opponent several stones larger than himself.

He stopped and watched as Archibald eventually bested the man.

Archibald saw him and hurried to his side.

" 'Tis glad I am to see ye."

"Any word of Lachlan?"

"Nay, though the Campbells ransomed Jamie. He is out now searching for Lachlan and news of his own Campbells. I was to wait here for ye." He paused, then asked, "How is the queen?"

"Heartbroken and surrounded by vultures. The council

is half for a French alliance, half for English, and cannot agree on anything. I fear that the new Earl of Angus is gaining her ear and promoting the English cause. I could not persuade her otherwise. For some reason, she chooses his protection and is siding with those who want a truce with England."

"She is King Henry's sister."

"Aye, but there's never been any love lost there, especially now that James is dead at his hand."

"More at James's own hand from what I hear," Archibald said bitterly. "More than ten thousand Scots dead. I fear for Hector and Lachlan and so many others."

"Are the Armstrongs helping in the search?"

"As much as they can. The border has been dangerous, and if Lachlan or Hector are in hiding, the Armstrongs do not want to alert the English that they may be alive. Jamie and several Armstrongs are posing as English borderers."

"Aye, Lachlan would be a fine catch for the English throne. Henry would love nothing better than to get his hands on a Maclean. We have always stood against the English." He paused, then added, "Is there any indication he might still live?"

"'Tis unlikely," Archibald said. "Most of the bodies were stripped of every piece of clothing and jewelry. They say all at James's side were killed. It was difficult to even identify the king's body."

"But no one saw Lachlan dead?"

"Nay, but . . ."

"And Hector?"

"We did find a Maclean who claims he saw Hector die. We have no' found his body."

Pain ripped through Rory. Both Hector and Archibald had been like fathers to him, far more so than his own had been. "We should find the place where Macleans fell."

I should have been there! He never should have allowed Lachlan to take his place.

Several burly men, dressed in heavy jacks, approached.

Archibald introduced him to the man who appeared to be the leader. "This is Tommy Armstrong. He has been doing everything he can to help us. He has contacted other border families and sent some of his men with Jamie."

Rory thrust out his hand. "Our thanks. The Macleans will not forget it."

"It will be easier to search now that the English army is leaving," the Armstrong said grimly.

"Were the wounded taken anywhere?"

"The wounded were ordered killed by the English."

"Jamie Campbell was taken for ransom."

"By a family powerful enough to defy the king. Not many are. Nay, ye would have heard by now, and I would have as well."

"Could he have been taken in by someone?"

"Who would risk death for doing so? Nay, I think not. The only chance is that he survived the initial battle and managed to hide somewhere. But the English have been scouring the countryside. There is little hope he survived."

Rory's heart tightened, cutting off his breath. He had not given up hope despite the odds. He had abandoned Lachlan when his younger brother needed him years ago. He hadn't realized how haunted his brother was until he returned from ten years at sea. Even then, Lachlan had risked his life for him, had almost died in the effort. Lachlan had shown far more loyalty to him than he had to Lachlan.

And now because he had not wanted to leave his wife and two bairns, his brother could be dead.

He would not accept that.

"I will go to meet Jamie Campbell."

"Nay. They will be back tonight. Ye can start looking again at first light." He looked over Rory's breeches, linen shirt, and doublet. "Ye look too much like what ye are. I'll find ye some new clothes. Ye may want to let your beard grow out."

He was shown a room and invited to eat supper with them. As hospitality demanded the invitation, courtesy demanded acceptance, though he would have preferred to be out looking for his brother.

The meal was loud and noisy and drunken. The Armstrongs were undistinguishable by rank or dress or language. They all wore the same attire: dark breeches, doublet, and jack. They drank with gusto and told tales of their bravery, and the cowardice of the English borderers.

Riders appeared after dark. There was a cry from sentries, then he saw the light of torches dancing in the night air as the party approached and the riders dismounted.

One of the men dismounted and hurried over to him.

It took Rory a moment longer to recognize Jamie. Rather than the plaid he usually wore, he'd donned the same rough garments as the Armstrongs along with the steel helmet that was so common on the border. Jamie took it off, and Rory saw him clearly in the moonlight. He was pale, and thin, his red hair darkened by some substance. The bright grin had dulled into an expression void of light.

Rory clasped Jamie's shoulder. "My God, but it is good seeing you."

"Too many others did not make it," his friend said somberly.

Jamie was obviously burning up with guilt. Rory understood. "I should have been there as well."

"Another casualty? I do not know what good that would have been."

"Lachlan—"

"Lachlan fought like the very devil. I saw him go down. He was swinging his sword."

"You have no hope for him then?"

"I had blasted little hope for myself, but I survived."

"When did you last see Lachlan?"

"He was at the left side of the king. I was on the other.

The king charged down the hill. As we engaged the English, we were attacked from the rear. We were surrounded. James fought like a madman. So did Lachlan. I tried to make my way to him, but a pike took down my horse. When I was on the ground, there was a sword at my throat, and I had no weapon." He was silent, then, "I should have died with the rest."

"Nay," Rory said, knowing guilt all too well. "That would have gained nothing."

"Except my honor."

"No one will question that. You have not asked how your wife is."

"I do not deserve her. I dishonored the Campbells. I live while the best and bravest of Scotland are dead."

"She does not feel that way." Rory paused, then added, "She's with child, Jamie."

Jamie looked at him with the startlingly blue eyes that were now filled with agony. Gone was the laughter, the teasing, the charm.

"She needs you," Rory continued.

"I cannot return until I discover what happened to Lachlan. I swore to you I would bring him back."

"Hector? Have you heard anything of him?"

"Nay. I fear the worse. You and I know he would not have left Lachlan," Jamie said. He paused, then added, "We went to the battlefield, to the place where the king and Lachlan went down. We found nothing. The reivers stole everything, including the baggage of the English army."

"There must be something," Rory protested.

"Aye, some bodies were taken to various churches. We've been to several on the Scottish side. Lachlan was not on any of the lists there. Now that the English army is mostly gone, the Armstrongs suggest I try Branxton Church. Mayhap they have a list of known dead."

"How far is it from here?"

One of the Armstrongs spoke up. "A night's ride."

"Then we go tonight. Archibald and I can go. You stay here and get some rest."

"Nay," Jamie said. "I will go with you."

From the determined look on Jamie's face, Rory knew he would not change his mind.

"Ye can have a hobbler while ye are here. Our horses may no' look so big," the Armstrong said, "but they can travel fast over long distances and go through boggy land that no other horse can. Ye would not be taken for a borderer on the horse you rode."

In minutes, Rory had changed to the rough clothes of the borderer, wishing mightily for his plaid. The jack was heavy, woven with steel strands, and the shirt rough. The helmet weighed heavily on his head. And as he mounted the small horse, he felt as if his long legs were dragging the ground.

They were silent as the Armstrong led the way through the ridges of sward and rough grass, then the bogs. Lit by a three-quarters moon, the bleak and lonely landscape helped Rory understand the hard and ruthless men who lived here. He knew of the border reivers, of course. King James had often vowed to try to do something about the lawlessness on the border. It wasn't only Scots raiding English but Scots raiding Scots as well.

But his family had also done some business with the Armstrongs, business that involved a bit of smuggling, and he had little right to question the morals of others.

Jamie rode over to him. "It is an inhospitable land," he said.

"Yet it has a stark beauty."

"I have no' your vision, Rory. I hate every foot of it."

The emphasis in Jamie's words was something else that was new. A bitterness that was alien to everything his friend was. He wondered what had happened to Jamie these past months.

Jamie lapsed into silence.

Rory turned his thoughts to Lachlan. Someone must have seen Lachlan. Someone must know whether he was dead or alive. He prayed silently that he would find some answers at the Branxton Church.

Chapter 15

ROBERT Howard felt irretrievably tangled in his web of lies.

He hated them.

He liked Thomas Charlton, regardless of his questionable acts as a reiver. He certainly did not want to deceive him. Holy Mother, but he didn't even know what he was lying about.

He'd thought about what Kimbra had said. In truth, he thought about her entirely too much. Yet there was nothing he could do. He was watched carefully. Every time he left the tower, he had a shadow nearby, and until now he hadn't had the strength to try to elude one.

Now, though, he turned his thoughts to leaving.

It was what Kimbra wanted.

It wasn't what he wanted. He felt oddly at home here on the border, both in Kimbra's neat cottage and with the rough borderers who seemed to seize life. He liked most of them, with the exception of Cedric, who seemed always around the corner.

He walked outside the tower, trying to regain strength in his leg, and had even engaged in sword play with a Charlton. He favored his leg and weakened much too fast, but for a few moments he held his own.

Later the Charlton brought the chessboard back into his room.

"I watched ye today."

"I did not do very well."

"Nay, ye did very well for a man with the kind of injuries ye have." He set the board down and put the black chess men in place. They had traded black and white this past week.

Robert's mind was not on the contest this time, and the Charlton won for the first time.

"Ye let me win?"

"Nay. I would not insult you."

"Then ye were not paying attention."

"Mayhap," Robert said, smiling. "'Tis time to be thinking of leaving if you give permission."

"Where would ye go?"

Robert shrugged.

The Charlton gave him a sharp look. "I can use more raiders if ye choose not to return to the Howards."

"I have no love for them—or loyalty," he said carefully. "I meant little to them."

"Then mayhap ye would like to go with us on a raid into Scotland? The Armstrongs raided one of our farms."

"I thought the English were still scouring the countryside for Scots," Robert Howard said.

"A few patrols, but they do not know the border and do not venture in most of it. And there is much to raid over. English horses. English cannon. English tents we've already liberated."

"I am flattered but puzzled. You know little about me."

"Ye will be watched at first, make no mistake about it. But I need men I can trust. Kimbra's Will was a leader. I have few now that other men will follow. Ye have the look and feel of one."

"You know nothing about me."

"I know your eyes meet mine," Thomas Charlton said. "Kimbra trusts you, and she does not do that easily. I had Cedric picked out for her, but she told me she would no' have him. I have since asked others about him, and though few would talk against him, 'twas obvious they do not like him." He paused. "My only daughter married across the border, the saints preserve her, but she did it against my wishes, and I have disowned her. My only son died during childhood. Will came close to being one." His voice broke slightly. Then he shrugged. "Your wounds show ye to be a man who does not run from a battle, even one that is not his."

Robert Howard tried not to show any emotion. Kimbra had mentioned that the Charlton had said something of the kind, but he'd dismissed it as fanciful. He should have known that nothing about Kimbra was fanciful. "You would trust me?"

The Charlton gave him a thin smile. "Nay, not completely. As I said, ye will be watched. But prove yerself, and ye will have a place here." He paused, then added, "I want Will's Kimbra to be happy. She has a light in her eyes when she looks at ye, and it's been gone far too long. But be warned, do not lie to me. Do not betray me. I take either as a personal injury. I will kill any man who betrays my trust."

His eyes had hardened, and the genial host and chess player was gone. In its stead was not an old man, but a powerful and ruthless one who ran one of the most notorious families along the border.

Robert Howard—the name was becoming more familiar now—merely nodded.

"Ye will join us then on the raid?" the Charlton asked.

It was not really a request, but a demand.

"Aye," Robert Howard said.

The Charlton poured them both a cup of wine. "To a successful raid," he said. "And a new Charlton."

It nearly choked Robert Howard on the way down. He was being offered everything he now wanted. Kimbra was obviously available to him if he proved his worth.

He wanted to stay. He wanted a home. He wanted Kimbra and Audra.

Be warned . . . do not lie to me.

He had done nothing but lie since he'd set foot into the tower.

After the Charlton left, Robert went to the window. It was past midnight and a three-quarters moon hung over the bare landscape. Sheep and cattle grazed outside the wall.

And beyond that was a warm cottage. Was Kimbra unable to sleep as he was? Did her belly ache with wanting as his did? Or did that happen with women?

A lone rider approached the wall at a gallop.

Robert watched as the gate swung open. The rider spurred the horse inside and dismounted. Several men joined him, and they hurried inside. Apprehension crawled up his spine. Had someone discovered who he was?

But no boots pounded down the hall for him, and after several moments he started to relax. Beneath him, a lad ran out to take the horse to be stabled. But as soon as he did, another worry plagued him.

There was urgency in the arrival. A raid of some kind? On the outlying areas?

The door was no longer locked. There was, in truth, no way for him to leave the tower without being noticed. He limped down the hall to the Charlton's room and encountered Jock, who ushered him inside.

He ignored Cedric's glare. "Something has happened?"

"A farm was raided," the Charlton said wearily.

"Kimbra?"

"Not Kimbra, but I have sent some men to bring her in. A farmer was stabbed when he tried to protect his cattle. They lost all their sheep as well as two hobblers." The Charlton's face was red with fury. "I am sending men after them."

"I want to go," he said. Oddly enough, he felt as if he himself had been violated, even though his head said something else. These were not his people. This was not his home.

"Not this time. The riding is hard, and ye must know the trails. Your leg is no' ready yet."

"But you said . . ."

"In a few days, Howard. Other Charltons will be joining us then. We will be strong enough to attack on their land, but now we may have a chance to bring back the stock. The cattle will slow the raiders down."

The Charlton looked among the men standing there, his gaze lingering on Cedric, then moving on to choose one man. "Richie's Will, ye pick fifteen men to go."

Cedric stepped forward to protest.

"I need ye here for protection," the Charlton said. "There has been one raid tonight. There may be others."

A mollified Cedric nodded. "As ye wish."

The man called Richie's Will left the room quickly. Robert followed the Charlton as he rose and went to the window. They watched as sixteen armed men galloped from the tower.

Robert grasped the stone wall as a new image seized him . . .

He was galloping along a path with a group of other men. He was with them, riding hard beside a man of great bearing.

Suddenly others blocked the road. He tried to lift his sword, but he could not.

The man at his side interceded, moved in front of him.
Then he fell, blood pouring out of his body . . .
He knelt next to the body, despair racking his body.
Father.
And he had killed him.

K IMBRA waited restlessly for word of her Scot.
Surely he'd had an opportunity to escape by
now. But if he had, she was sure Jane would have ridden
over to tell her. The same held true if he had been revealed
as an enemy.

She hadn't left her cottage or its immediate area in
hopes that he would make his way to her cottage. But each
day she waited in vain, and her apprehension mounted.
How long could he continue to play an Englishman without getting caught?

Both she and Audra continued working on their letters.
She knew the alphabet now and a few simple words. As
Audra fed the chickens, Kimbra drew the words the priest
had read from the crest in the dirt. *Virtue mine honour.* She
had remembered the shape of each letter.

She said the words softly, trying to remember the sound
of each.

"What is that?" Audra asked.

Intent in her study, Kimbra hadn't realized her daughter
had approached. It was too late now to erase them.

"It says 'Virtue Mine Honour.' "

"What does it mean?"

"That virtue is honorable," she guessed.

"What is virtue?"

"Good things like loyalty and kindness to others, bravery, honesty."

The last words stuck in her throat.

"Then you have virtue," her daughter said seriously.

But she did not. She robbed the dead, and she had withheld a valuable item from a guest in her house, and she had lied, and she had betrayed both her king and the Charlton. She could not even repent, because, given the circumstances, she would commit the same acts again. She certainly could not confess that to the local priest.

She would be damned forever.

But she could not say that to her daughter.

Instead she erased the words with her foot and went inside the cottage to make supper.

After a meal of the last of the stew she'd made with the mutton, she fueled the fire with wood, then sang a lullaby to Audra until her daughter's eyes closed. When she was sure Audra was asleep, she went outside. Bear was sitting there expectantly. "Go guard the road," she said with a brief scratch behind one ear. Bear lolled his tongue in pleasure, then obediently trotted down the path.

She sat down and looked heavenward. The night was clear, and a full moon was surrounded by a million stars. Ordinarily she would have appreciated the sheer beauty of it. But not tonight. Raiders liked a full moon to light their way along torturous paths. She shivered, more because of apprehension than the cold wind that was blowing.

Jane had said that since the English army left, the Armstrongs had started raiding again across the border. Her cottage had never been raided. It was deep in the woods and away from the traveled roads and trails. But she could not sleep. Worry was like a snake inside her. Worry for her daughter. Worry for the Scot.

Had the Charlton taken the Scot on a raid? Was he even well enough to make such a hard ride? If so, would he try to leave them and disappear into Scotland?

She must have dozed, because Bear's bark startled her.

She came awake quickly and ran inside. She'd planned what to do in the event of a raid. She woke her daughter and carried her in a blanket out to the stable. She led Magnus out of the stable and put Audra on his back, and she led both of them to a spot just inside the nearby woods. She securely tied the animal to a tree. "Audra, stay here," she said. "Take care of Magnus."

Audra, her eyes sleepy, nodded.

"No matter what you hear, stay. If I do not return for you, take Magnus and go to Jane's. Can you be a big girl and do that?"

Frightened eyes looked up. "I want to stay with you."

"Nay. Do as I say. Please."

"Aye," her daughter finally said in a small frightened voice.

Audra looked so small. It broke Kimbra's heart to leave her there, but hopefully she would be back in a few moments. She did not worry about animals. For the first time, she thanked God for the English who'd cleared out most of the game. She had seen none near the cottage.

Fighting back fear, she ran back to the copse of trees bordering the cottage and peered out from behind a large oak just as three riders approached. Bear, still barking, ran with them.

The rider took off his helmet, and relief flooded her as she recognized him as a Charlton. She walked out to meet them.

"Kimbra, the Charlton sent me. The Armstrongs raided several farms earlier tonight. One man was badly hurt. The Charlton wants ye and your daughter to go to the tower for safety, and he has need of your herbs, for the injured."

Relief flooded her. "What about my cow?"

"We will take her with us," he said.

"I have to get my daughter. I hid her in the woods. I feared you might be raiders."

"I will go with you."

Kimbra ran as swiftly as she could. She did not want Audra alone one more second than necessary. She found Audra leaning against Magnus for comfort. When she saw Kimbra, she ran to her.

" 'Twas just the Charlton, wanting us to return to the tower," she said.

"Are we going?"

"Aye."

"I will see Mr. Howard?"

"I do not know. He may be gone."

Kimbra lifted her daughter and carried her back to the cottage. She quickly bundled a second dress for both of them, along with an assortment of herbs the Charlton might need.

She fed the chickens and left additional seed for them, then mounted Magnus with Audra seated in front of her. Bess, bellowing with displeasure, was led by a long rope.

Kimbra's heart pounded harder with every furlong, both with expectation and fear. She wanted to see the Scot again, but not this way, not at the expense of an injured Charlton.

The first grays of dawn appeared as they neared the tower. There were more sentries than usual on the walls. Lads appeared out of nowhere to take their horses. She helped Audra down, then slid off the horse. A Charlton picked up Audra and carried her inside.

Claire was waiting for them and quickly led the three of them up to a bedchamber with a large feather bed. The Charlton soldier laid Audra on the bed, then left the room.

Kimbra sat next to her daughter. Fear still lingered from that terrifying moment when she left Audra alone. She leaned down and kissed her. Then she stood and left Audra in the care of a servant.

She looked at Claire. "I understand someone is wounded," Kimbra said. "I have brought some herbs . . ."

Claire nodded and led the way down two flights of stairs, then into a room off the hall where the family and visitors dined. Kimbra recognized the man as one of her neighbors.

His face was swollen, a cut halfway down his cheek, and there was a wicked looking slice on his side. His face was twisted with pain.

"Kimbra," he said. "They should not have brought ye to me."

"Of course, they should," she said. "Your family?"

"There's only my sons now. They were here at the tower for training, and now they've gone after my hobblers. Bloody Scots. Hope they rot in hell." He groaned as he tried to move.

"Stay still," she ordered. "I will get you something to help you sleep and keep away infection."

She hurried to the kitchen with Claire, and she mixed rosemary with wine and gave it to Claire to take to the wounded man, while she made several poultices of aloe and comfrey for the wounds.

When she returned, he had obviously drunk the potion. Some of the pain had left his face. She washed the wounds carefully before applying the hot cloth to them, her heart hurting as he tried to stifle a groan.

"He should sleep," she told Claire, "but someone should sit with him. If he has a fever, please send for me."

"I will," Claire said. "Now you get yourself to bed, or the Charlton will have my head. He has a soft spot for you. Said you remind him of his wife."

She was too weary for the words to make sense. She only wanted to get to the feather bed and hold her daughter in her arms, knowing both of them were safe.

For the moment.

Would the Charlton continue to have a soft spot for her, if he knew she was responsible for a Scot hiding within his own tower?

But she had one more question first. "Robert Howard? How is he?"

Claire gave her a rare smile. "He walks without crutches now. The Charlton plans to take him on a raid in two days."

"And those who raided the farm?"

"Armstrongs. Richie's Will is going after them."

Richie's Will was known to her as well. He was called

that since there were so many Wills in the Charlton family. It was a border custom that had confused her at first, men being called by both their father's and their own name to avoid confusion of so many like names.

"Cedric?"

"He is here to protect the tower."

Kimbra wished it was the other way around, but she knew Richie's Will to be a good fighter. Her own Will had said as much.

Kimbra climbed the steps to her chamber. It was on the other side of the Charlton's chamber from the Scot's. The thought of seeing him on the morrow warmed her, even though she knew Cedric would watch their every movement.

Still, anticipation bubbled inside her even as she took off her gown and laid down on the bed next to Audra. Her eyes closed, and her last thought was of the Scot.

RORY, Jamie, and the Armstrongs rode hard through the night. It was a rough and unwelcoming land to Rory, not at all like the green vales and blue lochs of the highlands. He already missed them bitterly and wondered how he had stayed away for the ten years he'd spent at sea. He'd hated Inverleith once, hated the legacy that had haunted all three of the Maclean brothers. He remembered how he had come home to face an undisciplined clan, a castle near ruin, and a demoralized people. Lachlan had been nominal leader, having lost a father after one brother disappeared on the continent, and the other—Rory—had chosen the sea. Rory had no notion, then, of his brother's torments. He'd only seen a brother who preferred playing the lute to managing a raucous clan bedeviled by Campbells.

Although Lachlan had proved himself when needed, he'd become the lonely wanderer as Rory had once been. What was it about the Maclean clan that made peace with themselves so difficult?

Dawn came. Gray tinged the horizon, slowly lifting the dark curtain as they left the great tangled ridge of the Cheviots, a rough barrier of desolate treeless tops and moorland.

In several more hours, they reached Branxton Church. There appeared little difference in the dress and speech of the people on either side of the border.

After leaving their horses in the care of one of the Armstrongs, they went inside. A priest approached them. "Are you here for confession?"

"Nay," said the Armstrong. "We are trying to discover the fate of a man who rode with King James. We heard the king's body was brought here. We wondered if any others were brought with him, or if ye have word of any wounded."

The priest bowed his head. "A sad time for both England and Scotland, God save their souls. The king was brought here, along with several other bodies. What is the name of the man you seek?"

"Lachlan Maclean."

The priest shook his head. "He wasn't among them. All the others were identified."

"Are there any lists of the dead?" Rory asked, unable to hold back any longer. It did not matter if anyone knew who or what he was. The English army was gone, and he was under the protection of the Armstrongs. There was also the promise of sanctuary inside the church.

The priest looked at him with surprise. "You are not from here."

"Nay," he said simply, not bothering to say more.

"Come with me," the priest said. He led them to a small room where a piece of parchment lay. He handed it to Rory. "'Tis all we have. Many of the dead, though, were carried back across the border to the church at Southdean. Some were taken to Graden Palace, near Grinton. Still others were buried where they fell."

Rory's eyes sped over the lists. The king's illegitimate

son, Alexander Stuart, who would also have ridden at the king's side. The chancellor of Scotland. The bishop of the Isles. The dean of Glasgow Cathedral. Fourteen lords of Parliament. Then there were nine earls and a number of lairds. He saw so many names of people he'd known.

But Lachlan's was not among them.

Jamie took the list and read it in silence, a muscle tightening in his jaw. "Is there any other information?"

"There may be at Southdean or Grinton."

"Lachlan Maclean wore a brooch," Rory persisted. "The crest of the Macleans. Will you ask around whether anyone has seen it or tried to sell it?"

The priest hesitated.

"There will be a donation for the church. A substantial one."

The priest still hesitated. Rory took some coins from a purse strapped to his belt and offered them to the priest.

The priest took them.

"I will draw the design for you," Rory said.

The priest led them to another room and a desk. He gave Rory a quill and bottle of ink, as well as a precious piece of parchment.

Rory sketched out a double circle with the clan's motto, then a tower.

The priest took it, then surprise flickered across his face. "I have seen this. It was encrusted with jewels. Rubies and diamonds."

"When?"

"Five days ago."

"Who had it?"

"A lad."

"Did he say where he got it?"

The priest shook his head. "No, but he wore the clothes of a reiver. The reivers went through the battlefield, taking from the dead. I thought he must have stolen it."

"What did he want from you? Absolution?"

"He wanted to know what the words on the crest meant. He couldn't read them. He wanted to know if I recognized them. I did not." The priest paused. "He told a most unlikely tale. He said he had killed a man on the battlefield and that in the man's dying breath he had asked the lad to return the crest to his family, but that the Scottish soldier died before he could tell him which family."

Rory's heart pounded. Could it be true? But it didn't make sense. No reiver would return such a precious object. He sensed the priest agreed.

"What did he look like?"

"He kept his helmet on. I thought that disrespectful. I could not see the color of his hair. His cheeks were freshly shaved, though muddied from riding."

"Riding?"

"I watched him leave. He rode a black hobbler. A handsome beast. Probably stolen."

"And he did not give you a name?"

The priest furrowed his brows together. "Nay."

"He was English?"

"Sometimes it is difficult to tell about borderers," the priest said, "but I believe he was English."

"He had to come here because he could not read," Rory said. He tried to decipher the puzzle. There was a border lad who could not read and rode a black horse. But he claimed to kill a trained soldier, which Lachlan most certainly was. Reluctant, yes. Incompetent, no.

"The tale is unlikely," he thought aloud. "Lachlan was a skilled warrior. A lad could not unseat him." He mused on. "And why would this lad surrender an object taken in fair combat?"

"I wondered the same thing," the priest said.

Hope flared in Rory. Someone was looking for Lachlan's family. For a ransom? To explain the circumstances of his death? He did not think someone would go to any trouble to do the latter.

He looked at Jamie.

Jamie nodded. They needed no words between them.

Rory glanced back at the priest. "I will make it well worth your trouble if you see the lad again and learn where he lives. You can send word to any Armstrong and ask for Rory."

The priest looked at the coins in his hands. "I will try to find him. God's blessing on you. English or Scot, this has been a sad time for the border."

Chapter 16

ROBERT Howard pulled on the jack that Will Charlton once wore, then fitted a steel helmet over his head.

Tonight they were to ride to the Armstrongs. He had listened earlier to the Charlton as he outlined the plan. They would meet another large group of Charltons near the border, then ride to the Armstrongs and take all the cattle they could gather.

Richie's Will had not caught up with the raiders of three nights earlier, but he had retrieved some of the cattle, which apparently had slowed the raiders.

Robert had been given a sword, and a bow and arrows. He had a dagger at his belt.

When he was ready, he started down the hallway, went to the steps, then stopped. He turned and went in the direction of Kimbra's room.

She had been here the past three days; days filled with temptation. He saw her in the corridors and in the hall where they all ate. They always seemed to have people with them, and their conversations had been short and polite. Each night he had to restrain himself from going to her room.

But Audra would be there, as well, and there were so many ears and eyes in the tower that he was sure word would spread within minutes. And all that time the image of the fallen man remained in his mind. Along with the stabbing guilt that he had done something terribly wrong. How could he go to her without knowing what demons lurked in his past?

Most of the men were gathered down near the stable, and by God's grace he was going to say good-bye.

He went to her room, knocked on the door. It opened immediately.

She stood there in her blue dress, the one that gave her gray eyes a blue lumination.

He stepped inside. "Where is Audra?"

"Down with the cook."

He opened his arms and drew her to him. "The last three days have been hell," he said.

"Aye."

"I hear the man you cared for is doing well."

She did not reply, just moved even nearer to him.

"God's tooth, but I have missed you," he muttered.

She didn't need words to answer. Her eyes told him that he hadn't been the only one in agony.

His lips smashed down on hers. No tenderness now, just raw, painful need. The emptiness in him was so vast, so agonizing, he tried to dull it with a passion that would fill all the cavities in his heart.

She responded as hungrily as he had, her hand going to his neck and drawing him even closer. Their kiss was explosive, as if emotions had been imprisoned so long they simply burst. Her body trembled in his arms, and he held her tightly.

He wanted to seize her and bury himself in her, but instead his fingers went to her cheek, running a thumb over the soft skin.

She stepped back, and her gray eyes glistened as they searched his face. "Be careful," she said in a broken voice, and he knew she was thinking about someone else who had left on a raid.

"I will."

"Leave if you have a chance," she said. "Go back to Scotland. Live and . . . be happy."

"I do not think I was ever happy," he said slowly.

"You remember something?"

He was silent. How could he tell her what he did remember, or about the hopeless guilt he'd felt when he'd had the vision?

"Nothing that told me who I was."

"What was it?" she persisted.

He shook his head.

She touched his cheek with such tenderness he almost told her what he had seen, what he had experienced. What would she think of him then?

"I must go," he said. "Stay here until you have some protection."

"Do you promise?" she said. "Do you promise to go back home?"

"Right now this is home," he said.

"But it cannot be. Someone will learn the truth. And someone is waiting for you."

"I am not wed," he said. "I *would* know."

"Why that and little else?" she asked practically. "You must find out for yourself. Someone will know you. You were with the Scottish king. You are obviously a noble. Someone in Edinburgh will tell you what you need to know."

"I will not have the chance. Thomas Charlton likes me well enough, but he also has men watching me. And I will not do anything to make them doubt you."

"The sooner you leave, the safer I will be," she said.

He leaned down and kissed her again. Tenderly this time. Lingering there with his lips on hers and his fingers wrapped in her dark hair.

Then abruptly he left before he made promises he could not keep.

*R*ORY and Jamie rode during the day and night to reach the Armstrong hold. The Armstrongs who'd gone with them remained behind to search for a lad with a black horse, first on the English side, then the Scottish.

Rory knew he and Jamie would be of more hindrance than help. The Armstrongs explained that few could tell the difference between the Scot and English borderers, but Rory's and Jamie's Highland speech would instantly be suspect.

When they arrived, the hold was full of riders, far more than when he'd left. His host approached him. "Our Armstrongs have been gathering. The Charltons plan to raid us. We will ambush them."

"How did you learn of it?"

"A traitor with the Charltons."

"It could be a trap."

"Nay, the man has his own reasons. Do ye want a bit of sport?"

Rory wanted only to discover the fate of his brother, but the Armstrongs had extended their hospitality and more, and he had a debt to pay. "Aye," he agreed.

Jamie nodded his assent as well.

"We will be leaving in several hours. Ye can get some rest while we wait for the others."

He and Jamie returned to the room they shared. But despite two days with little or no sleep, Rory couldn't rest.

Why was someone trying to discover the meaning of the words on the crest Lachlan had been wearing?

An ambush. He did not like ambushes. If he was going to fight, he wanted to do it man to man in the open. But the borderers, he had found, had their own ideas of honor. And he was their guest. That made their honor his.

ROBERT Howard had no problem keeping up with the Charltons, though the trails were treacherous. The horse he had been given was nimble-footed and responded to the slightest movement of his body.

The moon was past three-quarters, but light clouds were becoming more numerous, and he suspected they would darken the night before long. The breeze of earlier in the day had turned into a cold wind.

Despite his swollen legs, the Charlton rode at the front with Jock. Robert Howard was well aware that Cedric rode slightly behind him. Jock had told Robert the likelihood of violence during the raid was little. They would quietly approach the Armstrongs during the night and steal away with the cattle. With luck there would be no fighting.

But Robert suspected Cedric would take any opportunity to rid himself of a man he felt was a usurper who would take all he wanted. The man obviously feared he was taking Will's place in the Charlton's regard, along with Kimbra Charlton's favor.

Hours went by. Robert's leg began to ache, and he had to fight to remain in the saddle. Suddenly a shout broke the night silence.

Arrows struck a man in front of him, and he heard loud oaths from all around him. The Charltons milled about in confusion as swarms of horsemen charged them.

"Armstrongs!" someone shouted.

He took his sword from the scabbard and suddenly faced a man in clothing much like his own. The Armstrong wore a black feather in his helmet, apparently to identify himself.

The raider raised his sword, and for an instant Robert Howard raised his own sword in defense. *Another flash of memory.* Another sword raised in anger.

He forced the vision away and parried the first stroke. The Armstrong swung again. Again he was able to block the thrust. The raider was so close he could see his eyes. Steel gray.

Another blow he was able to deflect. But the eyes . . .

He saw an opening but shied away, just as another Charlton engaged the Armstrong.

Then he heard a shout. "The Charlton!"

He moved his horse forward just as instinct told him to look to his side. Cedric had raised his pike and was coming at him. Robert ducked to the side of his horse, and the pike went harmlessly inches over him.

Then the Armstrong with the gray eyes that seemed to burn in his mind took on Cedric.

He turned toward the Charlton who, with Jock, was surrounded by five men. He started to make his way to them when he saw an Armstrong with a pike make a run toward the Charlton.

He moved in front of it, his shoulder taking the brunt of the blow. He fell from the horse, agony ripping through him.

A cry rang out. The Armstrongs started to disappear into the night, a number of Charlton horses going with them, leaving the Charltons to tend to their wounded.

Numb with pain, he looked around for the tall Armstrong whose eyes had stopped him from striking. He was gone.

The Charlton knelt next to him. "Ye took a blow meant for me," he said. He took off Robert's jack, the movement causing him to stifle a groan. Blood poured from a jagged wound. Only the jack had kept it from going through him.

Jock was there as well and quickly tied a piece of cloth around it. "An ambush. They knew we were coming and which way," he said with bitterness.

"Aye," the Charlton said. "We have a traitor among us."

Those around fell silent.

" 'Tis only one stranger here," Cedric said.

"That one stranger may have well saved the Charlton's life," Jock rebuked him.

"Convenient," Cedric muttered.

"I doubt Robert Howard believes that to be true." The Charlton looked around. "How many down?"

"Seven," said one man who had just approached. "Another ten have lost their mounts."

"How bad are the injuries?"

"One dead. One almost. He will not live through the day. The others will live if there are no infections."

"We must go back," the Charlton said.

"We should go after them," Cedric said.

"Another day," the Charlton said wearily. "We need all the remaining horses to get home."

He leaned down and took Robert Howard's good hand and helped him up. "Ye will ride with me," he said.

*K*IMBRA felt as if her entire life had been spent in the process of waiting.

She kept remembering how she'd waited for Will on that last raid. She'd had an odd feeling when he'd left, something she'd never had before. She had that same feeling now.

She wished with all her heart she could have gone with them. She'd even thought for the quickest instant of time of disguising herself and riding with them. But that thought fled as quickly as it had come. She had Audra now.

Still, she remembered the excitement of riding along new routes, never quite knowing what was around the next turn. The captains planned the routes with great care, varying the path on each raid.

She did not sleep during the night, wandering down to the empty hall after Audra went to sleep. She found Claire in the kitchen.

"I have some of Thomas's best wine," Claire said. "Would you join me?"

"Aye."

"It gets lonely when they go," Claire said. "I wish I had your courage when you rode off with them."

"Courage is easier when you are young."

"You are still young, Kimbra."

"I do not feel young. I am tired of waiting for men who may not come back."

"The Howard?"

"I am tired of death and violence," she said, avoiding the question. "I want my daughter to be safe. I want the Charlton to be safe. And Robert Howard."

"They will be back. It is just another raid."

Then why was Claire in the kitchen in early morning hours? Did she, like Kimbra, have a sense that something was wrong?

"You care for the Charlton," she stated as a fact rather than a question.

"Aye, we all do."

"Do you love him?" Kimbra asked softly.

Claire didn't answer immediately. "We are first cousins. We cannot love each other in any way but as cousins."

The break in her voice gave her away.

"Is that why the Charlton doesn't remarry?"

"Men do not feel the same as women. They can love many times, but a woman . . . she loves once."

"I think she can love more than once," Kimbra said softly.

Claire's severe face softened. "Aye, but there is only one true love, and I do not think you have had that yet." She held up her hand to stop Kimbra's protest. "Will risked much in marrying you, and he enjoyed indulging you. You were an enchanting child, but I think you want more than that in a man."

A rush of anger flashed through Kimbra. Claire was wrong. She had loved Will, and he had loved her. Then suddenly she realized Claire was right. She had admired and trusted Will because he'd protected her, but she'd never felt intimately connected to him as she did to the Scot. As if they belonged together.

She could not tell Claire, however, why it would not, could not, ever be. She could not say that Robert Howard was not the bastard son of a reiver's family but certainly a Scot and probably one of high nobility.

"He will be all right," Claire said, as if sensing her internal agony. "I think we both should be abed." She paused, then added, "Grab whatever happiness you can find. God knows there is little of it on the border."

*R*ORY lagged behind the other Armstrongs who herded the stolen horses ahead of them.

Jamie rode up to him. "I see you unmarked this time. I lost you for a while."

"I fought a Charlton. There was something hellishly familiar about him, but I could not see his face under the steel bonnet."

Jamie frowned. "Familiar how?"

"Just . . . familiar. He seemed to recognize me and stopped when he had the advantage."

"Advantage over you?" Jamie said with disbelief.

"Aye."

"What are you saying?"

"If he hadn't been with English reivers, I would swear it was Lachlan. The way he sat the horse. The way he held his sword . . ."

"You said he stopped when he had the advantage."

"Aye. But if it were Lachlan he would have acknowledged me."

"If you have doubts, we can turn around and follow them."

Rory shook his head. "I just wanted it to be so. The reiver must have been distracted."

Yet as Rory rode back, his mind kept going back to the reiver. He'd sat a small bay horse. There had been nothing to distinguish him from the other reivers. He had been one among many.

It could not be Lachlan.

$\mathcal{H}$E was getting far too used to pain. He was among the least wounded, though his shoulder hurt like the blazes. The thought of Kimbra, of Audra at the Charlton tower made it bearable.

What he was not getting used to were the flashes that were coming faster now.

The Armstrong's face kept returning. Pictures flipped through his mind. The Armstrong—he had to be an Armstrong—standing next to a woman who held a bairn.

His friend? Or someone closer?

Blazes! Why couldn't he remember? Why taunting images?

After far too many hours, they arrived at the tower. Having been alerted by an advance rider, the Charltons left behind came running out. They took the wounded into the tower, where the physician, Claire, and Kimbra waited.

Robert Howard waited his turn, although Kimbra had rushed over and taken a quick look at his wound. "You cannot seem to keep out of harm's way," she scolded, her eyes alarmed at first, then quieting as she saw the wound. " 'Tis not so bad."

The Charlton stepped in. "He saved my life, moved in

between a pike and me. Take good care of him." He looked down at Robert Howard. "My thanks." Then he went among the other wounded.

Kimbra moved on, and Robert took pleasure in watching her quick, confident ministrations. At one point she argued with the physician who once more wanted to combat bleeding with more bleeding by his leeches.

It was the Charlton who stepped in and sided with her.

Finally she came to him. The pike had been blunted by the steel sewn into the jack, but it had still gouged a hole in his shoulder.

Servants had brought clean water, and Kimbra washed the wound, her fingers lingering on his skin as if reluctant to leave. Then she applied a familiar poultice to it. "Stay quiet," she said. "I will look in on you later."

"The others?"

"Two probably will not live out the night," she said.

"Any you know?"

"Aye. They rode with Will. How did you come to be ambushed?"

He shook his head.

"They are saying someone betrayed them."

The thought had surely crossed all their minds. How else could the Armstrongs know when and where they would pass? They might have guessed, having raided the Charltons, that there would be retribution. But a traitor was more likely.

He went up to his room. He had ridden all night and had had little sleep the previous night. He wanted to think. He wanted to see again that face from last night. He wanted to remember.

He knew now he could not make any plans without knowing his past. He was beginning to feel at home here, much too at home. And Kimbra? He wanted her with all his being.

If he thought the past was truly gone, mayhap he could

stay here and be content. But it haunted him, throwing out tempting morsels one at a time. How could he take a wife if one morning he woke and found he had another?

Concentrate. Go back to that moment. The gray eyes. *They were fighting. No, not fighting, training. The sword was heavy. He was but a boy. He did not want to train. He pleaded with an older man.*

I want to go into the church.

Not my son.

I will not fight.

You will!

The older man was the same one he had seen in an earlier flash, the one that lay on the ground, bleeding profusely. The sense of guilt flooded back with a strength that almost made him double over.

Then the important question: If he hated fighting, how had it come that he rode with his king into battle?

His shoulder throbbed, but it mattered little. He had to discover who he was, whether he had obligations. But how? He could not just ride to the Armstrongs and ask about a man with gray eyes.

A knock came on the door before it abruptly opened, and Jock walked in. "The Charltons believe there is a traitor. Cedric's brother is blaming ye."

"I've not been off the property," Robert said.

"He claims ye could have sent someone."

"Now who would that be?" he asked reasonably. "You and the Charlton are the only two I see." He paused. "Cedric's brother? Where is Cedric?"

"Cedric's brother said he followed them, hoping to get some of the horses back." Jock paused. "I thought ye should know what is being said. I do not believe it. Nor does the Charlton, who has told everyone ye saved his life. But there is muttering. Ye are a stranger. Cedric is not. And some see ye as a threat to their hopes. They will not challenge you directly but with a dagger in the back, or accident of some kind. 'Tis a note of warning. Be cautious, Robert Howard, and for Kimbra's sake, keep a distance, unless ye want her drawn into it."

He left, leaving Robert Howard—or whoever he was—feeling as if he had just jumped from the pot into the coals. His heart plummeted as he realized he might well take Kimbra and Audra with him.

Chapter 17

AFTER Kimbra finished tending the last of the wounded, Claire and the servants told her to get some rest.

She needed that rest, some respite.

Her emotions were churning about like clouds in a thunderstorm. She'd just managed to control them when she'd heard the Scot was injured. Thank the Holy Mother that, though painful, his wound wasn't far worse.

How many more lives did he have? He seemed to be spending them rapidly. Why in all that was holy did he persist in putting himself in jeopardy? As she'd watched him make his way toward the stone steps leading up to the chambers, guilt assailed her. She should be thankful he had saved the Charlton. But, dear Mother, the Scot seemed to be courting death. And now he had come even more to the attention of the Charlton, as well as the most ambitious Charltons.

The Charlton's favor could be a dangerous thing.

After she wearily washed her hands, she mounted the steep stairs, hesitating at the top of them. She turned to go to her own room.

But then she reversed herself, finding herself walking down to the Scot's room. She had not seen Cedric since the wounded came in, and no one else in the tower appeared to be awake. Certainly no one was in the hallway.

She hesitated at the door, knocked lightly, then went inside. If he appeared to be asleep, she would leave.

He lay on the bed, but she saw that his eyes were open. He sat up, his lips without the slow smile that so charmed her.

"Kimbra," he acknowledged, his voice low and husky.

"You should be sleeping."

" 'Tis hard to do."

"I can fetch you some rosemary."

" 'Tis not the pain, lass. I've had more memories."

"You remember your name?"

"Nay, but faces. I saw one tonight. He was riding with the Armstrongs."

She stared at him. "You saw someone you remembered?"

"I am not sure, lass. But his eyes . . ."

"And he was with the Armstrongs?"

"Aye."

"Was there anything else?"

"I saw a younger version of myself fighting him. But it was not a battle." His brows furrowed together. Each word seemed to be pulled from somewhere inside. "We were . . . training."

"A brother? Cousin? Someone who was fostered with you?"

"I do not know. The more I reach for a memory, the faster it fades."

"There are others?"

She watched him struggle with himself. Then, "An older man. My father. I think . . . I think . . . I was responsible for his death."

He stood, swaying slightly. She took his hand just as she realized he wore nothing but the long shirt. She had seen him naked before when she had first cared for him. Now, though, it was different.

Now her body was aware of his. Far too aware.

She took his hand, as much to steady him. Nay, that was a lie. It was not to steady him at all. It was because she'd yearned to do it since he arrived this morning. "I do not believe that."

"You know little about me," he said roughly. "About who and what I was."

"I know enough." She sensed a loneliness and despair in him that pierced her like a hot knife.

Her fingers tightened around his. "I cannot believe that you have done anything wrong. 'Tis not within you."

"I was ready to kill someone tonight. I probably did weeks ago during the battle. I *know* I am skilled at it. And I seem to be as good a liar. You do not know what I was. Or am. And the hell of it is, I do not either."

She knew the same desperation. She was a liar and a thief, and she hated herself for it, even though she'd felt she had no choice. She'd lied to the Charlton and to all the men who had ridden with Will.

She shook those thoughts aside, and her mind went back to the rider he'd seen. An Armstrong who looked familiar.

How could his ken be with the Armstrongs? Or was he an Armstrong himself? Surely if he was a member of that clan, someone here would have seen him at the games

most of the border families—both Scot and English—
attended. And his manners were far superior to any
Armstrong she'd met. His speech also was too fine for a
borderer.

"You are not an Armstrong," she said.

"How do you know?" His frustration and pain at sus-
pecting, but not knowing, was carved in his face.

She reached over and touched her lips to his. His good
arm went around her, clutching her to him almost desperately.

"I would have seen you. Or others here would have."

She released his hand and touched his face, trying to
smooth out all the new crevices, and ease some of the an-
guish and confusion she felt in him.

"Kimbra." His voice was a caress. His breath was feather
light on her forehead, the slight whisper of a kiss. Warmth
spread through her, like a hot summer's sun pooling golden
rays on a lake.

He stroked the side of her neck in gentle movements.
Her pulse quickened, and she trembled. She moved instinctively closer to him, the warmth turning molten.

The searing heat of their bodies radiated between them,
melding them into one. His lips hungrily traced the lines of
her cheek, then her neck, hesitating there. She lifted her
face to his, wanting more of the feelings and sensations
and emotions that shimmered between them.

Tremors shook her body. Careful not to hurt his bandaged shoulder, her arms went around him. Her heart thun-
dered, and she heard his as well.

His lips left her mouth, moved to her ear, where he nib-
bled, his breath sending shivers of pleasure through her.
His feathering kisses moved to her neck, to the pulse at her
throat, and she lifted her head up, her eyes misting as she
felt the tenderness in each caress. Yet his body shuddered
with restraint, even as its rigidity radiated his need.

She was consumed with wanting and feeling, and anticipation made her writhe inside. She heard something like a purr coming from her throat, and his lips parted in a smile so wistful it hurt her.

He went to the door, pulled the bolt close. Then he took a few steps to the bed and sat, bringing her down with him.

She wanted him with a need that erased every warning in her head. He had been wounded only hours earlier, and his shoulder must be agonizingly painful, yet he seemed more concerned with her than with himself. But then it had always been thus, from the first day she had brought him to the cottage.

Someone might come. The lock would prevent anyone from entering, but a locked door said much on its own.

If Cedric . . . or even the Charlton . . . ?

But surely there was no harm with lying next to him. Reveling in the fact he was alive!

He untied the laces of her dress, and suddenly she wore only her chemise. He pulled that off, wincing as he lifted his arm. The expression faded as his hands slipped up her body ever so slowly, exploring her back, her waist, and then her breasts.

He leaned down then, and his lips touched her nipple with exquisite lightness. Nothing could have been more seductive. His eyes blazed with the flames she felt, and the barely restrained passion was irresistible in its promise. She reached out and touched the corner of his mouth, then her fingers traced the strong, fine lines of his cheeks.

"It is not wise," he said softly, obviously wanting to be persuaded that it was.

She hesitated, but she was lost in those eyes of his, in the steady hold of them. "Nay," she agreed. "But I weary of being wise."

He smiled at that, then winced as he moved slightly.

"You are in pain," she said.

" 'Tis not the pain from the wound that haunts me."

"What does haunt you?"

He was silent for a moment. "Too many things, love."

"The images?"

"Aye, and how much . . . I want you."

"Is there ever a woman in those images?"

"Aye," he said reluctantly.

Unwanted jealousy ripped through her. "What does she look like?"

"She is not as bonny as you," he said. "She does not have that upturned nose and determined chin and wild dark hair."

"Do you love her?"

"I felt something. Love? I do not know."

"Then you must find her. You must leave this place and return to where you belong." It hurt her to say the words, but her conscience demanded it.

"I belong with you." He looked as surprised at his words as she felt hearing them.

"Nay, you belong somewhere else."

He caught her finger that was still wandering about his cheek. "I feel as if I have always known you, that we were meant to be."

"I am English. You are a Scot. I am a reiver's wife. You are obviously of high rank. We were *not* meant to be," she said.

"You do not know what I am."

"I can well guess! And I know that nobles have little care for those not of their rank. When you get your memories back, you will have little use for the widow of an English reiver."

"You do not think much of me, then."

"I know what nobles do."

"What do nobles do?"

"My mother. One promised everlasting love until she was with child. Then . . ." Her voice trailed off.

"Then?" he probed.

"He tried to kill her. He did kill her father. He wanted no bastards to embarrass a new fiancée. She escaped but she lived in fear every moment of her life."

He stared at her. "My God. You believe I would do something like that?"

She dropped her gaze. "Nay, but you might well be wed. Do you think a wife would welcome me?"

"I would never betray you."

"Would you betray your wife?"

A muscle throbbed in his throat. She knew he had considered the possibility. But rather than answer, his lips touched hers and offered unsaid promises. He was asking her to trust him.

She did not know whether she could, but for the moment she was being drawn back into a world of sensations. When he touched her, she did not care whether it was wise or not. And yet she tried. "I must go," she said in a voice that sounded hollow even to her.

"Aye, before I do something you might regret, love." His slight smile was infinitely wistful.

She touched his face again. She wanted to erase the look of haunting loneliness she so often sensed in him. She did not know whether it was from not knowing who he was, or something far deeper from the life he had before.

Mayhap someday she would regret it. But at the moment she did not care.

"There could be a bairn," he said softly.

She stilled. She would love his child, even if he left her. One with auburn hair and serious blue eyes.

She stretched out in invitation. Her lips touched his, and he pressed down hard on her mouth. As he kissed her, his good arm undid the cap she wore, and her hair came tumbling down around her face.

"So bonny," he whispered.

He ran his fingers along her skin, seducing, caressing,

stroking, yet she had an odd feeling that it was instinctive, not practiced.

Nonsense, she told herself even as heat from his body scorched her. His mouth fastened on hers, and their tongues met, explored each other until she thought she would cry out with the pleasure of it.

The last remnant of caution faded as he positioned himself above her. Still, he hesitated. "Kimbra?"

His voice was seductively low and husky. Will had never asked her permission. And never had her body so ached to join to another's.

"Aye," she said, her heart drumming. She felt his beginning probe, ever so slow and infinitely careful. Too slow and careful. Her arms went around him, and he entered deeper, then hesitated until she was mad with wanting. A deep, intense craving gnawed at the deepest core of her, and she moved shamelessly against him, savoring the contrast of her body against his hard one.

The very tentativeness of his movements when she could see the need etched on his face and feel it in his taut muscles made her throb with caring for him. Something was holding him back—his past, his present—and she did not want him to hold back. She arched upward, inviting him deeper inside.

The hesitation turned to urgency as he ventured deeper. Heat flooded her as his rhythm increased. Pleasure rolled through her like rumbles of thunder, each wave more powerful than the one before as the momentum mounted and she was swirled into a world of flashing lightning and bursts of splendor.

She cried out, and he thrust once more, igniting one final explosion that left her body sated. They both fell back on the bed. Her body glowed as it continued to quake with the aftershocks of their coupling. The turbulence faded, but a quiet fulfillment lingered.

She lay there, listening to his heart, to her own ragged breath intermingled with his.

She had loved Will, but she'd never felt like this before. He'd been a hasty lover, often leaving her unsatisfied. She'd never known it could be different, that it could be a beautiful, exquisite journey with each giving as much as taking.

She lay her head against his heart. She did not want to leave, but she knew she must. She had already lingered far too long. Neither of them could afford gossip. And one of the maids was looking after Audra.

"I must go," she whispered reluctantly.

"Aye," he said simply.

She forced herself to stand and put on her gown. She searched the floor for the pin that held her cap in place, found it, then scooped up her hair and twisted it in a knot before pinning the cap in place.

She turned to him. "Do I look respectable?"

His reply was that slow smile. "Eminently," he said.

She did not know what that meant. But his eyes approved, and she could do no better without a mirror.

"I will see how you are doing later," she said, "though I am beginning to believe you are indestructible."

"I do not think my body agrees," he said. He rose and went to the door. He opened it, looked outside, then nodded to her.

As she went by, he leaned down and gave her a whisper light kiss on her cheek. "I will no' let you go," he whispered, lapsing into a thick Scottish brogue.

She felt that kiss all the way to her chamber, and the words echoed in her mind.

If only it could be . . .

But it could not. She resolved that she would stay away from him in the future, because she lost all reason when he was near.

She could do that. She could!

* * *

HE tower hummed with activity over the next several days. There would be retaliation against the Armstrongs. But first the traitor must be found.

Lachlan found himself a hero in some eyes, a possible villain in others. He didn't think he was the first, and wasn't sure about the second. He was becoming more and more mired in deception.

He took his meals in the hall with the others. He occasionally glimpsed Kimbra, but she was either tending the wounded or with Audra, and he realized she was avoiding him. Even when Audra ran up to him, Kimbra hung back, her gaze going anywhere but to him.

He could not blame her. Neither could he go to her room. She'd had an excuse to come to his, but now there were many eyes on him, and he feared hurting her in any way.

His arm was healing well, and his leg was far better. He spent much of the day working with the sword and exercising sore muscles. He was constantly on guard against slipping into a Highland burr. He was only too aware he had done so the night he had made love to Kimbra.

Was she regretting it? Did she think that he would discard her as easily as she'd indicated? How he wanted to touch her again, to soothe away doubts. To feel her in his arms again.

The Charlton visited several times, each time pressing him about his military experience on the continent, on battles he had fought. Oddly enough, he could describe cities. Paris. Rome. He could even describe battles, though he did not even know if he'd participated in them. The knowledge was just in his head somewhere. He did not understand how he could remember some things, but things that should have been important, nay, essential, eluded him.

The third day after the raid, the Charlton appeared in

his room, the chessboard under his arm again. As they started the game, the Charlton peered at him. "What did ye see the night of the raid? Before ye joined me?"

"Just the raiders," he said. "I did not know they were Armstrongs then."

"Did any of our men act strangely?"

He thought about saying something about Cedric, but Cedric would only deny it and try to send suspicion his way. He could not afford more scrutiny.

"Nay, I was too busy defending myself."

"Cedric showed up last night. He said he was attacked as he tried to follow them and lost his hobbler." The Charlton's eyes met his. "He said ye had an opportunity to strike down an Armstrong and ye did not."

"Did he say what he was doing at that particular time?"

"Nay." The Charlton waited.

"I do not know what he was doing, either. I am surprised he had the time to see anything but his own opponent."

"Then ye did not spare anyone?"

"Nay. I turned away when I heard your name called."

The Charlton's face relaxed. "For which I am grateful. But Cedric is spreading gossip. He is saying that ye failed to strike because the Armstrongs were allies."

"Then I am sorry the Armstrongs did not feel the same way," he replied, glancing down at his arm, which was still bandaged.

"I had to have your answers. Cedric is trying to incite others against ye."

"I am a stranger, and Cedric is one of you," Robert Howard finished.

"Aye, but Cedric did not save my life."

"I had no opportunity to contact anyone," Robert Howard added. "Whereas I imagine Cedric did. Hasn't he been gone much?"

"On my orders."

Robert Howard shrugged. He had said enough. He would let the Charlton reach his own conclusions.

"Check," he said, moving his queen to take the Charlton's bishop.

The Charlton's brows furrowed together as he moved a knight to block her.

In three more moves it was over. "Checkmate," Robert Howard said.

The Charlton frowned. "At least it took you two more moves this time." He reset the pieces. "Another game?"

Robert Howard nodded, wondering whether the Charlton really wanted to play or whether it was simply a device to learn more about him. One could learn much about a man by playing chess with him. Was he cautious or reckless? Did he cheat or no? He was learning something about himself as well.

The Charlton played better this time, and the match was more equal. Robert Howard thought about purposely losing, then discarded the idea. The Charlton was a shrewd man and would realize it. The Charlton obviously did not like losing, but he had said he wouldn't like winning without earning it.

Robert Howard was two moves from winning when the Charlton looked up. "Have ye thought more about staying after your wounds heal?"

He had. And far too often. But as much as the Charlton was grateful, Robert Howard doubted he would tolerate the idea of an enemy in his midst. It would be far too likely then that he would be accused of being the traitor. And what would happen to Kimbra and Audra then?

"'Tis a fine offer," he said, "but I have roaming in my blood."

"What about Kimbra? I see the two of ye looking at each other."

He was stunned. He thought they had been so cautious.

"I do not know," he said. And he did not. He could take her and her daughter with him. To what? To where? With little or nothing? No name. No family.

Or he could search for his family and return for her. That had risks as well. 'Twas obvious she was a prize. One that might well be bartered by the man he now played chess with. It also frightened him that she lived alone. He was aware now, as he hadn't been before, of the dangers of the border.

"Ye can have her if ye stay," the Charlton said unexpectedly. "Ye can have her cottage." Although he had mentioned previously that he wanted Kimbra happy, he had never before made such a firm and generous offer.

"Would she have naught to say about it?"

"Aye, but I think she would accept."

"Others are courting her. They would not be pleased."

"It does not matter what others think," the Charlton said.

He was tempted. More than tempted. He wanted to accept. He knew Kimbra did not really believe what he'd said. He wanted to see the look on her face when he told her he would stay, that he wanted her. Not just for a night. But forever.

But what if he had another family?

"Think on it, lad."

The Charlton rose painfully.

"I do not understand why you would trust a stranger," Robert Howard said.

"Mayhap an old man's fancy," the Charlton said. "I need someone strong to take care of the Charltons when I die. There is no one now. I thought at one time Cedric, but he is a sly man, and I have come not to trust him. His brother is too much like him. There is no one else."

"I will think about it," Robert Howard said.

"Spend time with Kimbra and Audra," he suggested. Then he limped out of the room.

Robert Howard watched him go, wishing he was the man the Charlton believed him to be. He had the devil's own decision to make, and he feared he would bring disaster whatever he did.

Chapter 18

~~~

RORY could not dismiss the thought that he might have recognized the man behind the iron helmet several days earlier.

The image nagged at him as he and Jamie continued to search for word of Macleans and Campbells along the border. They found nothing at the last church they'd visited.

They went into a tavern. "I do not understand it," Jamie said. "Lachlan has just disappeared. And that lad . . . no one seems to have seen him."

"At least no one has recorded his death," Rory said. "I just wish we could find that lad. He must know something."

"The Armstrongs have searched everywhere except the Charlton lands. Not particularly wise to go there now. Too many of the Armstrongs are known personally to the Charltons."

Rory said nothing.

Jamie took a sip of ale. "There *is* your mysterious Charlton. Mayhap we *should* visit the Charlton land and satisfy that itch you have."

One of the accompanying Armstrongs stared at him with dismay. "They will no' be welcoming Armstrongs. Or any Scot."

"I think I understand that," Rory said dryly. "But surely there must be one Armstrong unknown to most Charltons. I will pay that man very well."

"'Tis daft. No Charlton would shelter a Scot."

Rory knew it was daft. But then he knew Lachlan, and how entirely likeable he could be, and how he had an uncanny ability to fit in any role he wanted, mayhap because he had done it as a child. He'd had to, to appease a father who had never approved of him. Lachlan, he'd discovered much to his surprise, was a survivor.

Jamie shrugged. "I did not see the man, but if Rory thinks there is a possibility . . ."

The four men rode back to the Armstrong tower and made a proposition to the Armstrong.

"'Tis madness," the Armstrong leader said. "But I like madness. I know two who might go. A man and a woman. For a price."

"I will make it substantial."

"So be it. I will have them here this afternoon."

KIMBRA finished wrapping the last wound and stood. She wanted to go back to the cottage. To her home.

Two men had died. The others should live. The physician had left in anger. But the servants who had assisted her could now do what had to be done.

The Scot was altogether too close here. Every time she saw him, her body hummed with desire. Heat pooled in the core of her. She longed to reach out and touch him.

And then there was Cedric.

She remembered the look on Cedric's face yesterday when she tended his wound. He'd just returned and had asked her to tend him. 'Twas little but a minor scrape, but his eyes bored right through her as he asked questions about Robert Howard. When exactly had she found him? What exactly had he said?

She had ignored the questions, concentrating instead on the wound that most men would not have even bothered bringing to her. It was as if he wanted to proclaim his bravery.

The next morning, she found the Charlton. "I wish to go home. I have chickens to feed. The garden needs tending, and we need more herbs for poultices."

"I can send someone to do that."

"Nay, they would not know what to fetch."

"It is still dangerous."

"The cottage is well away from the roads. We have never been attacked."

He sighed. "Ye may go. I will send someone to accompany ye, and there are already two men watching your cottage."

She found Audra, who did not want to go. Mr. Howard was here, and so were servants who constantly found sweets for her. "No," she insisted, "we should stay with Mr. Howard."

"Bess needs her home, and so does Bear," Kimbra tried to explain patiently, even as apprehension ran down her spine. Her daughter was becoming all too attached to the Scot.

"They like it here."

It was probably true. Bear was allowed to stay with Audra, and Bess was eating the best of Charlton oats.

"Mayhap Mr. Howard will visit us," she said. "But he and the others need our herbs. We have used all we have brought."

Audra surrendered then. "But we will come back?"

"Aye," she agreed.

With regret she gathered up what few belongings she had. She probably would not see the Scot again. He had more freedom of movement now, and he knew the danger here. She could only hope he would leave soon.

Even if her heart broke at the prospect.

She and Audra went to the stable for Bess and Magnus. One of the stable boys helped attach a lead to the cow. She went to Magnus's stall and found the Scot saddling him.

She stilled. Her heart skipped ahead.

He turned to her. "The Charlton asked me to accompany you and Audra," he said.

Audra beamed at him, then at Kimbra.

Kimbra did not want to admit she shared that spontaneous pleasure. "Are you well enough?"

"Aye. Your potions seemed to be miraculous." He wore a crooked half smile as if he knew something, or someone, had taken control of their lives.

She lost her speech for a moment. She wanted to protest. She had, in truth, been running away from him and her own feelings, but now they bounded to the surface.

He wore a doublet over a shirt and snug-fitting breeches. She wondered where he obtained them, probably from the Charlton, who had made it plain that the Scot was to have everything he needed.

The Scot's elevation from prisoner to favorite had stirred any number of reactions from others in the tower. Some were thankful to him. Others jealous. And there were questions. Too many questions.

He was one of two reasons she'd decided to leave the Charlton tower. Someone she hated and feared, and another she feared she loved. And now the latter was with her, his proximity causing shivers of a different kind than those caused by Cedric.

Had the Charlton planned this as a way to keep Robert Howard among the Charltons?

A stable lad saddled a second horse. The Scot tied bundles to both saddles, then helped her mount Magnus. He passed Audra up to her and mounted his own horse. He led Bess at the end of a rope.

The day was peerless. The skies were clear, the sun bright, and a gentle breeze cooled them.

"You really should not be riding this far this soon," she said.

"I think I rarely do what I should," he replied.

"And if you did, you would be somewhere else far away."

"Aye," he agreed, "but then you might have Cedric escorting you home."

"The Charlton would not do that to me."

"You thought differently several weeks ago."

"He has come to know Cedric better."

"Aye, I think he has."

He started whistling again. It was maddening. Carefree. When he should be concerned for his life.

They rode out of the gate and toward the cottage. Bear followed.

She was silent, though Audra chattered about the various people who had taken turns looking after her. Kimbra had seen little of her, having stayed with the wounded most of the time. Now she relished having her daughter in her arms and the quiet companionship of the Scot.

For the briefest moment in time, she was content.

They rode leisurely to the cottage. As promised, two Charltons were there.

One—Timothy—looked over the path that led to her cottage. Timothy approached them, appraised Robert Howard, and touched his forehead in respect for her. "Gibb's Geordie is in the stable."

"Have you seen anything?" Robert Howard asked.

"Nay, no one," Timothy replied. "What news do ye bring?"

"You heard of the ambush?" Kimbra asked.

"Aye, word was sent."

"Two more men died. Rob's Sim and Jack Carey. The rest are healing well."

"Bastards," Timothy said. "When are we going to strike back?"

"Soon enough, I think," she added.

"Why is he here?" Timothy nodded toward her companion.

"The Charlton sent him to accompany me. He saved the Charlton's life during the ambush. Took a wound himself."

"Are we to return?"

"Nay," her Scot said. "I will stay only a day or two. The Charlton wants the cottage guarded, and I do not wish to compromise Audra. I will sleep in the stable."

Timothy nodded, and they continued on down the path to the cottage and the barn.

"I will look after the horses and cow," the Scot said.

He dismounted and was at her side, lifting Audra down. Then he held out his arms to her, and she slid down into them. He held her for a moment, and heat shimmered between them. His eyes met hers, and she felt devoured by them.

"I want to help feed them," Audra said.

The Scot took a step back. "Aye, I would like the help," he said.

"But first you must feed the chickens," Kimbra said. "Run inside and get the feed."

Audra did as she was told, and Kimbra had the first moment free of young ears. "You must go while you can."

"With two guards here?"

"They were not told to keep you here. Ride to Scotland. To Edinburgh. This is the best opportunity you will have."

"There is no certainty I will find out who I am."

"You must try."

"Why?"

"Need you ask? Even if you did save the Charlton's life, you cannot stay here. Your future would not be his decision. It is the king's decision."

He touched her shoulder. "This is home," he said simply.

How much she wanted it to be. "It is not," she replied harshly. She had to say words that broke her heart. "You do not belong here. This was Will's cottage, and I do not want you here. You have no right. And the Charlton cannot give it to you."

His blue eyes met hers, and she knew he saw the lie for what it was.

"You will endanger both of us. Is that what you want?"

"Nay. I want . . . blazes . . . I want you. And Audra. Come to Scotland with me."

"I cannot do that. This is my home. It is Audra's home." But that was not the real reason. She wanted to trust him, but she knew what was real and what wasn't. How could she, the widow of an English reiver, go to Scotland with someone obviously a lord? She would be an embarrassment to him, her daughter an oddity. She could never be more than a mistress, and she would not do that.

He touched her face. "I will not let you go," he said softly.

"You are grateful."

"I am grateful, and I am in love."

"You neglect to mention you may also have a wife." She turned and almost ran to the cottage before he could catch her. When she reached the door, she looked back.

The Scot was watching her, his face still. Then he turned with the horses and went to the small stable.

* * *

IMOTHY and Gibb's Geordie ate with them as Bear stood watch. Kimbra made oatcakes and served cheese. Neither Timothy nor Geordie had been able to find game.

At the demand of the two Charltons, the Scot told of the ambush, how the Armstrongs appeared almost out of nowhere.

"They had to have been told," Timothy mumbled.

The Scot did not say anything.

After grumbling, the two left, one to watch the path that Bear was guarding, and the other to sleep in the stable.

The Scot stayed as they left. He sang a lullaby for Audra who went to sleep in his arms. He carried her into the bed and laid her there, tenderness softening his face. Kimbra thought how naturally he fathered her daughter, as if he had children of his own.

He stood, and they were close. Too close. She felt herself leaning toward him, and then his arms were around her. Not burning this time. More as if they simply belonged there. Passion simmered between them, but there was also a peaceful calm, a sense of belonging that, as much as she cared for Will, she'd never known with him.

My Scot.

He was that only for a brief time.

"Come," he said and took her hand, leading her to the main room. "I have something for you."

He released her hand and leaned down to the bundle he had dropped inside the door. He brought out a book and handed it to her.

"The Charlton gave it to me."

She took it in her hands. Felt the rich leather, then the vellum pages. Her eyes feasted on the illuminations inside, the elaborate drawings of animals. They were lovely, glorious pictures. She ran her fingers over a word. "I know these letters," she said.

"And before long, you will know all the words," he said.

Her heart swelled. It had been the one thing she had always wanted. A treasure. More valuable than jewels.

She traced the title with her finger.

"The Thrissill and the Rois," he said. " 'Tis the tale of the marriage of James IV and Margaret Tudor. The Charlton took it in a raid, and he said he had no interest in a Scottish tale."

His fingers ran over the book as well, hesitating on the title. She saw a muscle throb in his throat, then he started from the chair.

"What is it?" she asked.

"I am not sure. I did not look at it well when he gave it to me. You were ready to go. But it is familiar. I . . . I know the king and queen. I have been with them. I have seen them dance together. They were in love. And the man who wrote this . . ." His voice trailed off.

"The man who wrote it?" she prompted. This was what she'd wanted, for him to regain his memory. She wanted it, but she feared it as well.

"A friend, I think. I . . . blazes, I just have pieces."

"You said the Charlton gave it to you?"

"Aye. He asked me what I wanted, that he owed me a boon. I mentioned a book. I knew you wanted . . ."

He could have asked for anything, but instead he'd thought only of her. The thought sent frissons of warmth through her, even as she realized that one by one his memories were returning. She would lose him then.

How can one lose what one has never had?

She watched intently as expressions changed on his face. He was remembering more. It was like a wall had started to crumble. Each collapse caused others.

"Who was he?" she asked. "The man who wrote the book?"

"I do not know. I just see him in my head. A friend . . . I saw him at court. A scribe. More than that . . ." His voice faded away.

"What else do you remember? When did you see the king and queen dance?"

He shook his head.

"You still do not remember your name?"

"Nay."

"If you watched the king dance, then you must be known at court. You can leave tonight. You merely need to go to the Scottish court."

"Blazes," he said. "Why can I remember some things, but not all?"

"Read the story," she said. "Mayhap it will bring back more memories."

He closed the book and traced his fingers across the title engraved in the leather.

"You remember the letters I taught you?"

"Aye."

"Then you know what this one is." He pointed to the first letter of the engraved word.

"Aye, it is a *t*."

He led her through the other letters, and she was pleased she remembered them all. But then she had practiced while he had been gone, drawing them in the ground.

"The first word is *The*," he said. "The *t* and the *h* together sound like this."

He was a patient teacher even though she knew that memories were knocking at his mind. Nonetheless he sounded each word for her, explaining how the sounds fit together to make words. He led her to read the word *thrissill*.

She had not heard the word before.

"It is a prickly plant with purple flowers that grows in the Highlands," he said.

Something else he'd remembered.

Because of the book?

What would he remember if she showed him the crest?

It is too late now. He will no longer trust me if I produce it now. And the need was gone. He was remembering on his own. He would find his home, while the crest remained her only means to protect her daughter.

The Scot opened the book and started to read.

"Now fayre, fayrest off every fayre,
Princes most pleasant and preclare,
The lustyest one alyve that byne.
Welcum of Scotland to be Quene."

She listened to the tremor and rhythm of his voice. He obviously loved the words. He made her want to love them as well.

Hours sped by, as he led her word by word, making her sound out each one. Then the letters started running together.

"'Tis enough for tonight," he said, as if reading her thoughts. He seemed to do that entirely too often.

"Thank you," she said.

"Nay, it was my pleasure."

She believed him. It was in his voice, in his smile, in the warmth of his eyes. He was a natural teacher.

"We will continue tomorrow," he said.

"You should go." How many times had she said that? But she'd never meant it less than at this moment. She knew he should go. But her heart and soul wanted him to stay.

"I will sleep in the stable," he said. "I will not endanger your reputation further."

She did not want him to sleep in the stable. She wanted him next to her. She wanted the heat of his body and the comfort of his arms. She wanted so much. Instead, she held out the book to him.

"Nay, it is yours."

She clutched it in her arms. Next to Audra and Magnus, it was her greatest treasure. More important even than the crest hidden above them.

She could not speak.

He leaned over and kissed her lightly on the cheek, then

straightened. "That, lass, was the most difficult thing I've done."

"Kiss me?" she asked.

"Nay, kissing you so primly when I really want to consume you." His voice was hoarse with wanting.

She recognized it because she was raging with the same need. But she also knew he was right. They had risked conceiving the other night. The next day she'd realized the reality of that folly. She could barely take care of Audra. What if she were to die in childbirth? What then would happen to her daughter? All those thoughts had plagued her since she left his bed days earlier.

Never trust a noble. She trusted this man, but could she trust the one emerging from his memories?

As if he understood her inner turmoil, he took a step back.

She gave him one of two candlesticks in the room. His hand went over hers for a moment, and the heat from the flames was nothing compared to the heat that exploded between them. She thought the cottage might erupt with it.

But then he turned and left without another word.

She placed the book on the table. The candle cast shadows over the printed words and the illuminations as she turned pages. One was of a wedding gown. A picture of a man and woman looking at each other. She saw the love in the look.

An illusion? Did nobles and royalty marry for love?

She finally quenched the candle and went into the other room. She undid the laces of her gown and took it off, then, clad in her chemise, lay next to her daughter. She put the book at the end of the bed. She was not going to allow anything to happen to it.

Read. If he stayed long enough, she would learn to read. *And he might die.*

He most certainly would tempt her. Even now her body

ached with wanting, with remembrance of the night they had coupled.

She touched Audra's hair, and her heart shimmered with tenderness.

Her daughter came first. Always.

*H*E could have stayed. He knew that, and it made the leaving even more difficult.

It had been pure joy to watch the excitement on her face as she spelled out a word, to watch her eyes as the letters, then the words, came together. Holy blazes, but she was quick.

He knew now he had to leave, had to answer the questions both of them had. As much as he was tempted to stay here, he had to know what obligations he might have elsewhere.

She should be safe. The Charlton made clear his protection of her, and that should not change if he disappeared. They both would have been fooled.

He reached the stable. One of the Charltons was already asleep in the stable. He found a blanket that smelled of horse and found a place to lie. But sleep would not come.

New images were coming lightning fast. The moment he touched the cover of the book, traced the title with his hands, he saw the man he knew had written it.

He knew the man and woman of the title. He saw King James look with love at the beautiful woman at his side.

He saw the two on thrones. The king stepped down and touched a dark-haired man, taking his hand and putting it in that of a woman. His breath stopped.

The man was the one he'd nearly killed in the ambush.

Chapter 19

KIMBRA rose at daybreak while Audra still slept. She'd spent a restless night, wondering at the choices she'd made in the past weeks. Still, for the first time in a very long time, she faced the day with anticipation.

Anticipation that could well be dangerous. Even deceptive.

Still, it bubbled inside her as she exchanged her chemise for a clean one, then laced the front of her gown. The Charlton had given this one to her, and now she had three. It was unaccustomed riches. Even more so that someone else had washed them all before she'd left the tower.

She added wood to the fire. She would milk Bess, then fix porridge for breakfast. She had five to feed today.

Then she hurried out to the barn, only to discover that

the Scot had already milked Bess. The evidence was in the pail just outside the stall and in the drops of milk under the old cow.

She smiled at the thought of a noble battling old Bess. Then the smile faded as she realized she was alone. No one was in the stable, not Timothy, nor Geordie, nor the Scot. His horse, the one the Charlton had given him, was gone.

For a moment her heart stopped beating.

Surely he would not leave without telling her. Or mayhap something happened?

Her heart started to beat again, but she felt numb.

Do not be foolish. He *would* leave. Mayhap last night he remembered more than he had indicated. Mayhap last night *had* been his good-bye, a last gift that would stay with her all her life.

She looked around for Bear. She called him, then was relieved to hear his bark. Moments later he came running toward her and gave her a sloppy Bear kiss with his tongue. Geordie was with him.

"Mr. Howard?" she asked.

"He went hunting," Geordie said. "He took my bow."

Life seeped back into her limbs. He had not left. Still, her heart reached out to the Scot. *Run. Run.*

"Did he say when he would return?"

"Nay."

"And Timothy?"

"He just relieved me at the path. I thought I would sleep in the stable."

"I will have food soon."

"Thank ye, Kimbra. I will wait then."

Kimbra turned back to the stable, picked up the pail of milk, and returned to the cottage, Bear tagging along behind her.

Audra was in the main room, looking sleepy. She had pulled on her gown, but the laces had not yet been tied. "I am hungry."

"So am I, love. We will have honey with the porridge this morning."

Audra grinned.

The honey was a treat. Kimbra had found a hive six months earlier and had managed to get some honey from it, despite numerous stings. It was almost gone, and she'd been using it sparingly. But Timothy and Geordie were guests who were helping her keep the cottage.

After she finished preparing the meal, she told Audra to fetch Geordie.

The man ate as if he had not eaten in days. Audra watched him with fascination, barely eating her own food. He was a big man. More than six feet tall and with a solid girth. He had a lot to fill. He talked about his own two children, a son who worked at the Charlton stables and a daughter.

"Your Edie will be missing you," Kimbra said. Geordie's Edie was one of those who helped wrap Will's body after his death. She was as plain as her husband, but one of the kindest natured women Kimbra knew.

"Her mother ails. She's gone to look after her."

"I am sorry to hear about her mother. Did the children go with her?"

"Aye. 'Twas one reason I was sent here. The Charlton knew Will was my friend, and Edie yours."

"I am glad it was you." And she was. Geordie was an honest man with little guile.

"Edie and I have worried about ye here alone."

"I was alone when Will went raiding."

"Aye, but there are more raids now."

"I would have thought there was enough blood shed on Flodden Field."

"'Tis the nature of the border, Kimbra. Ye know that."

"Aye, centuries of killing and thievery," she said bitterly. "It cost Will his life."

"He knew the risks." He changed the subject. "What do ye know of this Robert Howard?"

"Only that he is a Howard. Why?"

"There is something odd about him. I cannot tell ye why. Just that I do not think he is what he says he is."

Her breath stuck in her throat. She had not expected that he, of all the Charltons, would sense something wrong. Cedric had, too, of course, but then he had wanted to find something wrong.

"Why do you think that?"

"I seen him look at ye, and ye at him," he said cautiously. "And 'tis easy to like him. But he is no' one of us."

"Aye, he is," Audra protested, and Kimbra suddenly realized she'd been listening to every word.

Geordie's face flooded red, as he realized, like she, that Audra had been listening intently.

"Mayhap he is," Geordie said, and reached for more honey.

The meal finished in awkward silence, and Geordie quickly made his thanks and left.

"You should not have said that," she told Audra. "You do not interrupt when you are with adults."

The rare rebuke brought tears to Audra's eyes, and she ducked her face.

Kimbra put her arms around her daughter and leaned down to kiss her cheek. "I know you want to defend Mr. Howard, and it is loyal and brave of you to do so, but you must be very careful. Cedric does not like him, and others are jealous as well. We must give them no reason to spur their dislike."

"Then we should look after him."

"I do not think he likes the idea of us looking after him."

"We look after each other," she said. "Why is that wrong?"

Why indeed?

Dozens of reasons came to mind, none of which she

could explain to her daughter. But she admired her daughter's simple and complete loyalty.

She took Audra to the garden, and they worked together to gather new herbs to take to the tower, and to Jane. They were nearly finished when she heard Bear.

Minutes later, the Scot rode up to the cottage, dragging a dead boar behind him.

Pleasure warred with dismay. Pleasure that he was back. Dismay that he had given up a chance to escape.

The Scot dismounted.

"You should have kept going," she said in a voice too low for Audra to hear.

He stared at her for a long moment. He seemed to be memorizing her face. "I wanted to leave you with food. Geordie said he would butcher it for you."

So he *was* going. It was what she wanted. What she'd prayed for. Yet the loss was now immediate and incredibly painful.

"He is probably a tough old boar," the Scot said, "but 'twas all I could find. The woods seem well hunted." He paused. "I did see some wolf tracks. They might be moving this way to find food."

Audra was looking at the boar with awe. Then she looked up at the Scot. "You left us this morning. We had honey."

"Then I am sorry I missed it," he said solemnly. "Tomorrow ye can have meat."

He looked down at his bloodied hands and clothing. "I must wash."

"I will take care of your clothes," Kimbra said.

"Nay, ye have enough to do. I can wash them myself."

She stared at him with surprise.

"I find I am not without skills," he said with the small self-mocking smile she was beginning to expect. Expectation did not change the impact, however. It never failed to touch her heart.

"There is a stream just beyond the trees," she said.

"Aye, I saw it."

She looked down at Audra, who held the basket full of aloe, rosemary, and bay. "Will you take them inside and wait for me? I must talk with Mr. Howard."

Audra looked from one to the other, then her gaze rested on the Scot. "Will you give me a lesson on the lute?"

Kimbra had nearly forgotten about the lute. It had been left at the cottage in the rush to leave for the Charlton tower.

"Aye," the Scot said. "This afternoon?" He looked toward Kimbra as if for approval, and she nodded.

"If," she said to Audra, "you wash the herbs well while I am gone. Bear will stay here and look after you."

"Where are you going?" Audra said. "I want to go, too."

"Not this time," Kimbra said. "We will be gone just a short time. Stay and keep Bear and Geordie company."

Audra's lip went out in disappointment, but she turned and went into the cottage, her small back stiff with indignation.

He led the hobbler inside his stall and unsaddled him. Then he joined her. She gave him two buckets, and she took two herself, then they walked together to the stream, which flowed from the waterfall she and Audra loved.

When they reached it, he stooped and washed his hands in the water, then turned to her. "I am not sure I can leave, lass."

"Why?"

He shrugged. "Many reasons. But mostly because I feel I belong here. And we have not finished your reading lessons, or Audra's lute lessons."

"Neither are worth your life."

"No one has suspected anything."

"One has."

He stilled. "Who?"

"Geordie. He suspects you are not what you say."

"He just suspects?"

"Aye, but I know him. He will keep looking for oddities.

Small things that might give you away. He can be like a dog with a bone."

The Scot looked at her. "You and Audra can go to Scotland with me."

He had mentioned that before. But it was impossible, no matter how wondrous it sounded. She wanted it. Dear God, how she wanted it. But she had a daughter, and he might well be wed and have a family of his own. Then where would she and Audra be?

He took off his doublet, then his shirt and rinsed the blood from them. She stood back and studied him. She had thought him too lean, but now she noticed the muscles. The new scars on his body contrasted with the older one. Both rippled as he moved.

He was incredibly attractive to her, especially when he turned those brilliant blue eyes on her.

"How did you kill the boar?"

"An arrow."

"The first one?" Somehow she knew the answer before he opened his mouth.

He hesitated, then said, "Aye."

Any other man she knew would not have hesitated. They would claim the first arrow regardless of whether it was or wasn't. It was the Scot's hesitation that told her it was true. She had never known a man who so hated to claim competence.

She knew how difficult it was to kill a wild boar. He was truly a warrior despite the gentle qualities she saw in him.

"Have you had more memories?"

"They come rapidly now."

"But no name."

"Nay."

This time she heard real regret. He was beginning now to feel emotions from the past. Despite his insistence that this was home, she detected the seed of longing in him. Not only longing, but a need to know.

"Go," she said.

His arm tightened around her. "I want to stay, but it would not be fair. Not to either of us. I must return to Scotland. I have to know who and what I was."

"Aye," she replied.

"I will be back," he said.

She leaned her head against his chest. She realized that he'd been struggling with himself as to whether he really wanted to return home.

"You were right. There are things I must know." He hesitated. "I think there are painful things. I cannot ask you to wait."

She was silent. She hoped her eyes did not tell him she would wait forever. That was her secret.

His gaze studied her. "You said something once about words. *Virtue Mine Honour.* It keeps running over and over again in my mind. It means something. Or I think it should."

She could not tell him that she had withheld something from him that was so important. He would despise her as the thief she was.

Fear was a terrible thing. She knew that now. It made one do things they would never do otherwise.

Give him the brooch. It will help him find his family.

He will not come back.

She was silent, even though her soul cried against that silence. *Virtue Mine Honour.* She had no honor.

Still fear persevered.

He tightened his arms around her as if sensing the confusion in her.

She wanted to feel his lips, his body against her. She wanted more, much more, but she had just lied to him, at least by omission. She deserved no more.

But then, without invitation, he kissed her, his lips fierce and demanding, and hers equally so.

In seconds they were on the ground, and he was disrobing

her, and she him. She knew he was leaving now. She wanted, nay, needed him beyond imagining.

His lips made love to her. Then he entered her, and this time the explosion came quickly.

AUDRA finished pounding the herbs into powder and very carefully placed them into small bottles.

Feeling quite abandoned, she went up to the loft and gazed out the window. She could not see her mother or Mr. Howard, but she did see Geordie riding off.

Then he was gone, too. She looked around the loft. It was where she had been told to go if there was immediate danger. She was to get into a small cupboard in a corner. If they had more warning, she and her mother were to go into the woods.

Now, though, she was just sulking. She'd fiercely wanted to go with her mother and Mr. Howard. She did not understand why they did not want her along.

She thought about getting in the cupboard. They would return and not find her, and for a few moments she would become important to them. Mayhap important enough that they would decide they both needed to take care of her.

She needed a father.

She did not remember that much about her own father, and that worried her. She should remember more. She squeezed her eyes shut and tried to recall him.

He had been big. And dark. She remembered that. But she could not remember his face, and that made her feel sad and disloyal.

She imagined, though, he was like Robert Howard. She had liked him from the beginning, although she realized there was some mystery about him. But he was kind and never, ever treated her like a baby.

Until just now.

No, she couldn't hide. Then they really would think she was a baby.

She started to explore, instead. She liked being up here. It was her refuge when she grew lonely. She would gaze out the window and make up tales from the clouds.

She reached under the pallet. She used to have some treasures there. A bead bracelet from a fair. A special stone. A pretty button. She thought they would be safe here. She found the box and opened it, disappointed that the treasures were not as grand as she remembered. Then she saw something caught above in the rope mattress. She reached for it and found it stuck. She tried to work it loose, then triumphantly pulled out a brooch of some kind. The colors were glorious. Red and silver and gold. She handled it carefully because it was so beautiful.

Why was it hidden?

Against raiders, she thought.

She could not bear to let it go. How had her mother come to have it? There was a wonderful story there. She was sure of it.

Clutching it, she climbed back down and placed it on the table.

Then she went outside to wait.

Chapter 20

$\mathcal{K}$IMBRA lay in the Scot's arms. She wanted never to leave them.

Her body still felt the tremors of lovemaking, but as marvelous as that had been, the tenderness now was even more so.

How could she let him go?

She ran her hand over his good arm, relishing the feel of it. The muscles that contrasted with the soft brush of auburn hair.

She had never known how lovely it was to be still with someone, to understand and communicate without words.

He brushed a curl away from her face and smiled at her. "You get bonnier every day."

Because he made her feel that way.

She took his hand and brought it to her lips. She tasted the saltiness of the skin and savored it.

He moved his head slightly, and their eyes locked.

"You told me a little about your mother. Is there any other family?"

"Nay."

"And her father?"

"A physician. Not like the one here at the Charltons. My mother told me he believed in herbs. He taught her about them, and she taught me."

"And her mother?"

"She died in childbirth when my mother was eight." She felt the familiar pang at the thought of a family destroyed.

Now she realized she had never trusted Will as she trusted this man beside her, and that shocked her into silence.

His own quiet silence was more demanding than words.

"And the man who fathered you."

"There were promises, my mother was in love. An old story. But when she conceived . . ." Her voice trailed off.

"Then what, Kimbra?"

"He did not want a bastard. Neither did his father, the earl. They came one evening and burned the cottage. My grandfather was inside. The earl must have thought she was inside as well, but she and the maid had taken a late walk and lingered to pick mushrooms. They returned to see the cottage ablaze. Her maid knew she was at risk, too. They fled to the border where the maid had family, and my mother worked as a maid."

"Do you know who he was?"

"Aye. I know the name. Burlington. A very powerful name. She lived in fear until she died. She taught me, though, about plants. She said it would be something I could always use. She used to take me to the gardens at night and tell me about the various plants. After she died I assisted the herb grower when I could."

"But she did not teach you to read?"

"Nay, she refused to teach me. She feared if anyone knew she could read, it might raise questions and possibly lead the earl to her. A maid did not read books. Neither did a maid's child. Not without questions."

"I am sorry," he said, his finger tracing her cheek.

"'Twas nothing of your doing. She taught me not to trust, especially nobles. And she was terrified of fire. She made me fear it as well."

"And your husband? Did he know?"

"Nay. He did not care about my past, and I did not wish to burden him with it. I feared he might go after Burlington. And I think he relished taking a wife that was . . . different. He was always the rebel." She could not help but smile at the remembrance.

"I think I would have liked him," he said.

"You would have. Everyone did."

He was silent for a long time, and she feared she had said something wrong, had told too much. She still did not know why she had told him what she had told no other living soul.

"I must go," she said, but her words were unconvincing, even to herself. "I left Audra in the cottage." As soon as she said the words, she knew it was even later than she thought. The first shadows of dusk were appearing. Audra would be safe enough. She knew to stay inside the cottage. And now there were two Charltons to look after her.

She stretched with pleasure at the warmth of the afternoon and the rare soft breeze that caressed them. She had finally uttered her darkest secrets to him, and he had not shied away.

He helped her up, then tied the laces of her dress. He had a quiet competence in doing that, just as he had in so many other things.

He kissed her. He had kissed her before. Passionately. Hungrily. Tenderly. But this kiss was different and melted every defense she had. This kiss was love. Promise. A sweetness that made her heart swell because it was understanding as well.

When he finished, he looked at her with the bluest eyes she'd ever seen.

"You know that it does not matter who provided the seed. 'Tis the people who love you that count, and I think your mother loved you very much."

"I was not that sure," she said. "At least I was not then. Now I know how difficult it is to raise a child on your own with no protection. She could have abandoned me, or left me at a nunnery. Instead, she chose to keep me."

"'Tis a fine thing, honor," he said. "In keeping you, she stayed true to that."

Honor. Virtue Mine Honour.

She knew then she had to tell him about the crest. "Remember when I found you—"

The words broke off as a flock of birds rose into the sky.

"Someone might be coming," she said.

"We had best return," he said, his hand back around hers.

She reluctantly agreed. She had never believed in false modesty, or making herself something she was not. But it would not be good for either of them if they were found this way.

How long had they been gone? He quickly pulled on his breeches and boots.

His hair was mussed, and she used her fingers to comb it. Her own was probably a tangle of curls and leaves.

He pulled her hair back and helped put the cap on. Then they brushed the leaves and earth off each other's clothes.

And grinned at each other like two wayward children caught in mischief.

Tell him. But it was a special moment with sunlight spilling over them, their bodies glowing with lovemaking and their hands intertwined.

Later.

They walked back together. They had left that way. It would seem strange if they did not return together.

Her body hummed, and her heart sang. She chased away the cobwebs of lies. He did care for her. Even possibly loved her. He would understand once she explained. For a few precious seconds, she even believed they could possibly have a future together. Then she shoved that idea away. It was enough to have these moments. She could not be greedy.

Audra sat primly outside. She jumped up as they approached, looking very much like an excited little girl with a secret.

"Look what I found, Mather," Audra said, almost dancing in her excitement.

"What, love?" Some young animal, she supposed.

Audra took Kimbra's hand and led her inside to the table, with the Scot behind her.

She saw the brooch immediately. 'Twas impossible not to, with the diamonds and rubies. She felt the blood drain from her face.

"What is it?" the Scot asked.

Audra pulled away from her and picked up the brooch. "It is so pretty."

Kimbra started to grab it, but the Scot reached out first and took it in his hand. It sparkled against his fingers.

He stared at it as if transfixed.

She could only stand and watch. It was too late now to snatch it away, or make explanations.

His hand closed around it, and he sat down. He opened his hand again, and she saw emotions cross his face.

He recognized it!

A muscle throbbed in his throat, and he bent his head.

Then he raised it and looked at Kimbra.

*   *   *

*L*ACHLAN Maclean felt his emotions tumbling as fast as the images flooding him.

The Maclean crest. It had been a gift from his brother, Rory, years earlier when he had helped his brother reveal a traitor. He remembered Rory's face now, and it was that of the man he had fought in the border skirmish.

He remembered his father. He remembered betraying him.

He remembered the name of the brown-haired lass that had appeared in his images. Maggie, his brother's first wife, whom he had loved from afar, as strongly as a young man could.

Other faces. Rory's new wife, Felicia, and Jamie Campbell, the first man to completely trust him.

Where was Jamie now?

They had been together when the battle started. Dear God, don't let him be one of the dead. Or Hector, who had taught him, fathered him, protected him, supported him when the other clansmen had called him coward.

Coward.

How was it that he lived when so many others died? *Had he run away again?*

Blazes, but he could not remember the battle itself. *What had happened?*

He fingered the crest again. It was a brooch that made fast the plaid he usually wore.

Then he looked at Kimbra. She'd had it all this time. It had been the key to who he was. If he had seen it earlier, would he have remembered? Or was it an accumulation of memories that needed one last piece?

Crushing realization flooded him. She hadn't intended to show him the crest, even if it aided his memory. Part of him understood why. She had a daughter to feed. But it showed how little she had trusted him, even after these weeks.

It was probably the only material item that had ever

meant anything to him. It had given him back self-respect and a sense of worth after years of being told he was weak and worthless because he did not like, or choose, war.

And yet in the end he had.

He looked at Kimbra, who stood absolutely still. Her face was rigid, and he saw misery in her eyes.

She had saved his life. Not once, but probably twice. He had trusted her completely. She had not trusted him. But then why should she? She knew nothing of him beyond scattered memories. She had reason to distrust nobility.

Yet he could not deny the rush of disappointment, the sense of failure. He had failed her, just as he had failed others. She had not trusted him to make good his promise to care for her.

"What is it?" Audra's small voice broke the silence.

The Scot looked down at her expectant face and knelt in front of her. "It is a crest, Audra."

Audra looked at it again. "Is it yours?"

"'Tis your mother's now," he said.

"Nay," Kimbra said in a broken voice. "I will have no more lies. It is his clan crest," she said.

"Clan?" Audra looked puzzled. "The Howards?"

He heard Kimbra's indrawn breath.

She stooped. "I said he was a Howard because he had lost his memory and did not know who he was."

Realization dawned in Audra's eyes. "He is a Scot?"

Kimbra nodded.

"You lied to me." Audra's lips trembled as she made the accusation.

"Aye," she said simply, not excusing herself.

"You said you would never lie to me. A Scot killed my father." She looked up at Lachlan, obviously torn about how she should feel when she had already given him part of her heart.

"I am sorry," he said.

"You lied to me, too," she said to him, tears forming in

her eyes, then she turned toward the door, which had been left partly opened, and ran out.

Kimbra ran after her. He stayed, the brooch still in his hand. He thought about going after them, but feared he would do more damage. He'd never wanted to hurt Audra. God knew he would give his life for her.

And her mother.

Audra would forgive her mother. Children did that.

He did not know if he could. Not because he was any better that she. He had certainly told a fair number of lies to the Charlton. But because he'd thought she had come to love him as he loved her. If she had, she would have trusted him enough to show him the brooch. She would have known that he would protect her and her daughter.

But she had preferred the brooch. And safety, and had allowed him to wonder who and what he was.

Rory would be near mad with guilt. He knew his brother and how much he'd suffered from too many losses already, all of which he took on his shoulders. He would blame himself for allowing Lachlan to go in his stead, regardless of how much Lachlan had wanted to go. *One more test for himself.*

He had almost killed his brother days ago. Or his brother could have killed him and been doubly damned in his eyes.

Likewise, Lachlan—his name was Lachlan—could never forgive himself if the challenge had gone the opposite way.

He closed his eyes and thanked God that something had stayed his hand.

He looked out the window to see Kimbra running toward him, her face panicked.

"I cannot find her," she said.

"You were right behind her."

"She reached the woods before me and just disappeared." She looked frantic. "I have never seen her this upset."

"Mayhap she is in the stable."

She ran toward the stable, calling for Geordie, and he followed. No one was there. She turned to him. "He said he was going to sleep."

Her face was frozen with fear. He remembered then what she'd said earlier. Geordie had mentioned suspicions about him. He remembered the flock of birds. Had he been listening and left in a hurry? Exactly what had they said?

But that meant nothing right now. What was important was a child who felt betrayed.

Together they started for the woods. Audra could not have gone far. Best to find her now.

"You go to the left, I will go toward the right," he told her. "Stop and listen. She will probably make noise."

She could not have gone far. He kept telling himself that as he plunged into the woods.

Chapter 21

AFTER what seemed like hours combing the woods, Kimbra knew fear such as she'd never known before. She thought she had known its every form. Fear of death. Fear of her mother being discovered. Fear of hunger. But nothing was like the terror that wrapped around her heart now.

She had never seen Audra as she was today, had never seen her face dissolve as it had earlier.

Above it had been the Scot's face as he'd realized she'd lied to him from the beginning, that she had never been more than a thief. There was no anger, only disappointment, which was a deeper cut.

But that mattered little at the moment as she ran through the woods, calling Audra's name. She heard the Scot's voice as well.

Dusk had turned into night.

Bear. They should have fetched the dog. But she thought she would find her daughter quickly. But there was no child, nor a sound.

She did not know how long it was before she met up with the Scot. He had to have moved quickly despite his limp. His face was creased with worry.

"I will return for Magnus," he said. "And Bear. We can cover more ground that way."

She looked up at the darkening sky. "She is so little."

"We will find her," he said.

"You said there were wolf tracks." She could not hold back the fear.

"We will find her," he repeated.

"I . . . did not mean to lie to her." She felt her heart sag more with every word. She had been so intent on protecting Audra that she failed to give her what a child needs most.

"We should go back and get torches," he said.

"You go," she said. "There is a full moon tonight. I know these woods. I will continue looking."

He looked reluctant.

"Go. Please. Hurry."

He nodded. "Do not go far from here."

He was gone before she could say anything. If there was anything to say.

She started moving again, calling out her daughter's name, then listening.

She started at even the slightest rustle of brush, the soft breeze that blew through the woods. "Audra!" she called. "Audra!"

But there was no answer, and she wondered whether her daughter—when found—would ever answer again.

"Audra!" she called again, this time raising her voice. The only answer was a scolding magpie. Almost blinded by tears, she stumbled past the waterfall and into the dense woods.

* * *

*L*ACHLAN moved as quickly as he could back to the cottage and saddled Magnus. Then he rode off to the path Timothy was guarding. He found them quickly enough. Bear barked until he discovered it was a friend. Timothy looked at him cautiously.

"Audra is missing. Kimbra is looking for her, but we need help. And torches."

Timothy did not waste time asking questions. He mounted his horse and rode side by side with him, asking questions.

"How long has she been gone?"

"Several hours now."

"And Geordie? Is he looking for her?"

"We cannot find him. Mayhap he went back to the tower. Kimbra thought Bear could trail Audra."

"Aye, he will find her."

They rode hard back to the cottage, Bear lumbering along behind them. When they reached the cottage, Lachlan dismounted and went inside. He gathered several torches and lit them from embers in the fireplace. They might need them this night.

When he returned, he gave both to Timothy. He leaned down and touched the dog. "Find Audra, Bear. Find Audra."

He prayed that the big dog understood. He had understood when Lachlan had fallen in the woods, and had fetched Kimbra for him. Surely he would understand now.

Bear looked up at him, puzzled.

"Find Audra," he tried again.

Bear went to the door of the cottage and pushed against it, then returned and wagged his tail.

"No, Bear," Lachlan said. "She is not there. She needs you," Lachlan said. "Find her."

Bear barked as if finally understanding. He turned and ran toward the woods.

Lachlan mounted and took one of the torches from

Timothy. The air had cooled, and clouds were thickening and moving across the sky, blotting out the moon.

The dog moved ahead, sniffing the ground, looking behind occasionally, apparently to make sure Lachlan was still there. Bear did not stay on the paths, and Lachlan and Timothy fought through underbrush as they struggled to keep up.

Both of them called out Audra's name. Lachlan felt the icy fingers of fear along his spine. He should have realized that Audra might equate him with her father's death. She had most likely been taught that Scots were demons without honor, just as he had been taught that about the Campbells so many years ago. The Campbells had been enemies then, not the English.

But he understood how strong hate could be when taught young. Even a lass as young as Audra knew it.

They had been searching an hour or more on horseback. She'd been gone more than four hours. The night was black, and Audra was probably terrified. Mayhap Kimbra had already found her. He prayed she had.

God help him, he should not have left Kimbra alone. Yet he'd understood her need to continue looking for Audra, and she knew these woods as he did not.

Bear ran ahead, and he lost sight of the beast. Then there was a sharp bark. Another.

A scream. A woman's scream.

He dug his heels into Magnus and disregarded the branches that cut through his shirt. He moved toward the sound. The bark turned into a growl.

Sharp yelps. He had no weapons with him, but then he heard another scream and spurred his horse forward.

The sound of animals fighting became louder. The snarls were sharp and angry. Lachlan pushed the nervous horse forward, then stopped as his torch revealed Kimbra backed against a tree, a long stick in her hand as Bear battled two wolves. 'Twas obvious Bear was getting the worse of it.

"Help him," Kimbra pleaded.

Lachlan shouted, a bloodcurdling sound, and threw his torch at one of the wolves, which yelped, then turned toward him.

"Take this." Timothy thrust a dagger into his hands, as he, too, sought to distract the animals with his torch.

Lachlan concentrated on the wolf near him. It had been bloodied as well, and was enraged. Most wolves would have run by now, but these two must be hungry enough to brave humans. The wolf near him lunged at Magnus's leg. From the saddle, Lachlan could not reach him. He jumped from the horse and hit Magnus's rump to get him out of the way, then turned and met the wolf with the dagger, slicing at the throat.

The wolf kept coming, teeth bared, when Bear attacked from the back. The wolf swung around to attack the new tormentor, and Lachlan plunged the dagger in the animal's back, then pulled it out and this time found the heart.

He looked for the other one. It, too, was still, an arrow through its head.

Bear was panting and whining. Blood was all over him.

Kimbra was still standing there, a bloody stick in her hand. She'd obviously tried to stave off the attack when Bear arrived.

He'd almost been too late.

He could barely breathe at the thought.

He walked over to her. She was still, her face paralyzed with fear.

Lachlan looked upward and saw Audra, who was clutching a branch. He raised his arms for her to fall into, but she did not move.

"Come to me," he said softly.

Audra hesitated, then fell into his arms. He held her for a moment, then set her down. Kimbra hugged her for a very long time, until Audra started to wriggle. Then Kimbra hurried over to Bear and inspected his wounds.

"Brave dog," she crooned. "We will get you home."

Then she looked up at him. "Thank you."

He nodded. He still hadn't repaid the debt. She'd saved his life twice. "There is no need for thanks. 'Tis the least I could do——" He stopped when he saw how rigid she was.

He started to hold out his arms to her, but she turned away.

Rebuffed, he lowered his arms. "You and Audra can ride with Timothy on Magnus. I will take Bear on Timothy's horse."

She nodded stiffly.

In minutes, he had taken the blanket from under the saddle and wrapped it around Bear. When he looked back at Kimbra, she was on her knees and her head rested on her daughter's. It was such a tender scene, heartbreaking in its impact, that he had to look away.

He mounted. Timothy lifted the dog up to him, and Lachlan settled him across the front of the saddle. He watched as Timothy helped Kimbra into the saddle, then Audra before leading the horse on foot.

Lachlan followed. Timothy and Kimbra knew this land far better than he. But the scene of mother and daughter remained in his head. Just as the brooch seemed to burn a hole in his soul.

Chapter 22

$\mathcal{J}$T was still dark when they arrived back at the cottage. To Kimbra's dismay, the area was filled with horses and riders.

Kimbra saw Geordie among them. Her heart dropped. She turned in the saddle to wave off the Scot, but he'd already seen them.

She saw him grip Bear tighter and ride ahead.

He knew what was going to happen, and he was not going to try to escape. Then she wondered, why had she thought otherwise? There was nothing of fear in him, nor dishonor, nor cowardice. She, on the other hand, had all three.

Jock strode over to meet them. He took the bridle of the horse the Scot rode.

"The Charlton wants to see ye," he said.

Lachlan nodded. "The dog was wounded by wolves

while trying to protect Kimbra and Audra," he said. "Kimbra needs to care for him."

Jock glanced at the dog. "The Charlton wants Kimbra as well. The dog can go with us." His voice was hard.

"He is bleeding," the Scot said. "At least allow Kimbra to tend to him before going on."

Jock looked undecided, then nodded reluctantly.

Two of the Charltons lifted the dog down, and Bear slunk to the ground. His fur was matted with blood, and now, so were Lachlan's clothes.

Kimbra dismounted, then went over to Bear, who whined softly.

"It will be all right," she crooned, hoping with all her heart she was right. For all of them.

She looked up to see the Scot dismount. He was immediately surrounded by three Charltons.

"Tie him," Jock said.

"I am not going anywhere," her Scot replied.

"Nay, ye are not."

Two Charltons pulled his arms behind him and tied them with rope.

"Who are ye?" Jock asked, his voice hard. "No Howard, I wager."

"Nay, though I did not know until just recently who I was. I lost all memory after the battle."

Jock snorted. "A tall tale." He stopped, then added curiously, "Ye said ye did not know until recently. How recently? And who are ye?"

"Maclean. Lachlan Maclean."

Maclean. The name stunned Kimbra, even as she sent Audra for water, needle and thread, and some pieces of cloth. She could not help but stare at him. Her Scot was a Maclean, yet she could not bring herself to call him that. She had heard the name mentioned occasionally. The Macleans were a seafaring family that was not above engaging in a bit of smuggling with the borderers. It was also one of the most important clans in Scotland.

Bear struggled to rise, and she put a restraining hand on him. "No," she said gently, just as Audra returned with the water and cloth and her sewing needle.

She blocked out the Scot then, and everyone else. Some of the wounds were deep. She turned to Audra. "Fetch some aloe," she said. In a very short time, Audra had returned with a bottle and helped Kimbra pour it into the wounds.

She looked up. "I have to sew the wounds. Someone has to hold him down."

Timothy stepped up. "I will do it, Kimbra."

She looked up and nodded. "Thank you."

He kneeled next to her and held the dog as she carefully sewed his wounds. He whimpered once, then was silent.

"Good Bear," she whispered when she tied the last knot. Then she looked up. "Can we use the litter in the stable for him?"

"Aye," Jock said, but she saw the hardness in his eyes before he turned back to the Scot, to the Maclean. Then his gaze went back to Audra.

"She did not know who I am," the Scot said. "She could not. I did not know myself."

"She knows ye are not English."

"Nay," the Scot said in a voice that reached her. "I took the clothes of a dead man when I saw the English kill the Scottish wounded and managed to crawl away. She thought I was English. I heard the name of Howard mentioned on the battlefield. I couldn't remember my own and took that instead."

"Geordie heard something else."

The Scot shrugged. "I do not know what he heard, or thought he heard."

"Were ye the one who warned the Armstrongs?"

"When would I have had a chance to do that?" he said. "I did not even know who the Armstrongs were then."

"So ye say," he replied, his eyes full of doubt.

Jock stalked away and neared Kimbra. "What did ye know, Kimbra?"

"That he was someone who needed help," she said sharply. "Just as those Charltons I've tried to help."

"The Charlton will want answers. So will the others."

She looked over at Geordie. He turned away. She felt a terrible sense of betrayal.

She stood. "I will get the litter. I do not think Bear can walk the distance."

"Nay, I will do it," Timothy said. "Ye stay here with the young lass."

Audra's hand crept into Kimbra's. Her daughter's eyes fastened on the Scot. "I did not mean what I said to him," she said, and tears glistened again in her eyes.

"I know."

Then Timothy was back. He and another man placed Bear on it and tied him there.

Jock helped her mount Magnus, then helped Audra up in front of her.

She watched as they boosted the Scot onto a horse, his hands still tied behind him.

His back was straight, though, and his head proud.

There was no fear there.

She remembered the words he'd uttered minutes ago. *She thought I was English.* He was protecting her yet.

For Audra's sake, she had to remember everything he'd said.

*L*ACHLAN sat straight in the saddle as a Charlton led his horse. He tried not to glance at Kimbra, but his eyes were drawn to her. He'd wanted to go to her when she'd tended Bear. He should have been the one holding Bear. And Audra shouldn't bear the guilt that was his. He'd been so mesmerized by the crest that he hadn't considered anyone else. Not when the memories started tumbling out.

He thought about them now. He knew that his life might well be forfeit. But he would die as a Maclean. He worried more about Kimbra and what would happen to her.

Strange, though, how easily he had fitted as an English borderer. He had liked the Charlton and many of his clan.

He loved one in particular.

The brooch meant nothing now. He'd been startled, both by the sight of it and the memories it had awakened. But when he looked at her, his heart ached with tenderness as he'd watched her minister to Bear with the same gentleness she'd shown when she tended him.

"Ye say ye are a Maclean?" Jock maneuvered his horse close to his.

"Aye."

"Ye were with the Scottish king?"

"I think so . . . aye." He remembered riding next to the king. He did not remember anything after that. He was still assimilating the memories. The process had been interrupted by Audra's disappearance, but returned on the ride back from the woods. He was Lachlan Maclean. He had two brothers. No wife. The brown-haired lass . . . she had been his brother's first wife, with whom he'd been secretly in love. But now he knew it hadn't been love at all, but affection for the first person who had thought he had value.

Then he'd proved he did not.

He was not going to deny now what he was. He could only try to keep Kimbra from suffering for helping him.

"What do ye mean, *think?*"

"I remember riding next to him . . . then . . . it is blank until I woke up on the battlefield."

"Do ye hold title?"

"Nay. I am a younger brother."

"But the Macleans would pay a handsome ransom?"

Not to die? "I believe so. I thought King Henry . . ."

"He wants Scots dead." Jock shrugged. "He does not

want to fight them again. I do not know what the Charlton wishes to do with ye. He was in a towering fury when I left. He does not like being taken for a fool."

"He is no fool. I truly did not know who I was."

"But ye knew ye were no Howard."

"I suspected as much," he said and saw Jock's lips turn up slightly.

Lachlan was silent. He had been warned by the Charlton. And he had lied, and lied some more.

Jock rode ahead, and Lachlan was left with memories that splashed across his consciousness. The castle at Inverleith. The training in arms. The books he loved.

Finally his father. Now he knew the source of the nightmares.

And Jamie. What had happened to Jamie Campbell? His friend had ridden with him. As had Hector Maclean and so many other Macleans. Where were they now?

He'd wanted the memories, and now he wanted them to stop.

They reached the tower. It had been forbidding the first time. It was much more so now. He was a Scot; there was a price on his head. He had brought Kimbra and Audra into jeopardy as well. His main concern now was protecting them, not himself. He should have died years ago. His father died in his place. The weight of that event had never left him.

Rory was nearby. He would be here for one reason, and one reason only. To search for him.

Audra and Kimbra would like him. He would like them. His brother appreciated unconventional, spirited women. He certainly had married one. Lachlan smiled at a memory that was solid and real now. Memories. He would never take them for granted again.

He slid off his horse and looked back for Kimbra. She and Magnus were lagging behind, probably because of the litter. He wanted to stay to see whether Bear had survived the journey, but Jock pushed him toward the door and inside.

He knew where he was going. Up the steps, and this time with his hands still bound behind him. He concentrated on every step and finally reached the Charlton's room.

The door opened, and he faced the man who would decide his fate. As well as Kimbra's and Audra's.

The Charlton was eating. He looked up and glared.

"I told ye never to betray me," he said.

"And I have not."

"But ye have lied."

"Aye." He saw no reason to lie now. It would, in truth, make his case worse.

"Ye are Scottish."

"A Maclean," Lachlan said. "But I did not know it when I was here."

The Charlton shifted in his chair. "And how can that be?"

"I lost my memory."

"But now ye have it back."

"Aye, but only since yesterday."

The Charlton stood. "I singled ye out. I look like a fool."

"For that, I am sorry. I never intended it. I was not given a choice about coming here."

"Impudent pup," the Charlton muttered.

"Kimbra had naught to do with it," Lachlan hurried on. "I lied to her as well."

"Ye did now?"

Lachlan did not like the way the Charlton said the words.

"She is guilty of nothing more than being kind. Do what you will with me, but hold her harmless."

"Macleans?" the Charlton said thoughtfully. " 'Tis said a Maclean is looking for a brother along the border."

"That would be Rory, laird and chief of the Macleans."

"I have heard of him. He did some smuggling."

"Aye, so have I."

"Where was your brother during the battle?"

"His wife had just had a bairn. I stood in for him."

"Your mistake," the Charlton said.

"Nay, to fight with brave men is never a mistake."

The Charlton slapped his hand against the desk. "Well said. I knew I liked ye." He frowned. "Ye present me with a problem, Maclean. My men know who ye are. The king wishes your death. Cedric is a vicious enemy."

Lachlan stood silent.

"The fact, though, that your brother is seeking ye means I might make a fast trade before the English lord admiral knows ye are here."

He eyed Lachlan speculatively, as if he were a piece of meat at a market. "I will send someone to see what their interest might be," he continued. "In the meantime ye will be guarded. I have no dungeon here, or ye would be headed toward it. I do not like liars."

"Kimbra? Audra?"

"I do not make war on women, but Kimbra must wed. She is far too willful. I will give her a choice, but it must be soon. Jock," he then called, "take the Maclean to his previous chamber. He is to be guarded day and night. No visitors. Not even Mistress Kimbra."

"Aye," Jock said and opened the door.

Lachlan had no choice but to go out the door, all the time the Charlton's words following him. *Kimbra must wed.*

He remembered the stricken look on her face when he'd spied the crest. There had been no doubt then that she had taken it and had meant to keep it. But 'twas a small enough price for his life.

The room was as he had left it. Stark and lonely. The door closed on him, and he heard a key twist in the lock.

The Charlton indicated he would ransom him. Lachlan

intended to demand that Kimbra and Audra be part of any bargain.

He still felt a stab of disappointment on learning about the brooch, that she had kept it a secret from him. Yet he knew desperation. Had felt it to the marrow of his bones. He knew she feared a marriage. She had been protecting herself and her daughter in the only way she knew. Who was he to say that was wrong?

The day went slowly. He looked out the window slit. He saw riders but no young woman with a child. Nor a great, lumbering dog. He prayed that Bear would survive. Audra loved him so.

He tried to remember everything, but too many memories were bittersweet. He could not remember truly being happy until he'd met Kimbra. It was odd that being without memory could make one happy.

Would the Charlton find his brother? Could Rory pay the ransom? He was only too aware that they were short of assets after the purchase of a new ship.

And how did Kimbra fare? Despite the Charlton's assertion he did not make war on women, he knew others within the tower had no such scruples.

He started pacing.

A Maclean. It still seemed impossible. She'd always thought him a noble, and yet the reality stunned her. He came from one of the most notorious families in Scotland.

No wonder he seemed to do everything so effortlessly. He must have had years of training. Years of education.

She had none of the latter. She knew letters now. A few words. But she was far from being able to read a book, or a document. She was a thief who had not only stolen his goods, but also kept his memory from him.

Biting her lip to keep from uttering a cry of despair, she

glanced down at Audra, who lay on a bearskin next to Bear, her arms around the dog's neck. Both were asleep, but she wondered whether she would ever sleep peacefully again.

The Charlton would be furious. Her Scot's life could well be forfeit. And if he survived, he would not trust her again.

If the Charlton forced her to wed, or banished her, she had only the gold ring to keep her daughter safe. And that, she feared, was not worth much here. That and Magnus.

Magnus. She bit her lip as she thought of selling him.

For her life. Nay, Audra's life as well.

She looked down at her hands. They were clenched together. And cold. So very cold.

She had wagered and lost.

Her Scot was in mortal danger.

Her own future was questionable. That made Audra's questionable as well.

By lying she'd lost everyone's trust, including Audra's.

But she feared the greatest price for her folly would be exacted from the Scot.

CEDRIC had watched with growing fury when Kimbra and the Scot were brought in.

For weeks, he'd suspected the man was not what he seemed. He had tried to convince the Charlton. Now Geordie would receive a reward instead of himself.

And Kimbra?

The Charlton had made it known lately that he would not give Kimbra to him, because Kimbra was against the match. A woman should have no say.

The decision had spurred his own pursuit of riches. He had deserved Kimbra. By the devil, he wanted her. He had to have her. Or, if not, make sure no one else had her.

Her rejection made his lust even greater. He wanted to teach her who was master. He wanted her to cringe under him.

And so once he learned of the raid, he had ridden to the Armstrongs while he was to be looking for escaped Scots. And he had made the devil's own bargain.

His life would be forfeit if his treachery was discovered. He also knew the Armstrongs would sell that information for a piece of gold if they thought him of no further use. He had to leave, but he was not going to leave alone.

He kept close to Jock. He was within hearing distance when Jock dispatched two men to take a message to Rory Maclean at the Armstrongs.

Maclean. So the Scot was a Maclean. Apparently the Charlton was going to defy the king and ask for ransom.

Cedric weighed his options. He could ride hard to the retreating English and report the Scot. But then he may not receive a monetary reward, and all the Charltons would learn of his perfidy. He would never be able to return.

The second option was to take the place of the messengers and take the ransom. It would be a handsome one, given the fact that Maclean was a powerful family. His brother Garrick would help.

He opted for the last. He and Garrick would kill the guards, deliver the note, then take the money to ransom the Maclean. When the money was not paid, the Charlton would be forced to turn over the Scot to the English. The family would demand it.

He would be wealthy. Kimbra and her daughter would be alone. He could hire men to take them.

The more he considered the plan, the more he applauded his own intelligence. The Macleans would have to give him the money because after their own ambush days ago they would fear retaliation by the Charltons.

Satisfied with himself and his plans, he found his brother, explained the plan. Garrick, as always, readily agreed.

He hurried to his chamber and retrieved his weapons. His bow, pike, and dagger. Then he hurried out to the stable.

He told the stable lad they were going hunting, not

unusual, since both of them were expert with a bow and arrow and were among the family's best hunters. He knew the perfect place to ambush the two messengers, both trusted lieutenants of the Charlton.

They rode hard to a pass that linked England to Scotland. It was but one of many raiding routes. It was also the shortest. And less used for that specific reason. Raids required more secrecy and surprise. But surprise was not required on this mission, and the direct route was likely.

They found a place atop the pass. It was still English land, and the two Charltons would not be as wary as they would be once across the border.

He tied up his horse and took a position among the gorse and stretched out alongside his brother. His bow was in his hands, several arrows at his side.

No one was better with a bow than he, not even Garrick.

Two arrows should take them down. Then if they were not dead, he would kill them.

The Armstrongs would be blamed.

He smiled to himself as he waited.

Chapter 23

Inverleith

"Are you sure?" Felicia Campbell Maclean asked.

"Aye," Janet Campbell replied. "And it is not as if you do not have enough help here." She grinned happily. "It will give me good experience when my own bairn comes."

Janet had appeared at Inverleith in the afternoon with a message from her husband. She had blushed when reading it. Or at least a part of it.

"He is well and he says they cannot find Lachlan's body, but that someone had seen the crest he wore. Someone knows something about him. They still hope to find him alive."

"I want to go," Felicia had said. "But the children . . ."

Janet's eyes had brightened. "I can stay with them. I would love it."

Anticipation bubbled up inside Felicia. She had been going mad not knowing about Lachlan. He had been her first friend here at Inverleith when she'd been kidnapped and feared the worst. He had been her comfort then, and later her protector. He'd almost died to see that she and Rory could wed and end the century-long feud between the Campbells and Macleans. He was as dear to her as her husband and children.

She'd felt guilty every moment she'd sat here while Rory and Jamie were trying to find both Lachlan and Hector. She wanted to be with them. She might be able to go places they could not. She had played the role of spy before.

She went into the nursery. She went to little Patrick first. He was two now and was waking up from a nap. He held out his hands to be picked up.

She hugged him for a long time, then sat down next to him on the small bed. "I love you," she said. "I have to go away for a little while."

"Go?"

"Aye, but no' for long."

His dark eyes, so much like Rory's, had the same inquisitive look. She was not sure how much he understood.

"Pater?" he asked.

"He will be home soon."

Patrick gave her a wide grin. He worshiped his father as much as his father doted on him.

"Be a good lad," she said.

"A'ways good lad," he said.

"Aye, you are. Take good care of your sister."

Another huge smile.

She gave him a big kiss and went to the cradle where Maggie was sleeping. She leaned down and touched her face. She was a beautiful baby with her red hair and green eyes. And a joy. Where Patrick had often been restless and fretful, Maggie slept and ate and smiled.

She had a wet nurse because Felicia did not have enough milk. Maggie would be fine for a few days.

She had never left them before. Not either of them.

Second thoughts assailed her. Would she be doing the right thing?

Then she thought of all the risks Lachlan had taken on her behalf. Rory had taken some money, but mayhap more would be needed. She would take her jewels. The Maclean jewels. It would be an excuse to give Rory, anyway.

Her husband would not be pleased.

She kissed Maggie, then turned to Janet who was standing in the door, a smile on her face. Her friend had so wanted to be a mother, but two years had passed without conceiving. Now she glowed with the knowledge she would be a mother.

In another hour Felicia was ready. Duncan, who captained the guard, had prepared an escort of four to go with her. She had protested at first, then realized the jewels were too valuable not to have a guard. The journey, she judged, would take two and a half days if they rode hard.

"Go to the Armstrongs," Duncan said. "Rory should be there." He looked up at her. "Are ye sure ye want to go? They may be on their way back."

"And they may not," she retorted.

Duncan merely nodded. They'd engaged in battles of will since he had been involved in her kidnapping years ago.

She tied her bundle to her horse. It included a second gown as well as a lad's clothing. The gown she wore now was a simple one that would not attract attention. Over it she wore a plain cloak.

She urged the horse ahead. She'd expected to feel the smallest bit of exhilaration. She didn't. She missed the children from the moment she left the courtyard.

Felicia gathered the cloak around her. The jewels were sewn into its hem. Pray God they would help.

Pray God Lachlan still lived.

The Border

Kimbra nursed Bear and sang to Audra. Her daughter wanted to go to the Scot. She wanted to, as well, but she could not say that to her daughter. Instead, she prayed that the Charlton remembered Lachlan had saved his life.

"He is not bad, is he?"

"Nay," she said.

"But a Scot killed my father."

"Your father killed Scots as well," she tried to explain. "And it was not the Maclean that shot that arrow."

Audra's eyes cleared, then hurried on to another question. "Does he have children?"

"I do not know. He did not, either. He could not remember."

"How can that be?"

"He was hurt very badly."

"I am sorry for what I said."

"I do not think he blames you."

"Can I see him?"

"I will have to ask the Charlton."

"Will you?" Audra's eyes were pleading.

"Aye."

A knock came at the door, then it opened.

Jock stood there. "The Charlton wishes to see ye."

She leaned down and kissed Audra. "Take care of Bear. I will be back soon." She hoped she could fulfill that promise.

She followed him to the Charlton's room.

Once inside, she stood silent as Thomas Charlton speared her with his eyes. "Did ye know he was a Scot?"

She had considered the answer to the question she knew

was coming. She had heard the Scot's explanation. She had her daughter to protect. Yet she found she could not lie. There had already been too many lies. "Aye," she said softly.

"Then he lied to me again."

"He wants to protect me. Surely there is honor in that."

"You lied to me before."

"I did not know who he was. He had a head wound. He remembered nothing. 'Twas my fault that he was at the cottage."

"Why did ye take him? Ye must have heard all Scots were to be killed."

"I thought at first of ransom." She took a deep breath. "I feared you would force me to marry Cedric. Or someone else. Mayhap if I brought you a prize . . ."

"But ye did not bring him to me."

"Nay. After I cared for him, I heard that there were to be no ransoms. I did not want him to die."

He looked at her sharply. "Ye love him?"

"Do I have the right to love someone of my choosing?"

The Charlton breathed heavily for a moment, then said, "Ye remind me too much of my first wife. Outspoken and stubborn." There was a softness in his voice, though.

"Will ye let him live?"

"If a fat ransom is paid," he replied. "I do not want a rebellion of my family, and rebel they will, if we get nothing for our trouble."

She did not remind him that it had been mostly her trouble. "Did he say whether someone would pay one?"

"He is the brother of the Maclean laird. I suspect a ransom will be paid. Someone has been seeking information about a Lachlan Maclean."

Brother of the Maclean laird. Not just a Maclean but the chief's family. He would be safe now. "And myself and Audra?"

"I want you wed because ye need the protection." His

eyes searched hers. "Ye did not answer my question. Do ye love the Scot?"

"Nay," she lied. It was over in any event. He would leave for his own home, his family. Most likely a wife. "I just saw so much death, and felt I had to try to save one. English or Scot."

"Ye are too soft for the border, Kimbra."

"Nay. I love the border."

"Ye do not care to see him then?"

She hesitated a moment too long.

A gleam came into his eyes. "Ye and Audra can have a few moments."

"I would like to see him alone first. I . . . there's something I need to tell him."

He nodded. "Do not lie to me again, Kimbra. I will not be so soft next time. If he had not saved my life, I would turn him over to the crown, ransom or not."

She backed away before he changed his mind.

In minutes she was outside the room the Scot had previously occupied. There was no dungeon in the tower. No cells. But it would be impossible for one to leave.

The door opened, and Jock, who had brought her, stepped away as she entered. The door closed behind her.

The Scot was standing. She imagined he had probably been pacing the floor. His eyes were difficult to read. There was no ready smile.

She had not expected one. It had been terrible of her to keep his brooch from him. He had lost days when he might have remembered. Remembered and escaped.

She wanted him to take her in his arms again. She wanted to lean against him and forget everything that had happened since they'd made love next to the stream.

"The Charlton said he will ransom you," she said.

"My brother will pay it."

"He is the Maclean?"

"Aye, unless my older brother returns. But he has been away more than seven years now."

"And your wife?"

"There is no wife," he said with a hint of a smile.

Relief flooded her, though she had no right to it. She had no right to him. "You . . . mentioned a brown-haired girl?"

"My brother's wife. She died a long time ago."

Something in his eyes changed. She had been more than his brother's wife.

"It is all back then? Your memory?"

"Not all. Not the moments during the battle. I do not know what happened to my king or to my best friend or the man who was a second father to me." His voice broke slightly.

"But you will go home."

"Aye for a while. I canna' stay here, not as a Scot. Having a Scot in residence might try my host's hospitality." There was a ghost of a smile on his lips.

They were talking like strangers. It was the first time since he'd discovered the crest. There had been, of course, those few moments after the wolf attack, but that had been pure emotion. Now he'd had time to think about what she'd done, how she'd kept away something that might have helped him piece back his life. Now he knew what she was.

She shivered.

He touched her shoulder then. "Will you go with me?"

She looked up into his face. She wanted to. Oh, how she wanted that. But how could she—an English reiver's widow—be accepted into his life, into his family? She was not only an enemy but a thief who robbed the dead.

She knew only too well that the Charlton had disowned his daughter for marrying a Scot of equal class. How would Lachlan's family view this liaison, even marriage, with a reiver's widow? An enemy and a thief.

She could not do that to him, even though her heart was

breaking. She looked up at him. "My home is here. I am an Englishwoman."

"I thought you feared staying here."

"The Charlton has assured me I can marry who I wish," she countered, fighting back tears.

"Then wed me. I have no wife."

"You are a Scot, and I am English. You are of a fine family. I am a reiver's woman. The Charlton disowned his daughter when she married a Scot. Your family will disown you. I could not bear that." She hesitated, then added, "You are grateful now, and I am grateful that you saved Audra. But gratitude is not enough for a marriage."

"Is that all you believe it is? Gratitude?"

"We are . . . drawn to each other. But that does not last. If you lose everything else, you will come to hate us."

He leaned down, and his lips touched hers, softly at first, then demanding as she responded. She stood on tiptoes as his arms tightened around her until she thought she could no longer breathe.

She could feel the blaze where their bodies touched, their lips met, and their eyes caressed in such intimate ways. She knew she should tear herself away, but she wanted this last kiss. This would not last, but for the moment she would embrace it. Never to know again the singing in her heart, the flight of that part of her soul that so craved him.

The kiss became frantic, a greedy fire needing fuel. A terrible thirst demanding relief. Their kiss turned searing, full of need, and she knew an ache so deep in her body, she wondered how it could ever be relieved. She memorized every second, and never wanted to let go.

He was the one who drew back, his blue eyes searching hers. "Drawn? Lass, I think it is far more than that."

She was numb, yet she knew what she had to do. No matter the intensity of their need for each other, it could not last.

He touched her face. "Do you not know I could never hate you? I could do naught but love you."

"It is impossible." She heard the words but didn't know who was speaking them. Mayhap someone bleeding from the heart. But she had to be wise for all of them. She could not destroy three lives. Possibly more.

His eyes grew still. "My family will love you," he said. "My brother would not care if you are English or Scot."

"How could they not?" she said in a voice that was all pain. She moved back from his touch. "All the Scots dead at Flodden."

She opened the door and almost knocked down Jock in the process. She saw his startled look, then her eyes glazed over and she almost stumbled.

Jock caught her. "If he hurt ye . . ."

"Nay." Then she fled back to her room.

*L*ACHLAN watched the door open and then close behind her. She did not look back.

He wanted to go after her, but he could not. Even if he had not heard the key turning in the lock, he could not. His body still thrummed from the passion that erupted in him. But she had no faith in him. And the two—or three—of them.

Mayhap she had reason. The circumstances of her birth had made her wary. But he had hoped she would come to believe in him.

He picked up the brooch from the table where he had laid it. He had meant to give it to her when he saw her. He'd had no chance. He looked at it now and thought about the doors it had opened in his mind. It had once meant everything to him. Now it meant nothing.

The sun suddenly hit the crest, and it seemed a live thing in his fingers.

He remembered the day Rory had given it to him.

They had returned to Inverleith after exposing a traitor to the crown, and Rory had won the right to marry a Campbell.

Three weeks after returning, Rory had found him looking out over the sea.

"Would you like to go to sea?" he asked. "Take my place as owner?"

"I know nothing about the sea."

"You will learn quickly enough. I have a good shipmaster. You would be doing the buying and selling. You have a head for books and numbers."

"You would trust me?"

"I already have trusted you with my life."

Nothing could have pleased Lachlan more. Neither the last declaration nor the opportunity to leave a place full of bad memories.

He nodded. "I will try it."

Rory then took something from his pocket. It was wrapped in rich velvet. "I commissioned this in Edinburgh. It just arrived."

He had taken the piece of velvet, opened it slowly, and saw the crest. A large lump lodged in his throat. He had never felt accepted as a Maclean. He'd always been the odd outsider, the strange one who preferred books and music to weapons and training.

This brooch said that, at last, he was a true Maclean.

It had been his most prized possession.

When he had seen it in Audra's hand, the memories had flooded back. All the emotions connected with it. Pride. Belonging.

Now it burned his fingers.

*R*ORY Maclean, Jamie Campbell, and an Armstrong had glasses of ale in a tavern on the English side of the border. The Armstrong ordered for them, and they took

a table distanced from other patrons so their words would
not be heard.

Rory knew he smelled of sweat and horses. The rough
material of his clothes chafed skin more accustomed to the
fine wool of his plaid. His beard had grown, and he disliked that as well. But it made him far less conspicuous.

They waited. Mary Armstrong was also traveling with
them. She had been given money to go to the village merchant for oats. And information.

This, according to the Armstrong, was Charlton land.

Three days had passed since they had left. The Armstrong had left word of the route they planned to take, just
in case there was word of Lachlan. Everywhere they went,
they asked about a lad and a black hobbler, as horses were
called here. They also asked if anyone had heard about a
ruby and diamond brooch.

So far all of their efforts to find Lachlan had met with
failure. He had been generous with his gold, and now it
was rapidly declining. If Lachlan or Hector still lived and
ransom was demanded, he would be hard put to meet it.

Rory stretched out his long legs and mournfully con-
templated the cup of ale. If it had not been for the lad
and the church at Branxton, he might have given up.
He'd had high hopes for this village, and his gaze had
gone to every man and lad they passed. None brought
back that fierce start of recognition he'd felt during the
fight days ago.

That scene continued to haunt him.

It had seemed like a sign to him. God's promise.

He'd wanted to come directly here, but there had been
other small villages on the way, and it did no harm stopping in them first. But now he wondered whether the journey was a fool's errand. The Charlton raider the other night
could not have been Lachlan.

They were just finishing the tankards of very bad ale
when the door opened and two reivers entered. They went

o the proprietor, obviously full of important news. "That soldier staying with Mistress Charlton. They say he is a Scottish noble. A Maclean, 'tis said."

In moments the tavern was buzzing with questions. Rory had to force himself not to join in. He allowed the Armstrong, whose accent was similar to the ones he was hearing, to make queries.

"He is alive?"

"Aye. Kimbra Charlton, Will's widow, apparently found him, thought he was English, and nursed him back to health. The physician said it was a miracle he lived. Either that or black arts. Given the fact he is a highborn Scot, it was most likely the latter."

Snickers broke out.

"Maclean, ye say?" someone asked.

"Aye, but pretending to be English. He even took part in that raid against the Armstrongs. He was the one who saved the Charlton's life."

"Probably set the ambush up hisself," one listener muttered.

Rory tried to hide his elation. So it *had* been Lachlan. God help him, what if he had killed Lachlan? Why had his brother not said anything? Why hadn't he turned and left with them? Why was he fighting the Armstrongs at all?

Loyalty. A Charlton lass had apparently saved Lachlan's life. Mayhap that had something to do with it. But surely Lachlan had recognized him, even though his own face had been partly covered by the steel helmet. Why had he not followed?

None of it made sense.

He and Jamie exchanged glances, rose, and left the tavern. It was filling fast, apparently to hear and discuss the news. They were strangers, and now that a Scot had been discovered in their midst, the villagers might ask questions of other strangers.

They saw Mary Armstrong walking rapidly toward them.

Apparently she'd heard the news as well. They mounted their horses and rode from the village.

When well away, they stopped and exchanged information with Mary.

"He is at the Charlton tower," she said. "I know it. It is much like the Armstrong tower. Ye cannot get into it."

"What do they plan to do with him?" Jamie asked.

She shrugged. "Some say hand him over to the English. Others want ransom."

"Who decides?"

"The Charlton. Thomas Charlton. He leads the family."

"The one they say Lachlan saved?"

"Aye."

"Do you know where this woman lives, this Kimbra?"

Mary smiled. "Aye. I asked. It seems that she has black hobbler as well."

He gave her one of his precious gold pieces. "My thanks. You can give me directions to her dwelling, and I'll decide then what to do. You can return home."

"I would rather stay, milord. I might be able to help."

"It could be dangerous. I doubt the Charltons care for Armstrongs at the moment."

She acknowledged the danger with a bob of her head. "I will go with ye," she said.

Chapter 24

~⊗~

ER heart crumbling, Kimbra returned to her own chamber.

As promised, Audra sat next to Bear, petting him. Bear's huge tail beat a tattoo on the rug that covered the stone floor. At seeing her, Bear rose to his feet and stood there, tongue lolling in front, tail wagging in back.

She kneeled and very carefully gave him a big hug.

He licked her face.

It was all right, though. She needed that affection.

"How is Mr. Howard?" Audra asked.

"It is Maclean," she said.

"*I* think of him as Mr. Howard."

He would always be the Scot to Kimbra.

"He is a lord, Audra, and I imagine an important man. He is not 'our' Robert Howard."

"But he will not leave us," Audra said stubbornly.

"Aye, he has his own home and family."

"Can we go with him?"

"Nay."

"Why?"

"Because he is a noble, and we are not. He is Scottish, and we are English. He has his life, and we have ours."

"Can I see him?"

"If the Charlton permits it. We should leave soon." She truly needed to be gone this day. There was Bess and the chickens. Her garden. Her herbs. She had promised Jane some bay leaves.

She swallowed past the lump in her throat. Though difficult, the cottage and her herbs had been *her* life and with Audra a satisfactory one. She had been caught up in a fantasy she knew would end.

"He was going to give me lessons on the lute," Audra persisted.

"Mayhap he still will. I will have to fetch it from the cottage." She grabbed at the chance to leave here, to return to the cottage, and do things she did every day. She would stop in at Jane's. Now she could tell her friend more. Not everything. But more.

It would keep her thoughts from the Scot and how she felt yesterday when he'd made love to her. And then today . . .

Was it only yesterday?

"I will ask the Charlton if you can see—" She did not know which name to use. She was so accustomed to thinking of him as simply the Scot.

She left the room and went to the Charlton's room and knocked, thought she'd heard something inside, and opened the door tentatively.

He was alone, and he motioned her in.

"May I have leave to tend the animals and fetch my daughter's lute? She will stay here. I will return before nightfall."

"I can send someone over to bring the animals in."

"There are items I need."

"Then I will send someone to accompany ye."

"I would like to go alone," she persisted. She could not explain why.

"It is not safe."

"It is daylight, and I will be back before dark," she persisted. She really wanted, needed, to be alone. "I have made the trip alone hundreds of times, and you know the raiders never strike during the day."

"If ye are not back, I will send men for ye," he finally relented.

She wasted no more time. She fetched her cloak, then went down to the stables. Magnus was already saddled. The Charlton must have sent word.

She was soon away from the walls, racing Magnus down the road. She wanted to flee from her thoughts. Had she made a terrible mistake? Her soul bled every time she recalled the Scot's eyes, the plea in them. The plea that she believe in him.

She finally slowed Magnus down. She would fetch the lute, and the ruby ring. She did not know when the Charlton would allow her to return. She would feed the chickens and milk Bess, then take Bess to Jane's. She would ask Jane to check the chickens the next day as well.

When she turned toward her cottage, she looked back and she saw a man on horseback. She recognized him.

So the Charlton had sent someone, after all. It unexpectedly warmed her. She realized it was because he cared about her. That had come as a surprise. She'd known he liked Will, but he had always seemed indifferent toward her.

She could live with her distant protector.

She knew now, however, how much she longed for a tall, blue-eyed Scot, instead.

* * *

$\mathcal{A}$UDRA did not have permission, but she went boldly to where the Scot was kept and told the guard she did.

He looked at her suspiciously. "Ye are not carrying a pike, are ye?"

"Nay."

"Did ye bring anything?"

She felt her face turn red. There was a sweet secreted in the sleeve of her gown. She pulled it out sheepishly.

He gave her a severe look. "There is no weapon in there?"

Not entirely sure whether he was serious or teasing, she shook her head.

"Well, then ye can go in," he yielded with a grin.

He opened the door, then he stood aside and allowed her to go in, and shut the door behind her.

The man she'd known as Robert Howard had been looking out the window. She knew because he'd halfway turned to face her.

"Miss Audra," he said in the soft voice he always used with her.

"Do you want to see me?" she asked forthrightly.

"Aye, always."

"But not my mother?"

"Why do you say that?"

"She is very sad. I think she cried. She never cries," Audra said solemnly.

He knelt on one knee. "I am sorry to hear that."

"Were you mean to her?"

"I did not intend to be."

"She said you are going away."

"Aye, I must."

"Why?"

"Because Scots are not welcome here."

"You are welcome at our cottage."

"Unfortunately you are the exception in thinking so."

" 'Xception? What does that mean?"

"Exception means that you think one way when everyone else thinks another."

She thought about that. "Like Mother."

He smiled. "Aye, like your mother."

"She went to fetch my lute. Will you teach me another song?"

"Aye, but you do not need me now. You know your notes. You can learn on your own."

"I want to read, too."

"Do you remember what I taught you? The letters as well?"

"I say them every night, so I will not forget."

"Can you tell me now?"

She did. She missed a *p*, but other than that was perfect.

He would send them books. Lots of them.

He didn't want to send them. He wanted to be there when they opened them. He wanted to see the same delight on their faces that he felt at opening a book.

He wanted to hear Audra read out loud. He wanted to see Kimbra bent over a book, her face intent.

Blazes, he did not want to lose either one of them.

She is very sad. I think she cried. She never cries.

He had stood at the window and watched her ride away. He had known she rode away from him.

His heart was riding away as well.

"You say your mother went for your lute?"

She nodded.

He'd watched her ride off alone. What was she thinking? He saw the sudden concern in Audra's eyes and knew his own apprehension must be obvious.

"She will be fine," he assured her, even though his own heart was pounding. Cedric was out there. Armstrongs were raiding. God only knew what else. Damn the Charlton for letting her go.

He tried not to let his own worry show. "Would you

like a story?" he asked. "One of a lad who went to sea?"

"I would like that very much," she said primly.

"Then I will tell you of Dan, a boy not much older than you who was a cabin lad . . ."

And all the time he told the story, he kept thinking of Kimbra riding alone.

She was so sad.

How could he possibly let her go?

He couldn't. He'd been a damned fool to let pride blind him to what should have been obvious. He'd obviously hurt her by his reaction to seeing the crest. And still she was trying to protect him. She feared who she was might turn his family against him. She didn't realize that not having her would hurt far more.

Even as he told his tale to Audra, he prayed the Charlton would let him see her again, that he would not be too late.

*T*HE cottage did not look as welcoming as it usually did. She had just ensured the Scot would want naught to do with her again. She saw little now to commend the future. She didn't even have the crest. Not that she wanted it now. She wished she had never seen the infernal thing.

She took Magnus to the stable, unsaddled him, and gave him some oats. Bess mooed plaintively, and she milked the cow. Finished, Kimbra left them then and went to the cottage. Just as she was about to open the door, a tall man stepped in front of her. She whirled around, and another had appeared behind her.

Unease crawled up her spine. Armstrongs?

They could be. They looked like any borderer, but they were not Charltons. She would have recognized them.

"Mistress Charlton? Kimbra Charlton?"

The voice from the man in front of her was soft, courteous. It sounded much like the Scot's when she first found

him. It did not go with his rough clothing. It went with the
fine plaid that the Scot had worn before she had cut it from
his body.

"Aye," she said cautiously.

"Is there a lad here?"

Surprised, she looked up. "Nay." She thought about saying her husband and his very large older brother, who were
out hunting, would be back momentarily. But if he knew her
name, then he probably also knew she was a widow. She
studied him. He had dark hair and gray eyes.

She turned around. The man behind her was almost as
tall with red hair. He was uncommonly handsome.

"Mistress," he acknowledged. "We are not here to harm
you." He spoke with a heavy brogue, one far greater than
that of either her Scot or the dark-haired stranger.

She turned back to the dark-haired man.

He looked around. "You are alone?"

She did not answer.

"I understand the border is dangerous," he added, obviously taking her silence as an answer.

Was he one of the dangers?

"What do you want?" she asked.

"Do you know a man named Lachlan?"

"Why should it matter to you?"

"He is my brother."

She was stunned. This man looked nothing like Lachlan. But he must be the Maclean, chief of the Macleans.
She'd heard at the tower that he had been searching for his
brother.

He was risking much by coming to this side of the border.

She had no reason to lie. The Charlton now knew her
Scot was a Maclean. She did not want this one to try to do
something that might put Lachlan in danger.

"Aye, I know him," she replied cautiously.

"I am Rory Maclean. This is Jamie Campbell."

"Jamie Campbell?"

The redheaded stranger moved around to stand next to Rory Maclean. "I was with Lachlan at Flodden Field," he said. "I was taken for ransom. Is that what happened here?"

"Nay." 'Twasn't the whole truth.

"Is he safe at the tower?" Rory Maclean broke in. "Is he well?"

"Aye. He is now, but he was badly wounded. He might have a limp." She had lost her fear of them. What she wanted was more information.

"Thank God," the Maclean muttered, and she realized that Lachlan meant much to these two men. The redheaded one had even risked recapture and death to find him.

"The Charlton has sent a messenger to the Armstrongs asking for ransom. He heard someone was looking for Lachlan."

The Maclean stared hard at her. "I heard that King Henry was warning borderers about keeping Scots for ransom."

"He is, but the Charlton had taken a liking to . . . to the Scot."

She thought again about the man following them. How far behind had he been when she approached the cottage? Had the Charlton asked him to come all the way, or wait on the road?

"It is dangerous for you. A Charlton was following me."

"Someone is watching down the road," Rory Maclean said.

Fear curdled inside her. "I do not want a Charlton hurt on my behalf."

The one named Jamie looked at the Maclean and abruptly left. The two men seemed to communicate without words, and that surprised her. Even on the English border she'd heard of the great feud between the Campbells and Macleans.

She turned back to the Maclean. "Come inside," she said.

Once inside, he looked around the small cottage. It had been big to her, but it must seem very humble to him.

Rory Maclean was one of the most intimidating men she'd ever met. Those gray eyes gave nothing away. His lips were stern, unsmiling.

"You have the Maclean crest," he said without preamble. "How did you get it?"

She was so startled she could not reply. Then she fought for time. "Why do you think . . . ?"

"A priest said a lad riding a black horse asked him to read the words."

"There are many lads and many black horses."

"No' so many," he replied. "It was you?"

She did not want to answer. She sought to divert him, instead. "Would you like some ale?"

"I would like some answers more," the Maclean said. "What happened to Lachlan?"

"I found him in the woods," she said, repeating the story she'd told everyone else. She did not want Lachlan's brother to know she was little better than a grave robber. "He was wounded. I brought him here."

"How badly?"

"He nearly died. He had many wounds. There was a blow to his head. His leg was badly hurt, the ribs had been damaged. He'd lost much blood."

"And now?"

"He has a limp. I do not know whether it will last."

The Maclean muttered something.

"You healed him?" he asked then.

"Nay, your brother healed himself. He was determined to live."

"He fought with the Charltons. Why?"

She looked at him with surprise. "How did you know . . . ?"

"I fought him. I was staying with the Armstrongs. They asked me to come along. During the fighting I thought I recognized one of the . . . enemy but I was not sure because he was wearing a helmet. He raised his sword against me, then suddenly stopped as if . . . surprised, stunned."

He paused, then continued, "But if it had been Lachlan, why would he not have said something? Why was he fighting for the English?"

"He lost his memories. He did not know who he was," she said. "He would not have known who you were. There must have been a second when he realized something about you was familiar."

She paused, then continued. "When I found him, I knew the English had ordered all Scots killed. I told the Charlton he was English, a man named Howard. I taught him the border speech and gave him my husband's clothes. As he started to get better, the Charlton feared his presence here might compromise me and moved him into the tower. Then the Charlton took a liking to him and wanted him to join . . . the family."

The Maclean sat down abruptly.

Her heart turned. The Scot had faced his brother and had not known it. No wonder Lachlan had been angry. If she had given him the brooch earlier, mayhap he would have regained his memory and might never have faced his brother. It was just lucky that he'd stayed his hand. Or brother might have killed brother.

The Maclean was staring at her as if he knew as well. "Why did you take the brooch to the priest?"

"I did not say I had."

"Nay, but you did."

She was weary of lying. "I wanted to find out who he was."

"Why?" he asked abruptly.

"So he could go home."

"Not because of ransom?"

She flushed. But she was not going to lie any longer. "Mayhap at first."

"And then?"

"And then I just wanted him to get well."

"How did they find out who he really was?"

She flinched. "Someone overheard us talking and realized he was a Scot. At the same time, he suddenly got his memories back. Most of them."

He nodded. "And a ransom is being asked?"

"Aye. The Charlton is risking the king's wrath. The English ordered all captured and wounded Scots killed, particularly the nobles. They wanted no repeat of the battle."

"Then why . . . ?"

"Your brother saved the Charlton's life during that battle with the Armstrongs. The Charlton also likes him. But the other Charltons would resent incurring the king's disfavor without reward. He had heard that you were on the border, asking about . . . Lachlan."

The Scot stood, towering over her. "I thank you for caring for him."

The door opened then, and the Campbell came in.

"The Englishman has been taken." He looked at her. "He has a lump on his head and will be bound, but he will live."

"Thank you," she whispered.

She listened as Rory recounted everything she had told him.

The Campbell listened intently, then grinned. "Our Lachlan an English reiver? My God."

The derision as he said "English reiver" made her flinch inside.

Rory glanced at her, then realization dawned on the Campbell's face.

"My apologies, mistress," the Campbell said. "I meant no disrespect. It is just that Lachlan has never liked warfare. At one point, he wanted to be a priest."

Her Lachlan? A priest?

"Why was he at Flodden Field?" she asked, bewildered.

"He took my place because my wife had just had a bairn," the Maclean said, guilt in his voice.

"He does not remember what happened at Flodden," Kimbra explained. "Nothing after the battle started."

"He fought beside the king," the Campbell said. "I was just a little way from him. He fought hard, then we were surrounded."

A knock at the door interrupted. She opened it to a man in border clothing and a woman.

The man paid little attention to her. "We should go."

The woman stared at her. Kimbra started as she recognized the woman from the battlefield.

A broad smile spread over the woman's face. "I hoped I would see ye again to thank ye."

The Maclean cleared his throat. "You know each other?"

Kimbra and Mary exchanged glances. Neither wanted to say why they were on the battlefield that night.

"We have met," Kimbra explained shortly.

The Maclean obviously had more questions, but he turned to the Campbell. "We must go now. I want to be at the Armstrong tower when the demand comes." He turned back to Kimbra. "Come, mistress, you will go with us."

She backed up. "No. I have a daughter at the tower. There is a cow here that must be milked."

"I am sorry," he said in a harsh voice. "I cannot risk anyone knowing we were here. The man following you did not know who we are. You do. If one Maclean is valuable, another and a Campbell would be even more so."

"I would not tell anyone."

"I cannot take that chance," he said. "You will be returned as soon as it is safe."

"I will not go."

"You *will* go. Mary will assure your safety."

"My daughter . . . she is but seven . . ."

"She is safe at the Charlton tower?"

She stared at him hopelessly. There was no sympathy

there, no mercy. He was not like his brother. Or perhaps he was. She had seen glimpses of that hardness in Lachlan.

"'Tis your choice," he said impatiently.

"I will go with you. But only because you are forcing it. You are a barbarian."

"So I have been told," he said. "Gather what you want to take. We will leave shortly."

Chapter 25

HE journey seemed interminable. Kimbra could not stop worrying about Audra and what her daughter's reaction would be when she did not return to the tower, as promised.

The Maclean set a hard pace, traveling through the afternoon and twilight and now night. He stopped only long enough to rest and water the horses.

It was approaching dawn when they finally reached the Armstrong tower. She was exhausted, but pride and anger had not allowed her to show it. She could be as strong as they.

The Armstrong with them had ridden ahead to tell the chief of their pending arrival.

The tower was much like the Charltons' tower, built more for defense than for beauty or comfort.

She refused proffered assistance from Rory Maclean and slid down on her own. She stood there in the courtyard of the clan that had killed her husband and raided, killed, and thieved from the Charltons for decades. Several men came up to the Maclean and the Armstrong reiver who had accompanied them.

They made way for a man who strode toward him. She did not need anyone to tell her he was chief of the Armstrongs. Alexander Armstrong. Chief. Laird. Thief and murderer.

He reached the Maclean. "There has been a message about your brother. A demand for ransom. Come inside, and ye can read it."

He looked curiously at Kimbra. "And who is this?"

"Kimbra Charlton. She assisted my brother after the battle," the Maclean said, adding with a warning tone, "and she is under my protection."

"A bonny lass is always welcome here," the Armstrong said. "And protected."

"I do not think the widow you raided last week believes that," she retorted sharply.

"Ah, a spirited lass. What do ye plan to do with her?"

"Return her. I just could not allow her to run to the Charltons. Mayhap the person who brought the message can return her."

"He is sleeping now. Ye can read the demand and get your answer ready."

The Armstrong gave orders to take and feed the horses, stopping to admire Magnus. He had his hand on the rein. "A fine hobbler," he said. "He reminds me of one I had years ago."

The Maclean moved between them. "The horse is under my protection as well," he said. "The lass will not suffer for assisting my brother."

"Aye," the Armstrong said, though his eyes glittered with avarice.

They went inside then, and the Armstrong ordered a servant to show her a room and provide food and drink.

She had little choice but to follow.

$\mathcal{R}$ORY had not liked taking the woman.

He simply had not seen any other choice. If he became a prisoner as well, the ransom could well be more than the Macleans could pay.

He was not quite sure of the woman, either. He had seen the looks between Mary and Kimbra Charlton. He knew from talk that both clans had been part of the looting of bodies after the battle. The thought repelled him.

But the woman, regardless of motive, had evidently saved Lachlan's life. He would not see her incur a loss because of it.

He followed the Armstrong into a small drawing room. He picked up a piece of parchment and read.

The Charltons demanded ten thousand pounds within a week, or his brother would be turned over to the English.

He had nearly that amount but not quite enough. He had not really believed that Lachlan was being held for ransom, or the demand would have been sent directly to Inverleith.

He would just have to offer what he had.

He exchanged looks with Jamie.

"We can offer to send what we have now and promise the other in a fortnight."

The Armstrong spoke up. "If the English learn that the Charlton is holding a Scot, particularly a Maclean, they will send soldiers for him. Rumors spread quickly. 'Tis best to get him back as soon as possible."

Rory wished he had taken more time to raise funds, but he had been in a hurry, and hard money had been difficult to obtain, especially in the days following Flodden. He had spent most of his available funds on a new ship and had little on hand. Nor had he been able to borrow any on short notice. The government had been in confusion. He had not wanted to wait.

"Would they take a note?"

"From a Scot?" The Armstrong grimaced. "Ye jest. I would not take one from the English."

He looked directly at the Armstrong. "Would you take a note from me?"

"I would, but I have not that kind of wealth. Ours are in horses and cattle, and I can spare neither."

"Then I will try to trade myself."

"What would that accomplish?"

"Lachlan took my place. I can do no less. He fought in the battle. I did not."

"Why do we not try the offer first?" Jamie said. "Offer what we have, promise the rest, and see what happens. Mayhap he will accept. The woman said the Charlton was fond of Lachlan. Blazes, 'tis hard not to be fond of Lachlan, but to charm an English reiver into . . ." His voice trailed off as he glanced at Rory.

"What do ye mean?" the Armstrong chief said.

Rory wanted to kick Jamie. It would do their case no good if the Armstrongs knew that Lachlan had fought them, loss of memory or not.

"He is likable," Rory interceded. "That is all."

The Armstrong searched his face, then shrugged. "I will send for the Charlton messenger," the Armstrong said. "In the meantime, ye can write out the offer." He pushed over a quill and parchment.

They were offered a cup of ale. Jamie accepted. Rory did not. He wanted to be clearheaded as he wrote his reply and spoke to the messenger. Lachlan's life was at stake.

In several moments the messenger arrived at the doorway. He was a compact man with dark features and a scowl on his face. His face was red, as if he had been drinking.

"I have a reply for Thomas Charlton," Rory said.

"He will want some of the ransom in gold coins," the

messenger said. "Not promises from a Scot. I cannot go back without, and if I do not . . ." He left the threat hanging in the air.

Rory did not like the man. He did not look directly at him, and there was something in his eyes. But he had little choice.

"How much?"

"A thousand pounds."

"How do we know we can trust you?"

"I have the Charlton's own letter."

Rory did not like it. He liked nothing about this. He thought about asking him to take the Charlton lass with him, but there was something about this man . . .

He nodded. "I have the money. You can leave shortly after I pen my reply."

The messenger nodded.

It was done.

*K*IMBRA *had not returned!*

Lachlan stared out the window as pale streaks of gold announced the approaching dawn.

Jock had told him late last night that she had not returned. There were suspicions that he might know something, that she might have confided in him.

He knew she would never willingly leave Audra alone. He also knew he could no longer sit here and wait.

Her face haunted him.

Had the Armstrongs intercepted her? Cedric? The thought curdled his soul.

Audra must be scared. More than scared. Terrified. And lonely.

Blast the locked door.

He pounded on the door.

No one answered.

He pounded again.

It opened. It wasn't Jock but a very resentful Charlton. He'd apparently been sleeping, because he wiped his eyes with his hand. "What are ye hammering about?"

"I want to see Thomas Charlton."

"He may not want to see ye."

Lachlan was out of patience. "Ask him."

The guard slammed the door, and Lachlan did not know whether he had made himself clear. He wished now he'd just hit him.

He had a moment of chagrin. For someone who once loved peace, life seemed to be carrying him to an entirely different place.

Lachlan was ready to try to tear down the walls when the Charlton entered the room. His face was drawn, and he looked older. "I'd sent someone to watch over her. My men found him bound and gagged. He said he was attacked and knocked out."

"Were they Armstrongs?"

"He believes so."

Icy fear twisted around his heart.

"Audra?"

"She's sleeping. She does not know yet."

"Let me go," Lachlan pleaded. "I can find Kimbra. You said my brother is across the border with the Armstrongs. If she is there, he will help me secure her release. If not, he will help me find her."

"I cannot do that." The Charlton sighed. "My Charltons would not have it. Why could ye not be what I thought ye were?"

"I could have stayed here, and happily," Lachlan said. "But I would no' be accepted now. We know that. 'Tis Kimbra and the wee lass I worry about. She said she did not wish to go with me, but she is not safe here. Not with the raids, and not with Cedric prowling around."

The Charlton searched his face. "Ye love her."

"Aye. I do not think she trusts that." He hesitated, then

dared, "She fears my family will disown me as you dis
owned your daughter."

The Charlton suddenly looked older. "I was wrong, bu
it is done."

"Some things can be undone. Pride is a lonely compan
ion," Lachlan dared again.

The Charlton's eyes hardened and he did not answer.

Lachlan changed the subject. "Where is Cedric?"

"He is not here, but surely ye do not think he took Kim
bra. My man said it was Armstrongs."

"You said he *believed* they were Armstrongs."

"But he also said there were many, and no other Charl
ton would have joined Cedric in something like this."

"Mayhap it was not such a large group. And he has a
brother."

The Charlton shook his head. "I cannot believe it of
him."

"He has made it plain how much he wants her. Release
me," Lachlan pleaded. "I can go to the Armstrongs and find
the truth of it."

The Charlton looked at him sadly. "If I allowed ye
to leave without ransom, I would no longer be chief,"
the Charlton said. "I will be seen as weak. And there is no
one else to take over. Not yet. I cannot let that happen.
None will believe Cedric has done such a thing."

Lachlan tried again. "My brother will pay a ransom. I
swear it. It may not be all you ask now. Rory just purchased
a new ship and cargo. But you will be paid."

"I would take less. 'Tis always good to ask more."

In any other circumstances, Lachlan would have smiled.
But now he could not. Worry about Kimbra ate through his
gut.

He stared hopefully at the Charlton.

"I cannot release you now. It depends on yer brother
now," the Charlton said. "Is he a worthy man?"

"Aye."

"Then ye both should have been English," the Charlton said.

He walked out, leaving Lachlan angry, frustrated, and more afraid than any other time in his life.

T HE moment Rory met the messenger from the Charltons, the hackles on his back rose.

He considered himself a good judge of character, and there was nothing about Cedric Charlton that gave him good feelings. He certainly did not want to give the man gold, and yet those were the instructions.

The gold would lead to a meeting. The Armstrongs had first suggested the border itself. But Rory doubted the Charltons would agree. They would remember an ambush only too clearly. The Branxton Church might be a fair compromise. He would risk going onto English soil, but the church was a sanctuary. There would be enough Armstrongs along to get them out, if it was a trap.

But the English woman said the Charlton had a liking for Lachlan. He prayed she was right.

He thought about going himself, but the Armstrong distrust was contagious. He was a prize. Archibald or an Armstrong would not be.

He went up to see the woman. He knocked, and the door opened immediately after his knock, as if she had been standing just inside, waiting. She had braided her hair, and her gray eyes looked luminous. Until they saw him. Then they became all hostility.

"I want to go to my daughter."

"You will. The Armstrongs received a messenger from the Charltons. I will do whatever it takes to get Lachlan home." He hesitated. "I am sorry it was necessary to bring you here. You can go home now with the Charlton messenger."

She simply nodded.

"Are you ready to leave?"

"Aye."

When they reached the courtyard, the horses were saddled. The English emissary started when he saw Kimbra Charlton.

The blood drained from Kimbra's face.

"Kimbra," the English reiver said. "I did not expect to see ye here."

"Nor I you." She glared at him. "You seem well at home here."

He reddened. The barb obviously hit home. Rory wished he understood the meaning of it.

"The Charlton sent me," the Englishman blustered.

Rory saw the doubt in her face, but she held her tongue.

"I need a few words with Mistress Kimbra before she leaves." Rory took her arm, drawing her toward the stable.

"You seem disturbed by the man the Charlton sent."

"I do not think he sent him."

"He had the letter with the Charlton seal."

The doubt didn't leave her face, and it wriggled into Rory's mind.

"I cannot understand why he is here. He is not . . . to be trusted."

Her assessment agreed with his own instinctive one.

"Then why is he here?"

"I do not know. Just do not trust him if you wish your brother back. He hates Lachlan."

She said his brother's name easily.

"Why?"

"He is jealous. He wanted to be the Charlton's favorite. He wanted to have . . . me." She rushed on. "Not because of me. Because he wanted my cottage and Magnus."

He absorbed that. He had been suspicious of her since he met her. But now he found something appealing about her. Had Lachlan also found it so?

"Mayhap you should not go. I have suggested a meeting

at Branxton Church. You can wait and go with us then."

"Nay, I must get to my daughter. I will go. I can take care of myself."

She said it stoically, as if she knew she was going into the jaws of evil.

In that moment, he saw much of Felicia in her: the same stubbornness, the protectiveness of those she loved, the unflinching strength.

The wariness he'd felt before faded. Reiver woman or not, she had a rare dignity. "Archibald, and an Armstrong, will go with you. He will look after you."

She only nodded, but he saw something in her eyes that worried him.

He held out several gold pieces. "For looking after Lachlan."

She backed away. "Nay," she said and turned her back on him. She walked back to the horses.

He followed, feeling like the worst of villains. He had obviously insulted someone who had helped—mayhap saved—his brother.

The Englishman looked apprehensive as they approached.

"Your name?" Rory asked curtly.

"Cedric Charlton."

He handed a heavy pouch to Archibald. "There is a thousand pounds in gold, along with a message. The captain of my guard will accompany you, along with an Armstrong."

Cedric frowned. "The Charlton wants no Scots on his land. He said I was to return alone."

"I am sure he will relent this one time, considering the amount of gold involved." He paused, then added, "Mistress Charlton will accompany you as well. Unfortunately I had to . . . detain her when she saw us. She tells us she has a daughter who must be missing her."

An odd light came into the Englishman's eyes.

Rory's doubts grew stronger.

"If anything happens to her, or the funds, I will hunt whoever did it to the ends of the earth," Rory said coldly.

Cedric ignored him and went to one of the horses and mounted. Rory noted he was well armed, but then so were Archibald and the Armstrong.

He watched them ride off, then went over to Jamie, who had been standing nearby. He told him what Kimbra had said.

"Do you think we should go with them?" Jamie asked.

"Not you. You've been a prisoner already. I'll follow."

He went to the Armstrong. "Is Cedric Charlton a traitor to his clan?"

"Nay," the Armstrong said, but Rory saw the lie in his eyes.

"I will follow them," Rory said. "At least to Charlton land." He turned to Jamie. "Stay with the ransom money. If I do not return, you pay it yourself."

"I want to go—"

"I need you here," Rory cut him off. "I have no time to argue."

Jamie nodded.

HE Charlton was in a towering fury when he entered Lachlan's room.

"We found the two men I sent to the Armstrongs," he raged. "They are dead. The message I sent to the Armstrongs was not on them."

Lachlan's heart plunged. "Where were they?"

"Not far from the border. We would not have found them had we not been searching for Kimbra."

"There was no sign of her then?"

"Nay," he said reluctantly. "I fear ye may have been right about Cedric, though it tries my heart sorely. One of my men saw both Cedric and his brother ride out just before the messengers left. They have not been seen since."

"Would that have given them time to take Kimbra?" Lachlan asked.

"I do not know. They may have help from the Armstrongs."

"Will you accept my parole?" Lachlan asked. "The Armstrongs would not dare to touch a Maclean."

"My Charltons will not be pleased to let ye go."

"They will, if I return with Kimbra and the ransom. And the traitor."

"Aye, that should satisfy them," he said. "How can I be sure ye will not just return to Scotland? Or that your brother will pay the ransom once ye are there?"

"My word," he said. Then he thought of the crest. It was certainly not worth ten thousand pounds or anything close to it, but it was valuable.

He went to the bed where he had placed it as a constant reminder of his foolishness. " 'Tis our family crest. It is probably worth a thousand pounds."

The Charlton peered at it closely. " 'Tis a fine piece of work. *Virtue Mine Honour*," he read, then looked at Lachlan suspiciously. "Have ye had this all this time?"

"Aye," he lied.

"A Scottish noble risking his life for a reiver's widow, an English one?" the Charlton said doubtfully.

"She is not just a reiver's woman to me," Lachlan said, "but even if she was and she had helped me as Kimbra has, I would spend every penny I had to keep her safe."

"Then ye are an unusual Scot. And an unusual man. Ye have your parole. Ye can pick among the hobblers. Do ye want many to go with ye?"

"Nay, I do not want another battle between Charltons and Armstrongs," he said. "And I cannot believe the Armstrongs would harbor a traitor for long."

"Come to the armory and take what ye will," Thomas Charlton said. "And ye will need a guide."

Chapter 26

KIMBRA rode as far away from Cedric as she could.

She still did not understand how Cedric had obtained the letter. Surely, the Charlton had not gone addle-headed.

She certainly did not trust him, nor did she trust the Armstrong riding with them. She'd learned to distrust and detest Armstrongs long ago. The death of Will and the recent ambush on the Charltons had only confirmed her opinion.

But if nothing else, the tall Maclean appeared competent, and if Archibald Maclean appeared a bit old, he also appeared alert. He was certainly armed well enough and wore his weapons with experienced ease.

She thrust aside her misgivings. She *had* to get back to Audra. How very much she wanted that.

And her Scot. That would be bittersweet now. He would

be leaving on their return, and she likely would never see him again.

They reached the border after hours of riding. She was exhausted from the ride the day earlier. So must have been the Maclean, though he showed no sign of it. The Charltons were still six hard-riding hours away.

She dozed. Suddenly, a cry. Her eyes snapped open.

The Maclean ahead of them tumbled from the horse, an arrow in his back. Then the Armstrong raced off. An arrow downed him, but his horse kept running.

She tried to follow, but before she could turn Magnus, Cedric grabbed the reins from her hand.

His brother suddenly appeared from behind a hill. He went after Archibald Maclean's destrier, while Cedric held Magnus's reins. She looked down at the Maclean. She thought she saw him move, but said nothing. Better that Cedric thought him dead. In truth she needed to distract him from the Maclean on the ground.

In one movement she swung her leg around and slid off Magnus.

She scrabbled up a steep incline, using her hands to pull her up, then she looked behind. He was approaching, one hand still on Magnus's reins. She picked up a stone and threw it at her horse.

Stung, Magnus reared, jerked away from Cedric's hold, and galloped back toward the border. She heard Cedric's loud curse. He now either had to follow a horse he had always coveted or give her time to hide. 'Twas easy to do here.

Taking advantage of his confusion, she started to climb again. She heard him below her. *So he had given up on Magnus.* He wanted her more than he wanted the hobbler. She stopped and looked frantically for another stone. She saw a small one, picked it up, and aimed it at him, throwing it with all her might.

It hit him in the face, drawing blood. He cursed again, but he did not stop.

She scrambled upward, but he caught her ankle and pulled her down. She saw his fist coming at her face, then everything went black.

C EDRIC cursed her with every ounce of his being.
    He put his fingers to his face, and they came away bloody.

She was unconscious. He knew they had to get away from here. Her horse was galloping back to the Armstrongs. They would realize shortly that something was wrong.

He leaned over and felt her pulse. She was unconscious, nothing more. He picked her up and carried her down to where his horse waited.

His brother returned with the destrier.

He should just kill her now. If not for her, he might have Magnus as well as the gold.

Then he remembered she had saved Lachlan Maclean's life. Mayhap Lachlan could convince the brother to pay a hefty sum for hers. He brightened. After today, he would have no home on either side of the border. He would need funds to go somewhere else.

Cedric tied Kimbra on his own mount. "Kimbra's horse got away. We will go west along the border," he told Garrick. "We can cross it if need be and say we are Armstrongs. Ye scout ahead."

His brother knew the border as well or better than anyone else. He had made enough trips, both with the Charltons and on his own. He knew every cave, every wooded spot, every bog.

Cedric thought about killing Kimbra and still asking ransom, but he wanted her now more than ever. And he wanted Lachlan's head. If not for the Scot, Kimbra would have married him. He would have become the Charlton's favorite, mayhap even his heir. But once the Scot appeared, she had planted seeds of distrust in the old man's head.

Cedric mounted the destrier. "Follow me," he told his brother, and holding the reins of the horse he'd tied Kimbra to, he turned west. The mountains there were particularly rugged, and the horse trail difficult to follow.

He turned around. She had not gained consciousness yet.

But soon she would know who her master was.

𝒪NE of the Charlton's men, a man named Davie's John, guided Lachlan through the labyrinth of trails to the border.

The two of them rode hard, and Lachlan came to appreciate the small hardy horses with sure feet as they crossed the treacherous paths.

Davie's John moved his horse closer to his. He had volunteered to guide Lachlan. "The border is just on the other side of the pass."

They turned toward the pass. Watchful, they started through it. Lachlan had nearly reached the end, when he saw two bodies on the ground. One looked familiar. He slipped from the hobbler.

Archibald!

An arrow jutted out his back. Lachlan's heart nearly stopped. Archibald and Hector had been the only two constants in his life.

"Archibald?" *Dear God, please let him live.*

The man moaned.

Lachlan knelt down. The arrow had gone through Archibald's body.

Archibald opened his eyes. "Lachlan," he said. A pained smile crossed his lips. "We feared ye had died."

"Nay, I am still among the living. What happened now?"

"A Charlton brought a demand for ransom. Rory sent a thousand pounds in gold as . . . good faith." Archibald struggled to continue. "Kimbra Charlton . . . we found her . . . she was sent back with the ransom. An Armstrong and I were to accompany them."

"A Charlton?" Lachlan's pulse raced. "His name?"

"Cedric."

Hate washed over him. He'd never known real hate before. He felt it now.

"The woman? Kimbra?"

"He took the lass with him. She tried to run . . . I think mayhap to distract him from me."

Cold fear lodged in Lachlan's heart. Apparently Cedric had slain two of his own clan members. He would not hesitate killing a woman, nor hurting her in the worst possible way.

But he could not leave Archibald like this, either.

"Go, lad," Archibald said. "Go after her."

"I cannot leave you," Lachlan said, though his heart was breaking. He would do what he could for Archibald, then see whether he could follow the tracks. He looked up at the sky. It would soon be twilight, then dark.

He turned toward Davie's John and saw the man leaning over the other fallen man.

Davie's John shook his head, then came over to them. "He is dead. An Armstrong by the look of him."

"They took Kimbra," Lachlan said.

"I will get help," Davie's John said. "Someone who can track." The Charlton mounted and left at a gallop.

Lachlan stayed at the side of his mentor, the man who'd been more a father to him than his own father had been. He said a silent prayer, then studied the arrow. By God's mercy it must have missed a lung, or he would be dead now. But one movement could kill him.

Archibald groaned, tried to move.

"Nay, stay there," Lachlan said. "Tell me everything you can."

"There were . . . four of us, Cedric, an Armstrong, myself,

and the lady. Then I felt as if I were hit by lightning. Someone rode down and went after my horse. That's all I know,
lad. I knew that if I moved again, they would kill me, so I
played dead . . . hoped they would say something . . ."

"Did they?"

"Border. West. That is all."

"How many?"

"Just two that I saw. I did not get a good look. Just heard
them. Lad, I had a thousand pounds for yer ransom." He
looked at Lachlan. "How did ye . . . ?"

"I was given my parole after they found two men dead
near the border and Kimbra Charlton missing." His face
felt like stone, his heart torn in two by the choice he was
being forced to make. But he knew Archibald would die if
he did not tend him.

"The lady?"

"Aye," Lachlan replied gently. "Now say nothing more,"
he said. "I am going to break off the arrow head and pull it
through."

"Go after them. Yer brother is not far behind me."

"When I finish with you."

He broke off the head and gave Archibald a piece
of wood to bite. He did not have to tell him it would hurt.
Then he went to Archibald's back, braced himself, and
pulled.

The arrow came out. And blood.

Lachlan pulled off Archibald's shirt. He tore it and
bound the wound.

He heard a shout then, and looked up. His brother was
walking, then running toward them, holding the reins of a
horse limping badly and leaving a trail of blood.

Rory clasped him tightly, then looked down at Archibald
on the ground. His eyes were closed.

"Archibald said they were ambushed, that Cedric Charlton took the money and Kimbra. I have to go after them."

Rory closed his eyes for a moment. "Blazes," he said, "she warned me about him. I should have listened more closely. I was following, but the horse threw a shoe."

"Stay here with Archibald," Lachlan said. "I am going after her."

"No," Rory said. "It was my mistake."

"She's going to be *my* wife," Lachlan said.

Rory stared at him in astonishment.

"Aye," Lachlan said. "Give me your weapons."

Still looking stunned, Rory handed him his sword, dagger, and bow and arrow.

"I have sent for help," Lachlan said. "Archibald said they mentioned going west along the border." Then he grabbed the reins of the horse he'd borrowed from the Charlton and dug his heels in the hobbler's sides.

*K*IMBRA woke to stabbing pain in her face and nearly everywhere else. She'd been tied to a saddle and swayed back and forth.

How long had she been unconscious? Where were they going? What happened to the Armstrong? To Archibald Maclean? Then she remembered the arrow through his back.

She tried to raise her head enough to see where they were going. Pain ripped through her.

Audra. Her heart cried for her daughter. She would know her mother was missing by now. Who would look after her? Mother her?

That agony was worse than any physical one could possibly be.

She had to stay alive for her daughter. No matter what Cedric did to her, she *had* to stay alive.

She did not know how long it was before they stopped. She only knew that the sky was darkening and shadows were getting longer. The ropes holding her to the horse were untied. Her hands and wrists remained so, however. They had already cut deeply into her wrists.

She was jerked from the horse and landed on the ground. She looked up to see the smile on Cedric's face.

"Not so much the lady now," he said.

She wanted to spit at him. But now the important thing was to stay alive for Audra's sake.

"No words? You always had enough before."

Her cap had come loose, and he pulled her to her feet by her hair and dragged her to a tree and tied her to it.

"Ye will be silent," he said, "though it should be a long time before anyone knows what happened. If they ever do. Money and a thief gone missing. Yer Scot's ransom will not be paid. He will think ye took it. Mayhap the Charlton will get tired of waiting and hand him over to the English. All this while ye and I get better acquainted."

"The Charlton would not believe it."

"Why should he not?"

"They will find you and hang you."

"Ye say that with such viciousness, Kimbra. Ye are in no position to do so." He brushed her cheek with the back of his hand, even with gentleness, then struck her hard. "I have much to teach ye, and ye will learn quickly."

Then he left her and went over to his brother. He said something to Garrick, who then mounted his horse again and rode off.

"We do not want visitors," he said, "though I think it will take a day or more before they find that Scot."

She wanted to tell him that the Scot lived, that Lachlan's brother was behind them and probably had found his friend by now. She wanted to remove the smug look from his face.

Oh, how she wanted to do that.

Instead she was silent. She hoped Rory Maclean was the man his brother was. She hoped . . .

She hoped she would see Audra again.

Cedric looked disappointed at her lack of response. He walked away and unsaddled his hobbler. Then he started back toward her.

West Along the Border

The two brothers had apparently thought Archibald dead, but he was a tough old soldier.

Lachlan galloped in the direction Archibald had indicated, but soon slowed. He slipped down from the horse. The path was clear, but would they have kept to it?

He led the horse, looking for recent tracks. The way was rocky, but occasionally he saw the imprint of a hoof. Then evidence of a recent passing. The dung was still fresh.

He speeded his steps. It would be nightfall before long, and he had no torch with him. The sky was clear, though, he could already see the luminous outline of a part moon. He prayed he could see enough to continue.

The night grew darker. Though the path was visible, the ground was not. He feared they might have taken another path, or route. Just as he was about to despair, he noticed first by smell, then by sight, horse droppings. It was warm.

He must have gained time on them. They could not travel too quickly with Kimbra along, and if he knew her as well as he thought he did, she would not be a compliant prisoner. The other thought, that Cedric would want to take his pleasure of her, drove him on.

He heard the snort of a horse and covered his own mount's mouth. "Quiet," he whispered, not knowing whether the horse would obey. The animal stomped one hoof, then quieted.

He tied the reins of the horse to a tree, then advanced on foot. He decided to try the bow and arrow first, but his dagger was in a sheath at his waist.

Lachlan moved into the woods and circled, all the time listening for any sound not in keeping with the mountains.

He finally heard the horse again and moved toward it, hoping his own horse would remain silent.

Then he saw the figure in the moonlight. Cedric's brother, Garrick. He was sitting on a boulder overlooking the trail.

He took his bow off his shoulder and notched an arrow. *Now!*

His fingers would not let the arrow go. Then as if sensing something, the man turned toward him.

He ambushed Archibald. He took Kimbra. Lachlan's hand loosed the arrow. The figure crumpled and fell. He went over to the body and nudged it over with his boot. The arrow had pierced the heart.

Cedric should be nearby. Lachlan smelled smoke and moved toward it.

He heard a cry then. A woman's voice. It struck straight to his heart.

Be strong, Kimbra. I am coming.

KIMBRA struggled against the ropes that burned and cut into her wrists and ankles.

She watched as Cedric built a small fire. When he turned toward her, she lashed out with her bound legs and managed to kick him.

Even as she did so, she knew it was unwise to madden him any further, but it was more instinctive than not. She would not give up easily.

She had aimed for his manhood, but he moved just quickly enough that she hit his legs, knocking him down. He cursed, rose, and slapped her, knocking her head against the ground.

He stood over her and ripped her gown.

She screamed and tried to kick him again.

Cedric tore pieces from her gown and used the cloth to tie her bound ankles to one tree, her wrists to another until she was stretched out.

Nearly naked now, she felt his hungry gaze on her. He blood pounded, and she shuddered with humiliation. And rage. She could only watch helplessly as he lay his dagge down and unlaced his breeches. She twisted against th bonds, but they only dug deeper into her.

"At last," he said. "I will enjoy this, my lady," h mocked. "I will show you what a real man does."

He lowered himself onto her, and she tried to twist away as his rancid odor assaulted her. Waves of revulsion swep over her.

She heard a shout, and a body hurled itself on him knocking him away from her. She saw the auburn hair ii the light from the fire.

Lachlan.

Dear God, he was far from healed. Cedric was strong as an ox.

Surprise had helped him, stunning Cedric for a mo ment, but as Lachlan raised a dagger, Cedric deflected the blow and rolled over on him. The dagger tumbled from Lachlan's hand.

Both men pummeled each other, though she did no know how Lachlan kept fighting. Then she saw the dagger Cedric had dropped just before assaulting her.

She fought the bonds. The cloth binding her rope-bound wrists to the tree started to give, and she pulled with all her strength, despite the agony of ropes cutting through her skin. Then suddenly it gave.

Her hands were still tied together, but she could move She scrambled for the dagger, grabbed it with her two hands, then cut the ropes on her ankles.

Cedric was over Lachlan, punching him.

She yelled out to distract him. As Cedric turned toward her, Lachlan used his legs to knock him over. She pushed the dagger toward him. He grabbed it and plunged it into Cedric Charlton.

Cedric moaned, tried to move, then was still.

"His brother," she whispered. "He is out there."

"He's dead," Lachlan said, his voice and breath coming in rasps. He cut the rest of her bonds, gently taking her hands and staring at the deep cuts. "May he roast in hell."

He took off his jack, then his shirt and wrapped her in it.

She saw then that he was bleeding as well. She did not know whether it was a new wound or the opening up of the one he'd received when he fought the Armstrongs. She thought of him fighting the wolves for Audra and her, and now attacking a man so much superior in strength. Without a thought. Without reservation.

A noble who was truly noble.

"You keep getting wounded," she said.

"I have never been a good warrior," he said.

"Nay," she said softly. "You are the best kind. One that hates killing but does what's necessary. You did not fight the Armstrongs, but you moved yourself in front of the Charlton to save his life. That takes far more courage."

His breath was still raspy.

He was silent for a moment, then said, "I let my father die." He swallowed hard. "We were attacked, and I could not raise my sword against another. He was badly wounded and died a week later. The clan knew . . . or suspected."

He stopped then, but she heard the agony in his voice, and she remembered the nightmares he'd had. Now she knew why.

"Is that why you were at Flodden Field?"

"Aye. I killed one Maclean laird. I hoped to save the other. And now I do not know if I fought or not."

"You did. Your friend Jamie said you fought like a tiger next to the king. You never left his side."

"You saw Jamie?"

"Aye, he kidnapped me."

"I thought Cedric . . ."

"Nay, it was your friends. They were looking for you, and did not trust me not to reveal their whereabouts."

Lachlan scowled. "Rory did not tell me that. The Macleans have a bad habit of kidnapping women."

She reached for his hand, wrapped her fingers in his. "What do you mean?"

"Archibald helped kidnap Rory's wife. He wanted a wife for my brother and thought one lady would be perfect for him. Unfortunately—or fortunately for us—he kidnapped the wrong one. 'Tis a long story, but you will like her."

Her fingers stopped moving against his. He seemed to assume she would be going with him. But nothing had really changed, except the danger of Cedric was gone. She was still who she was, and he who he was.

"Wait," he said and brought his finger to her lips. She listened, then heard a soft whistle, the sound of a morning bird, but it was not morning.

Lachlan whistled a similar call.

Minutes later two men rode into the clearing. She recognized Rory and Jamie immediately as they dismounted. Jamie went over to Cedric. Rory went to his brother and stood over him, then leaned down, offered his hand and helped him up. Then gave him a bear hug.

"You have nine lives, brother. Thank the saints. We saw the other man on the trail. I did not know you are that good with an arrow."

"Archibald?"

"He should live if there is no infection. When your hobbler ran back to the Armstrongs, Jamie and several other Armstrongs came looking for us. I took one of their horses."

Then he looked down at Kimbra, his eyes going over her bloodstained clothing and her torn wrists. "My apologies, mistress. I should have listened more closely to you."

"Aye," Lachlan said. "She saved my life, not once, but twice. Three times now. I do not know how she did it, but she managed to get partly loose from where Cedric had tied her and passed a dagger to me just as Cedric was ready to finish me. Her wrists . . ."

Jamie came over. "He is dead. The dagger went into his heart. Just as the arrow went into the other scoundrel." He looked at Lachlan with great admiration. "For someone who doesn't like to fight, my God, but you are good at it."

She noticed the compliment did not make Lachlan smile. If anything, his lips tightened. He was, indeed, a reluctant warrior.

Rory urged Lachlan to sit, while he and Jamie looked for wood to add to the fire. When the blaze gave more light, he sat next to each of them and silently tended their wounds with such gentleness that she changed her mind about him.

"Hector?" Lachlan asked.

"We could find nothing of him."

She saw the pain on Lachlan's face. "Who is Hector?"

"He was at Flodden Field," Lachlan said. "He was like a father to me."

They were silent for a moment, all of them mourning a friend.

The grief on both Lachlan's and Rory's faces was stark, and she ached for both of them and all the others who had died that day.

And she knew Rory was most definitely Lachlan's brother. They both lived—and loved—well.

LACHLAN spent the rest of the night with his arms around Kimbra. He did not care what the others thought. He had come too close to losing her.

Rory and Jamie had taken Cedric's body somewhere. Lachlan did not care where or how, and then they had taken one look at Lachlan and silently retreated out of sight and sound.

They lay together, both too hurt to do much more than revel in the truth that they were still alive. And together.

He ached to be inside her again, to send both of them on that incredible journey they had shared just days ago. Just the thought sent heat racing through his body. But they both were too bruised, and she had come so close to being raped.

He knew only one thing now. He *had* to persuade her to come with him. He knew what she did not know: that Rory and the others would readily accept her. She had saved his life, not once but several times, and that made her one of theirs. But how to convince her?

He had never met a woman so stubborn. Unless it was Rory's wife, Felicia. He smiled at the thought of the two of them together. No man would be safe.

He tightened his arms around her. He thought she was asleep. He hoped she was. The pain from those wrists must be agonizing. He would not sleep. He wanted to be aware every moment, to feel her next to him, to hear her soft breathing, which came from such a valiant heart.

If only she would believe in him enough to be his wife.

Dawn crept through the trees, sprinkling rays from a morning sun. He had evidently dozed off, because he saw her gray eyes looking at him with such tenderness that he thought his heart would burst. He leaned down and kissed her cheek, and she snuggled closer to him.

Rory was tending the fire. Jamie was nowhere to be seen.

His brother turned, gazed at him with the somber expression he wore too often since the death of his second wife. Felicia, his third, and their bairns usually brought a smile to his face, but Rory still considered the world cautiously. "Jamie went hunting," he said. "I found some water. As soon as we get something to eat, we will return to the Armstrongs."

"Nay," Lachlan said. "Kimbra will want to see Audra."

"We can send her back."

"Like you did the last time? In any event, I gave my word to the Charlton. I do not intend to break it."

Rory sighed. Then nodded. "Most of the ransom is still back at the Armstrongs. I found the gold, though, that your Cedric stole. We can take that with us."

"Us?"

"I do not intend to let you out of my sight until we return to Inverleith," Rory said.

"But . . ."

"You think he is honorable. We will have to rely on that," Rory said.

Jamie rode in then with two rabbits, and quickly skinned and cooked them. They all ate, then Rory and Jamie saddled the horses.

They rode east on the trail that had brought them there. Halfway there they met a troop of Charltons, led by Thomas Charlton. They were immediately surrounded.

The Charlton approached them, his eyes going from one man to another.

Then he spoke to Kimbra. "Thank God you live. Cedric?"

"Dead. Both he and his brother."

"By whose hand?"

"Mine," Lachlan said. "He killed an Armstrong and wounded a man from my clan. He took the ransom money and Kimbra."

"Good," the Charlton said. "It will save me the trouble of doing it." Then, "The ransom?"

Rory joined them. "I am Rory Maclean. I have a thousand pounds in gold. The rest is at the Armstrongs and will be delivered as I think it is safe."

"Ye question my honor?"

"I do not know you," Rory said.

The Charlton smiled. "Ye can have him back now. I trust *him*."

"I will not leave," Lachlan said. "Not without Kimbra."

He looked at the Charlton. "I want your permission to wed her."

Kimbra had listened to the conversation with dismay. "Should you not ask your brother first?"

"It does not matter what my brother says. I wish you to marry me, not him."

She glanced at Rory, obviously expecting an objection.

Rory then grabbed the reins of her horse and led her some distance away. Lachlan followed, and she was only too aware of the Charltons looking on curiously.

"Why do you wish to break my brother's heart?" Rory asked Kimbra when they stopped.

Kimbra's hand trembled on the reins. "How could you, your family . . . want me? I stole the crest. I . . . stole from the dead after . . . the battle. I am English. A reiver. I even went on raids."

To her surprise, Rory threw his head back and laughed. "Holy Mother, but you sound like my wife, Felicia. She impersonated Jamie's betrothed, then dressed up as a lad and got into one scrape after another. But she has a warm heart." His voice softened. "And so, I suspect, do you." He paused, and added, "How could we not want the person who saved my brother?"

"Go away," Lachlan said. "I can do my own talking."

Rory grinned. "Aye," and he rode back to the Charltons.

Lachlan turned to her. "I love you, and Audra. I captain a ship. If you are not happy in Scotland, we can go anywhere. We can even come back here if you wish." He hesitated, then plunged on. "I have never known what being happy was—of belonging someplace—until I met you."

Lachlan paused, then said slowly, "There is something I should tell you first," he said. "My family was cursed many years ago. A hundred years ago. One of my ancestors, another Lachlan, chained his wife—a Campbell—to a rock in the sea, hoping the tide would kill her. It did not. Some fishermen found her. But she died of a lung sickness, or a broken heart soon after. A curse was made by a Campbell: 'No bride of a Maclean will live long or happily, and every Maclean will suffer for it.'"

He paused. "And no wife did live long, and all Macleans did suffer," he said. "Then Rory, who had lost two wives, fell in love with a Campbell and they wed."

"Felicia?" she said in a small voice.

"Aye. The curse may not be broken. I cannot say. It is one reason I wanted to be a priest. I did not think I could ever take a bride. But I believe Rory and Felicia, in their marriage, broke that curse. I cannot be sure. Nor can I be sure whether I will hesitate when I am needed."

The story was heartbreaking. She realized the courage it must have taken for Rory's Felicia to wed. Not only because of the curse but a hundred years of hatred. Could she be less?

She held out her hand to him. "You have always been the brave one of the two of us, whether you realized it or not. You will now have to be brave enough for three."

"I love you, Kimbra. And Audra."

The words—spoken softly and lovingly—curled around in her heart.

He leaned over and kissed her long and tenderly as shouts broke out among the Charltons.

Then, together, they rejoined the Charltons.

The Charlton grinned. "We will have the wedding at the tower, though I will sorely miss Kimbra's potions, and her remedies." He hesitated, then added, "I might invite my daughter and her barbarian of a husband."

Kimbra grinned at him. She was bubbling inside with joy. Then she turned to Lachlan with a question in her eyes.

"Aye, love," he said, then turned to the Charlton. "We accept with thanks."

She looked startled, then pleased, at the endearment.

He planned to use it often.

How odd that war had brought him peace. Enemies friends. And a future he'd never dared dream.

He looked at Rory and thought he saw a tear there, but that was nonsense. Not Rory.

Not when his own heart was singing. Looking at Kimbra's face, he knew she had a song there as well.

He reached out and took her hand. Home, he knew, would be wherever she and Audra were.

He'd finally found it.

Epilogue

AUDRA bobbed with excitement.

Kimbra knelt beside her. "You look beautiful."

"I know," Audra said with confidence. "I have never had such a pretty gown."

"'Tis not only the gown," Kimbra said. "As Lachlan says, you are a very bonny lassie."

"He says it about you, too. 'My two bonnie lassies,'" Audra chanted.

"Aye," Jane said. She had just finished braiding Kimbra's hair and twisting it into a knot at the back of her head. Jane had been ecstatic at being asked to be in the wedding, to stand up with Kimbra.

A knock came at the door of her tower room, and Felicia Maclean walked in.

She wore a blue gown, the only one she had with her. But it brought out the blue of her eyes. To Kimbra's surprise, they'd taken an immediate liking to each other. They'd sensed in each other similar spirits.

There had not been the slightest censure of her, only a warm embrace when Felicia had appeared at the tower just hours after she had arrived with Lachlan. Apparently Felicia had arrived at the Armstrongs just after the kidnapping and had defied every Armstrong warning not to travel to the Charlton tower.

Felicia heard Lachlan's story with amazement and gratitude and told Kimbra she would always have a place in her home and heart for saving Lachlan. Then she gave her such an impulsive hug that Kimbra believed her.

Kimbra had even confided her fears to Felicia. That sometime Lachlan would come to despise her.

"Lachlan never judges," Felicia replied. "At least no one but himself. He is the kindest, gentlest man I have ever met, and if not for Rory, I would try to take him from you. Not," she added, "that it would be possible, not the way he looks at you. And he adores Audra. I hope you have more children. Mine would love to have cousins."

Felicia was like a boulder rolling down a mountain. Nothing could get in the way of what she wanted, or she rolled over it.

Now her future sister-in-law eyed her with approval, then stepped back. "You and Audra *are* bonny," she said. "Thank you for making Lachlan happy." Felicia gave a brief hug. "Time to go."

The wedding was in the chapel. Kimbra wore a gown that had belonged to the Charlton's wife. She and Jane had worked a day to make it fit. They had taken another dress and used the material for Audra's gown. There had been no time for more.

They wanted no invasion of English soldiers, and the wedding was to be small and quick. Under the circumstances the priest, not altogether happy with the situation but dependent on the Charlton for his living, waived the bans.

A knock on the door. It was time to go. For a moment, Kimbra's legs trembled. She still worried something might change Lachlan. He might realize her complete unsuitability for him. They had talked about where to go and decided first to Inverleith, then she and Audra would accompany him on the ship to Paris.

If Audra liked shipboard life, he would continue to master a ship. If not, they would decide then where to go.

But she could not really believe he did not want to return home to Inverleith.

She went down the tower steps to the small chapel in the tower. The door was open. Audra went first, fairly dancing down the aisle. Felicia and Jane followed.

She passed the Charlton who sat with his daugher, son-in-law, and their three children. He beamed at her.

When Audra reached the altar she went to Lachlan and put her small hand in his. He leaned down and said something to her, which caused her to giggle.

Then it was Kimbra's turn.

Lachlan was waiting for her. Rory and Jamie stood next to him. But she gave them only a passing glance. Her eyes went directly to the man who would be her husband. To the auburn hair and blue eyes, and straight body, and the smile that made her ache inside.

He would love both of them. And any children they were blessed with.

She reached the altar and put her hand in his, and unconditionally gave him her heart and accepted his. Warmth spread over her. Warmth and wonder that this man could be hers.

Unafraid, she turned to the priest.

In 1988, **Patricia Potter** won the Maggie Award and a Reviewer's Choice Award from *Romantic Times* for her first novel. She has been named Storyteller of the Year by *Romantic Times* and has received the magazine's Career Achievement Award for Western Historical Romance along with numerous Reviewer's Choice nominations and awards.

She has won three Maggie awards, is a four-time RITA finalist, and has been on the *USA Today* bestseller list. Her books have been alternate choices for the Doubleday Book Club.

Prior to writing fiction, she was a newspaper reporter with the *Atlanta Journal-Constitution* and president of a public relations firm in Atlanta. She has served as president of Georgia Romance Writers and board member of River City Romance Writers, and is past president of Romance Writers of America.